The Seeker

The Hero:

Book One

T0282972

G. R. Linden

ISBN-10: 1515167348
ISBN-13: 978-1515167341

The Seeker

For Dan

CONTENTS

.

ACKNOWLEDGMENTS

I would like to thank all my friends and family for their support . Especially my parents without whom this would not have been possible.

Prologue

Where Many Threads Begin with an Ending

Our story begins one ominous evening in October. The thirteenth of October to be exact; as it is always important to be precise where the subject of time is concerned. A radiant full moon hung high in the night sky; silently watching over Friday night revelers as they stumble away from a nearby pub and into the foggy evening.

The name of that particular pub, its relevance, and the relevance of some of those stumbling patrons will be explained in due course; for now, we must presently deal with the two rather seedy gentlemen standing on a nearby levee.

The older of the pair wore a dark blue fedora low on his brow. The collar on his ankle-length grey trench coat had been flipped up, so that the only feature that could be made out against the midnight dim was a single eye of icy blue.

The aged man carried with him a silver-tipped walking stick in his left hand and in his right he held a briefcase as black as the gloved hand that gripped it.

Opposite him, standing at the fog's edge, was a man who, while much younger in age had years of wisdom in his eyes, decades of pain in his face, and a broad set of shoulders that seemed to slouch just barely under the weight of the world. In his left hand, he held a manila envelope, the contents of which would set the world aflame.

It seemed as if time stood still as he stared into the light blue eyes of the man in the dark grey overcoat. This was a moment of destiny.   As he had come to understand at great cost such moments were seldom trumpeted and were rarely grand events. Instead, they were ominous, easy, and quick. The consequences though? Those were painful and long-suffering.   As these thoughts crossed his mind, the man with the envelope chastised himself for being so

1

cynical. Once not so many years ago, he had been a good and honorable man.   This night would seal that man's death.

"Is it done?" The question was little more than a whispering rasp as it left his lips. The man in the dark grey overcoat made no movement save a slight arch of his brow.

"Well answer me. Is it done? Do we have a deal?" The words managed to escape his throat even as he tried to have them back. He was bound now by laws that went beyond this world.

"Even now that you've reached this place you're still full of that righteous anger that has proved to be your undoing time and time again."

"And responding to a straightforward question with an irrelevant non-answer is why you don't get invited to parties. Now, do we have a deal?"

"This briefcase contains all that you will need and all the knowledge available to me. We have a deal if you have what I want."

"The envelope has the information you seek."

"Then we have a deal"

So shook the world.

Chapter 1

The Third Thread

The alarm on Raphael's phone felt redundant to him as he lay awake staring at the ceiling, counting the cracks in the plaster. A red hue of early morning light penetrated the curtains that had been pulled only partly shut the night before. As Raph fought to shield his eyes from the diffused glare a long yawn escaped his lips.

Wakefulness was a struggle made all the more difficult by tossing and turning of the previous night. He felt as if he was the victim of a plot whose chief conspirators were the sun, his phone, and his own mind. The final betrayal was the most irritating and the hardest to rectify. Sometimes Raph really just wished he could turn his brain off for the night.

But alas he could not and as a result rest was quickly becoming a scarce commodity in his life and he hardly needed the blaring sound of an old-fashioned landline with a disabled snooze button to remind him of that.   He reached a lazy hand out to silence his so-called 'smartphone' as he forced himself to sit up in bed. Cracking his neck, he headed to the shower resolved to put another sleep deprived night behind him. The release of endorphins helped get him going, but Raph's

4

inability to get any kind of quality rest was really starting to worry him.

It had been like this for a few weeks now, ever since his nineteenth birthday. To celebrate the occasion Raph had gone out with a few of his friends bar-hopping. Nothing too wild, just hanging out at some of the student-friendly joints on Maple Street. One of the many advantages of growing up in New Orleans was the fuzzy nature of its drinking laws. Twenty-one tended to be more of a suggestion than a law. And yes, there had been a plethora of Irish car bombs, but he knew how to handle his liquor and in every other regard he was a straight shooter, so he didn't think that could be the cause of what he was feeling. No hangover known to man left you sleepless for weeks after the fact. The question was stuck in his head now. *Why can't I sleep?*

He stepped into the shower and let the cold water run down his body. There had been a woman that night, staring at him, just at the edge of his vision. Every time he tried to get a look at her she had faded back into the crowd. Maybe she had just been a figment of his imagination, a little birthday wish fulfillment. He supposed that could be the reason for his insomnia. It wouldn't be the first time he had lost sleep over a woman.

Raphael was tall, coming in at six feet four inches, and built like a linebacker, which made sense since he had been one in high school; but he'd never been good with the ladies. 'More than a little awkward' was what his best friend Billy would call it, and Billy was an expert on awkward.

It's possible she could be the cause. Despite not even seeing her face she had made an impression on him. He felt a pulling sensation in his bones even just thinking about her. Like they had been tuned to the same frequency and were calling out to one another. That was a silly thought. Raph supposed that he was right in calling it wish fulfillment. Just a lonely guy creating a mystery girl out of thin air. *Get a grip on yourself. Figments of your imagination do not make for girlfriends.* He ran a hand through his short, close-cropped hair and shook his head at himself.

Raph turned off the shower, toweled himself and continued about his morning routine, brushing his teeth then dressing. He skipped his usual shave. Not that it would make much of a difference in his appearance, his five 'o'clock shadow tended instead to be more of a five-day shadow. He often envied Alistair his jet-black goatee. One day his cheeks would shed their baby fat and he would grow a beard. Today was not that day. He took a quick mental inventory decided he was ready to face the morning.

As he headed down the stairs the smell of bacon

wafted up to him from the dining room. "Aww, I thought I managed to get up before you for once Alistair." His voice was teasing but had just the slightest air of truth to it. As he expected Raph turned the corner to find a full plate of bacon, eggs, and Andouille sausage on the dining room table along with a glass of orange juice. One look at that and his stomach growled; reminding him why the meal was called breakfast. The disappointment he had voiced at not being the first to awaken this morning was forgotten, a small thing compared to the anticipation of a deliciously filling spread.

Raph was still amazed at how, no matter what time he got up, Alistair always had breakfast ready and waiting for him. He had tried more than a few times on special occasions to surprise him, father's day, his birthday, and so on; but Raph had quickly realized the futility of his attempts. He had even gotten up at four a.m. one random Tuesday morning in March when he was fifteen only to find blueberry waffles, eggs benedict, fresh squeezed orange juice and a nice little hallmark card telling him he was wonderfully thoughtful. Bleary eyed he had almost started screaming until he'd tried a waffle. In five minutes his plate was clear and well forgotten were his own plans for the morning.

The memory left him with a wry grin as he took his seat at the table. In front of his plate was a note, neatly folded, sitting like a name placard. Flowery, ornate cursive script made it appear more like artwork than a set of instructions, yet the card remained easily legible despite its elegance.

Raph,

> *Had to run a few errands this morning. Need you to open the shop. Thanks, Enjoy your breakfast.*
>
> *Alistair*
>
> *P.S. Don't let Billy break anything.*

The shop was the *Portent's End*, a bookstore for whom customers were almost as rare as its contents. At least that was the joke that his godfather liked to use when he'd had a few too many glasses of brandy. Alistair had owned the small shop for as long as Raph could remember, it was the pride of his existence. For Raph, the *Portent's End* was home. He had spent the vast majority of his youth wandering its stacks, ravenously consuming the contents of its shelves.

When Raph had elected to put off going to college, Alistair's reaction had summed up his feelings perfectly: "Quite Right, Who needs stuffy academics and overly air-conditioned rooms when you have your choice of masters to learn from right here. Shakespeare, Einstein, Pythagoras take your pick we have them all." Alistair's support had meant a lot to him; he was, after all, the only family he had left.

Raph's parents had died in a car accident when he was just a baby. He was so young in fact that he didn't even remember them other than a vague notion he held onto that they had been kind people and good parents. The truth was Raph really had no way of knowing if either of those things were actually true or if they were just a fantasy he had created for himself.

The only real thing he could say for sure about them was that before they died they had named Alistair as his Godfather and left instructions in their will that if anything happened to them he was to be the one who raised Raph.

Alistair had no children of his own and as far as Raph knew had never been married. He was the closest thing to a father that Raph had really ever known. They fought occasionally, as parents and their children are prone to do, but there was no one that Raph trusted or loved in this world more than Alistair. That feeling was made even more special by the fact that his parents must have felt exactly the same when they had been alive if they had chosen to leave their only son with him.

Raph gathered his things and stepped out into the warm autumn air. It was a short walk from his home on Napoleon to the Portent's End on Magazine Street and this was the perfect weather to enjoy it in. Raph had hardly made it to Prytania when he realized that he had miscalculated the sun's warmth and that his sweatshirt was really too much to be walking around in. Wanting to be free of its suffocating confines Raph started to pull it up over his head when he tripped on the uneven pavement and found himself hurtling toward the ground.

Then suddenly he wasn't. "Thank you so much. I'm not usually this clumsy." The apology flowed out of him as he struggled to get the sweatshirt over his head.

"I really am so sor….." Finally free from his cotton blend prison Raph's sentence came to a screeching halt as he found himself face to face with one of the most beautiful creatures he'd ever come across.

Her eyes shone like two emeralds in the morning sun. A sharp contrast to the soft sheet of porcelain that was her skin. Her features were soft and without abruptness. Each part of her subtly morphing into the next, not a line wasted. Her lips were full and pouty, painted a seductive crimson that surely should have been outlawed by any sensible society. They opened now to reveal a smile that seemed destined for mischief and misdeeds, the edges daring you to join her. These dangerously alluring features were framed by a shoulder-length tangle of wildfire, an external manifestation of the suggestion in her eyes.

"You should be more careful. We wouldn't want

anything to happen to that 'aww shucks' face of yours now would we?"

Some words we use our entire lives without ever really understanding the essence that they are trying to convey. Then we encounter someone or something that embodies that essence so perfectly that we realize that this was the occasion the word was created for and all the previous times we had used it had been grossly inappropriate. When this woman spoke Raph finally understood the meaning of the word sultry.

With a start, Raph realized that he had been standing there mouth agape for what seemed like an eternity. Self-conscious he attempted to adjust his now disheveled clothing and gather his wits.

"I....um... I'm really sorry." The Cheshire Cat had nothing on the smile she favored him with then. The chills he felt were strangely at odds with heat that seemed to be suffocating him.

"Yes, you said that already.   Not great with words, but the pretty ones rarely are. If you turn any redder you may just explode."

Her tone was playful if patronizing, but Raph only really heard one part of that sentence. *She thinks I'm pretty.* While it is sure to be true that other women had held similar opinions of him over the years, to this point none had made those thoughts known to Raph and thus he found himself completely unprepared for the rush that came when someone you find incredibly attractive says that you yourself are easy on the eyes.

"Well clumsy, does saving you from horrible disfigurement earn me a name or do I have to go on calling you pretty?" Raph's mind finally started working. Not fully, but at least enough to remember his own name.

"Raphael, my name is Raphael, but most people just call me Raph." The blush had not left his cheeks and he was sure that she knew his reddened face was not simply a result of the heat. Her eyes seemed to find his no matter where he directed his gaze. Not that he was letting his gaze go far, he had embarrassed himself enough without letting her see him taking a good look at her. Though Raph was quickly coming to the conclusion that she would relish the opportunity to catch him in just such a look.

"Ok ', Raphael, My Name Is Raphael But Most People Just Call Me Raph,' my name is Faye. It's a pleasure to meet you." Her extended hand took his into its soft embrace. "Oh my, what a firm grip you have. Strong, confident, reassuring and yet very delicate. My mother always said you could tell a man by his grip. Too strong and he had something to prove. Too soft and he had nothing worth fighting for. Just right and he might just be mister right. But then my mother always was full of silly sayings about finding the right man. She was a bit of a traditionalist that way." She paused as her words floated on the air. Raph wanted to say something but found himself entranced by the rhythmic melody with which she spoke. "Alas I am a traditionalist myself in a few ways and I fear as a result I must be going. Goodbye Raphael, I'm sure that we will encounter each other again soon enough."

The screech of tires and a cacophony of honking horns behind him startled Raph. He turned to see a mess of cars and frustrated motorists unsuccessfully attempting to navigate a four-way intersection. He turned back to Faye. She was gone.

****

The remainder of Raph's walk went by in a flash, his heart still pounding from his encounter with the mystery woman. The key slid into the door and unlocked the rusted bolt that served as the only security the Portent's End needed. It was another one of Alistair's quirks that he refused to invest any money in an alarm system.

"They cost too much money, besides who's going to rob a bookstore?" He would say.

And sure enough, the Portent's End had never had so much as a speck of graffiti. The other shop owners marveled at the phenomenon and Alistair attributed it to positive thinking.   "If you know something to be true, the universe will adjust itself so that it is." Raph had learned better than to argue with results and besides he liked the idea that Alistair had a knowledge of the universe that evaded others.

He hit the switch and the lights came up gradually in the store, the bulb in the back right corner blinking out 'conk' in Morse code. Or at least that's what he imagined it did. Raph didn't actually know Morse code he just liked to pretend he did.

The musk of old books greeted him as he ventured into the back room, the smell of memories and lost time. The store was of medium size and because it was a rare bookstore it was laid out a bit differently than your local repository of used romance novels.

A display case featuring some of the more impressive, delicate, and expensive pieces of the store's collection lay on your left as you walked in with the register positioned next to the door. Behind the case were a small walkway and a work area for Alistair and Raph to use when they lacked customers, which was fairly often.

The display case was not the only place that Alistair had decided to show his most valuable wares. The floor of the front room felt like a museum with books on stands under glass covers all over the room. Next to each book was a little placard explaining the history of the work as well as any interesting information concerning this particular edition.

Raph had asked once why Alistair didn't put the certificates of authenticity on display as well, instead of keeping them filed away behind the counter. He responded by saying that a person should be able to know if something is real or not without a piece of paper telling them so.

Moving back from the more hallowed aspect of the front room, you would take a half step down into the stacks. Here the store became more traditional in nature, with large shelves full of first editions that had not yet earned the reverential treatment of a glass display.

It was a sizable collection, sorted meticulously by genre and cross-referenced by century and region. The kind of collection any book lover would salivate over.

At the very back of that maze of literary wonder was another door that led to a small hallway. The hallway had three doors. On the left a private restroom. On the right a small storeroom. And straight ahead an exit out to the alley behind the shop.

To Raph the Portent's End was more than just the sum of its parts, it was a monument to all the dreamers of this world. To everyone who was brave enough to tell a story to the anonymous masses and talented enough to get those masses to remember what they had to say. It was his church, his school, and his home.

That thought brought a smile to his lips as he went through the various daily tasks he needed to complete before the store was ready to do business for the day. For others, the work might seem a mundane humdrum of monotonous tasks performed hundreds if not thousands of times, but for Raph, it was a daily ritual in line with a priest preparing a sanctuary for the arrival of his congregation. And so with great reverence and joy, he went about his work. And before too long he was ready to begin the day.

The morning was fairly uneventful. Mr. Higgins swung by to pick up a first edition copy of Ralph Ellison's *Invisible Man* that he had been waiting on and Raph managed to sell a signed copy of *Gatsby* to a walk in.

He spoke honestly to both men when he said their purchases were among his favorites and he was glad that they had found a good home. Although even if they were going to a bad home Raph would not have been overly distraught.

No matter how much he loved the books that surrounded him business is business and they were not doing so well that they could afford to judge those willing to pay the prices that they asked.

All in all those two sales were enough receipts to make it a pretty profitable morning. At least profitable enough that Raph wouldn't feel bad when Alistair eventually did show up. The bell chimed and Raph raised his head in time to see the giant grin on Billy Bordeaux's face.

"Did you hear? A guy in Belgium supposedly stumbled upon an original 1485 hand-transcribed copy of *La Morte D'Arthur*. Can you imagine? That's got to be worth millions right? Oh man, I wish something like that would happen to me. This is like the coolest thing ever" The words came out in a jumble traveling at light speed. Raph laughed while Billy caught his breath.

"Ya, Billy it's pretty cool alright." Raph's smile was genuine but he chided himself for not sounding more engaged. It was cool, he just had other things on his mind right now. But Billy blustered on right ahead as if Raph had given the most gushing agreement he had ever heard. Billy was like that.

"I know, just imagine, going through Alistair's things. A secret hideaway attic you never even knew about. You open a dank chest of rusted metal and darkened wood and what should you discover? But the lost works of Shakespeare or an ancient copy of Beowulf in the Old English. You know what we should do? We should start going to antique stores and garage sales and looking for old books!"

Now Raph really did have to try hard not to laugh out loud at Billy's exuberance. "Um, Billy we already do that remember? This is a *rare* bookstore, in fact, that's probably where Alistair is right now, some old garage sale in Slidell on a hot tip."

"Oh ya, but still............." Billy trailed off and let his eyes take a quick inventory of the store, confirming the information Raph had just shared with him. "Alistair's really not here today?"

"No dude you're safe"

"Well, it's not like I care. He just always thinks I'm going to break something." Almost on cue, Billy's right hand sent a precariously perched box full of ballpoint pens flying through the air.

"Well, that was clearly a bad spot to put those." Raph had meant the quip to be self-deprecating. It really had been a bad place to put them, laziness more than anything, and it was better he figured that out with Billy than with a customer. But from the red in Billy's cheeks, it seems he had taken it as a dig at him. Trying to take out the sting as he moved to help Billy get the scattered pens back into their box he tried the same tactic but a little heavier on the self-deprecation this time around.

"I think Alistair just gets mad because you make it so he can't leave a job half finished. He does like his tea breaks. To be fair I think you serve to customer proof us. I'd rather know it's a bad place to leave something because of you than in front of a potential sale." That seemed to do the trick. Billy smiled at him and Raph gave him a big grin back.

They were best friends. More than that really, they were brothers.

That was another one of Alistair's favorite sayings: "Family is who you chose."

Billy and Alistair were the only family Raph had ever known and Billy's own family made a concerted effort to have nothing to do with him. The funny thing was that it was only random chance that had brought them together.

Raph and Billy had first met over a dozen years ago when Billy had wandered into the Portent's end one day looking for Young Jedi Adventure books and promptly succeeded in knocking over a stack of eighteenth-century romance novels that Alistair was in the process of re-shelving.

Billy was so scared when Alistair turned around that he proceeded to fall backward and knock over a pristinely and rather recently displayed collection of twentieth-century dystopian literature. Billy had been on the verge of tears when Raph had given him his copy of The Hobbit and told him not to worry about it. He returned three days later raving about how it was the greatest thing he'd ever read. They had been best friends ever since.

The journey from boy to young man had not

done Billy any favors in the coordination department. Now at twenty, he was not what you would call tall, though not all that short either. He stood a head and change shorter than Raph, but that missing bit of height had turned horizontal and inserted itself into his waistline; so that portly was the tactful way of putting it. The ruffled mess that was his curly dark black hair gave him the look of a walking bowling ball. As a result of his girth, Billy had a horrible habit of knocking things over without ever realizing what was happening. That, coupled with a natural genetic predisposition to clumsiness that had somehow managed to dodge natural selection over the course of millennia, made Billy a metaphorical bull in a world shop full of fine china. Very delicate, very breakable china. Alistair was fond of referring to him as chaos theory incarnate. But for all of that awkwardness, Billy was a good man, far more fierce in defense of a friend than in defense of himself.

As Billy began returning the pens he had knocked over to their rightful position on the sales counter Raph debated whether or not to tell him about his morning encounter.

Faye. It was a beautiful name for a beautiful woman. And that voice. He could still hear her in his head. Like an echo in his memory sending chills down his body.

Raph decided against telling Billy about her. There wasn't much to tell and he'd spent enough time talking with Billy about women to know they'd only end up in a co-dependent downward spiral. If you've ever spent time with two nice but awkward young men who have an incredibly hard time finding success in their dating life then you understand Raph's reluctance to discuss the matter with his best friend. When you win the lottery you don't want to rub a friend's face in it, especially if there's a good chance that you might have misread the numbers.

"Anyway, I just came by to see if you wanted to grab something to eat. I have a Groupon for Theo's that I need to use." Billy said as he struggled to fit the last pen into the box so it would close.

"I could eat." Not telling Billy was the right move. If he ever saw her again he could bring it up then. But for now, the topic of women was best avoided.

Instead, Raph put the closed sign up in the window and the two headed to lunch and talked some more about *La Morte D'Arthur* and whether or not the stories might have been based on a real person. Still, he was smiling.

Faye.

It really was a beautiful name.

Chapter 2

Trust No One

The afternoon had been a bit of a disappointment. Raph had opened the Portent's End back up immediately upon returning from lunch. All toll the shop and been closed less than an hour. And in the three hours since then not a single customer had come in. On top of that Alistair had not yet returned from whatever activity he was pursuing.

Raph tried calling him a couple of times but his godfather's phone just kept going straight to voicemail. Meanwhile, as he often did after a satisfying meal, Billy had taken to the stacks in the hopes of ferreting out some Asimov or Lovecraft that he had yet to read four or five times. It was all rather monotonous and it had Raph on the verge of closing early when he heard the jingle of the welcome bell. He raised his eyes to find he finally had a customer.

The man stood tall, nearly Raph's height; with taut leathery skin that almost seemed as if it had been sewn together in the shape of a human face. A horrible thin sticky comb-over covered his obvious baldness and sunken eyes radiated contempt. A set of yellow, crooked teeth completed a look that could best be described as plague survivor. Emaciated was the word that stood out in Raph's mind.

He forced himself to meet the man's eyes. It was not easy. Raph felt physically ill just looking at him. Then, as he often did, he felt ashamed for being so judgmental about a complete stranger. Especially one who hadn't even spoken yet.

Maybe he's a perfectly nice guy. Maybe he's got some kind of sickness that makes him looks this way and jerks like me judge him before he even gets a word out of his mouth. But Raph couldn't shake the feeling deep inside that said something was wrong. *Or maybe this guy is every bit as bad as he looks.*

He put on his best fake smile and spoke the words he had said a thousand times "Welcome to Portent's End, where we specialize in rare and antique books. Is there anything in particular that I can help you with?"

The man returned Raph's attempt at a steady gaze and unleashed a toothy grin that actually made his whole face seem that much more disgusting.

"I was looking for the proprietor, Alistair Fox, is he in?" Raph supposed he should have been prepared for the sound of nails on a chalkboard. It was the only voice that seemed appropriate for the man.

"I'm afraid he is out on some business and I don't know when he'll return. Is there anything I can help you with?" The emaciated man pulled back slightly and looked around the shop. It was only then that Raph realized just how close they had gotten to each other. His eyes finished scanning the store and came to rest on Raph's face again.

"I very much wanted to discuss a matter with Mr. Fox. I suppose I will come back another time."

The man made no movement towards the door. Normally Raph wouldn't have pressed but he hadn't made a sale all afternoon and something inside him very much made him want to help the gentleman.

"If you like, but I can assure you that I have full autonomy to conduct any store business while Mr. Fox is away." It was true. To a point.

The man raised an eyebrow and his glare seemed to intensify. "Oh well, that's quite a bit of responsibility for an employee; to conduct any store business. Alistair must trust you a great deal. You two are close then. You've known him a long time?"

"He's my godfather, I've known him since I was born." He spoke the words absently. A rehearsed answer to the question he was most often asked. He didn't stop to think that this conversation had gotten very direct and very personal very fast.

"A good friend to your parents then? How did they meet?" The man's inquiries gave Raph an uneasy tingling in the back of his mind. That he felt the need to answer them only made the sensation worse.

"They were close enough to leave me in his care. The rest is a long story and probably best told by Alistair." It was as evasive an answer as he could muster. It took a great deal of energy to keep his mouth shut and not let the words just flow out of him. The whole thing was decidedly odd and more than a little uncomfortable.

"How is Alistair? It's been years, really, since we've gotten together." The high pitched screech took up the cause again, trying a different tact.

Raph's instincts had begun to gain a foothold. There was something wrong with this whole exchange. He decided it was time for the gentleman to leave.

"Oh, same old Alistair. I was about to close up, but I could take a message for him if you'd like. If you'd just give me your name and a way to reach you I'll be sure he gets back to you as soon as he gets in."

The man scrunched up his face. As if something unexpected had happened that was worth considering but he did not resist the cues as Raph walked around the counter and opened the door for him.

"No, thank you. You've been very helpful, but it's been a long time since I've seen Alistair and I'd like to keep it a surprise that I'm in town. I'm very much looking forward to seeing the look on his face. Well, I must be off. Remember now not a word to our friend Alistair about me popping in. That's a good lad." With that, the man took his leave.   As soon as the door was shut behind him Billy emerged from his hiding place among the stacks.

"Okay, now that was one creepy dude. Where do you think he knows Alistair from?" Billy's eyes were fixed on the store's entrance, probably afraid the man would walk back in and hear his forthcoming disparaging remarks.

"I don't know. It's hard to imagine Alistair spending time with a guy like that, but it's not like I really know anyone from his life before me. It's just not something that we talk about."

It was the truth, Raph really didn't know that much about Alistair before he had come to live with him. He'd brought it up a few times, but Alistair insisted there wasn't much to tell: "A bit of tomfoolery and a dash of deviance my dear boy. The same as any man who has earned his age. Not much to speak of really."

Alistair was not much of a sharer.

Billy, on the other hand, couldn't seem to stop himself from staring at the moment.

"Dude was creepy with a capital creep. And that voice, you'd think he'd have to practice to make it sound like that. I thought my glasses were going to break. I was gonna be all like 'It's not fair!'"

Billy threw his hands up in the air in mock anguish.

"'There was time now!' Swear to god, with all the books around, it would have been perfect."

Billy's pantomime seemed to bring back the warmth that had left the room and Raph found that he now had a wide grin on his face. "Be nice. If he really is a friend of Alistair's we may end up seeing him again. Maybe even have him over for dinner."

"Oh man, an entire meal listening to that voice. I'd rather eat dinner with my mother. And that's saying something. Could you imagine? I think I still have that pair of earplugs from last Jazz Fest. Better fish them out before I get caught unawares and bleed out through the ears. Alistair would never let me live that down." Billy wasn't often one to talk trash to someone but once he sunk his teeth in he did not let go easily.

"Only you would wear earplugs to Jazz Fest. Sorry, you and babies. And I don't mean that figuratively. Literally, you and babies are the only people I've ever heard of wearing earplugs out at the fairgrounds."

Billy pretended to be taken aback. "Hey, do you know how many cases of Tinnitus are caused by that gospel tent every year?"

Raph stared at him in blank astonishment.

"Neither do I but I have no intention of becoming just another statistic. I have sensitive ears. And I'm an auditory learner. You wouldn't want me not to learn things, would you? We all deserve to learn Raph; because the children are our future and we have to teach them well. So when you're against my earplugs, you're against the children. Why do you want to keep the children from learning Raph? That's more than just wrong, it's cruel. And I know you Raph, you're my friend, you're not a cruel man. So support the children, don't mock the earplugs."

Raph had to brace himself against the counter he was laughing so hard.

****

Shortly after Billy had settled on Creepy McWeirdface as a suitable pseudonym for their strange encounter, Portent's End found itself swarming with customers. Well, maybe not customers, Raph thought with a smirk, one had to buy something in order to be called a customer. But there were browsers aplenty and really rare books didn't tend to be impulse purchases. So he watched as they browsed answering questions and being as helpful as possible.

Billy kept himself hidden. He wasn't much for strangers unless he thought they could teach him something. Then just try to get him to stop asking questions.

The rush lasted for about an hour and tapered off fairly suddenly when a warm autumn thunderstorm began to make itself known outside.   By the time the crowd had dwindled and disappeared Raph had largely forgotten about his strange afternoon visitor.

Instead, a cute girl in a sundress had him more focused on his mysterious morning encounter. With his luck, he would not be bumping into Faye again. Not getting her number was turning into the biggest let down of his week. Looking at his watch he saw that it was now nearly six thirty and past time to be calling it a day. Raph stepped out from behind the counter and decided to take a walk around the shop to make sure he wasn't going to lock any straggling browsers in with him when he closed up.

Raph was nearly to the back when the door burst open, the bell clanging with ferocious intent. A howling wind and heavy rain assailed the hitherto untouched atmosphere of the bookstore.

Alistair was there, drenched to the bone, looking like a man possessed.

"Raphael!" he called out with a desperate roar. "Raph m'boy are you here?"

"I'm right here. What's the matter? You're soaked come in out of the rain."

"No time for that nonsense. Has anyone been here? Asking after me?"

His Godfather's sudden, dramatic entrance had startled Raph and the panicked questioning was throwing him further off balance.

"Well now that you mention it, there was someone

earlier. He was a bit odd really. Alistair, what's going on? Shut the door you'll ruin the inventory."

"Bigger things to worry about than old books. The man Raphael, what did he look like?"

"He looked sickly; yellow teeth, sunken eyes, skinny. Alistair, what's going on? I've never seen you like this before." *Bigger things to worry about?* The *Portent's End* was Alastair's life what could be bigger than safeguarding its contents? Raph was genuinely beginning to get scared now.

"The games afoot and I'm two moves behind. Or at least that's what they think. I play the long game Raph, always have." His vision seemed to hone in on his godson. "Yes, a very long game indeed."

And then he was gone again lost in the infinite space of his thoughts.

"There's time yet, there must be. Watch the shop, act completely normal. Nothing is amiss. That's a good lad. Remember, trust no one." Like a shadow, he faded back into the night and was gone. Raph went to shut the door. And he could hear Alistair's voice call back in the night.

"Trust no one."

****

"Trust No One."

The words rattled around inside Raph's head. What was going on with Alistair? Surely if he was in some kind of trouble they should call the police. But what kind of trouble was he in? He spoke that thought allowed and let it sit in the air. It was Billy who spoke first.

"Well, maybe he took out the wrong kind of loan." Raph raised an eyebrow and Billy took that as an all clear to continue.

"Think about it. How much do you really make in this store? I'm in here almost every day and I hardly see anybody. "

"We're not like other bookstores that's the point." Raph could feel himself growing defensive.   "We only need a few sales a day to keep going."

"C'mon Raphael," Billy always used his full name when he thought he had a winning argument. "You're a smart guy, do the math.   What's your average sale worth?"

"I don't know off the top of my head five hundred, five fifty maybe."

"Let's say six hundred to be safe. And you make about fifteen sales a month. So that's nine thousand dollars a month. Your overhead can't be less than four thousand and it's most likely closer to six. Three thousand a month for the two of you doesn't cover the way you live and I haven't even gotten to what your taxes and insurance would be. Something is off financially about this place. I've always thought so. I just didn't think it was my place to bring it up. But now, what if he's in debt to the wrong people trying to keep this place open?"

"That doesn't seem like Alistair. Besides, I think he's got family money or something." Raph was stalling while he tried to do the math that Billy suggested. He'd never really thought about it. Whenever they had needed money they had it. But now looking back Raph couldn't remember Alistair ever saying no or telling him that something was too expensive. He had from time to time asked Raph if what he was asking for was the wisest way to spend his money, but Alistair had always been making a point about something silly that Raph hadn't thought through all the way. Like the time he'd wanted to buy a replica Highlander sword off eBay.

"No, I'm just forgetting something. There's no way that I've gone this long without asking any of these questions." Raph didn't believe it even as he said it.

Billy was relentless. "Does Alistair ever let you help with the books?" Raph looked around. "The accounts I mean."

"Well no but…….. He has a system."

"And when has Alistair ever refused to teach you something? And what about the fact that you don't have your own bank account? Alistair used to give you wads of cash for your allowance and now he gives you wads of cash for your salary. There's something off dude. You know that."

Raph and Billy stayed in the shop for another hour discussing fanciful scenarios concerning the connection between Alistair and their disturbing guest. Finally, Raph started to shut things down for the night.

Most bookstores were simple: take care of the till, take out the trash, turn out the lights, and lock the door. Easy Peazy, Lemon Squeazy. At the Portent's End, things were a bit more complicated. Because of the delicate nature of their merchandise, it was necessary to check the hermetic seals and temperature controls on each of the glass cases. Alistair insisted on taking accurate readings at open and close. It wasn't a difficult task but it could be a tedious one. Luckily Billy was with him tonight and the whole exercise went that much faster with someone to talk to, so after a lengthy discussion about the greatest science fiction shows in television history and two tangents concerning who would they would most like to see play the next Doctor the job was done and they were ready to head out.

"So what are we doing tonight?" Billy asked as Raph was locking the front door. "I'm kind of in the mood for a marathon of something after all that TV talk."

Raph put the keys in his pocket and they started the short walk home. "Ya, I could be up for that I guess. I'm pretty hungry. Order a pizza and watch some Firefly?"

"I'd rather we get some chicken tenders from Balcony Bar instead. I could do Firefly or you know what how about The IT Crowd?"

Raph looked up at the sky as a blue light flashed inside the grey clouds above. "Looks like we're about to get a..."

He was cut off by a deafening boom that seemed to come out of nowhere to explode in his ears. It was followed a fraction of a second later by a concussive blast of hot air that threw Raph off his feet and into the air.

The last thought he had was *this is going to hurt.*

Then everything went black.

Chapter 3:

Lightning and Fire

Thunder echoed in his head as Raph attempted to open his eyes. He could feel the blood flowing like fire from the cuts on his body. The world was spinning around him and refused to be made sense of. He had been next to some kind of explosion. A gas main? A terrorist attack? He didn't know, but every instinct he had told him to find somewhere safe to figure it out.

He stretched out his hands, tried to push himself upright, and found his legs rather uncooperative. The impact of his ribs against the pavement sent a sharp jolt of agony through him, strong enough to be discerned from the cacophony of pain that the rest of his body had become. It did serve to tear his senses out of their stupor and back to the here and now.

Thank God for small miracles was the thought that ran through his head with only the smallest trace of sarcasm.

Raph forced himself to crawl behind a nearby upturned mini-van and began to take stock of his surroundings. He could hear car alarms going off up and down the block and chunks of asphalt and sidewalk were scattered all over the street. Flames superheated the air around him, causing him to mix a good deal of sweat into the blood and dirt that covered him.

Next, he did a quick check of himself. Small cuts everywhere but nothing that seemed too deep. He felt around his head. It didn't seem to him as if it was bleeding from anywhere but it still hurt. *Possible concussion then.* He felt a sharp painful twinge in his left wrist when he put it to his scalp. *Sprained wrist, might be a fracture.* Now he turned his attention to the legs that had just abandoned his efforts to stand. He gently worked himself into a crouch to see if they would hold his weight. They did without a problem. *Well, that's good at least.* Having decided that he was not going to die from any of his injuries in the immediate future Raph started to stand up and look for Billy. Before he could make it to his feet he heard a bone-chilling cry.

"We've come for you Arthur-Son. Time to Die." The voice was a high pitched death shriek made all the more frightening by its sadistic playfulness.

And Raph recognized it.

Slowly, Raph positioned himself to peak around the corner of his seven-passenger shield. He could make out two figures dressed in all black striding through the bedlam, their heads constantly in motion scanning for movement in the chaos.

The shorter was a hand taller than Billy and possessed of broad shoulders and a wide gait. The taller of the pair would have stood eye to eye with Raph, gaunt and wiry in a way that invoked emaciated death. It was the man who had been in the *Portent's End* earlier.

Raph didn't believe that it was a coincidence these

two imposing men were strolling through the rubble screaming death threats. He didn't know who or what they were after but the smart thing would be to find Billy and keep their heads down until this was over.

Looking beyond the black-clad figures, Raph could see something moving by one of those piles of rubble. *Billy!* The realization almost made him stand up and shout. Almost. Instead, he froze and gathered his wits. Billy was most likely not going to handle himself well in this situation. He was either going to do something stupid out of fear or out of a misguided belief that he had to help Raph. Either way, Raph needed to get to him fast if he wanted to make sure that his friend made it through this in one piece.

The explosions had been some serious business. Which meant these guys were most likely carrying guns to go with their bombs. So that ruled any kind of confrontation out. There was no way to signal Billy to creep around to where he was without being seen. Plus these guys were getting closer every second, which meant Raph couldn't be certain that his hiding spot was going to stay hidden that much longer anyway.

In the end, it was more the lack of options than confidence in his own idea that compelled him to act. Raph grabbed a sizeable chunk of debris that still looked light enough to throw and crouched next to the tire of his makeshift bunker. He just prayed it was the oldest trick in the book for a reason, otherwise, this might be a rather short-lived rescue attempt.   He waited until the two men had turned their bodies away from him and he threw the hunk of concrete as hard as he could at the building across the street.

Raph didn't wait to look at his throw before he sprinted towards the next line of cars. He heard a sizable thump and crash that meant he had struck true. He turned his head to check if he had the desired effect. And he froze.

The two men had fallen for his simple ruse and their response had been to shoot fireballs from their hands at the direction of his erstwhile projection. The thought bore repeating in Raph's head as he stood there frozen without cover staring at his potential assailants. *They shot fireballs. From their hands. And blew up a car.*

Unfortunately for Raph the two men were not nearly as impressed by their pyrotechnics display as he was. It only took them a second to catch on to his trick and a second was not nearly enough time for him to regain his composure.

"There you are Arthur-Son. Have you decided to meet your end standing up after all? I have to admit I'm a bit disappointed. I expected more from one of your lineage." The tall one seemed to be taunting him but Raph had very little comprehension of what the man was saying or what was going on. The one thing he did understand was that he was in danger. So he ran. Or at least he tried to. Air constricted around him, first binding his legs together then his arms to his sides. Impossibly his feet began to leave the ground. Raph didn't understand how but he was sure this was the work of the Emaciated man.

It was the Brute's turn to gloat now. "Look at him. Frozen like a pup in front of a lion. You know I don't think he's ever seen real magic before. What a terrible

world this must be." The two were focused entirely on
Raph. Eyeing him like an animal at the zoo. No, more
like a kid frying ants with a magnifying glass.

"LEAVE HIM ALONE"

Billy was running full speed at the two wizards with
what looked to be the remains of a stop sign. With
surprising power, he swung at the Emaciated man and
knocked him to the ground. And Raph was free of his
invisible restraints. Not wasting a second he rushed
headfirst into the brute executing a perfect tackle like the
all-parish linebacker that he was. The two went flying to
the ground in a heap. Raph rolled off and tried to grab
Billy to make a break for it but the Brute grabbed his
right ankle and pulled him back to the ground. Stunned
Raph kicked instinctively and hit something solid. The
brute gasped for breath and relaxed his grip enough for
Raph to scramble away.

"Enough!"

Raph's head jerked around to the voice. The
Emaciated man was there. And he was holding a sword to
Billy's throat.

"Stay where you are. No more running. No more
fighting. Or I kill the fat one."

"Fine. You win. What do you want?"

"What do I want? I want you to die Arthur-Son. I
want you to die hopeless and alone and in unbearable
agony. I want you to beg for the nothingness of
extinction. That is what I want Arthur-Son. And you will
oblige me."

With that he threw Billy twenty yards into a four-
door sedan and sent a burst of wind towards Raph that hit

him in the chest like a hammer, knocking him to the ground. Raph slowly got to his feet. Only to be knocked back by another burst of wind. Raph got to his feet again. And was knocked back. Again. And again. And again. This went on until his body was bruised and nearly broken. He had been beaten almost thirty yards down the road. Far enough away that he could try to make a break for it. But that would mean leaving Billy behind. And that was something Raph couldn't do. And so Raphael Carpenter, nineteen years old, prepared himself to be murdered by forces he couldn't comprehend for reasons he didn't understand rather than abandon his friend.

And that's when the lightning came.

Angry bolts hurled with purpose.

To bring fear.

To show rage

To rain down destruction.

The ground shook.

The sky rumbled.

The very air shivered and gave way

And that's when the thunder spoke.

"You Come Here! To My Home! To My Place of Power! AND THREATEN MY FAMILY!" The voice was full of rage and power.   It filled the night air with its presence, announcing that terror followed in its wake. It was a song of salvation. The cultivation of a lifetime of righteousness. The end of fear itself.

It was Alistair's voice.

Thunder cracked and water poured forth from the heavens, quickly extinguishing the fires that raged in the streets. All save two. Two sets of flame standing opposite

Alistair struck out at the torrential downpour as if they meant to fight back. Raph could not believe his eyes. The fires seemed to twist and separate from their origin points until they were floating in mid-air. The miniature suns burned above his two would be killers bathing them in sickly light.

"Do you think we're afraid of you old man? A washed-up traitor exiled to a backward world without magic? We are Shak'Tah'Noh. We are Death." And right on cue, the two enormous balls of fire hurled towards Alistair splitting into thousands of pinpoint missiles of heat and flame.   Raph tried to shout a warning of some kind but the cry caught in the sudden dryness of his throat. He watched silently as Alistair stood motionless, making no effort to escape the fate speeding towards him. Then, suddenly the night was dark again. Raph sucked in a deep breath. Each second felt like an eternity. Lightning flashed. Alistair roared. With superhuman speed, he closed the hundred yard gap between himself and his opponents.

"I stood on the fields of Velek Nor when the earth ran red with the blood of the Tah'Mer."   More lightning fell upon them; striking in rhythm with Alistair's quick stride. From underneath his coat, he produced a metallic rod. Free of its confines it expanded to the length of a quarterstaff.

"I was at Balktier, at the fall of the Lion's Gate." A quick spin and Alistair struck the stouter man in the kidney. He whirled again and took the now bent over assailant off his feet with a sweep of his legs. "I was named First Knight of the Table while your mothers wept at the thought of conceiving you." Without looking Alistair moved to parry the sword coming toward his back. "The Queen of Dellian dubbed me Servant of the Seven Worlds, Protector of the Infinite." Parry. Thrust. Twirl. Alistair moved with lethal elegance, easily knocking away the gaunt man's attempts to get under his guard. The slightest stumble on the ruined road by his opponent was all he needed to finish it.

"I am Alistair Ret'Mier, the Fox of Avalon. Last Light of the Fallen. You are Death?" Knees. Wrist. Head. Three blows in quick succession and the emaciated man fell in a heap. Alistair spit on his fallen foe. "Then I defy you. Again."

The thunder stopped and the lightning moved towards the horizon, becoming a source of illumination rather than an imminent threat. Raph rushed to Billy's side and pulled him to his feet.

"I'm okay" was what Billy said. Looking at the state of him Raph wasn't convinced. He put Billy's arm over his shoulder and helped him over to where Alistair was standing over the bodies of the men he had so soundly dispatched of.

"Are they dead?" Alistair raised his eyebrows at the question. He clearly thought that it needn't be asked.

"No. I left them alive. The Shak'Tah'Noh are often as dangerous in death as they are in life. Besides mercy has its own rewards. They'll have to wake up in order to report what happened here. That will buy us precious time. Time we are wasting standing around here. Quickly now." Without another word he turned and started walking back to their house.

Despite Alistair's insistence on speed he never accelerated his pace beyond what Billy could manage. He walked with quick, certain strides about ten yards in front of the boys. His head was constantly in motion, looking for danger in the dark. And now that the lightning had faded it was a deep dark. Midnight in the dead of winter dark. By Raph's estimation, it couldn't be much past eight by now, which made this dark seem unnatural. He didn't like it. Most days he would have dismissed these thoughts as a flight of fancy. Today was not most days.

Despite Raph's reservations about the night, they made it home without incident. Alistair stalked into the kitchen and instructed Raph to put Billy on the sofa. He did so and took a seat himself. And as the adrenaline began to wear off he began to feel more pain than he ever remembered feeling before in his life.

Raph gently pulled up his shirt to reveal a mass of purple and green where pale white skin should have been. Dropping his shirt back down every inch of him was loaded with hurt. His eyes grew damp as he fought back tears. Raph looked over at Billy on the sofa to see that he was not alone in his struggle. Between the initial explosion and fighting for their very lives, they had endured more in the last hour than they had in their entire lives. Raph did not think that they were the better for it. When you threw the fact that apparently magic was a thing. A real, actual, tangible, thing. It was a wonder they both weren't in shock. That made Raph think he might actually be in shock but not having ever been in shock before he couldn't recognize it for what it was. It was a relief to stop thinking about it when Alistair came back into the room holding two mugs

"It's all right boys. I know the pain has set in. It'll be better in a minute. I've got just the thing." He handed a mug to Raph then walked over to Billy and helped him drink from the other one. Raph took a deep swig.

"It's hot chocolate." While Raph was absolutely a fan of hot cocoa on almost any occasion this, to him at least, seemed as if it would be the exception.

"Yes its hot chocolate, but it's also got a special little ingredient that will make you right as rain in no time. I call it Healing Cocoa. Catchy right?"

Raph decided tonight was not the night to be skeptical and drank his cup as quickly as he could without burning his mouth. Sure enough by the time he had reached the bottom he was indeed feeling a lot better.

After they had finished their first cups Alistair had gone back to the kitchen to pour them each another with a warning that they should drink these a bit slower than they had their first serving. He left them alone in the living room while he scurried about the house. Raph tried to ask what he was doing but gave up after a few minutes of being completely ignored. A glance at Billy said he wasn't much for talking right now either. So Raphael sat there quietly and drifted off to sleep.

He awoke to an intense quiet conversation between Billy and Alistair. "No, it's okay. I know why you didn't want me around now. You knew this day would come and you thought I'd get Raph killed. And I almost did. I'm just stupid and useless. No wonder my family hates me."

Alistair bent slightly and looked Billy straight in the

eye. "William Bordeaux you are a good man and a loyal friend. Your actions tonight were more than enough to prove what I have known all along; that you have a noble heart and are as true to Raph as any blood born brother. And if you did not know how I felt about you until now then that fault was with me and never with you. But your bravery has brought with it a severe choice. We run from the most dangerous men you could possibly imagine. Murderers and Torturers who seek our deaths by any means available to them. And they know your name. You can come with us; take an uncharted path of danger and battle with our lives ever in the balance. Or you can stay here. Changing your name and going into hiding knowing that they will only stop looking for you when we are dead. Dangerous still but by far a safer option. I leave the choice to you. But, before you decide, know this: Raph and I will both be better for your company in the days ahead. And that is a fact."

Billy looked at Raph then to Alistair then back to Raph again. "You're the only two people who have ever loved me. Where would I go if not with you?"

Alistair gave a quick nod and that was that. But for Raph, it was a sadder moment. For a second he felt as if Billy was expecting an answer to his question. And he was fairly sure none of them could have come up with one.

"Raphael, could you help me with this?" Alistair was fiddling with the large bookshelf on the far wall. Raph stepped over to help him move the large oaken frame away from the wall and into the middle of the room. Alistair stepped back to the wall and reached out his hand feeling for something. Sure enough, after a moment he found it and the wall opened up to reveal a set of stairs heading down to some hidden basement.

"Dude, your house has a secret passageway. How awesome is that?" Billy's response was fairly typical him and he seemed to have shaken off the emotion of only a moment ago. Raph wasn't totally convinced.

"Just something that I had tucked away for an emergency such as this," Alistair spoke with a casualness on par with saying he kept a flashlight in case the light went out. Raph was very much starting to wonder just how long Alistair had known his life might be in danger from crazy fireball wielding wizards. As if to cut off the thought before Raph had time to give it voice Alistair began urging them on with renewed vigor. "Come on now, time to go, before anyone has a chance to figure out where we've gone."

The three of them took to the stairs with Alistair at the rear practically shoving them along. The basement was dank and musky. With brick walls and a concrete slab, it was the definition of nondescript. When they reached the bottom Alistair went into a cubbyhole hidden underneath the stairs and pulled out three sizable travel packs and handed one each to Raph and Billy, slipping the remaining pack on himself. Billy smiled realizing that Alistair had planned for him all along. Raph, on the other hand, frowned again wondering just how long Alistair had known this day was coming. He slipped his pack on without comment and walked over to where Alistair was standing on the far side of the room.

"I need you, boys, to be quiet for a minute,

absolutely still. What I am about to do is incredibly difficult and will require all of my concentration."

Billy looked at Raph with a questioning glance and all he could muster was a shrug in return.

They stood there in silence while Alistair simply stared at the brick wall in front of them. He had the same blank look on his face that he got when he was doing the Sunday crossword. Raph was about to inquire if he could help when a blue light appeared at the center of the wall. It began to spread, like oil slowly covering a frying pan. Coating it until there was no wall just an ocean of blue light.

"Um, Alistair......" Raph had thought he was done being genuinely shocked this night. He had been incorrect.

"Yes, Yes. Big blue portal in the basement appearing out of nowhere. You are suitably awed and impressed. Now through the portal hippity-hop, if you don't mind, it's rather difficult to keep open you see and I'd rather not die from the effort of saving our lives. Yes, there we go one foot in front of the other."

Raph looked at Billy and saw the apprehension in his eyes. Then he looked to Alistair and saw the strain on his face. Finally, he looked ahead. He stepped forward and let his vision fill with blue.

Chapter 4

Through The Looking Glass

Raph emerged to find himself standing in a clearing the size of a football field under the blaze of a summer sun. He felt funny, like a battery that was suddenly overcharged. Every particle of his body radiated energy, and it wasn't only him. Raph was acutely aware of every atom in his vicinity. He felt the grass reaching for the sun, the subtle shifts in the currents of the air. And he felt it as Billy and Alistair joined him on this side of the portal.

He barely had time to look back before Alistair flew past him at a dead sprint toward the tree line. As he ran, he shouted back at them "Hurry lads! Run!"

Not needing to be told twice, the boys mustered all haste to catch Alistair. They had just made the fallen tree trunk Alistair had ducked behind when a deafening roar erupted from the portal. The blue pool of energy expanded outward then quickly collapsed in upon itself, sending a concussive wave out in all directions. And just like that, it was gone; leaving behind nothing but flattened grass and felled trees here and there at the edges of the field.

"What was that?" Billy shouted loud enough to be heard over ringing ears.

"When we crossed over we ripped a hole in the fabric of reality. I think that was a pretty light explosion considering. Don't you?" His tone did not seem joking in the least. Raph was forced to run through events in his head. The sum of which made him afraid.

"Alistair, what do you mean crossed over?" The words came out in a hushed whisper, his words trying not to alert his breath that it had a stowaway.

"We are on another world." Raph was staring into Alistair's eyes, hardly noticing the vice grip Billy now had on his arm. Alistair continued in a voice hard enough to break steal. "A world where we are strangers and in danger. A world where the slightest misstep would see us all dead. Remember you've known me your whole lives and that you trust me. Do what I say, when I say it and there is a chance that we might just survive this."

Then he gave him a look that Raph had never seen before. It was a look of pity.

Alistair took his pack off his shoulder and set it down on the grass in front of him. From it, he pulled a pair of heavy, dirt brown cloaks. Without looking up, he tossed the cloaks to Billy and Raph.

"Put those on."

Raph wrapped the cloak around himself and fastened the silver fox clasp it at the neck. Billy was having trouble with his so Raph reached over and fastened it as well. When he looked up, Alistair was wrapped in a cloak of his own; a mixture of green and brown with faint traces of gold and silver running through it. It was also fastened by a small fox except Alistair's fox was gold with emerald eyes. He was now perfectly camouflaged while retaining a rather regal look about him. Raph had to admit to himself that it was an admirable wardrobe selection.

"Come along, we need to keep moving. I'll explain what I can as we go." Alistair set off into the trees and did not look back to see if they followed. Raph turned to look at Billy for the first time after what seemed an eternity. Billy was scared. Terrified in a way that Raph imagined was reserved for soldiers caught behind enemy lines or kidnap victims. But there was something else there too. There was a look of grim determination. Raph did the best to mirror it in his own face. A slight nod and they moved quickly to follow Alistair through the trees.

As they traipsed through the forest conversation was light. Despite Alistair's promise to explain as they went the only inquires he didn't deflect were ones of immediacy. Everything else received cryptic delayers or a warning that they must not make too much noise. After a few hours of this Raph gave up on his questions and decided to focus instead on this brave new world he found himself in. It was no secret that Raph was a city boy and had a limited knowledge of foliage and other such outdoorsy things, but as far as he could tell there was no real difference between this world and his own. At least where trees and grass were concerned.

Raph thought about his surroundings and he felt like he was more in touch with them. The feeling of awareness that he had sensed when he first walked through the portal was there again.

In fact, Raph realized the feeling had never left him. It was like putting on a pair of sunglasses. You noticed the change when you first put them on but forget that your vision is tinted until you actively think about having them on again.

Raph saw what he thought was a large oak tree about thirty yards ahead of him. He focused his thoughts on it. The tree came alive in his mind, each molecule illuminating itself like a tiny light bulb. As he got closer the molecules reached out to him, reverberating through the atoms in the air, until all illusion of space between himself and the tree disappeared. It seemed right to Raph. A remembrance of something long forgotten, but what it was he was remembering he couldn't say.

Raph was drawn out of his thoughts by a sharp cry from Billy and the sizable thud that followed on its heels. He turned to find his friend flattened out across the forest floor. The oak tree long since passed.

"You okay?" Raph asked as he reached out a hand to help Billy to his feet.

"I tripped" was the only response he could muster.

"I know dude. Don't worry about it." Raph turned to shout for Alistair but found his godfather standing behind him. "We have to stop Alistair. I don't know how time works around here; but by earth standards, we've been scared, confused, and on the run for almost a solid day. We need food and sleep."

Alistair took a long look around, giving each degree of three hundred sixty degrees turn its due diligence. When he was satisfied he spoke calmly as if they were

simply out for an afternoon hike that the boys hadn't
gotten into shape for.

"All right then, we'll rest. Five hours for food and
sleep. Then we follow the moon."

With that, he set his pack down and smoothing out a
spot for his bedroll.

Raph watched his Godfather's casualness with a bit
of confusion.

"Aren't you going to cast wards or something?" If
they were truly in danger he would think that Alistair
could muster up some sort of defensive spell. Only
exhaustion kept him from thinking about the
ridiculousness that had made 'defensive spells' a normal,
real-world thought.

"Wards?" The answer was both nonchalant and
quizzical. It was the tone Alistair used when he wanted
you to dig deeper with your questions.

"Well you're a wizard aren't you? Shouldn't you be
able to cast spells?"

"Ah, I see the confusion. I was a wizard once, that's
true, but 'wizard' is not a vocation. It's a rank. Like a
general but with less paperwork. Don't get me wrong.
There was still a great deal of paperwork. Why I
remember one time a fresh-faced lad about your age
spilled a whole pot of peeled potatoes into some freshly
prepared chutney; now this wasn't ordinary......."

"Alistair. Wards? Protective spells?" Raph could feel
the irritation building inside him. He hated not knowing
the rules of this new life he was living. He hated Alistair
knowing and not sharing. But mostly he hated that he
didn't even know what he didn't know. Ignorance was

not bliss. It was frustrating and more than a little disconcerting.

"Ah yes well, see the thing is spells are a creation of Hollywood. Real magic doesn't work that way. Magic is simply you asserting your will over the world around you to manifest the desired effect. Some people use trinkets and potions and incantations and whatnot to help them with harnessing that will. But still, it is the belief in the process rather than the process itself that possesses the power."

Billy's face lit up as he heard Alistair's words. "So if that's true anyone can do magic." The excitement in his voice was palpable.

Alistair knew as well as Raph did where this conversation was headed. "It is true that there is no special trait that marks one out as being able to use magic and anyone could learn it in theory but it is incredibly difficult and very few ever master themselves enough to use it with any efficiency."

"But if they worked hard and studied and dedicated themselves to it, it could be done right?" There was a tenacity in Billy's voice that suggested he would not be letting this go. Ever.

"Billy theoretically anyone can play the piano and with enough practice and dedication, anyone can become a master. But we both know that the reality is for all those who begin studying the piano an incredibly small percentage become masters. It is best to keep reasonable expectations." Alistair was being kind and tactful but he was clearly skeptical of Billy's chances of mastering such a rarified skill set. Billy either didn't notice or was so accustomed to people doubting his abilities that any new incredulity left him undaunted.

"Alistair, you'll teach me how to do magic, won't you. Please?" Then Billy gave a quick look to Raph and must have felt like he had left him out because he added "Both of us"

Alistair seemed resigned in his response. "Yes, I will try." Then with more confidence in his voice. "If you can be taught I will teach you."

They ate in silence after that. Alistair instructed the boys to get some rest and with that, he turned over and went to sleep.

****

Raph stood at the mouth of a great cavern. Three suns hung in the sky. At dawn, dusk, and noon. The heat was unbearable. The beauty unspeakable. Burnt orange filled his vision with hues of purple rippling out from the twin horizons. Lightning crackled and thunder roared appearing out of nowhere, for as best Raph could tell there was not a cloud in the sky.

What do you think? Is it beautiful because it is dangerous? Or is it dangerous because it is beautiful."

Raph turned to see Faye standing a few feet away, staring into his eyes. She wore a simple white gown that seemed to be untouched by the winds raging around them.

"Where are we?" It wasn't the only question in his head but it seemed the most pressing.

"We are at the crossroads. Some call it limbo. Others call it purgatory. All peoples have a name for it, even if those names distort its true purpose." Her voice

was not the same as he remembered it. It seemed harder, less inviting. As if the heat had been sucked out of it.

"What is its true purpose?"

"Ah, now if I told you that, that would be cheating, wouldn't it. Even bringing you here is overstepping a bit. But I was never really a fan of rules." She stepped closer to him, slowly as if afraid to startle him. She needn't have worried. Raph's eyes were locked on hers and he stood transfixed by her presence. Yet he felt that was doing a far better job of maintaining his mental faculties in this encounter than in their previous one.

"So why bring me here? What do you gain?"

"Well, that's not very nice, assuming I have something to gain." She was standing directly in front of him now. Tilting her head up at him as she spoke. "Maybe I just want to help. Maybe I like you. Maybe I think we should be allies instead of enemies."

"Why would we be enemies?"

"Always the questions with your kind. Poking, prodding, gathering as much knowledge as you can as if it were coin to be earned and spent later." Faye stepped away from him and Raph knew he had made a misstep.

"Please, I'm not trying to be difficult. I just don't understand what's happening here." She turned back to face him. One sun above her, one burning on both sides, and all around lighting rained down from the cloudless heavens.

"My dear boy, that's the point."

Raph snapped awake. Terror filled him as sunlight flooded his eyes. He counted to ten and took a quick inventory of his surroundings until he felt confident he was back where he belonged in his bedroll in the party's camp. Billy and Alistair slept only a few feet away. Billy was snoring. *But this isn't where you belong, is it?* Raph thought to himself. *No more than you belong on that strange dream world. You belong back in New Orleans spending your days working at the Portent's End.*

But even as he thought it, he knew it that it wasn't true. Despite the strangeness and despite the danger he felt like something inside him had finally awakened. He felt fuller, healthier, and he really didn't want to go back to the way things were before.

It was, in fact, that sense of heightened awareness that led him to believe that what he had just experienced was more than just an ordinary dream. Even as he had that thought it caught him off guard. A dream is a dream. And certainly, his subconscious had a lot to deal with right now. It would stand to reason that he would be having some weird dreams for the next long while. But two things stood out to him. First after weeks of not sleeping and not dreaming he easily fell into a deep enough sleep to dream out here in a forest under a strange sky with the sun still shining above him. The second was that regular dreams fade. Whereas every second of this one burned brightly in his mind.

Raph rolled over and tried to get back to sleep. He couldn't. And so he laid there staring up at an unknown sky waiting for someone else's sun to set so he could get back to living a life he was completely unprepared for. He had to try very hard not to scream.

Alistair and Billy awoke a couple of hours later. Raph kept quiet about his dream. He seemed to be developing a habit of that when it came to his interactions with Faye. Both the real and imagined ones. But he wasn't too inclined to be sharing with Alistair right now and there was no way that a trippy more-than-a-dream conversation would do anything other than freak Billy out. So Raph said nothing as they cleaned up camp and began their journey towards the rising moon.

The trio moved slowly through the darkened forest. While it would be true to say that Billy was the slowest of the three, Raph knew that he would not have been moving all that much faster on his own anyway. Alistair moved with his usual grace and Raph had to struggle to keep track of him as he deftly maneuvered the forest. The endeavor was made harder by that fox-clasped cloak of his. Raph only hoped that his own cloak gave him as much camouflage as Alistair's.

Of course, even if it did, it wouldn't have done him much good. Neither Raph nor Billy were anywhere close to being considered a woodsman. The night was quiet and they stood out like a car alarm in a library. Traipsing about, breaking every branch along the way and stumbling over tree roots every few feet. And while Raph wouldn't consider himself an expert in such matters, it seemed that when you were being hunted by people who want to kill you it would be best not to be both glacially slow and ridiculously loud. Nonetheless, they continued through the trees with the moon as their only illumination. Following Alistair as best as they could and trying not to think about things too hard.

Hours passed as they fought their way ever deeper into the forest's heart. Slowly but steadily the expansive sky above them gave way to a claustrophobic canopy of faded leaves and menacing branch. The ever constant moon that had guided their early evening had become an ever less frequent visitor, capable of pointing out only their most severe missteps. At one such brief visit of the moon, Raph realized the shape he had been following for the last twenty minutes was actually some sort of raccoon. He stood there, dumbfounded and waited for Billy to catch up to him.   When he turned to explain the situation he saw Alistair there, clear as day, gesturing for them to follow. And so they did.

That proved to be the last bit of decent light that they were going to get. Even with his eyes adjusted to the night, Raph could see nothing. He kept his ears open, trying to keep track of Billy and Alistair by listening for their footsteps. Trying to keep track of Alistair this way was a futile exercise, but Raph had some small successes when he listened for Billy behind him. He tried to work his way back to the noise but it seemed to just keep getting farther away until there was only silence.

He attempted to reach out to his surroundings as he had earlier with the oak tree, but Raph could find nothing around him that he could connect to. All he felt was dark and alone. Despair began to overtake him. Alistair was probably long gone, unaware that the boys had lost his trail. Billy was somewhere out in that darkness too, almost certainly feeling just as lost and alone as Raph did at that moment.

A low growl rumbled in the dark.

Startled, Raph jumped at the sound. He tried to take a step back and slipped on a loose branch and fell flat on his rear.

The growl grew into a roar and hot sticky breath coated Raph's face. Terrified he scrambled backward until his back was flat against what felt like an enormous tree trunk.

Still, he could see nothing in the blackened forest. Raph sat there silent and still, waiting for a sign that the night-cloaked beast had left him.

Another roar. This one right in front of Raph. Warm air rolled over him, drenching him in saliva as it hit. The great beast snorted and fire flew up from its nostrils. The sudden flash of light blinded Raph and he put up his hands in an attempt to shield his eyes. The hot flames burned intensely. Raph felt like he was trapped too close to a furnace. Then, suddenly, it was gone.

Raph's body ached from his tenseness, but it was a solid hour before he let himself relax. He decided that the sun would be up soon enough anyway and that it would be far smarter to simply stay put until he had some light rather than gallivanting about a ridiculously scary forest in the dark while large probably fire-breathing creatures that may or may not want to eat him were lurking about. Whether this decision was smart or indeed even rational who's to say, but it was the only thing Raph was emotionally prepared to do at this point.

About the time he came to this conclusion Raph began to imagine that the forest was calling his name.

"Raph! Raphael! Raph where are you?"

This hallucination continued and he could swear that it was getting louder and even sounded a little like Billy.

"Raphael? Can you hear us? Raph?"

Finally, Raph was forced to face the reality that the voices were, in fact, reality and not fanciful illusion.

"I'm over here! Over here!"

He repeated the cry a few more times.

By the third shout, he had managed to find his voice again.

"This way Alistair! He's over here."

And finally, there was light. Not the blinding light of a sudden fire in the night but a soft reassuring white light that allowed his vision to adjust without pain. Even still it took his eyes a few moments to trust this sudden turn of events.

Billy and Alistair were there and all three of them were surrounded by a dome of light that seemed to be moving, keeping Alistair's staff at its center. Raph was still propped up against the tree trunk. Alistair was kneeling beside him checking him for injuries. At this point, Raph was just grateful that he was alive and not alone. The fact that he had managed not to piss himself in fear was just gravy on top. He looked up at Billy and tried to muster a smile to let him know he was ok. Judging by Billy's reaction, Raph was fairly sure he had been unsuccessful.

"Well, you're all right. Just a little shaken I'd guess. I'm sorry. I should have kept a better eye out. But in my defense, it's not like you to lose your cool in the dark Raph. " Alistair's apology seemed more like an accusation to Raph but he was too exhausted to get angry.

"There was a creature. It breathed fire. I thought it was going to eat me." The words took a great deal of effort to get out.

"Oh, a dragon. Well yes, that would scare the wits out of you. They're not supposed to be in this neck of the woods so to speak. It's a wonder it didn't eat you." He paused, pondering the information for a second. "Well, it's gone now. Let's get moving before it comes back."

"That seems like a really good idea to me." Billy chimed in while looking rather horrified. Alistair simply smiled and held out his hand to Raph. With a bit of effort, he got to his feet.

"Right then. Off we go." was all Alistair said as he turned and began walking. The dome of light that sheltered them moved with him, still centered on the staff he carried. Raph and Billy hurried after him, staying close, anxious to keep as far away from the dark as possible.

Shortly after dawn, they came out of the forest onto a field of green and yellow. This was a great relief to both Billy and Raph, but when they stopped for a moment to catch their breath and enjoy their small victory Alistair simply kept walking and they were forced to catch up. Another hour's march through open country found the three of them approaching a small farm. To Raph's surprise rather than avoid the clutch of dwellings Alistair hastened towards them. Raph and Billy hurried to keep up. As they approached Raph could make out a young man working in the fields. And from the way he set down his till and ran towards the big white house he had apparently spotted them as well. He came back out of the house with an older gentleman who looked on expectedly as the party followed them straight to the front porch. When they reached the porch Alistair walked up to the pair of men and shook their hands. Then Alistair turned to them and said simply.

"We have arrived."

Chapter 5

Answers and Questions

Fifteen minutes later they were seated in a small living room on what were some ragged but rather comfortable chairs. The older of the two men had ushered them in with an overabundance of reverence despite the fact that Raph and Billy understood absolutely nothing that he said.

The language he spoke seemed like some strange amalgamation of Latin and Old English. It was just familiar enough that Raph felt like he should be able to make it out or at least identify what language was being spoken but far too different to wrap his head around. As soon as Billy and he had sat down Alistair had told them to stay put as he walked into the adjoining room with their hosts. Raph didn't mind being told to sit and relax but he also didn't much care for being left out of the loop.

He was listening intently attempting to make some sense of what was being said in the next room when Billy leaned forward and spoke softly to him.

"Raph, I know I said that I was in this to the end and I am; but have you really thought what we are in for? We are on another world where we don't speak the language and have no idea what's going on." The fear in Billy's eyes struck Raph like a slap. It hurt more because he knew that the same fear was showing through on his own face.

"We didn't imagine those two guys trying to kill us and we aren't having some shared delusion. We are on another world and that by itself suggests we didn't have many other options. Alistair says we're safe in this house so while we're here it's time to press for some answers. But I've got a feeling this is going to get a lot worse before it gets better. Which means we've got to keep up our courage. Alright, buddy?"

Alistair returned with their hosts right as Raph finished speaking. It was hard to tell if his words of encouragement had been of any help to Billy and unfortunately any further conversation on the matter would have to wait. It was time to see if Alistair was finally prepared to tell them some things.

"Here drink this." Alistair handed each of them a small vial full of an orange liquid. Raph took it carefully in his hand and marveled at how cold it was to the touch. Billy's face had grown even paler. Raph was fairly sure that if it got any whiter they were going to have to invent a new color pallet. Raph had said it was time to start asking questions and now was as good a time as any to push the issue.

"What is it?" Billy stopped halfway to drinking his when Raph asked his question. Alistair waited until he had settled into a sturdy looking dining chair across from them before he answered.

"It's a specially made potion that will enable you to understand any other language you encounter. It also allows you to respond in said language. Basically, it's a universal translator. This size dose will last a month or two, and by then I should be able to buy or make some more. Well, what are you two waiting for? Drink up. You're being rude to our host."

Their hosts had taken a seat on some humble chairs by the hearth. They didn't look quite as eager to talk as Alistair suggested but Raph was beginning to feel as if he was, in fact, being a bit rude. On the other hand, he was becoming increasingly irritated with Alistair's constant disdain for anything other than unflinching obedience.

"Yes, forgive us for not blindly ingesting whatever you put in front of us. I think we've had enough things that were figuratively hard to swallow on this journey without adding something literal to the equation thank you very much." Raph was surprised at the edge he heard in his own voice but was unwilling to back down.

Following instructions blindly was not in his nature and Alistair should know that considering he's the one who taught Raph to question everything. "Besides I thought you said this wasn't how magic worked. That it was about asserting your will over the world. That potions and wards and all that weren't necessary." Alistair looked to their hosts and said a few sentences. The pair stood up and left the room leaving Alistair alone with the boys.

"Yes, you're right I did say that. But also no, there's

more to it. It's complicated." Alistair pulled out an old wooden pipe and set about cleaning it while he talked.

"Let's see if I can find the best way to explain this to you. The universe you know, with the earth you grew up in, is one of an infinite number of universes. These universes began exactly the same way. But every time an event occurs that has more than one outcome the universe expands and divides to account for each of the different paths that could have been taken. Sometimes these events are large and are the difference between a star collapsing or a species emerging. Sometimes these changes are minuscule, the difference of blinking now or a second from now. If you take that idea and project it out over everything that has ever occurred over the course of history; that's how many universes exist. Which, as I said, is infinite. Since every action creates another set of infinite decision trees. That is the truth of the universe and a truth that is not without supporters on your earth. Are you following me so far?"

Raph saw Billy nodding furiously and wondered how much of that was from comprehension and how much was just from sheer awe. Raph had read enough Max Tegmark to understand that in an infinite universe there would be an infinite number of worlds that had the same conditions for life as earth, but the idea that the universe itself would divide in some kind of cosmic mitosis every time someone made a choice blew his mind. Struggling to keep up he nodded as well.

"Good, then I'll continue." Something in his voice reminded Raph of a teacher who thought his students should be asking questions. Alistair kept on with his lesson nonetheless. "What your own scholars have not come up with is the notion that some of these other universes are reachable to each other. Not all universes mind you, though again the number of universes that are connected are infinite as well. Universes that are too close to the original and universes that are too far apart fall outside what we call the Tand-Roth zone. You could not travel to a version earth that could not support human life for instance, or to an earth where the only difference is that you wore a blue shirt on your first day of school rather than a red one."

To say Raph's head was spinning would have been a bit of understatement. Billy was looking at Raph for reassurance that he wasn't the only one out of his depth. He wasn't. Tand-Roth Zone? Since when had Alistair become a quantum theorist? And why did he keep saying 'your earth' and 'your scientists'? Realization dawned on Raphael.

"You're not from our earth are you, Alistair?" Billy's head whipped around to stare, his mouth agape. Only a slight twitch at the ends of his mouth betrayed any kind of emotion from Alistair.

"No Raph, I'm not. I'm from here originally." It was a statement, but the look in Alistair's eyes said he meant it for an apology. Billy was having a hard time processing the new status quo. Raph pressed for more answers.

"And where is here exactly?" Raph's tone was harsher than he intended and he could sense a kind of resigned hurt emanating from his godfather.

"Here is Avalon. And yes, before you ask, it is the same Avalon of Arthurian myth. But I'm afraid it is a much grimmer place than legend would have you believe. This is a world caught up in the egos of war and the realities of politics."

It struck Raph that every time he thought that their situation couldn't get more outlandish right then the universe or, as it appeared now, universes decided to step up their game. At this point the idea that mystical Avalon of Arthurian legend was a parallel world he had fled to in order to avoid assassination barely phased him. Billy, on the other hand, could always be counted on for an unsuitable response.

"That....is...so..." The shock on his face apparent he struggled to get the words out ".....COOL!!!!!" It wasn't the reaction Raph had been expecting. "So where is the round table, and Camelot, and Merlin?! Oh, Alistair tell me you know Merlin!"

Alistair finally cracked a smile at this. "Merlin has been dead a long time and while I may be older than I look I'm not that old. As for the rest, well they are as much legend here as they are on your world. There is a prophecy about King Arthur we have here. And it does hold some sway."

"We know the prophecy Alistair, it says in Britain's hour of need King Arthur will come again and save them." Raph had known the story since he was a boy. "That's why they call him the once and future king."

"That is the prophecy on Earth, yes. It's a bit more parochial than the one we have here. On Avalon and a great many other worlds, it is said that a descendant of Arthur will rise, find the Grail, and save the whole of existence from the end of all things." Alistair's eyes did not leave Raph's when he said this.

And then it struck Raph like a freight train. "Arthur-Son."

Billy looked at him confused and Alistair leaned back in his chair.

"That's what they kept saying. Arthur-Son. That's what they called me. The Shak'Tah'Noh." Now realization dawned in Billy's eyes as well.

"They think I'm the one in the prophecy. They think that I'm a descendant of King Arthur." Raph looked straight at Alistair and didn't bother to hide the rage that was building inside of him. "And you do too."

"You are a descendant of Arthur. This I know for certain. If you are the one spoken of in the prophecy I cannot say. But that is irrelevant for right now. What matters is that they believe it and they will kill you to achieve their objectives."

Raph was stewing in rage and self-pity, reevaluating his entire life, seeing it from a completely new perspective. Because of that, he didn't ask the obvious question. Billy did that.

"What are their objectives?"

"Why, the end of all things of course" was Alistair's response.

Raph stared at his godfather, waiting expectantly for him to continue. Unfortunately for Raph's temper, Alistair seemed to be expectantly waiting for the boys to react. The nonchalance was too much for Raph and words starting pouring out of him before he could think.

"That's not an 'of course' Alistair. You can't just say 'The end of all things' ominously then throw in an 'of course' afterwards like it's some same old same old because you're a fan of being cryptic and melodramatic. Explanations. Exposition. Context. These are things that I need if I'm even going to have a chance at comprehending what my life has become. So please, for me, will you just tell us what you mean without coating it in three layers of menace first? What do you mean by the end of all things? And what, precisely, do I have to do with any of it." Raph realized he was standing and his face was bright red. He carefully sat back down but never took his eyes from Alistair. Raph admitted to himself there was probably a better way than huffing and puffing to get the answers he wanted. He also admitted to himself that a little huffing and puffing felt pretty damn good to him right at that moment.

"I don't have all of the answers, Raphael. It has been the sacred duty of my family to watch your lineage, protect it, and teach it the ways of the universe when you came of age. I thought we were safe in isolation. And more foolishly, I thought the Shak'Tah'Noh defeated. They are nihilists of the worst order. They believe in no morality, no code of ethics. They do not seek power or riches. They simply want to put an end to existence. They want a return to the void. To nothingness, formlessness. Some among their numbers are men who were once good but gave into despair. But most are cruel, jumped up thugs who care not one bit for ideology. They seek only to make the world share their pain. Pawns. But dangerous ones." Alistair took a deep breath before continuing. "I don't know what their plan is, but if they want to stop you from finding the Grail then it seems to me that finding the

Grail is exactly what we must do. And we must do it
before they find a way to kill you."

The room was quiet then. Raph felt as if the weight
of the world had just come to a crashing halt on his
shoulders. Billy sat back stunned. And Alistair looked at
him with pity for the second time in his life. Raph did not
care for the look one bit. The silence was deafening. Raph
looked at the vial full of liquid that he still held in his
hands. With a great sigh, he raised the vial to his lips and
drank it down in one gulp. It was pretty awful but he'd
had cheap tequila that was worse. Billy sputtered and
choked a bit as he drank his own vial.

The older of the two men entered then with a tray
full of bread and cheese and their tea. Alistair stood up
from his chair, looking grateful for the reprieve.   "Ah,
Brun good. You always knew how to lay out a spread.
And I'm sure the lads will appreciate a bit of a tea chaser
right now. Come let us leave the boys to their meal. We
have much to discuss and they have much to digest."

Raph and Billy sat in silence after the two men
exited. Raph was sure that Billy wanted to talk about
everything that they had just been told and he appreciated
his friend letting him sit quietly and reflect upon the
avalanche of information that had just fallen on him. A
knock came at the door and their respite proved to be
short-lived. The younger of their hosts poked his head in.

"Hello? Have you taken the potion now? Can you
understand me?"

"Yes, we can understand you." Raph kept his tone
neutral. These men were clearly doing them a kindness
but he was not in the mood to make new friends at the

moment.

"Excellent." Without another word he walked in and sat down in the large oaken chair Alistair had been occupying. He leaned forward expectantly, big doe eyes darting from Raph to Billy to back to Raph again. He reminded Raph of a puppy dog looking up at two masters; unsure of where his next treat was coming from, but certain it would appear at any moment. When it became apparent that they were not immediately going to explode into conversation their host took it upon himself to get them started.

"My name is Lux."

"Raph."

"Billy."

Raph took a second to examine the man. He was more mature than he had looked to Raph when they first saw him. Now it was clear he was at least Raph's age if not older. He stood about six foot and was lean. Not skinny so much as wiry. He had sandy blonde hair that screamed surfer dude and deep almond eyes that surely would have made him a hit with the ladies of any world. All in all, he seemed like the kind of stereotypical twenty-something actor they would get to play the heartthrob in some high school melodrama.

"So what's it like?"

"What's what like?"

"Being on an adventure! Traveling to another world! It must be amazing."

"It's um…. It's something all right." Lux's exuberance caught Raph a bit off guard. For Billy though it seemed to be the jolt he needed.

"It's super scary. But also pretty cool." That seemed to be the answer that their new friend had been expecting. His face broke into a wide grin.

"And the Fox. What's he like? Is he really like they say?" That question didn't really do much for Raph's mood and it showed in his response.

"I don't know. What do they say he's like?"

"Why the cleverest mage there ever was." Raph could tell that Lux was expecting some sort of recognition. "The scourge of eight. The champion of Balktier. The Last Light of the Fallen. My father tells stories of when he served in the Traveler's Wars. Hopping from world to world, a never-ending stream of impossible to win battles and always it was the Fox who brought them out alive and victorious." He looked at their blank faces quizzically. "You really don't know who you're traveling with?"

"No I guess we really don't." was Raph's only reply.

****

Lilith Fey was not a woman who was easily intimidated. In truth, she was far more accustomed to being the intimidator. But this man, in this place....

She shuddered. Better not to dwell on it. He had invited her here as a peer following the old forms. It showed her respect. The self-styled "Leader of the Lawless" did not like rules. It was a trait they shared. But where she had good reason to disdain rules her host simply felt they made him predictable. Of course for that same reason, he may have obeyed the forms because no one would have expected him to. Whatever his true motivations; Jack Smith, the Bard of Bedlam, the

Purveyor of Pandemonium, was a man to be wary of.

She counted it a double honor that his booby-trapped
abode had only tried to kill her three times. Enough to
show she was worthy of his interest but not enough to
indicate he actually wished her harm. It was as flattering
as two pendulum axes and a trap door could get.

The residence was quite impressive if you could get
past the imminent threat of death and dismemberment
long enough to appreciate it. Lilith stood in its center, a
large round room with a domed ceiling.

"I want in." So much for pleasantries, she thought to
herself ruefully. Well just because he wanted to get right
to it didn't mean that she couldn't do with a little foreplay.

"It's good to see you too Jack. I was grateful for your
kind invitation." He was lounging on a decadent love
seat, white shirt untucked and only partially laced. His
unruly black hair accentuating his green eyes and boyish
grin. But what caught Lilith's attention was the way he
filled out the leather breaches that he wore. Another day,
on another man and Lilith, might have gotten a few ideas.
But not today and not this man.

"I'm sorry how rude of me." Jack stood and gave her
a deep formal bow full of flourish. "Welcome. Your
presence does me great honor. Forgive my ill manners but
I was overwhelmed by the complexities of your beauty
and the ease of your grace. I am afraid that I am a poor
compliment to the regal bearing of a lady such as
yourself, but I vow that I will ever strive to make do. So
again, in humblest manner, do I bid you welcome to my
home." Finished with his honeyed words, he straightened
from his bow and looked her straight in the eyes.

"I want in."

"My dear Jack, I'm afraid I have no idea what you
are referring to."

"Oh now don't take that tone. You're far tricksier
than I am of late Lilith. Or should I call you Faye?" He
paused to let that name sink in. "Looking as you do it's
hardly fair for the boy. I'll bet you didn't even have to bat
your eyelashes. Which is a shame. I hate to see good
eyelashes go to waste. Perhaps you should practice your
feminine wiles on me. You know what I say, a busy
tongue is a sharp tongue. We wouldn't want you to grow
dull. I can't stand a woman who grows dull."

"I'm as sharp as ever Jack. And if you don't want to
find out exactly how sharp you'll refrain from interfering
in my affairs." She kept her voice playful and soft but
inside she was panicked. How had he known about her
visits to the boy? And how much exactly did he know?
"And since when do you care for the plans for others?"

"Oh my dear Lilith, I'm bored. I just want to have a
little fun. And you should be happy. I've decided that I
want to be on your team for the great game to come." He
paused and tilted his head at her. "I'm sorry my mistake,
it has already begun. The fox runs free while the hound
chases his own tail. The cogs turn and the empty return.
Men plot. Women scheme. And, at the center of it all, the
lion must learn to roar. Thus the field is assessed. And yet
here I sit, not even knowing which game you've chosen
to play. I'm not the only one to wonder. There are other
great players sitting in the wings, waiting to take the
stage. And they do not enjoy playing the fool nearly as
much as I do."   He smiled a dashing smile and put up his

hands in mock surrender. "I will make it easy for you and lay my cards on the table. The boy must find the Cup. On that, we agree. What happens after that?" He gave a shrug that could have taught steel a lesson in cold indifference. "I love a good surprise."

"You plan to help him? Play one of your tricks?" She had tipped her hand and she knew it but this was too good an opportunity to pass up. "How?"

"Why with subtlety and great panache. How else?" He was frustrating, as always. It was another lesson her mother had taught her, never bandy words with a scoundrel. And Jack Smith was king of the scoundrels.

"All of this pretense is maddening. The boy should be ours by right. He is a creature of magic and chaos if ever one lived." Too honest. But honesty was the most dangerous tool of a talented liar.

"He is a creature of choice. The embodiment of what could be." Jack might have well said that the sky is blue for all the confidence in his voice.

"Exactly a natural ally." Was he. His line had never been one before. That was the point of her machinations after all.

"Oh? On how many worlds does man choose to spurn the mystic for the rational? How many peoples choose tyranny over anarchy? Be careful in your assumptions Lilith. They will get you killed." That was it. She gave a twinge of a smile and he knew he had said more than he should. She could see the realization in his eyes for a second but to his credit, he showed no sign of his mistake anywhere else. He resumed his position on the love seat and tapped it twice inviting her to join him.

"So are we going to make passionate, world breaking love or are we done here?"

"We're done here. " Lilith turned and walked out. This meeting had proven more fruitful than she had expected. She wondered how many times Jack's house would try and kill her on the way out.

****

Billy was in over his head. He knew it. Raph knew it. Alistair knew it. In fact, anybody who even remotely glanced in his direction knew it. He was scared and tired and completely unprepared for this new world he found himself in. He wanted to cry his eyes out and never stop. He wanted to go someplace where no one would ever find him and curl up in a ball. He was that terrified. And yet as he sat listening to everyone else make plans he realized that he had never been more excited in his life.

Magic and knights and parallel worlds. It was as if all the imaginary games he had played when he was a kid had come to life. And here he was on a real-life quest with a famous wizard on Avalon. He was going to die. Billy wasn't completely delusional. Magic may be real, but this was still life and not fiction. Happy endings weren't guaranteed and he was the least prepared for this adventure out of everyone. But at least he was here and not back on earth with his mother, wondering if Raph was dead or alive; always wondering what if.

If only she could see him now. Well, she probably would have still said he was a disappointment and a sidekick. His mother was a real piece of work. But Billy didn't care, Raph was his best friend and treated him with respect. If other people wanted to think of him as Raph's sidekick then that was fine with him. It wasn't really true and even if it was it was a hell of a compliment. Lost in thoughts of terror and excitement he didn't realize that the conversation had turned its attention to him.

"Sorry, what?"

"I said…" Alistair's tone was a mixture of impatience and indignation. "Do you think you can manage that pace? Honest now. You're not in the best of shape and we have long hard miles ahead of us. Once we leave here we will be vulnerable and must stick to the plan. That means we must keep up our pace. I don't mean to be mean or inconsiderate but I have to know that you can keep up or we have to change the plan to accommodate."

It was an embarrassing thing to be asked. Especially in the presence of the two people he cared most about and two complete strangers. He didn't hate Alistair for the question. It was a fair one and all of their lives might depend upon it. But that didn't mean it didn't hurt his feelings.

He could feel his muscles ache just from the nights walk here. This was three or four hard days on the road. With no stopping unless to grab some sleep. He'd never been one for exercise and even when he'd tried it because he knew he'd needed it people would always chuckle and snicker at him. So he just let himself be fat. He'd never really thought his life might depend on his physical fitness. More than that Raph's life might depend on it. Which meant he was going to have to push his body harder than he ever had before. It was his own fault. So it was his burden alone to carry.

"I'll be fine."

"You're sure?" Raph had that look of concern that seemed to be his default face when looking at him. That more than anything else made up his mind.

"I'm sure. "

"Good that's decided then. We make for Ardoth at first light. If we cover 35 miles a day we should make it to the city by sundown on the third day. Brun, you've been too kind already but we must ask for four days rations for the three of us if you can spare it."

"Pardon, but I think your math is off a bit M'lord Fox. They'll be four of you on the road. I'm too old to go adventuring but as long as there's been a Ret'Mier there's been a Traal following them. My boy knows these woods better than anyone and I don't think he'll be happy stuck on a farm his whole life. On top of that, the worlds changed since last you were here. It might be handy to have someone around who's a bit more knowledgeable about current events. He's come of age and good with a bow. His place is with you. Just as mine was all those years ago."

Billy watched as Lux looked at his father with unadulterated glee. He wondered what it was like to have a father who cared for you so much that he was willing to give you up so that you could have a chance for a happy life. Billy's own father had given him up but he was fairly sure Billy's happiness hadn't been his motivation. The two men hugged for a good long while and it fell to Alistair yet again to be the downer of the group. He coughed and the men broke off their embrace.

Alistair took Lux by the shoulders and looked him straight in the eye.

"The road will be dangerous and I do not yet know where it leads. It may be a long time before you see your home again. If you ever see it again at all. But I won't say that we couldn't use you. Is that what you want?" Some of the joy faded from Lux's face then and he looked back to Brun.

"Father, this is what I wish but are you sure? The idea of never seeing you again......"

Brun cut off his son with a wave of his hand.

"Follow the Fox without question or hesitation. Never stand ideally by when innocence is threatened. Be kind and fierce in equal measure. Remember that you always have a choice. Do these things and you will see me every time you look into a mirror."

Lux turned to Alistair and spoke with an enthusiasm tempered by the wisdom he'd just received. "I'm coming with you."

"Then to bed all of you. We leave at dawn."

Chapter 6

Travelers

The next morning saw the party out the door before the sun was over the horizon. Brun and Lux had said their peace the night before and it seemed to Raph that neither wished to linger over their goodbyes now that the time for leave-taking was upon them. So with no great fanfare, they nodded their gratitude to Brun and made for the road.

Thirty minutes into their journey they come to their first fork in the road. The bookseller in Raph was amused at so obvious a metaphor. Luckily for his poetic side, Lux promptly took them right without so much as a second's hesitation. This became a familiar routine as the day wore on.

Lux explained that Ardoth was a city in constant flux, forever caught between the Northern Kingdoms and the Southern Alliance. It was known to alter its allegiances, by sword or pen, every decade or so. Because of this precarious and ever-changing position over the centuries both the North and the South were constantly trying to find new hidden paths with which to smuggle goods or surprise an unsuspecting enemy with. The result was that Ardoth had developed a complex road system in and around the city. Whatever the history, Raph thought it worked out quite nicely for their purposes.

The first day's journey was long and hard but uneventful. Despite his protestations that he was doing just fine, they had needed to slow down in order for Billy to keep up in the later hours of the day.

Still, Raph was impressed with the willpower of his friend to keep going long after his body had to be screaming for him to stop. The sun was well past set when they finally stopped for the night. Lux scouted out a nice camping spot about a half mile off the road. Far enough away that someone wouldn't accidentally stumble upon them in the night.

Alistair allowed them a small cook fire and the group devoured a surprisingly tasty soup that Lux prepared them from their rations and a few roots he had found. It wasn't exactly a crawfish boil but what could you do.

Soon they found themselves talking quietly amongst themselves. For a moment it seemed as if they were just four guys on a camp-out without a care in the world.

"Tell us a story, Alistair."

Raph wasn't sure what had compelled him to make that particular request but it seemed normal for a boy's godfather to tell him a story around a campfire and Raph was a fan of anything that seemed the slightest bit normal at the moment.

"Ya Alistair tell us a story. Please?" Billy took up the call timidly.

"I would be honored to hear a story from the Fox's own lips." Alistair harrumphed and broke out in a smirk at that last remark. But Raph knew that Lux had hit a soft spot by playing to Alistair's ego so Raph followed suit.

"C'mon Alistair you always tell the best stories."

"Tell us a story about Avalon. It'll be educational and fun." Leave it to Billy to try and use the word educational to win someone over. Alistair might have had the same thought because his smirk had become a full-blown grin now.

"All right, All right. Settle in and I'll tell you a story." He waited for the boys to get comfortable on their bedrolls and a suitable quiet to fall upon them before he started, in a solemn baritone, to tell his tale:

"A long time ago, before you and me, before Arthur and the Grail, before civilization had even begun on Avalon or Earth, came eight men and women of enormous wisdom and understanding. There was Tarth who put his faith in an ordered universe. Tarth's closest companion was the maverick Zha who believed that the universe's true beauty lay in its fundamental randomness. There were Lani and Aman who believed the universe was balanced between the forces of the feminine and the masculine. There was Level-headed visionary Jer, who believed anything possible through science and technology. His opposite was the oldest and most beautiful among them, Terra, who believed that everything they had discovered was a gift from a living, conscious universe and should be treated with the appropriate reverence. The youngest of the collective was Gias, a devout seeker of truth who was second in wisdom only to their leader Galed. Galed who saw all of these fragmented philosophies and brought them together in common purpose.

They were a group as devoted to each other as they were to the pursuit of knowledge. And that pursuit took them to a radical discovery. They discovered that they could bend reality to their will and by doing so could open portals to other worlds. Worlds where different choices had been made, where humanity had taken another path, where the laws of nature as they knew them did not apply. This revelation was beyond any of their wildest dreams. Together they decided to explore these other worlds, learning all they could, cataloging their discoveries for future generations. And so the eight became the first Travelers; men and women capable of moving between worlds, hopping from one reality to the next. Whether they were truly the first to discover this power or simply the first amongst those worlds reachable by us I cannot say. I doubt even they knew in truth.

So they traveled, encountering every imaginable type of civilization as they did. Societies devoted to law and order. Societies both matriarchal and patriarchal. Some devoted to science and the pursuit of the rational and some steeped in faith and myth giving honor to the mystic. Some completely devoid of structure altogether. Most of the worlds they encountered were primitive compared to their own. Their inhabitants struggling to comprehend the visitors from another world. Some called them gods, others devils. Over time a few of the eight grew arrogant, believing themselves superior to the worlds they visited. There was talk that they should take a more active role in guiding these worlds towards a more civilized future. But just what the nature of this direction should be, quickly became a matter of contention amongst them. Rifts began to form. Differences became disagreements. Disagreements became rivalries. Rivalries became open hostility. The eight shattered. Abandoning the path that they had agreed upon; they sought out worlds to influence and shape, places where they could consolidate their power and plot against the others. All in the name of the greater good.

Only Gias and Galed stayed true to their original goals. They continued to Travel. Searching for truth and understanding in the worlds that they saw. Ignorant of how far their brethren had fallen. Until one day the pair came to a world incredibly similar to one they had visited before. So much so that Gias was incredulous as to the assertions that this was not, in fact, the same world. He demanded to be brought a child named Olvir, whom he had befriended on their previous visit only to be told that the child had died some time ago. Drowned in a river.

It seems that their visit to the first world had been the cause of some excitement and so the children of the village had forgone their usual trip to the river that day to see the strangers from another world. But on this new world, they had never come. So Olvir had no reason not to go to the river that day. He had slipped, hit his head on a rock, and fallen beneath the current.

Despair came over Gias. He had spent all this time, searched all these worlds for universal truth. For some deeper understanding of infinity. Finally, he had found it and he did not like what he saw. He went to Galed and told him of his epiphany. That any moment of joy creates an infinite tree of despair. That choice is an illusion that we give ourselves. That we are just part of the universes fractal geometry. That we are here not because we choose to be, but because we must be in order to account for this particular set of probabilities. Galed tried to calm his friend. If every choice is accounted for, he said, if all possible outcomes exist then that means that our choices are all that matters. We are the sum of a unique set of outcomes and no other version of us exists that is exactly like we are in this moment. That makes us special. It means we get to strive to be our best. Always knowing in the process we vindicate all the versions of ourselves who made lesser choices.

But Gias refused to see the universe the way Galed did. Worse he realized that his mentor had possessed this knowledge all along and not shared it with him. So he ran. To the farthest stretches of what the eight had explored together and beyond. He sought isolation to think on what he had discovered. He found it, on a desolate world useful only as a junction to other realities.

Galed wished to follow him. To counsel Gias and help him process the enormity of the knowledge he had gained. But he had ignored the rest of the eight too long, hoping that they would realize their follies and make amends when finally faced with the reality of what they were doing. But an open war was now being raged amongst the other six. The destinies of many worlds were being subjugated to the whims of his former friends. Galed knew he must make a choice. And so Galed went to war."

Alistair stopped there and reached for his canteen. Raph could feel the silence gripping him. Pulling at him but he dared not move for fear of breaking the atmosphere of anticipation that had settled over them all. Alistair took two long swigs of water looked each of them in the eyes then continued on.

"It was a fearsome struggle that would go on for centuries. The others had secured strongholds, raised armies, and designed weapons. Whole worlds worshiped them as gods. But there was a reason Galed had been their leader, had been called the wisest of them all. He understood the secret to Bending, the term they had come to use for their manipulation of reality. We are all connected and collectively we shape the reality that we see around us. While the others sought to impose their will upon the universe, Galed simply understood it for what it was. And in doing so had access to power beyond anything the others could imagine. Still, he was one man against a thousand worlds and he could not fix the damage that had been done overnight. Slowly and methodically he conquered world after world only to set them free. Allowed once again to pursue their own destinies they rallied behind Galed. Perhaps if the six had combined their forces they might have stopped him, but at this point, the only thing they hated more than Galed was each other.

But, as Galed planned for a major offensive against Tarth and Jer, the last two significant threats to the free worlds, word reached him that Gias had finally reemerged, the final force in what would become known as the War of Eight or the Infinity War. Where the others conquered, ruled, influenced; Gias and his servants only destroyed. He laid waste to every world he touched leaving nothing, not even ruin, behind him.

Now here is where what is known and what is believed begin to blur together. Some say that Galed's spies came to him having discovered Gias' plot, others hold that the universe itself cried out to Galed for assistance, while still others believe that so great was Galed's wisdom that he needed no signs, no warning as to Gias' intent. He simply knew what his friend would try to do. Whatever the source of the knowledge, Galed knew that Gias sought the end of everything and that only he could stop him. Abandoning all other plans, he made haste for where it seemed Gias was headed, a lifeless world of storms and desert that they had visited long ago. From here Gias intended to end all suffering the only way he knew how, by ending reality itself.

Galed met his protégé in epic battle. The universes trembled as they fought. Bursts of power and destruction rippling outwards. Whole worlds extinguished, gone as if they had never been. Gias finding power in his madness, Galed in his acceptance. Both drawing upon a view of infinity that no mortal had ever glimpsed before. Finally, Galed found his opening and struck a fatal blow at the cost of his own life. The others knew what had happened. They knew that their arrogance and stubbornness had almost lead to the end of existence itself. Their pride would not let them admit that they were wrong, but they were no longer absolutely certain that they were right either. And so an uneasy peace fell upon them. No accord was struck, no treaties signed, but no more battles were fought. Galed's sacrifice had brought the Infinity War to a close. Thus ends the tale of the eight. The story of a man who understood and a man who didn't."

Alistair finished with a flourish. Billy and Lux broke out in quiet applause, faces beaming with delight. Raph sat quietly meeting Alistair's eyes. It was an excellent story and the telling of it had been phenomenal but Raph doubted that Alistair had selected this tale at random. He'd wanted them to hear it. It was related to what they were up against.

"Alistair, how was Gias going to destroy all reality? Your story didn't tell us." Alistair smiled and shrugged at Raph's question.

"I don't know. The stories don't say. It has been the subject of scholarly debate for millennia. Perhaps Gias took the secret to his grave. Perhaps he didn't. Let us hope that we do not find the answer in our lifetime."

Something about the way Alistair said that last sentence made sure that Raph did not sleep well that night.

* * * * * * * * * * * *

It was just short of evening on the second day of their journey when Lux returned from one of his regular scouting trips at a dead run. Winded he grabbed Alistair's arm and took him aside. The two conferred quietly before Alistair turned back to address Billy and Raph.

"We need to get off the road. There are soldiers coming." Alistair let a long pause punctuate those words. "They shouldn't have scouts out this deep in the heart of their own country but nonetheless we do not want to encounter them on the open road."

Raph and Billy quickly followed their guides into the trees that lined the highway. It wasn't until they were tucked into a snug little alcove underneath some bushes that Raph noticed the ground underneath them had a slight shake to it. It was a few minutes before the first soldiers began riding into view.

To say that Raph was impressed would be to say that the night was dark. This was martial pageantry on full display, a comparison for which a boy from Orleans Parish simply didn't have.

At the head of the procession were a series of men and women on horseback. From the flags and the attendants, Raph figured them for knights.

He was on Avalon after all.

But if they were knights their armor was not what he would have expected. Instead of large bits of plate mail, like the kind that he had grown up watching in fantasy movies, these knights were decked out in all manner of fanciful leather and chainmail.

At their front rode a big barrel of a man on a great black horse. He wore an intricately crafted leather brigandine stitched with a myriad of crests and symbols to give it the look of a mural or mosaic. Leather shoulder pieces extended out and down, their flaps covering most of the man's arms to his elbows which were themselves padded. Those actually reminded Raph of something he used to wear back in his ball-playing days. Fierce looking gauntlets began at his forearms and ended in fists that held the black stallion's reins tightly. On the hands of the gauntlets were more of the symbols and crests but these were more segmented from one another. Less like a

painting and more like a collection of stickers or decals.
The middle and ring fingers of the right gauntlet were
also decorated but Raph could not see well enough to
make out in what fashion.

Not to be left out, the leather guards that protected
the knight's legs were covered in what appeared to be
landscapes. They were not peaceful, layered, or even
remotely cohesive tableaus.

No these landscapes violently clashed with one
another, mountains giving way to ocean giving way to
field with no apparent care for geography or order. The
pictures ranged from the enormous man's thigh down to
the tip of his boot, which was a long way by any
reckoning.

The man passed them and Raph let his eyes take in
the other members of the procession. He realized that
what he had mistaken as a hodgepodge of styles and
armors was actually one style executed in various
fashions. These other knights had also decorated the
armor on their chests, hands, and legs. Some of the
markings and pictures were different, and some were
similar if not the same. The only constant was that none
had has many markings as their leader.

Women rode among them as well which surprised
Raph. Not that he had a problem with a woman being a
knight. It was just that everything he had ever read about
knights and chivalry kind of screamed 'we don't let our
womenfolk fight.'

But these women could fight and Raph didn't have
to see them in action to know it. Their armor was
different than the men's. It was not that ridiculous fanboy

bikini mail that you'd see at a cosplay convention; but it was clearly sleeker then what the men wore, less ostentatious, with fewer broken lines and decorative pieces meant to intimidate. Undoubtedly feminine, undoubtedly deadly.

Raph gawked at all the knights, men and women, as they rode past. It hadn't really sunk in until this moment, with these riders, that he was on a different world. He knew he was down a rabbit hole with scary monsters and bad guys trying to kill him. But as strange as it was, the world itself didn't really feel any different than Earth. Here, now, watching these people march towards a battle he knew that he would never see the universe the same way again.

As the knights moved further down the road the regular soldiers began to come in to view. On foot, they marched in lines five wide and ten deep with an officer on horseback at the lead of each such section. The soldiers marched with precision. Legs moving in unison, their heads held high against the setting sun.

As they came closer Raph could hear a gentle, morose singing coming from the men as they marched. Soon he was able to make out the words:

Here we are at the end of days
In the land of rot
In the world of haze
Bring us now to our final doom
Our resting place
Our father's tombs

We grow tired

The night grows long
So we sing our funeral song
We are Living
We are Dead
We march to the battle
To the field of red

The Gods of the Grave pick up our song
And we keep marching right along
Singing We are living
We are Dead
We march to the battle
To the field of red
Bring us comfort
Bring us strength
Bring us steel of any length

The song went on like that for an hour, looping and repeating every few verses. Raph thought that by the end well over five thousand soldiers had passed them by. He felt as if he had been in a trance, hypnotized by a simple, sad melody. When the soldiers were finally out of sight and earshot Billy started to stand but Alistair put a firm hand on him to keep him where he was.

Raph had to remind himself to breathe. Now with nothing to distract them their hiding spot was beginning to feel claustrophobic to all of them. But Alistair held them there. It was another full hour before he let them stand.

"That should be long enough. We'll be just fine now." Alistair said with an air of disinterest. As if they hadn't just spent two hours trying to remain perfectly still and silent. "No worries to be had at all. In fact, I think just over there is a perfect spot to set up camp for the night. Come on all let's get to it."

And in a flash Alistair was off, making his way away from the road and into the trees. His Godfather did his best to bound around and talk a good game, reassuring them all that they had no need to worry and the danger had passed but Raph noticed that while he was doing all of that Alistair never raised his voice above a whisper.

****

Alistair woke them well before dawn.

They had lost time the previous day as a result of their close encounters of a soldering kind and would need to make it up today if they hoped to reach Ardoth by nightfall. They took only long enough to cover up their campsite before setting off on the road.

Remarkably making it through another night without having their throats slit in their sleep seemed to have relieved a great deal of the tension from the night before. They joked and laughed when some of Lux's punchlines got lost in translation. Raph thought it was nice to see them all in high spirits throughout the morning. Even Billy, who had clearly been struggling with the pace of the last two days, seemed to face the day with a renewed vigor. He even had enough energy to indulge his curiosity and ask questions.

"Alistair I forgot to ask last night, but I was wondering about the armor the people on horseback were wearing? What did all those pictures and stuff mean?"

Lux chimed in before Alistair had even gotten his

mouth open to answer.

"Oh, that's easy. Knights put the crest of any house that has given them guest right on their chests so that the man who does battle with him knows whose friend he plans to kill. On the left hand are all crests of all the notable foes that the knight has defeated in fair combat and on the right hand are all the crests of all the ones who have defeated him. This is so his foes will know the measure of the man they wish to kill. On his legs are all the worlds he has done battle on, so that his foes may know the path he has traveled to bring him to this fight."

Raph chimed in with a question of his own that he'd been pondering about. "What about the fingers? The first man we saw yesterday had two of his fingers decorated as well."

"Yes, I saw that too. I think it must have been Damon the Bruiser. I've never heard of another man who would have had two fingers painted. If he's here then there must be a great battle coming. Which means war between the North and the South again." Lux, reasonably, did not seem excited at the possibility.

"A very astute observation," Alistair said to no one in particular.

"Okay, but what do the fingers mean?"

Alistair answered this question himself. "It means he has killed Benders. He has faced those who can shape reality to their will and emerged not only alive but victorious. Any warrior might get lucky and slay a Bender who is distracted, tired, or sloppy but a man who has two fingers painted? That is a very deadly man."

"Good to know. The next time somebody flips me

off remind me to check for a smiley face, see if the guy's serious or not." That got a smile from Billy but just a raised eyebrow from Alistair. He'd become a tougher audience since people had started trying to kill them all.

It was at this point in their journey that they began seeing other travelers on the road more and more frequently. So far they had avoided major thoroughfares and highways, managing to travel incognito simply by being the only ones on the road. As they got closer to Ardoth however the disparate mishmash of roads began to come together into what Alistair called "a more sensible, straightforward system." Which meant their choice of roads had narrowed down to just one. Alistair said it was called The Unwinding Road because of all the roads that spun out of it.

Alistair said there was no use in trying to hide or avoid the crowds at this point. He pointed out that it would be far more suspicious if they popped out of the woods in front of the city gates instead of traveling the road like any other law-abiding citizen. Besides, it wasn't the city guard who wanted them dead.

Raph was inclined to agree with these points but he was still self-conscious about being around so many people. He was sure one of them would realize that he didn't belong on this world and tell all the rest. Then they would point and talk until the Shak'Tah'Noh came for him. It was a ridiculous thought. Knowing that didn't stop Raph from thinking it. But as the came over a small hill all thoughts left him.

G.R. Linden

Chapter 7

Of Blood and Heirs

Raph felt the breath catch in his throat. The city of Ardoth was beautiful. Four spires, two white, two black, reached high into the air. As tall as any sky scrapper Raph had ever seen. Taller if he was honest with himself. They seemed designed to draw the eyes upwards towards their topless heights. So much so that he had to consciously think about looking down in order to see the rest of the city.

Not to say that the city of Ardoth needed to draw attention from itself. Ardoth was situated like a three layer cake with those unbelievable spires completing the analogy like four over-sized birthday candles. Of course if it the city was a cake you would have needed an oven the size of Arkansas to bake it. Ardoth was a huge, sprawling metropolis. Only his distance from the gates allowed Raph to see the curves of the city walls.

The bottom layer was wide and flat. Here no buildings stood taller than the walls. The effect was an even, multi-colored smoothness all the way from the outer wall to the first of the elevated inner rings.

The middle layer, segregated by its own wall from the first ring below it, was not as uniform as the lower level. Many of the rooftops stood above the tops of its walls. Not by much, but a few reached as high to challenge the buildings on the uppermost level of the city. They were large square buildings. And other than their height they seemed quite unremarkable to Raph.

The top layer was where the real grandeur could be found. The innermost ring of Ardoth stood high on a hill surrounded by its own set of interior walls. A great many buildings of all sorts poked their heads out above the city walls with spires and peaks of their own. Raph thought that they should have looked like a joke compared to the four great towers, a pale imitation of another's glory. But instead, somehow they served as perfect compliments to works that most would have thought stood on their own merits.

Outside the walls was a deluge of people set up in some kind of tent city. The sprawl was very much akin to the roads leading towards Ardoth. Close to the walls, the tents were arranged in neat rows with clear organization and structure but the further out you went the more the tent city became a disorganized mish-mash, with people setting up according to their whims rather than by efficiency.

They moved past the outskirts of the tent city. And he could see that Billy was just as curious as he was. Lux, on the other hand, was looking straight down at the road as if he expected it to jump out and attack him. Raph didn't know much about what they were in for but out of

Comment [G]: Inserted: ,

all of them, Lux was the one with the most recent experience in the area. If he thought that keeping your head down and avoiding eye contact was a good idea it probably was. So Raph followed suit. Unfortunately, he didn't find his shoes all that appealing.

"Pull your hoods up," Alistair ordered them in a harsh whisper. Raph obliged despite thinking it was far too hot to be wearing a hood.

As they followed the road towards the city gates the sea of people pressed into them. Raph had to struggle and fight just to keep close to the others. Now he could see past the sea of humanity and focus on the individual faces in the crowd. Raph had never seen refugees first hand but he didn't need to be Sherlock Holmes to deduce that's what these people were.

They looked ragged.

Few had clothes that weren't torn and even those looked like they were wearing third generation hand-me-downs. Most clung tightly to some bundle or another, afraid that if they loosened their grip even a little someone would rip it from their hands. Dirt covered all the faces. Raph understood about the hood now. The four of them weren't exactly clean but compared to this lot they would have stood out like a bald spot on a Yeti.

The wall of flesh began to part and Raph thought they might have caught a break but he soon realized that the procession was merely breaking into three lines. He stuck close to Alistair and saw that Billy and Lux did the same. Lux started reaching into his cloak for something but Alistair stopped him with a gesture.

"I'll handle this."

99

Comment [G]: Inserted: ,
Comment [G]: Inserted: ,
Comment [G]: Inserted: ,
Comment [G]: Inserted: ,
Comment [G]: Deleted:e
Comment [G]: Inserted: ,
Comment [G]: Deleted:.
Comment [G]: Inserted: -

Now Raph saw Alistair reached into his own pockets and pulled out a bundle of papers. Ahead of them, Raph could see three stations. At each sat a man flanked by two guards. Billy leaned in and whispered quietly into his ear.

"What's going on?"

"Ardoth's version of airport security I guess."

"Oh." Billy thought for a second, then panic seeped in and his whispering got a bit more frantic. "Oh! But Raph we don't have any kind of ID. What are we going to do?" Raph thought it was a fair question but he was guessing that the situation wasn't exactly going to catch Alistair by surprise.

"Just be cool and keep your head down. Whatever Alistair says back him up."

"Okay, sure." Billy's voice didn't exactly sound reassured but Raph trusted that his friend knew enough to know freaking out wouldn't help any of them.

Raph watched as a family approached one of the tables. A few words were uttered and an envelope was pushed across the table. The man sitting there motioned to the two guards. There was a scene as they put chains around the entire family and carried them off.

No one remarked on it. In fact, Raph noticed that all conversation had stopped altogether. He could still hear people talking but it was distant. Beyond the gates, he could hear the bustle of the city and behind him, he knew people were jostling and joking around, but right where he was it was as if a dome of silence had fallen over them. Nervous eyes and shuffling feet. No one wanted to end up like that family. Raph certainly didn't and he wasn't even sure what was going to happen to them.

Comment [G]: Inserted: ,
Comment [G]: Inserted: ,
Comment [G]: Inserted: ,
Comment [G]: Inserted: ,
Comment [G]: Inserted: e
Comment [G]: Deleted:l
Comment [G]: Deleted:a

The Seeker

He didn't like it, there was a sensation in his gut that he should try to do something to help, but this wasn't his world and he didn't know the rules. And Alistair had always taught him that he should never break a rule unless you knew why it was there in the first place.

Finally, it was their turn. A guard standing to their left motioned them forward. Alistair moved towards the middle table. Raph, Billy, and Lux followed him.

"Papers?" the guard asked in a way that suggested he had done this a thousand times today and he would do it another thousand times tomorrow. He was a burly fellow with a tangle of black hair that made it hard to distinguish between the hairs on his head and the ones on his chin. He had a fierce look in his eye that made Raph nervous.

Alistair leaned close to whisper to the man

"The hounds hunt......"

The guard looked up at Alistair. His eyes bulged wide at what he saw. To the man's credit, he recovered quickly enough that no one else had noticed his shock. But if Raph had to guess he thought he had just seen a dead man. He leaned in and said as softly as he could without being overheard

"...but I still run."

Alistair nodded but the man was already looking down again. Stamping our fake papers without a second glance and shoo-ing us on our way just as he had with the party before us. And as simple as that they were inside the city gates. Raph had a feeling that getting out was going to be a whole lot trickier.

****

101

There are a lot of things that you could say about Jack Smith. You could say that he's a liar and a cheat. You could say that he's a charmer and a scoundrel. You could even say that he's a delight at dinner parties. But you could never say that he's boring. Certainly, the blonde lying next to him wouldn't. She'd been nice. Her sheets were nicer. Silk. It was rather luxurious. Too bad about all the blood. But what had she expected? Cuddles? A woman of her position ought to have known better than to trust old Jack. Then again he had told her his name was Elan or Edam or something like that so he guessed that he couldn't exactly blame her. It was the nature of the universe after all. These things happen.

He rang the silver bell that sat on the nightstand next to the bed and walked out on to the balcony. The nice part about seducing the help is getting them to clean up after the messes you make. A cool breeze was blowing and gave his bare torso goosebumps. The sun was setting and an array of orange and purple hues made up the early evening. Lights were being lit across the city, like little fireflies just beginning to wake up from a long slumber.

He enjoyed looking at it. To him, each lamp represented a life. Fiery, hot, unpredictable. And in the end, extinguished. Just like all the ones that came before and all the ones that would come after. He had not been on Avalon in a long while. He forgot how well it burned.

Two of Ardoth's legendary spires framed his vision of the city while the remaining two stood behind him. Making him feel as if they were looking over his shoulder. That feeling of being watched could drive a lot of people crazy. Not Jack. He enjoyed an audience.

Comment [G]: Inserted: ,

Comment [G]: Inserted: ,

Comment [G]: Inserted: ,

Besides, there was a reasonable chance that he was insane already.

He wondered how many of them would die this time. Maybe all of them. It was possible. In truth it was more than possible, it was probable. That didn't sit well with Jack. A little death and destruction were one thing. After all anybody worth knowing had been a part of some murder and mayhem at some point. But the fun of all that was to see what happened afterwards. To watch people adapt and grow. To become something new. To be surprised. And that was what got to him. If you killed everyone off then there would be no one left to surprise you. Nothingness was boring and predictable. It was too ordered.

He had meant what he'd said to Lilith. He would help the boy find the Cup. He would just do it in his own way. That would make a game of it at least.

A high pitched wail came from inside the room.

"No, no, no. That won't do at all. We can't have hysterics from the help." He sighed as he left the balcony reluctantly. Jack tried to remember the girl's name. He was really terrible with names. Sandra...Kendra....

"Madeline, you poor dear come here. I didn't mean for you to walk into such a terrible shock." He strode towards her and opened up his arms. She ran towards him, tears running down her cheeks. Her head nuzzled into his chest and she wrapped her arms around him with a desperate ferocity.

"I just... I didn't....I've never seen a body before." The words came out between heaving sobs. Jack had to concentrate not to be distracted by the motion of her

breasts against his naked skin. He assumed from the
crying that Madeline wasn't the kind of girl who liked to
have a good time while there was a corpse in the room.
Which was too bad. Jack was always a little horny after a
kill.

"I did it for us, Maddie. I did it so we could be
together." Oh, what cliché tripe. Her eyes lifted to meet
his, and he held her gaze. A long, meaningful look that let
her see his pain and his love. Jack was always amazed at
how often this worked. Not all women got sucked into
this routine true, but enough of them did that his puppy
dog eyes never lacked for work. And here his big brown
doe eyes had done their job again.

"I know my love, it had to be done. It was just a
shock to see the Lady like that." She broke their embrace
and composed herself, wiping the tears from her eyes.
Jack held her hands gently and led her out towards the
balcony.

"Take a breath, relax. Look down at the beautiful
city. It's ours now. The whole world is ours." Madeline
did as he said, leaning over the edge to look down at the
people below.

Which is what made it so easy to push her over the
side. Her scream didn't last as long as her fall. If Jack had
to guess it was probably hard to maintain enough breath
to scream at that velocity. Quickly and calmly he walked
back into the bedroom. The rest of the servants would be
here shortly. He pulled out his knife and gave himself a
cut on the forehead. Deep enough to bleed but shallow
enough that it wouldn't leave a scar. He was slow and
careful. As anybody as good looking as himself would

104

Comment [G]: Inserted: ,

Comment [G]: Inserted: ,

Comment [G]: Inserted: ,

Comment [G]: Inserted: ,

Comment [G]: Inserted: e ey

have been under similar circumstances. He picked up his goblet and chugged the wine inside. A waste really for such a good vintage. But sacrifices must be made.

> **Comment [G]:** Deleted:y
>
> **Comment [G]:** Inserted: -
>
> **Comment [G]:** Inserted: ,

The wine contained a mild, fast-acting sedative. He would be unconscious for two or three hours. Long enough for someone to search the girl's quarters and find the unrequited love letters he had planted there. The narrative would be established before he ever woke up. Poor serving girl falls in love with her Lady's new husband. When she walks in and finds them together she goes into a jealous rage killing her Lady then herself in her despair.

All he had to do was tell how he had tried to protect his beautiful bride but had been struck and fallen unconscious. Jack's eyelids began to grow heavy. He sprawled himself out on the ground awkwardly. It had to be realistic after all. As he faded to black he thought about how much fun he was going to have when he woke up. A heartbroken widower with all that money of his dead wife's to spend. Oh, how the ladies would eat that up. Lying there on the floor waiting for the servants to find him Jack had to use his last moment of consciousness to make sure he wasn't smiling.

****

The room was stuffy and cramped. Sweat beaded together all over his body. Raph was a Louisiana boy. He'd grown up in heat and humidity sure, but he'd done it in the twenty-first century where air-conditioning came standard. Spending a couple of hours out in the heat was no big. Being baked alive in a tiny oven with two other dudes with no end in sight was another story.

It had been three days since they had arrived in Ardoth and Raph was growing impatient. Actually impatient was the far too polite way of putting it.

As soon as they had made it through the city gate Alistair had hustled them off to an inn he claimed was safe and forbidden the boys to leave for fear of them causing a scene and being discovered.

He feared no such thing for himself it seemed, as he spent every waking hour out and about; leaving before Raph managed to get out of bed each morning and coming back long after the sun had set.

As if trying to irritate Raph a bit more, he refused to share with them exactly what he was doing. Raph had pressed him upon his return the previous night and had gotten nothing more than a dismissive "When there's time, m'boy, when there's time." He found the response more than a little patronizing. It didn't seem to be much use though. Raph had learned long ago that you would know what Alistair wanted you to know when he wanted you to know it. It was a rather annoying habit for a man who claimed to have spent his life in pursuit of knowledge.

That was the thing though wasn't it. Everything about Alistair was a claim. A mythos that he created while he hid away on Earth. And wasn't that a ridiculous sentence to string together. Raph's entire world was different now. And not only because 'world' had become 'worlds' in a blinding flash of blue light.

Alistair had raised him, was the closest thing to a father he had, and he'd been lying to him this whole time.

Comment [G]: Inserted: '
Comment [G]: Inserted: '
Comment [G]: Inserted: '
Comment [G]: Inserted: '

Alistair wasn't some quirky bookstore owner. He was a wizard. A wizard with secrets. Had Raph's parents known about all of this? Was that another one of the secrets he was keeping? If so Alistair had a lot to answer for. And there would be answers.

That thought process having suitably pissed him off it was no wonder he was rather susceptible to Lux's suggestion that they go out exploring anyway. Not being completely stupid Raph grabbed his cloak and put up the hood. On their way out he attempted to convince Billy to join them but as per usual, he declined for fear of upsetting Alistair. Raph decided it was just as well that one of them was remaining behind. He wasn't entirely sure what Alistair would do if he returned and found them all missing but was fairly confident it would be bad for the entire city, and most especially bad for Raph himself.

He put his hood up as he walked out the front door and tried to take it all in.

"Aren't they amazing?"

Raph had to agree with Lux. They were amazing. He had gotten a good look at the four spires that towered over them as they had approached the city but nothing really compared to standing underneath them. They were Ardoth's central feature and no matter where you were your eyes were constantly drawn back towards their heavenly heights. Which was fitting since the ground below could be called a hell on earth and you would not accuse the speaker of hyperbole.

Beggars in rags and blankets covered the streets and the smell was an assault on the senses. The stench reminded him of Bourbon Street during Mardi Gras but a

Comment [G]: Inserted: ,
Comment [G]: Deleted: ;
Comment [G]: Inserted: ,
Comment [G]: Deleted: l

hundred times worse. This was more than just piss and vomit. If Raph had to guess, there were corpses under some of those blankets. He hurried after Lux, hoping he would never get the chance to confirm those suspicions.

Lux moved easily through the crowd, and Raph had to put some effort into to keeping up. They were staying in Low Town, what the locals called the lowest of Ardoth's three levels. Judging from the rundown buildings, some no more than poorly constructed huts, this had not been the nice part of town to begin with. Now that it was full to the brim with refugees it was clear that its two major features were crime and poverty.

Raph walked with purpose and kept his eyes on Lux, trying not to gawk at his surroundings. No matter what planet you're on its best not to look like a tourist while in a bad part of town. It was hard though. Raph felt as if he was stuck in some way to intense renaissance fair where everyone refused to break character. Except that wasn't quite right either.

Eventually, they came to the Mid-Town gate. Guards were posted here but no one was checking papers and people came and went freely.

Lux must have seen Raph's hesitation at the sight of the guards because he came close enough to whisper.

"It's okay. You don't need papers to go through the gates during daylight. As long as we get back to Low Town by sunset we'll be fine. Nobody will stop us. Come on. We're almost there."

"Almost where? I didn't realize that we had a destination in mind."

"I'm taking you to the Farchnad."

Comment [G]: Inserted: ,

Comment [G]: Inserted: I

Comment [G]: Inserted: .

Comment [G]: Deleted: ,

Comment [G]: Deleted: i

Comment [G]: Inserted: e

Comment [G]: Inserted: ,

"The what?"

"The Farchnad. Come on you'll see."

Raph followed Lux as he snaked his way through the bustling crowd. They passed through a massive archway and came to a humongous open-air market.

It was the aroma that first captivated Raph. The mixture of spices and incense teased his sense of smell. An exotic and mysterious bouquet of fragrances that allowed his mind to leave behind the rankness of Ardoth's other, more unseemly districts.

Vendors were set up everywhere and Raph even recognized some of the things that they were selling. Carrots, celery, beets, and it seemed as if every third stall had a barrel of apples for sale.

There were also quite a few things he didn't recognize displayed as well. Bright orange fruits that looked like potatoes, giant blue strawberries, and winged Chihuahua-like animals hung up like chickens.

In addition to the food vendors, there were artisans and craftsmen. Selling knives, clothes, and various trinkets and doodads.

Lux grabbed Raph's arm and pulled him over to a table of kid's games. Lux tried to show Raph how to play a simple game involving a wooden ball tied to a wooden cup by a string but Raph's attention was drawn to a wooden board with hand-crafted wooden figurines that bore a striking similarity to a game of chess.

"What's this?"

"Oh, that's a Mah'Na'Ret board."

"Mah'Na'Ret?"

"Something about the heart, the mind, and the soul.

Comment [G]: Inserted: -
Comment [G]: Inserted: ,
Comment [G]: Inserted: ,

It's a game with three different sets of rules. Dad always wanted me to learn how to play but I never got into it. Too much to keep track of. Come on, that lute player is about to start."

Lux was off like a shot and Raph had no choice but to follow and leave the curious game behind.

He caught up to Lux as the lute player started his first song. A catchy, folksy number about a farmer trying to catch something called a wently.

Raph smiled at the sight of buskers and fortune tellers. They reminded him that home was not all that far away.

It was hard for Raph to tell what was local and what wasn't but there was enough difference in the styles and designs of the vendor's goods to indicate to Raph that they came from a myriad of places and cultures.

He turned his attention from the merchandise being sold to the people doing the buying and selling. They were, after all, as foreign to Raph as the wares they were haggling over.

Unlike Low Town which was exclusively home to the poor and really poor, Mid-Town encompassed people from every walk of life. The clothing was the biggest give away. It seemed to Raph that the more money you had the more colors you could afford. And some of these people very much enjoyed showing off their wealth.

Raph was enjoying watching the various peacocks strut self-importantly around the square when he heard a cry come from one of the side streets. He turned his head and about fifty yards down the way he saw five men standing over a woman. The shortest of the five stood closest to her and was saying something that Raph couldn't make out over the distance.

Raph started walking in that direction, watching the scene unfold. He was the only one. The rest of the dwindling crowd was pointedly avoiding looking at what was happening while attempting to be somewhere else as quickly as possible. More than one person had simply turned around and walked in the other direction.

"Raph we should go" Lux had caught up with him and put a hand on his elbow.

Raph removed the hand and kept walking. The short man raised something above his head and brought it down fast. Striking the defenseless woman. And that really pissed Raph off.

"Hey, what do you think you're doing?" He yelled as he sprinted towards the girl. The man raised his arm to hit her again. Raph got there just in time, grabbing the upraised arm and throwing the smaller man to the ground. "Knock it off, jerk."

"This is none of your concern, peasant. Leave us now and I will forget that you laid hands on me." The man's entourage had lifted him back to his feet and he looked out for blood. Raph assumed if it wasn't his, it would be the girl's. That left Raph with two options. Leave the girl to her fate or stay and take the brunt of what was about to rain down on them.

The thing about Raph was that for a wide array of reasons he really didn't like bullies.

It made the decision quite an easy one.

"You know where I come from we treat our ladies with respect. We've got this little thing we like to call a sense of honor. From what I've seen so far I would hazard a guess that you wouldn't know much about what that entails." Raph stood bold and defiant. He was outnumbered but only one of the five men was even comparable to him in size. A little arrogance and some showmanship and he might be able to talk himself out of this. But only if he could present a position of strength.

"Are you saying that I am without honor?! Do you know who you address bloodless? I am Xan'Tah'Mer, Grand Emissary of The Northern Kingdoms to the city of Ardoth. This insult will not go unpunished. I will flay the flesh from your bones while you watch me rape this sad, mongrel whore to death." It was roughly then that it occurred to Raph that he was frequently wrong about the rationalizations he made for his actions. He considered the possibility that perhaps humility would have been a better play, under the given circumstances.

On the other hand, the knowledge that this guy was the high muckity-muck of whateversville didn't change the fact that Raph really, deeply, incredibly disliked bullies.

"Now that is the best invitation for an ass whopping I have ever heard. Alright, I haven't been in a fight since a couple of Pikes decided to feel up a perfectly sweet shot girl without her permission; but this kind of feels like the same thing." Xan pulled his sword from its sheath. "Or not." The four men behind Xan also pulled out their swords. It was at that point that Raph came to the conclusion that he may have overplayed his hand.

"Uh Lux, little help here." Raph removed his cloak to gain some freedom of movement. He didn't think it

112

Comment [G]: Inserted: ,

Comment [G]: Inserted: k

Comment [G]: Inserted: ,

Comment [G]: Deleted:h

would help much but he thought it made him look like he knew what he was doing.

Apparently, something caught Xan's eye because he straightened out of his battle stance. "You are a servant of The Fox. I didn't know any of those still existed."

Seeing an opportunity Lux seized upon it. "He is more than a servant. He is Heir to The Fox."

"So you have some blood to you after all. Then we will settle this in the old forms. As custom befits our station. I invoke Sha'Dral." Raph felt a chill at the word. "You have three weeks to prepare for your death little fox. Take the whore. I hope she was worth your life." With that Xan'tah'Mer, Grand Emissary of The Northern Kingdoms to the city of Ardoth, spun on his heel and walked away with his entourage in close pursuit.

"Well that seemed a bit anti-climactic" was Raph's comment to no one in particular. He turned to see that Lux had gone a rarefied shade of pale. "What? I'm not complaining. Just seemed like a lot of drama for not much of a result. Are you okay miss?" He held out his hand to the young woman in order to help her up. His gentlemanly gesture was ignored, and she climbed to her feet on her own.

"Thank you, sir, for the kindness, but it isn't right Tah'Mer fussing over one as myself. I deserved what I was getting my lord and nothing less. I'd hate to think of the blood being spilled because of me. It just isn't right for a handsome lord like you to die on my account."

"First of all stop calling me lord. My name is Raph. Secondly, nobody died, and nobody's going to die. It's all over now. Three weeks? We'll all be long gone by then.

Comment [G]: Inserted: ,
Comment [G]: Inserted: led
Comment [G]: Inserted: ,
Comment [G]: Inserted: ,
Comment [G]: Deleted:t
Comment [G]: Inserted: ,

Finally, I don't care what you did, no one deserves to be treated that way."

"Gone m'lord? But you can't go anywhere. The Sha'Dral, Begging your pardon m'lord, I don't pretend to know much about the ways of my betters but I thought to break such a vow was to lose one's soul."

It was then that Lux finally spoke up. "She's right Raph. You're bound by magic not to leave the city before the duel is finished. To do so is to forfeit. And since it is a duel, a forfeit means death. It is the ancient way of the Tah'Mer."

"How does that make sense? I'm not one of these Tah'Mer. All he has to say is a word and all of a sudden I'm in a fight to the death?"

"The laws of the Tah'Mer are found in the covenant. A powerful magic binds all the Tah'Mer to what was written there"

"I'm not a freaking Tah'Mer, whatever the hell that even means!"

Chapter 8

Frayed Knots

"It means 'of Merlin' short for Sha'tah'Mer or 'blood of Merlin'. And you became bound the laws of the covenant the second you claimed to be my heir. I had hoped to avoid exactly this kind of incident when I asked you to remain here at the inn." Alistair had been waiting for them upon their return. It had taken all of five seconds for Lux to spill everything about their unfortunate escapades. Alistair's anger had turned rather quickly to worry and concern when he had gotten the whole story.

"I'm afraid that you have no choice now. And whatever other plans we have made must be put aside. If you leave the city before the duel you will die. If you do not meet at the appointed hour you will forfeit and you will die. And if you go into this battle unprepared to kill or be killed you will die. So it appears you have some training to do."

Raph was having a hard time forming the words to

express the ludicrousness of the situation he was in. Billy was sitting in the corner looking like he was trying very hard not to cry. Raph didn't really blame him. He felt like crying himself right now.

"Alistair I can't learn how to handle a sword in three weeks, let alone become a talented enough duelist to take on what I assume is a highly trained individual." He was starting to regret not joining the fencing club in high school.

"Who said anything about a sword?" Alistair gave him a perplexed look.

"Daggers, lances, whatever they use around here. If it's sharp and pointy there's a good chance I don't know how to use it properly. And flippant remarks aren't going to change that."

Raph watched as Alistair took a deep breath and put on his calmest 'this customer clearly doesn't know what he's talking about, but we really need this sale' face.

"Sha'Dral is a battle of wills. It's for Benders. You wanted to learn magic, well now you will have to and fast. More dangerous than swords perhaps but easier to close the skill gap between gifted amateur and seasoned expert in the time allotted."

"IT'S A MAGIC DUEL?!? Well, now I truly am good and fuc..." Something hard and invisible flicked him on the wrist. "OW!! What the hell was that?"

"You may be an adult and we may be on a parallel world where fate seems stacked against us and the threat of an ugly death lurks around every corner, but I'm still your Godfather and you will still do me the common courtesy of watching your language when you're around me."

"Really? You want to lecture me on my swearing right now? That's the conversation you want to have? 'Cause I really think we've got bigger things to worry about."

"Civility must be kept even in our darkest hours otherwise there's not much point to it in the first place."

"Fine, I'm sorry. But you can understand why I'm a little prone to vulgarity at the moment. Alistair, I don't know the first thing about magic. I don't have a shot at living through this thing."

"Thank you for the apology. I appreciate it. And you're wrong on two counts. First, just because I didn't call them magic lessons doesn't mean I haven't laid the groundwork for what you'll need to know. And second I honestly believe that you have more than a shot at living through this."

"Alistair I appreciate the faith but I think we need to be realistic about this."

"I am being realistic. What you need to be is optimistic. It's all a matter of confidence m'boy."

Billy emerged from his self-imposed exile at the far side of the table and smiled. "Well, that's good Raph's never been short on confidence."

"Really? 'Cause I'm running kind of low on it right now." Raph was starting to think that they were in denial. At least Lux still looked suitably depressed.

"Don't worry by the time the duel rolls around you'll be filled to the brim. But we can start worrying about that tomorrow. We have other problems right now." Alistair had returned to overly concerned face.

"Other problems? Being completely unprepared for my magical duel to the death doesn't rate?" Raph mustered all his skepticism for that one.

"Not right now it doesn't, no. And neither does your penchant for colorful phrasing. No, our biggest problem right now is that the entire city is going to be talking about this in a couple of hours."

"Why?"

"Because Sha'Drals are not all that common. No more than a few a year if that. People tend to hesitate before challenging others to a 'magical duel to the death' as you put it. And considering you managed to find the highest-ranking member of the Northern Kingdoms while the Southern Alliance is preparing for war, there is a good chance that some of the nobility around here are going to have a vested interest in its outcome. By tonight you'll be famous, by tomorrow you'll be a serious player in city politics whether you want to be or not. Maintaining our anonymity is out of the question now. "

"So what do we do?" the question came from Lux this time.

"We do the complete opposite. Lean into the skid as it were."

"I don't understand." Lux again. The confusion plain on his face.

"Alistair's saying that if we can't stay hidden we might as well become so famous that if the Shak'Tah'Noh come after us people will notice. But that assumes that they don't care if people know about them." Raph had to admit it wasn't a bad idea. And it was especially hard to criticize considering that this was all

Raph's fault.

"I think they might. If they move now Avalon will unite and rally the other worlds against them. If they wait a few weeks....." Alistair trailed off and Billy picked up the thread.

"There will be a war on and no one to care what they do. It makes sense." Alistair gave Billy the acknowledging nod of a proud teacher. Raph had to shoot Billy a look to get the grin off his face.

"Okay we have a strategy now but that's not the same thing as a plan. Exactly how are we going to raise our profile?" Raph still wasn't sure about it all but he didn't have a better idea so there wasn't any point in arguing.

"Leave that to me. I am called the Fox for a reason. And it's not because of my devilishly good looks. Well not just because of them anyway. Lux, I'll need your help."

"You will?" Lux still looked confused. Raph hazarded a guess that he and his father didn't move with quite this level of verbal velocity back on the farm.

"Why certainly I will. What was it your father said? That you were more up to date on current events than myself? Well, time to put that knowledge to work. It will make up for your part in coaxing Raph out of the inn this morning against my explicit directions. Or did you think I had let that particular part of your story slip my memory in the deluge of other difficulties presented?"

"No sir.... I....uh....yes sir...." Raph felt bad for Lux. He'd been on the receiving end of Alistair's forceful personality. It could be more than a bit overwhelming.

"Splendid then, that's settled." Alistair beamed as Lux lowered his head in resignation.

"So what are we supposed to do then?" Raph asked as he gestured to Billy and himself.

"Billy can do whatever he wants so long as he stays in the inn. You will need to go to your room and spend the night in quiet meditation in preparation for your first lesson. Which will be at first light tomorrow morning." Alistair's tone brooked no argument. Raph argued anyway.

"I'M GROUNDED?" He was way too incredulous and insulted to control his volume.

"RAPHEL IGNATIUS CARPENTER! You have ignored my instructions once and as a result of your rashness put yourself and your friends in even more mortal peril than we were already in. Which is remarkable considering I hadn't thought that there was a realm of grave danger that we hadn't yet taken up residence in. But you found it. So if you will take a minute and think that just possibly I know what I am about then maybe you will do what I ask rather than let your childish stubbornness get us all killed. Come, Lux, we have things to do."

Alistair stood and made for the door. Lux shot Billy and Raph worried look and hurried after him. Raph watched them as they walked out without looking back. Billy reached over and put a hand on his shoulder.

"Raph...."

"Don't." Raph stood and went up the stairs to his room feeling like a complete ass.

****

"The game is a simple one, Billy Bordeaux." Billy had tried to explain that the man, at least he thought he was a man, could call him by his first name; but he was starting to think that whatever Alistair had done to let his mind translate things automatically was a little bit off. "I am surprised that it is not played in the land of your hearth, all I have encountered know some version of Mah'Na'Ret, even if they manage only a crude approximation."

Large hands reminiscent of bear paws moved with the deftness of a surgeon, quickly and easily arranging the pieces on the board. Billy had met Tai in the common room of the inn. With Raph upstairs sulking and Alistair and Lux doing who knows what Billy had been stuck sitting at a table by himself drinking a variation on red wine, the locals called Karsh. Drinking alone in a crowded room was always a little depressing. Doing it on a parallel world where saying the wrong thing to the wrong person could get you and your best friend killed is particularly isolating. Billy had noticed Tai sitting by himself at a small table in the corner whittling wood with great care. It seemed nobody really liked talking much to him either so once Billy had imbibed a suitable amount of liquid courage he'd gone over to talk. Tai had been excited when Billy asked about the small figures he had been making. It had taken little effort to convince the man to play teacher.

"I will explain as we play. The rules are complicated. It may take many matches to fully grasp them. As for the game itself, there is a saying on the tongues of my people. 'A man will master Mah'Na'Ret but once in his lifetime, he must pray the stakes were worth the cost.'"

Billy paid close attention as the man laid out the rules of the game. It seemed that Mah'Na'Ret was a pretty literal name. It meant "mind, heart, soul" in the language of the old spells. Not that he grasped what language of the old spells meant, but it seemed a good guess that it was flowery talk for language a lot of people didn't speak anymore. Billy figured it was a lot like Latin and left it at that. The game had three sets of rules that the challenger could choose from; heart, mind, or soul. The pieces and the board remained the same for each set of rules but the pieces had different restrictions on them based upon the rules the challenger had selected. It was at this point that Billy asked how the challenger was determined between two players.

"The challenger is whichever player has the losing record in all the times the pair have played. No matter the recent record. A man could win ten in a row and still be a challenger to a man who beat him a score straight before that. Similarly, it matters not how well they play against others. If an enlightened one, a champion player if you will, plays a boy of five and loses the enlightened one is the challenger until he regains the winning record; even if it takes a lifetime. "

"But what if you are playing an opponent for the first time?"

"Ah, that is easy. If two have never played or then the younger of the pair is the challenger. If their records are tied then the older is the challenger. Always that has been the way."

Billy was fascinated. Apparently, it was custom to

commit every opponent you have ever faced and your record against them to memory. It was considered great insult not to know how you stood against another player. Tai said that it was not unheard of for such an insult to end with blood on the board.

As the challenger, Billy chose Mah, or heart, for his first game. It didn't last long and Billy got the sense that Tai had been going easy on him.   They played a few more teaching games before Billy got enough of a handle on the rules that their conversation could drift to other things.

"So Billy Bordeaux, what brings you to Ardoth?" It was an innocent enough question but Billy knew that answering it truthfully was out of the question. He didn't particularly like lying to someone who had been kind to him but he didn't see that he had a choice.

"Just traveling through. But with tensions the way they are we thought it might be best not to be on the road right now." Vague, non-committal, and touching on a bigger, wider, juicer topic. Whether it was because of his weight, clumsiness, or his general lack of charisma people tended to take Billy at face value. The truth was that he was an incredibly talented liar. Growing up in his family it had been a necessity. The skill served him well again here.

"Yes, yes. Tensions. That's a polite term for it. Stupidity and bullheadedness are the more accurate ones." Tai took a long swig of his own cup of Karsh. "The Tah'Mer are always playing games with people's lives. Fools. Fools everywhere from Candar to Kernow. Fools that think their blood puts them above the rest. It's unconscionable. And it's not just the Northern Kingdoms with their Right to Rule nonsense, the Southern Alliance for all its talk of justice and fair governance is just as corrupt as the north."

Billy could see whatever it was that Tai was talking about was getting his blood pressure up.

"What do you mean?"

"Why this silly war of course. You know how this all starts." Tai looked at Billy expectantly. Then the look became thoughtful before settling on knowing.   "Oh, my. Maybe you don't" A soft chuckle began to grow in his chest before Tai let it out as a full blow roar of laughter. "Just Traveling through indeed. Ha! Very good young Billy Bordeaux. Very good indeed."

"I don't know what you're talking about." Billy flushed embarrassingly. Apparently, he wasn't a very good liar after all.

Tai had managed to suppress his mirth down to a conspiratorial smile. "Of course you don't. 'Just Traveling.' How exceptionally clever. It's all right. Your secrets are safe with me." Tai gave him what Billy could only assume was an extremely awkward wink.

Well, Billy thought, *it's usually better to let people think you're smarter than you actually are than to look like you don't know anything.* It was one of the few life lessons that Billy's mom and Alistair agreed on. So Billy decided he might as well roll with it. Better that than admit he had no idea what Tai was talking about

"One more match?" Billy hoped a change of subject would help cover his ignorance.

"Yes, I believe I have one more good game in me.

Do you remember the traditional invocation   before we start?"

Billy racked his brain for a second before exuberantly muddling through the strange phrase.

"*Callen*a *Fayier.*"

Tai beamed proudly at Billy.

"And so we begin."

****

Raph rubbed his eyes and tried to concentrate on what Alistair was saying. He had woken well before the sun had crested the horizon and as soon as he had come downstairs Alistair had hustled him off to a secluded open area behind the inn. Raph had been sitting there for over an hour staring off into space before he broke down and asked what sitting out in the morning cold had to do with magic.

"First you need to stop referring to it as magic. The correct term is Bending. And it's far less about ability and far more about your state of mind. Bending is a combination of the mystical and the rational. Focus on the world around you. Close your eyes and hold that picture fast in your mind."

Raph sat quietly, eyes shut, focusing on forming an image of the world around him. He could hear Alistair pacing as he lectured in a soft, dulcet tone.

"The first step is to believe. This is the easiest of the three steps. You believe that the world is a certain way. You have faith that the outcome you want will occur. Sometimes individual belief is enough to affect the world around you. Most of the time it is not. It allows for doubt. Doubt is the crack in the armor that allows the other side to win. Do not belittle belief, however. In an individual, it may not pose much of a threat, but in large numbers, it is extremely powerful. And extremely dangerous." Alistair paused to let the warning sink in. Raph didn't need to be told that beliefs could be dangerous, he'd grown up in the South.

"The second step is knowing. To know something is to understand it. To accept it as fact. That doesn't mean that it is a fact. Just that you know it to be. This is more powerful than believing because there is almost no doubt. Your perception of reality will warp and change so as to confirm what you know. Knowing can be dangerous too but mostly to the self. If you are certain that you know something and it is the wrong something you will destroy yourself before you have time to realize your mistake."

"The third step is being. It is far more powerful than knowing or believing as it is passive acceptance rather than active assertion. You open yourself up to the universe and in return, it opens itself up to you. This is what you must achieve. It is possible to Bend using belief or knowing but it is unreliable and weak at best. To be a powerful Bender you must learn how to simply be."

Raph pondered the words while maintaining his vision of the outside world in his head.

"Alistair I thought Bending was a matter of quantum mechanics, not metaphysics?"

"Can't it be both? The multiverse is a complicated place full of wisdom and wonder. As Clarke said 'Any sufficiently advanced technology is indistinguishable from magic'. We are the universe and the universe is us. We are made of the same materials. We speak the same language. It's just that we are like toddlers mastering the rudiments of vocabulary and the universe is a professor of literature at Oxford. Tell me what you see inside your mind."

Raph focused on the mental image in his head and rattled off what he saw there.

"I see a small alcove. Ten feet by ten. Cobblestone floor. Brick walls. Hay scattered about the ground. An alleyway on my left. A wooden door directly in front of me."

"Is that all? Concentrate. What else can you see?"

"That's it, Alistair."

"Very well open your eyes." Raph did as he was instructed. "What did you miss?"

"Um. The two barrels in the corner. The stack of wood in the alley. I didn't have the hay quite right."

"Forming a picture in your mind is more than just what you see. You have to incorporate your other senses as well. The way a place smells. The way it feels. Also, you forgot something else rather important."

"What?"

Alistair chuckled. "Me."

"Oh."

"Let's try it again."

Raph closed his eyes and focused on his surroundings. It was going to be a long day.

****

It was going to be a glorious day. The sun was warm. The fruit was fresh. The women were naked. All in all, it was hard to ask for anything else. Why Jack was even forgoing his usual expensive taste in wine to indulge in something from the vineyards of Gent. Karsh it was called, apparently, it was all the rage these days in Ardoth. Jack still preferred a good white wine but for a warm day like today it the karsh was a suitable substitute.

Of course, all of that was a prelude to the real enjoyment of the afternoon. Three days had passed since his new bride's tragic death had brought their wedded bliss to a sudden end. His plan had worked to perfection and no one had thrown so much as a suspicious glance in his direction. He was the just handsome widower drowning his sorrows in women and wine as any proper noble would. That he was the sole remaining heir to his wife's estate and its corresponding wealth was a small comfort in this his hour of abject loss.

What would be of great comfort, what Jack had been after from the very beginning, was the position that he was about to inherit from his dear, sweet whatever her name was.

Three days had passed and that meant the council had taken the appropriate time to mourn their loss. It also meant they'd had plenty of time to investigate him. Jack was certain that they would be by today to officially offer him his seat. In fact, since they should have finished their morning session by now he anticipated that his wait would be one of minutes, rather than hours.

Unfortunately, that did not allow him time to indulge in a dalliance with the redhead he'd been eyeing for a few minutes. One of the new serving girls he had brought on following his wife's death. Jack very much admired her outfit which consisted of a daffodil in her hair and nothing else.

He frowned at the thought of being responsible but sent the staff away just the same. Sometimes being especially cunning had its downsides. Jack changed into something a bit more appropriate for a mourning widower overcome with grief. Just as he finished dressing one of the servants announced the arrival of the council's representatives. Jack's timing was impeccable. As it often was.

They were waiting for him in the drawing room. Waiting for him with the impatient looks of those who were not accustomed to waiting. Good, he could use that.

There are many people who believe that the truth of a lie lies with the lie itself. That is a falsehood. The truth of a lie lies in its presentation. A thousand micro-transactions occur before ever a word is spoken. Anyone can tell a fib and hope they get away with it. A true artisan weaves together a pallet of sounds, smells, and subtle movements that paint a picture so vivid that by the time it's complete all it needs is a name. And Jack was the most gifted painter who had ever lived. On this or any other world. It was time to make an entrance.

He threw open the doors and began acting like the drunkenly morose sycophant they assumed him to be. "Sir Geir and Lady Tam you do me and my late wife great honor by coming to offer comfort to my household in its time of mourning." Jack made sure to add the slightest slur to his words. Not enough to be unseemly but enough to be detected and noted by the trained ear.

It was a flourish intended for the Lady Tam more than for the Knight Protector. She had a reputation as a formidably clever woman. Whereas Sir Geir, while politically competent, was far more renowned for his military prowess.

"It is you who do us the honor Sir, by offering us your hospitality even while the burden of grief weighs upon your house." Sir Geir also had a reputation for unwavering politeness. Jack would have called it stiffness but that would just be Jack being polite.

"This is not a social call. We are here to discuss a matter of importance with you." The elderly woman also had a reputation for being blunt and to the point.

"Of course my Lady, it would be my humblest pleasure to assist you in any way that I can." He gave an obsequious little bow with a hint of a tipple. Lady Tam gave the air an irritated sniff. Sir Geir stepped in to keep the conversation moving forward.

"As you are no doubt aware the death of your wife has left a vacancy on the council. Being that she has no other heirs the responsibility of filling that position falls to you. Under normal circumstances, it would be your right to abdicate your responsibility and an election would be held to choose a lord to be elevated in your stead. However..."

"However?"

"However such elections take time and the council would not be able to take any actions until the post was filled. Given the current tensions between the North and the recent arrival of their emissary to Ardoth, it would be an inopportune time for the council to be paralyzed by ancient laws." Lady Tam obviously cared for Sir Geir's 'politeness' as much as Jack did because she felt the need to follow up with her own frank assessment of their situation.

"What the Knight Protector means to say is that despite what you may want or what some of us may think you are joining our little club, because, detestable as it may be, it is the least detestable of our current options." Which was exactly what he had been hoping to hear.

"I cannot say that I was unaware of my wife's duties or the possibility that they would pass to me in the event of her death but I will admit that it had always been my intention to set them aside and allow someone more capable than myself to take up their burden." Half true anyway.

"As the Lady Tam has said that just simply isn't a viable option at the present moment." Jack stifled a yawn. This man was so boring. He might actually have to be drunk they next time they meet or else he might be prone to do something homicidal.

"Then I will endeavor to do my best to be worthy of the honor that you bestow upon me." Lady Tam looked skeptical. She also looked like she didn't care to linger any longer than needed.

"Good that's settled we will take our leave. You will be expected at the council chambers in the morning. Good day."

"And a Good day to you Lady Tam. Sir Geir."

"Good day. And again our truest condolences for your terrible loss."

Jack nodded and rang the butler to show them out.
He saved his smile for after his visitors had left.

****

The door to the inn burst open with a large crash. A

woman stood in the doorway taking a long, hard look around the common room as she let the occupants of its half-filled tables stop and take a long, uncertain look at her. She was short, standing perhaps five foot four if Raph was generous. Despite her height, she was a big woman. Not fat, but thick and muscular. She wore her auburn hair up in a bun. Her face was round with rosy cheeks and a small mouth. She wore a no makeup and simple traveling clothes of gray and brown. A long, thin staff was strapped to her back.

She walked with presence towards the bar. She knew that the inn's patrons were staring at her, it was right that they should, and she didn't give a damn that they did. She shot a death stare at the innkeeper that was cold enough to freeze magma. She waited until he seemed suitably withered before asking her question.

"The Fox, where is he?"

Raph gasped. And apparently gave himself away. He looked at Billy and Lux and motioned to the two that it was time to leave. It was too late. In three quick strides, the woman had crossed the room to where they sat.

"The Fox. You know him. Where is he? Lie to me and you will be dead in thirty seconds." It was a cliché, but it was a cliché that Raph believed. He was about to tell her everything when he was cut off.

"I'm right here. Try not to scare the boys too badly. They have delicate constitutions." The woman turned and Alistair towered over her. She reached up and slapped him.

"How did you know it was me?" Alistair stood unfazed by the abrupt attack.

"Because you are the only man wise enough to know that note would bring me here and stupid enough to send it anyway." Alistair smiled at this.

"I apologize. But our time is short and our need is dire. We face the Shak'Tah'Noh and the end of all things. We require your assistance." She stared at Alistair for a long moment, her face impassive. Raph usually prided himself in his ability to read body language and emotions but he had to admit to himself that he had no idea what their new arrival was thinking or whether she planned on joining them or killing them.

Finally, she spoke in a tightly controlled whisper, limiting her volume so that only Alistair and the boys were forced to endure the cold fury of her words.

"I told you once Fox, I want nothing to do with your crusades. And that goes double for all your wily machinations. Even if I believed you, the Shak'Tah'Noh don't interest me and the end of all things would be a blessing. Why shouldn't I just kill you all now and wait for the end to come?"

Either the boys were becoming more accustomed to the ever-present possibility of their imminent demise or they were so scared that none of them could move a muscle. Raph didn't want to think about it long enough to figure it out. He just watched and waited to see how Alistair would respond to the very clear, very believable threat.

When Raphael had been a freshman in high school his favorite teacher had been gunned down in a drive-by shooting. Just collateral damage in someone else's war. Raph had been devastated and had responded poorly to having another important figure ripped from his life so senselessly. After a few weeks of feeling sorry for himself and lashing out at everyone within shouting distance, Alistair had sat him down to talk. He told Raph that nothing ever made these events okay and that some scars stayed with us for a lifetime, but it was the way we bore those scares that would eventually define us. For Raphael, the words themselves weren't important. He had heard them many times before and had always felt them to be rather obnoxious trite to tell an orphan. What was important was the way Alistair said them. With all the sympathy that one man could hold, he looked Raph in the eyes. And it was then that Raph saw that every act of self-pity and self-destruction he committed wounded Alistair in his very soul. And that was because Alistair loved him with the whole of who he was. That conversation had profoundly changed Raphael and helped turn him into the man he was today.

When Alistair leaned down and put his hand on this woman's shoulder, and spoke to her using the same voice he had used all those years before, that was the memory that came flooding back into Raph's mind. And realization dawned on him. Alistair may have been lying to him all these years, but he was still the same Alistair. A great man full of wisdom and wit that loved him. Anger that Raph didn't even know he was holding on to washed away at that point.

"Because Bea that's not who you are. I know you are angry. That you desire vengeance and peace. And you feel like you would pay any price to get them, but you won't. You will stand with us. You see the faces of evil men in your nightmares. We seek the darkness that gave form to those faces. You fight to avenge innocence lost. We fight to preserve the innocence that still is. But mostly you will join us because without you that nineteen-year-old boy sitting there, my godson, will likely die and that is not something that your conscience can afford. So I say again, we face the Shak'Tah'Noh and the end of all things. We require your assistance."

Impassive, she stood there. Her gaze slowly moving from Alistair to Raph and back again. Her eyes felt methodical, almost clinical upon him. But there was something else there too. An empty sadness, too deep and too cold to be casually dismissed. Even so, Raph thought he felt her soften just for a moment when she looked at him.

"No, I will not be played, Fox. No matter the circumstances. Tell anyone what was in the letter you sent me or send another of its like and I will return to do what the Shak'Tah'Noh seem unable to." She turned to the rest of them, still frozen in their booth. "Whatever games you are caught up in remember that while the Shak'Tah'Noh are deadly, the Fox is clever. And that cleverness can be far more dangerous in the long run." She turned and headed for the door.

"Good day to you too Beatrice. Always a pleasure to see you." Beatrice did not let Alistair's very pleasant last words slow her down as she exited the inn.

Chapter 9

Pages

Billy wasn't sure he liked where all this was headed. Sure on the surface of things it all seemed fantastic and wonderful. Magic duels and parallel worlds, what's not to like. The reality, however, was a whole other thing entirely. It was bad enough when they were running away from terrible things that wanted to kill them. But now they were waiting around for people to kill them. That seemed like a markedly worse idea.

He had desperately wanted to train with Raph and Alistair. In Billy's mind, it would have been a double win, a chance to learn magic and a way for him to learn to defend himself. Personally, he thought it would be nice not to have to quiver in fear every time they got into trouble.

But given the circumstances, Alistair had said it was best if he wasn't forced to divide his attention between two pupils. The key to potentially saving the multi-verse had three weeks to become proficient enough in Bending to survive a duel to the death with a highly skilled nobleman out for blood. And Billy, well Billy was just kind of around. It made sense, but just because he understood didn't mean that he wasn't disappointed.

He told himself to look on the bright side, at least now he had plenty of time to play Mah'Na'Ret with Tai. The enormous man, Billy still wasn't entirely convinced he was a man in the traditional sense but he didn't know what else to call him, won every time of course. But Billy was getting better with each game. Besides for him, it wasn't really about winning or losing anyway. Tai seemed to know something about everything. And considering at this point Billy seemed to know nothing about anything, their games were an excellent learning experience.

He'd even managed to catch enough of Raph's interest to explain a bit of the game to him. Raph had been too tired to play of course but at least they'd gotten to talk about how cool it was. Billy thought that if he ever did get back to Earth he'd make a fortune of teaching people how to play. Not that Billy really cared about money, he just thought it would be nice to be successful at something.

Tai set up the board. Their current record stood at thirteen to nothing in favor of Tai. Billy would be the challenger for the foreseeable future. He chose heart and the game began. He started out well but when he lost nearly half is pieces to an attack he hadn't seen coming he realized that his early success had been a ruse meant to sucker him into an attack.

"I can't believe I didn't see that coming."

"Mah'Na'Ret is a game built on deception young Billy Bordeaux, like all great games of strategy. You must learn to not be so transparent about your objectives. Boldness wins battles, but prudence wins wars. The key is to get your opponent to commit his resources before you do. That way you can force him to meet you on your terms. Remember what this game represents: Mah'Na'Ret; heart, mind, soul. Heart is the most straightforward of the three. A game of bold choices, where risk is rewarded and a successful gamble or two wins the day. The Mind is a game of moves and countermoves, a back and forth of plans within plans. Laying trap after trap while maneuvering yourself into position for the endgame. And finally, the soul is a war of attrition. No one loss is enough to cost you the match but enough small ones and victory will be out of reach long before you realize it. The truth though is that the best players, the true masters of the game, use elements of all three versions of the game. Blending the three together creates opportunities that would otherwise be missed. Balance, hard to find, but essential to maintain. Take the upcoming Sha'Dral for instance between your friend and Xan'tah'Mer."

"You've heard about that?" Billy's question was answered with a bellyful of hearty laughter.

"Heard about it. Ha! Billy Bordeaux your humor lightens my heart and steels my soul. Yes, I've heard of it. The whole of Ardoth has heard of it. I'd dare say that it's on the lips of every servant and noble in the kingdom. A stranger of the Blood fights a prince of the north to the death over a serving girl. I do not know how it is in the land of your hearth Billy Bordeaux but here gossip is as fine a currency as coin and as well used."

"Oh," Billy really wasn't sure what else to say to all that.

"Now what was I saying… Oh yes, the Sha'Dral. Xan is well known for his cruelty. He is arrogant and bold. But he lacks the cunning of his older brother. And his soul is too far gone to give him help of any kind. No, he will depend on his heart for victory. A black heart for sure but a powerful one full of fire. What of your friend? What will he fight with?" Tai looked at Billy expectantly. Billy tried to think hard about what Tai was asking. And after thinking hard about it for a minute he still had nothing. In fact, he was slightly more confused than he had been.

"I don't know I haven't thought about it in those terms before. I don't really understand. I thought the Sha'Dral was a magic duel."

"A Bending duel yes." Tai nodded

"Uh right Bending. What does bending have to do with Mah'Na'Ret?"

"A very good question Billy Bordeaux. One that would be good to get an answer to. And I believe I know where you should start."

****

"Alistair we've been at this for a week. I don't see how all of this is going to help me win my duel." Raph was exhausted. After their first lesson on visualization Alistair had started adding various physical elements. First, it was pushups, then it was pull-ups, and now Alistair had him taking laps around Low-town before asking him to close his eyes and visualize, for the thousandth time, every exact detail of their little training grotto. Raph was seriously beginning to fear that the next step of his training was going to be to climb one of the Four Spires of Ardoth blindfolded while Alistair asked him to count the strands of hay that had fallen onto the floor of the stable.

"That's because you lack the vision and foresight that I myself possess in spades." Alistair stared at him with steely reserve, his face betraying no emotion. But deep down inside Raph knew that his godfather had to be enjoying this.

"Funny. Really funny.   But I'm being serious. I've got two weeks left and I don't know anything more than I did when I started this." Raph was also fairly frustrated. While he had to admit that he was in the best shape he had been in since high school football had ended, he highly doubted a good cardio workout was going to save him from being electrocuted to death by force lightning. All in all, Raph had been hoping that his tutoring was going to be a little more Hogwarts and a little less American Ninja Warrior.

"Shame on you Raph. I raised you better than this. You've seen Karate Kid. Wax On, Wax Off. Have a little faith. Besides today we try something a little different. Take a seat." Alistair gestured to the floor and Raph sat down cross-legged on the cool cobblestone.

"Now, in your mind visualize the room just as we've practiced. Every color, every smell, every texture. Map out every detail in your mind." Raph closed his eyes and did as Alistair instructed. Emptying his mind of all other thoughts he brought the room into focus, recreating every minute detail with perfect cerebral clarity.   The smell of the manure in stables, the roughness of the wooden support beams, the bright light of the sun. All of it coalesced into a perfect sense memory of the courtyard around him.

"Hold that image in your mind. Now open up your essence to it, go beyond what your surface senses. Feel the energy of this place. Feel the molecules in the air and the wood and the ground. Connect them to your own molecules."

Raph could feel it then. The same feeling that he'd had when they first emerged from that blue portal. That he'd felt again when he'd passed by that old oak tree in the forest. Everything around him brimmed with energy. And all of it was connected to him. There was no space between himself and the walls around him. Just a chain of atoms and electrons connected to his own.

"Good. Now remain open to that energy while you change the picture of the room in your mind. Instead of sensing air above my head I want you to see water. Communicate that image through your molecules in your body through the molecules in the air between us to the molecules above my head. Tell them that they are water, that they have always been water, and that they will always be water. Let the atoms all around you feel your energy, feel your certainty that this is what is. Concentrate and allow the universe to manifest your will."

Raph did as Alistair instructed and focused on the picture in his mind. The air above Alistair's head was really water. He made himself believe that it was true. He made himself know it to be true in his very bones. The air above Alistair was water. It was a fact. He reached out to the energy surrounding him and explained it to the atoms of the air. They were wrong. They weren't air. They were water.

Raph focused on that thought as seconds dragged into minutes dragged into what seemed like forever. Raph had no idea how long he'd been sitting there with his eyes closed trying to turn air into water before Alistair finally stopped him and told him to open his eyes.

"Now explain to me what you did. Step by step." Raph shifted his weight to his other leg before he answered. Cobblestone was not a comfortable surface for prolonged sitting.

"I pictured the room as it was, then I opened myself up like you told me to." Alistair nodded along with him as he spoke.

"And what did you feel?"

"I felt everything. All the atoms of the air, the protons in the wood, the electrons in the cobblestone." It was the best way Raph could think to describe it. The truth was that the feeling went far beyond the vocabulary he had at his disposal. "I felt all of it. Alive and overflowing with energy."

"Good and then?"

"Then I did as you asked and pictured the air above you as water. I reached out to the molecules their and asked them to rearrange themselves to be water and not air." Alistair's lip turned upward into a smile.

"Apparently they didn't listen. Do you know why

you couldn't turn the air into water?"

"No, I thought I was doing everything the right way."

"You made a mistake that speaks highly of you and, I must say with some godfatherly pride, your upbringing. You asked the universe to change for you rather than try to force it to change. If you had demanded it change instead of asking it to you might have achieved some success."

"I thought about that, but it didn't feel right."

"I didn't say it was right. I said you would have achieved some success. Those who learn to bend the fastest often take this path. Forcing the universe to submit to their will. Their early achievements convince others they must be powerful but in the end, they are often found wanting against one possessed of a true understanding."

"But if asking is wrong and forcing is wrong what am I supposed to do?"

"You are supposed to be. It is not a matter of permissions. You are the universe and the universe is you. When you wish there to be water where there is air, you do not acknowledge the air. The water is there, it has always been there, it will always be there. Do you understand?"

"I think so."

"Close your hand into a fist." Raph did as he was instructed. "Now did you ask your hand to become a fist? Did you demand it to? Or did you simply want it to be a fist and so it was? The world around you is just as much a part of you as your hand is. Treat it as such. Now try again."

Raph took a deep breath then closed his eyes. He pictured the room around him; the smell of the manure in stables, the roughness of the wooden support beams, the bright light of the sun, and the water above Alistair's head.

"Excellent. Well done Raph." Raph opened his eyes and saw a few gallons of water hovering over Alistair's head just as he'd seen it in his mind. His eyes went wide in shock and the water came tumbling down all over Alistair, drenching him. Alistair let out a yelp of cold shock as Raph burst into a fit of laughter. But it was Alistair who had the last laugh as it took him only an instant to dry himself off.

Once Alistair was dry he raised an eyebrow to Raph. It was the only warning he got before a bucket's worth of ice water came pouring down on his own head making him scream bloody murder. Alistair let him shiver for a minute before drying off Raph's clothes the way he had his own.

"Good. Now again."

****

A kind of faded grey filled the sky above Jack while all sorts of repugnant odors emanated from the earth around him. Anticipation filled the air, excitement and adrenaline mixed with fear and trepidation. He had to fight to keep the smile he felt he felt creeping over him from reaching his lips. It was one of his favorite things in all the universes, two opposing armies camped across from each other anxiously awaiting battle. The slightest incident, an odd accident of chance, could set alight a powder keg of chaos. It was an electric calm, like the

brief palpable pause before two lovers plunge into carnal
delight for the first time. All it would take is one shot
fired at an inopportune time, or perhaps a mysterious fire
and manic shouts of sabotage.

Jack drew his thoughts back from their reverie. As
much as he would love to indulge himself and touch off a
little madness there was a larger picture to be considered.
Just because one was an anarchist didn't mean that one
couldn't be a disciplined anarchist. After all being a slave
to one's nature is just as abhorrent as being a slave to
societal norms.

"And what is the makeup of the Northern Kingdoms
forces?" Jack already knew the answer to his question,
but it was important to keep up his charade and it seemed
the sort of question a man in his position should ask. It
wouldn't do for the brand new dilettante and black sheep
of the Namahsii to appear to be well informed on his very
first assignment. Such a thing might raise eyebrows.

The young man looked nervous, how was he to know
that the council had sent Jack here merely as an attempt to
keep him busy and out of their hair for a few days.

"M'Lord the majority of the forces are of Candish
origin. Three divisions of infantry accompanied by two
divisions of horse. They are joined by a division of
Sadeeni horse and Macurian infantry. As well as a
division of mixed irregulars from the other kingdoms. But
all of that pales to the real force we fight. May the Eight
have mercy they've dispatched a full battalion of Benders
to this battle." Of course, given that report, the
nervousness might just be a result of his trying to cope
with a very real expectation of death and dismemberment

in the coming days.

"Now, now Captain you mustn't get discouraged. The might of the Southern Alliance will see us through the day just as it always has before. I'm sure our forces are more than adequate to handle such numbers." A tall, portly man stepped forward from his place at Jack's side to clasp the Captain's shoulder and give him a reassuring smile. The officer looked far from reassured.

"I'm sure Sir Dense is correct concerning our eventual victory, but just to satisfy my curiosity how do our own capabilities stack up against such a force?" It was only natural that Jack would get to ask the very question he had come here to answer for himself. Fortune tended to make a regular gift to him of such moments.

"Sir, we have two divisions of Ardothi infantry, one division of Boonwahee horse, one brigade of mixed irregulars, one regiment of Veruinnian horse, and two platoons of Benders."

"So you're saying they outnumber us more than two to one with three times the Benders." The gravelly voice came from Jack's left. Sir Glaive was a man of middling years whose hairline had long ago retreated from the stern features of his face. The man was short but was possessed of superior presence and a voice that commanded respect. He also tended to cut through all the flowery words and get to the point. All in all, Jack was beginning to like the man.

"Yes, M'lord." The captain did not look pleased to be held to a straight answer.

"Well, that sounds like a rousing victory speech if ever I've heard one. Perhaps the captain would be so kind as to enlighten us to the Wizard Carl has planned to combat such overwhelming odds?"

"I'm not at liberty to discuss that sir"

"Nonsense, that's the very reason we're here in the first place."

"If you gentleman will follow me the Wizard's command tent is right this way." Jack followed to follow the young captain with Sir Glaive and Sir Dense stepping into line behind him.

It only took them a few minute to reach the Wizard's command tent, an ostentatious looking thing that would have looked far more at home in a Laytarian pleasure caravan than in an army camp. While Jack could never be accused of not enjoying the pleasures in life at least he understood there was a time and a place for such decadence and the battlefield was not one of those places.

The captain held open the main tent flap for the three visiting dignitaries and Jack entered to find the inside of the tent to be just as opulent as the outside. At the center of the room was a large table of gilded gold covered in reports and maps strewn about in a most disheveled way. On both sides of the table stood an assortment of Benders and lords casually chatting and sipping at their wine, all neatly sorted into small groups according to social standing.

In the center of it all was a great bear of a man standing well above six foot in height and standing nearly as much in width. A wild orange beard ran down to the man's overstuffed belly. The orange and grown dull with time and was now mixed with a fair amount of gray and a generous amount wine. The man's armor was of fine material and solid design but had clearly been forged in thinner days. He stood with a massive turkey leg in one and a goblet of wine in the other. His green eyes sparkled when they caught sight of Jack and his fellow new arrivals.

"Ah, finally we are joined by our auspicious dignitaries. Please come in." He gestured to some padded benches nearby. "Sit, please enjoy some wine." Sir Dense moved past Jack and took a seat while Sir Glaive gave Jack a look and a shrug before doing likewise. Jack couldn't help but be unpredictable.

"Wine would be excellent Wizard but if you don't mind I'd rather stand. A long day's ride has left me with a sincere desire to remain on my feet."

The Wizard Carl met Jack's response with a grin. "Of course, of course. I find that true some days myself. Very well let's get started. Let me tell you all how we are going to smash those damn Northerners to ash."

Arrogance and decadence. A finer pair for the work ahead he could not ask for. Jack took a goblet from one of the nearby cup-bearers a smile began creeping up inside him again as he listened to the Wizard's plan. This time he didn't fight it. It helped him to blend in. After all, how could any of these fools know that they weren't smiling at the same thing?

****

If there was a heaven, Billy had found it. The Great Ardothi Library was absolutely breathtaking. Vastness was an inadequate word to describe it. Rows and rows of books with no end in sight in any direction ranged out before him. Above him was a domed ceiling so high he could just barely make out the frescos that covered it in vibrant color. As impressive as the paintings were, they held Billy's attention for barely a moment before his eyes returned to the stacks before him.

To call them bookshelves would be doing them a disservice. They were so much more than that, grander in every way. They were decorated with facades that Billy was certain depicted great scenes of Avalon's history or literature. Billy's best guess was that each row stood two hundred feet high. At the end of each row was a spiral staircase made of iron that the mere sight of was enough to give Billy vertigo. Every ten feet or so a narrow walkway jutted out from the shelves where patrons could disembark the staircase and peruse the section's selection. It was, without a doubt, the greatest library he had ever seen. All these books and he had never read any of them. Raph was going to be jealous.

"Ahem" Billy jumped at the sound of someone clearing their throat. He forced his eyes away from the literary feast before him and found that he had wandered in front of some sort of help desk where a young woman was looking up at him.

"Can I help you?" She had bright blue eyes accentuated by the gold half-rimmed spectacles that rested comfortably on her nose. Bushy dark brown hair went down past her shoulders. Her small mouth and dimpled chin completed the mousy look.

"Yes, sorry I've never been in here before and it's all a bit overwhelming." Embarrassed Billy lowered his head and stared at his feet.

"I know, isn't it? Sometimes I have to pinch myself

just to make sure it's not a dream and I actually work here. All of these books. Sometimes when I'm supposed to lock up I stay late and just wander around the stacks pulling out books at random just to see what I can find. Ohh I shouldn't have told you that. I don't even know you. Please don't tell anyone I said that. I'm sorry. I tend to babble when I get excited." He looked up to find her giving him a weak smile.

Billy was more than a little overwhelmed. This was the longest he'd ever been in a conversation with a pretty girl. Like, ever. He was going to have to try very hard not to screw it up.

"Umm… Don't worry I won't tell anybody. I mean even if I was going to tell somebody I wouldn't have the faintest clue who to tell anyway. Not that I would. Tell, I mean. I mean your secrets safe with me." Billy cleared his throat. "I'm Billy. I babble too."

"Hi, Billy. I'm May. It's nice to meet you." She held out her hand and Billy took it, praying that his palms weren't too horribly clammy. An odd expression came over her face as they began to shake, but she quickly recovered with another smile. He knew it. His hands *were* too clammy. He felt like he was going to die of embarrassment.

Looking for a distraction and a quick way out of their handshake Billy stepped forward to the stacks and pointed up.

"So how high does it go?"

"A hundred and fifty-seven feet. After thirty feet we make the patrons wear harnesses. Anything after ninety feet is strictly staff access only."

"How many books is that?"

"Millions upon Millions in ten thousand languages from over a thousand worlds. It is one of the largest collections in the entire multiverse."

"You know about the multiverse?" Billy tried to hide the open astonishment on his face.

"Of course I do silly. Everyone in Ardoth knows about the Travelers and other worlds. It's only in the Northern Kingdoms that they try to keep that information quiet. I've always found that odd actually. For a group that relies so heavily on the memory of Merlin to rule they deny the biggest piece of his legacy, opening us up to other worlds."

"Merlin was the first Traveler?"

"On Avalon yes, at least that's what the history books say. I have to say you're the oddest Traveler I've ever met."

"I'm not a Traveler. What makes you say that?"

"Well, for one thing, most Traveler's won't deny being one. Especially when it's completely obvious that they are. Secondly, I've never met a traveler who couldn't tell the story of Merlin from heart."

"I'm really not…..." Billy tried to get out a denial but May cut him off before he could figure out what to say.

"It's okay. I want to be a Traveler someday. My father says he won't allow it but I figure once I'm older he won't be able to stop me. He'd rather I played the nice courtly lady and marry some rich foreign stiff but I want adventure. You're a Traveler, you understand."

"I'm really not. I'm not anything special at all really.

I just wanted to come and read about it. Traveling and Merlin that is. If you have any books on them that would be great please."

"Oh really, I could have sworn that you were one. I'm sorry I get carried away on my flights of fancy sometimes. C'mon I know where all the best books are I'll show you."

And with that, a whirlwind enveloped Billy and took him into the heart of the great Ardothi library.

****

Alistair had kept Raph practicing well into the evening before he allowed them to call it a day. After hours upon hours of attempts, Raph had only been able to replicate his success with the water twice. Though both times it was in a limited capacity. When Alistair finally did call it quits the moon was high in the sky as they walked into the Mended Eagle's common room. Immediately upon entry, the Bartender pointed them out to a young lad in very fine clothes, who hurried over to present himself to Raph.

"You are Raphael Carpenter, Heir to The Fox?" Alistair coughed at this but Raph responded as if he hadn't heard.

"I am." The lad pulled a piece of parchment out of his bag, cleared his throat and began to read aloud from it.

"By decree of Sir Allan Geir, Defender of the Towers and Knight Protector of the city of Ardoth you are hereby ordered to appear before the Namahsii at the Sun's zenith three days hence so that it may sit judgment in your dispute in accordance with the venerated tradition of the Sha'Dral. Heed this summons or forfeit." The boy, he couldn't have been more than twelve, looked sheepishly at Raph but held his gaze.

"Well I had planned on going for a nice long walk through the city, maybe stop somewhere for a drink, meet a nice girl, invite her back to meet the family have three kids and call it a day but I suppose I could move my schedule around, do all that another day." Lux, who had walked over from his seat in the corner to meet them while the page was reading, rolled his eyes and stifled a laugh at Raph's flippant response. Alistair, on the other hand, looked none too pleased with his answer and the poor young page seemed utterly perplexed by it. Raph let out a long sigh and tried again. "Please inform Sir Geir and the…. Namahsii…" he stumbled a bit over that but Alistair nodded so he kept going "…that it will be both my honor and my pleasure to appear before them tomorrow."

This reply seemed to be much more in line with what the page had expected. Raph had another thought and reached into his pocket and pulled out one of the silver coins Alistair had given them and pressed it into the boy's palm. He looked down at it and his eyes went wide.

"Well, what are you waiting for? Get going." The prompting came from Lux. The page stammered out a few "By your leaves sirs" and left still staring at the coin in his hand.

Once he was gone the room relaxed considerably and Alistair burst into laughter with Lux quickly joining him. Raph was about to get indignant but Billy beat him to it.

"What? What did Raph do wrong?"

"Wrong?" Lux composed himself long enough to answer the question. "He didn't do anything wrong exactly." He looked at Alistair and burst out laughing again.

Raph was really quite confused now. "Okay, so what's so funny then?"

"Well basically….." Alistair wiped tears from his eyes and spoke through wheezing spurts. "You just tipped the mailman a hundred dollars."

"Oh. Well, I guess that is pretty funny." Raph joined in on the laughter with a chuckle of his own. "So my over tipping aside what did I just agree to?"

Alistair let his laughter trickle down to a small snicker before he answered.

"Nothing I haven't been expecting for a little while. The Namahsii is a kind of ruling council made up of seven members from across the Ardothi hierarchy including the Knight Protector. The law says that they are obligated to summon the duelists before them to discuss the Sha'Dral no matter what the circumstances. But what with all of the extraneous factors surrounding this duel I would guess that all seven of them will be there with a somewhat heightened interest in the proceedings."

"Okay, so what am I supposed to say to them when I'm there?"

"Did events unfold exactly the way you relayed them to me?

"You know they did."

"Then you tell them the truth. As for the rest, if I had to guess they will be far more interested in learning about what I've been up to than about you. I have a bit of a reputation with this group you see. They'll be rather curious about anyone that has been proclaimed my heir."

"And what should I tell them?"

"Absolutely nothing. Anything more than that and they won't believe that you're my heir."

Chapter 10

The Namahsii

When Raph was fifteen he'd completely forgotten about a biology test until the day before. The test was on human anatomy: bones, muscles, the circulatory system, and all that good stuff. Heavy on memorization and not something he could just fake his way through. So he'd stayed up all night studying with Billy trying to memorize every detail of the text. He'd never studied so hard in his life for anything.

Until the last three nights anyway, over which Alistair and Lux had crammed every piece of Ardothi culture and protocol into his head with no regard for what might be getting pushed out. This in addition to his daily Bender training. Sleep had not entered the equation. He hoped it worked because he had a feeling he was going to need better than a C plus if he was going to keep his neck.

Raph stifled a yawn as they walked through some of the seedier parts of the city. Since their arrival in Ardoth a week ago thing just kept seeming to get worse. Low-Town was crawling with desperate refugees begging and stealing in a desperate effort just to make it through the day. Raph had never seen anything like it. Not even in those Post-Katrina days. Ardoth was a city on the verge of exploding.

Raph, Billy, and Lux had left the Mended Eagle around mid-morning in order to give themselves time to reach High Town. The Lord Protector sounded the punctual type and while Raph doubted that tardiness would get his head chopped off, it didn't seem totally outside the realm of probability either. Alistair had stayed behind with the collective understanding that he served the group better as their hole card. Raph told himself the phrase collective understanding meant they had all agreed to that strategy. The truth was that collective understanding meant Alistair had told them what he thought was best and none of the rest of them knew enough about what was going on to argue the point.

In his absence Lux had taken up Alistair's role as quizmaster, throwing questions of etiquette at Raph in a way that made him feel like he was in a batting cage getting pelted with fastballs.

"And what do you do if the Third Lord of the Towers calls you by your family name?"

Raph wanted to throttle Lux but it wasn't his fault. He was just trying to help. "Do I bow my head obsequiously? Because I feel like the answer to half these questions is to bow my head obsequiously."

Lux gave him a disapproving look that was undermined by the man's boyish features. It made Raph wonder what he must look like when he tried to make a stern face.

"You need to focus. There's a lot riding on you not screwing this up. Myself included." Lux had a point. And Raph felt a little bad that he wasn't taking all of this as seriously as he could be. But only a little bad.

"Ya, Ya I got it. If the Third Lord of the Tower refers to me by my family name then I speak in the plural because it is understood that I am speaking not just for myself but for the whole of my family line both past and future."

"Good. Now…" Lux continued the rapid-fire questioning until they reached the High Gate. Raph thought he did fairly well for himself but he was far from perfect. Lux grimaced at each wrong answer while Billy remained completely silent as they walked, clearly engaged with thoughts of his own.

Billy left them at the High Gate and headed towards the library. He was spending an awful lot of time there of late and Raph was beginning to worry about it.

Billy had a tendency to bury himself in books when he felt like his world was spinning out of control. And while Raph could understand why he would be feeling that way at the moment, they couldn't afford for Billy not to have his head in the game right now. He hadn't said anything so far because he'd been a bit jealous of Billy and didn't want to rob his friend of the little enjoyment he had these days. But, it was time to have a talk with him, friend to friend, and get his concentration back on the here and now.

And with that thought, Raph took his own advice and forced himself back to the present. The streets of the High Town were rather vacant, with only the occasional servant hurrying to and fro on some errand for the upper city's elite.

The houses here were astounding. Most stood at least three stories tall with some rising as high as seven or eight stories. They came in a wide array of styles. Some were stark sentinels with very little adornment, quietly inferring their superiority through sheer mass. Others were possessed of every sort of lavish décor you could imagine; gargoyles, corbels, balustrades, and all other sorts of ornamentation mish-mashed together in nothing resembling any combination Raph had seen on Earth.

It reminded him of taking the streetcar down St. Charles back home. Not the architectural elements. Not by any means. No, Raph much preferred the elegant southern homes to what he saw here. But the gravitas, the presence of these mansions was palpable on the streets. And Raph guessed that was their true intention.

They had been walking through those stately manors for about a quarter of an hour when they came to their destination. Sitting on the highest point in Ardoth, perfectly equidistant from the four grand towers that stood vigil over the city's inhabitants, was the House of the Namahsii. In contrast to the other buildings of High Town, it stood only a single story. It seemed small and insignificant next to the surrounding buildings. But it said something else to Raph. These people didn't need to show off their wealth and power. It was a sobering thought.

They walked toward the front gate, which was manned by a squad of soldiers in traditional garb. Raph remembered what he had been taught and spoke in a strong, commanding voice.

"I am Raphael Carpenter. Heir to the Fox. I have been summoned by the Lord Protector to appear before the Namahsii and so I have come." The words came out crisp and clear and Raph was rather pleased with himself. At least he was until he received a response.

"Wait here." The guard captain's curt words were anything but friendly. It put Raph slightly on edge. Preparing to walk into the lion's den was a little different than actually walking into the lion's den. He kept his focus straight ahead and tried not to think about the trained killers who had taken up position on either side of him.

Raph and Lux stood there in absolute stillness for a good ten minutes before the captain of the guard returned with another set of soldiers in his wake.

"The Namahsii have called and you have answered. This is the first step on the path to wisdom. Follow the steps of those who come before and in doing so find the heart of wisdom itself. Listen, Learn, Live or perish in the suffocating darkness of your own ignorance. The choice is yours and yours alone."

The captain turned his back to them and began a quick time march towards the compound. Raph walked quickly to keep pace and after a moment's hesitation, he heard Lux's steps following behind him.

They entered through two large, finely-crafted

wooden doors. Three long hallways of white marble stretched out from the small alcove beyond the doorway. One in front and one to each side. The captain escorted them up the middle hallway and opened the door to a small waiting room.

To Raph's surprise, they found Xan already in the room. It appeared as if Raph was not the only one caught by surprise. Apparently, Xan hadn't thought that he would be expected to mingle with lesser beings than himself. He recovered quickly. The insufferable man deciding that he didn't want to miss the opportunity to preen and mock his opponent.

"Well if it isn't the foxling. Here to tell your side of the story no doubt. One would think the Namahsii would have the wisdom to accept my word as fact but I hear they are not as sharp as they used to be."

Despite being in no mood for it Raph forced a smirk on to his face. "Oh good. You know I trust my instincts, but it's always nice to get confirmation. You are actually as big of an asshole as I thought you were." Xan's eyes grew tight in anger. It was nice to know that asshole translated.

"Watch your tone foxling." Raph rolled his eyes at the threat. Hoping that the proper protocol was to remain standing Raph leisurely took a seat on one of the marble benches.

"Or what you're going to threaten me to another duel to the death? I'm frightened. Petrified, really I am. I'd hate to go two outta three. I'm more of a winner take all type of guy."

"Snark is the resource of an inferior mind. Careful

foxling, your peasant is showing." The self-satisfied smirk Xan wore was possibly the most grating thing Raph had ever seen in his life.

"It's meant to. After all, I wouldn't want to be mistaken for a man of your stature." Raph walked over to the much shorter man, closing the distance and leaving no doubt what Raph meant by the word stature. If the insult landed Xan didn't let it show.

"No, you wouldn't. One should never pretend to a civility that one was not born to."

"Civility? Is that what you call it here? Abusing your station and treating the hard working people of this city like trash to be used and discarded? Man, what I wouldn't give to introduce you to a guy named Robespierre." Raph's cool was quickly dissipating.

"Used and discarded. I quite like that. I think once I have killed you I shall find every peasant whore in this city and use and discard them as I see fit. That way I can be sure to find the one that you so foolishly gave your life for." Raph's cool was gone.

"Oh for the love of god. How one dimensional of a person can you be? Don't you have hopes, dreams, and deeper motivations? Are you compensating for a childhood trauma? Something, anything that points to you being more than just a completely flat, static asshole? I mean seriously who says stuff like that? I think we need to get you help. I think you're mentally unbalanced. Is there a history of inbreeding in your family?"

Xan came at him then, ready to take a swing, when the captain of the guard returned through the doorway.

"Xan'tah'Mer the Namahsii have summoned you.

Those who would wish to be wise would do well to heed their call."

Xan collected himself, turned and walked through the door the captain was holding open for him. He stopped and threw one more disdainful glance at Raph before entering. The Captain closed the door behind them and Raph began to worry about what would be the exact nature of the lies that Xan would tell to the Namahsii. Raph went and joined Lux on the bench he had staked out. Raph had a feeling it was going to be a long wait until it was his turn.

****

Lilith Fey shivered just a bit as she made her way through the damp catacombs. The thought occurred to her that she really needed to meet with a better class of people. Or conversely, put herself in a position where people had to come to her. Lilith promised herself that this would be the last time that she would present herself as a supplicant. She knew that it would not be a promise that she could keep but it the thought was enough to steel her for what was to come.

Finally, after an unnecessarily long and winding path, she arrived at an alcove the size of a small sitting room carved out of the rock. There sitting cross-legged waiting for her were three white robed women. The only light came from luminescent minerals in the walls of the cave. Lilith had never known if it was a real mineral that had the effect or is it was simply one the sisters bending.

She knelt down before them, spread her arms wide with her palms facing the sky, and began the ritual incantation.

> *"I am the Fey.*
> *Born into Contradiction*
> *The duality of the two selves.*
> *The Fire and the Darkness.*
> *Passion, Love, Warmth.*
> *Longing, Loneliness, Need.*
> *Too close to the flame and I will burn.*
> *Too close to the void and I will fall.*
> *I accept what is.*
> *I accept what was.*
> *I accept what will be.*
> *We are the Fey*
> *We open ourselves to the Infinite*
> *The wonder of creation within and without.*
> *We see the unseen*
> *We know the unknowable*
> *We believe in belief.*
> *We are the Fey*
> *We walk in the Twilight of Men's Souls"*

Lilith felt enrapturing power rush through her as she delivered the words. So much so that it was difficult to let it go as she spoke the last. A ceremonial goblet of silver was passed around with each sister drinking deep of the water it held. When it came to Lilith she too took a long sip of the water it held before placing it down on the hard rock in front of her.

"What is. Is." Lilith spoke the words quietly and with great reverence.

"What is. Is." Came the ritual response from her

sisters. A second was given for all to recover from the power of the incantation before they got down to business. But only a second.

"You have been away from us for too long Sister. Your absence disturbs us." Lilith's old teacher Yelena was the first to speak. By one who did not know her well her words could be interpreted as a rebuke, but Lilith could hear the warmth buried beneath the stone. At least one of her order had missed her.

"I apologize for my absence Sisters. Events have begun to unfold that require my attention. Our attention."

"This has been told to us before. By another of your line." Corra. There was no warmth there and there never would be

"And in doing so led us to great catastrophe." The last Sister to speak was someone Lilith new only by reputation. Rea. Young to be afforded such responsibility. Her's was a rising star amongst the Fey.

"It is true that my Great Grandmother made mistakes. Great and terrible mistakes. But when she said that a time of great change was coming she was not wrong just as I am not wrong now."

"And what would you have us do with this information? Would you have us go to battle? Would you have us hide? Or is it as simple as submitting ourselves to your whims?" Corra was a woman of middling years and for her, it was a mask of serenity that would best maintain her beauty. When she grew irritated the lines on her face began to show. The lapse in her outward appearance did not slow her down, however. In fact, it almost seemed to spur the greying woman on to greater indignation. "The

Fey have long memories girl. We remember the Grail and all its seekers. This one is no different from the rest of his lineage. No different from Arthur. No different from his father. We will observe, as we always have."

It was the answer that Lilith had been expecting but not the answer she had been wanting. Still, it meant that the arrangements she had been making were not unnecessary ones. It was nice to know that one's efforts were not going to waste.

"And what is the point of observation?"

"To learn" Rea.

"To gain wisdom" Yelena.

"To achieve understanding" Corra.

"To what end? What is the point of knowledge if it is not used? Wisdom if it is not shared? What is the point of understanding the universe if we sit apart from it?"

"And what can we learn if we are constantly involved? What can we change if we go blindly traipsing about? What right do we have to change the destinies of others? No, we have taken that path before. The path of your great-grandmother. It led us to ruin then and it will lead us to ruin again." Even Yelena spoke against her. Lilith had been prepared for that but it hurt none the less.

"This your sisters' command. You are forbidden from contacting the boy. You are forbidden from interfering with the politics of Avalon. And you are forbidden from pursuing the Grail. Hear our words and obey for in this we speak for all the Fey." Corra meant her words to be final. Ironically they would also be her final words.

"Well, I find that regrettable. Luckily I took the

liberty of having one of my agents poison the water we just shared. To be more accurate I had her lace the cup we just passed around with a very specific poison that I happen to have already taken the antidote to. The irony was really far too luscious to do it any other way. Don't worry it's not going to kill you. It's just going to make sure you can't Bend or move a muscle while my men do what needs doing. With your avid stance in favor of observation, I thought that you would be excited. Farewell sisters. Perhaps, in another lifetime, you will make better decisions."

Lilith rose to her feet and headed for the cave entrance. The sunlight felt glorious on her skin. A squad of her most trusted guards waited for here there. No the kind of men to get squeamish about things. They would have already dealt with whatever hidden security her sisters had brought with them.

"You'll find them inside, paralyzed. You have three hours until they can move again. Do what you will. When you're done chop off the heads and the hands and bury them somewhere far from here. The rest should remain in the cave. Use the device I gave you to collapse the cave. Leave no way in. Understood?"

"Yes, mistress."

"Good. Hurry along Captain. I have plans to make."
****

Without a watch, it was hard to tell time effectively but Raph guessed it had been about an hour since Xan had been called before the Namahsii. While Raph had taken up pacing back and forth in front of the door Lux was sitting patiently on the same bench he had been sitting on since they had arrived.

Raph hadn't quite figured out what to make of Lux yet. Sometimes he was as impetuous and impish as Raph could ever be and other times he was so straight-laced and obedient Raph wanted to strangle him. That's not to say he didn't like the guy, he did. Raph just wasn't overly fond of not knowing how a person would react to a situation. He just couldn't figure out which way Lux would jump and that bothered him a bit.

The door opened and all other thoughts left Raph's mind.

"Raphael Carpenter the Namahsii have summoned you. Those who would wish to be wise would do well to heed their call." The Captain's volume and cadence were identical to when he had summoned Xan. Raph was unsure whether that was sad or impressive. Formally Raph answered the Captain the way Alistair had taught him the night before.

"Wisdom is what I seek. I will heed the call." Raph said the ritual words that Xan had skipped hoping to gain even the smallest bit of favor over his opponent. But the captain simply nodded and gestured for Raph to follow him through the doorway.

Raph stepped into the wide white chamber and found himself facing seven blue-clad figures arrayed in a semi-circle in front of him. Summoning all the showmanship and confidence he knew he strode to the small raised platform that had been centered before the council.

"Raphael Carpenter, you come before the Namahsii today in order that we may validate the challenge of Sha'Dral that has been laid before you. As you are not of

Ardothi origin you are bound by no oath or law to answer our questions. Know, however, that we reserve the right to interpret those omissions in any way that we see fit." The man sat in the center position of the seven which was slightly raised from the rest. His voice spoke with an air of command. That calm, cold power that was accustomed to being obeyed. He was clean-shaven with a strong chin and regal nose. His hair was black with a distinguished grey around the temples. Sir Geir then, First Lord of the Towers, Knight Protector of the City of Ardoth. The longest-tenured Knight Protector in some two hundred years according to Alistair. Not a man to be trifled with.

"I understand." Raph bowed his head obsequiously as he had been instructed.

The older woman sitting to the left of Sir Geir leaned forward and spoke with a voice as clear as crystal and just as civilized.

"I very much doubt that. But we shall see." The Lady Tam, Second Lord of the Towers. Alistair had described her as the shrewdest of the lot, loyal to Ardoth and her family and nothing else. A woman for whom the end always justifies the means. Dangerous. "Please describe to us, in your own words, the events leading up to Xan'tah'Mer issuing his challenge of Sha'Dral. "

Raph had been prepared for this question and had decided that his best course of action was to try to keep his explanation as succinct as possible.

"Xan and his compatriots were physically accosting a young woman. I intervened. He called me a great many names, some of which being of a right and moral upbringing I still do not fully grasp. And then he threatened to kill me if I did not leave immediately. I told him that the young lady was under my protection and that he was welcome to try. He and his four companions drew swords. My companion, who is sitting outside, finally caught up with me and let slip who I was. Xan changed his tune and challenged me to Sha'Dral. That's about the long and short of it."

"So you admit to starting the altercation." Wide shoulders, a stout nose, and a well-groomed beard. Manu Garret, Third Lord of the Towers. Not a fan.

"No, Xan began the altercation when he began beating the woman. I merely interceded on her behalf. I do not know the customs here, but where I come from it is expected that we should give aid to those unable to help themselves. Without me, she might be dead. I acted in accordance with my conscience."

"That does not match the account given us by Xan'tah'Mer. He says that the peasant in question was infatuated with him and he was merely trying to disabuse her of certain uncouth ideas when you interfered, needlessly escalating the situation." The Lady Tam kept her face expressionless, which actually made it the second most pleasant face before him. With the exception of the man to the far left, who was grinning from ear to ear, the rest of the Namahsii seemed rather displeased with him.

"Then Xan'tah'Mer is lying." Their outrage was palpable. Apparently calling someone a liar was a breach of etiquette. Whoops.

"You would dare challenge the honor of one of the Tah'Mer?" This was Sir Garret.

"Not much to challenge if you ask me. If he had any

honor we wouldn't be here in the first place." Raph was well aware of the fact that his flippant attitude wasn't helping. What he was surprised by was how much he just didn't care.

"Such impudence. You speak to the Namahsii boy. You will show us respect." The handsome man sitting next to the Lady Tam spoke this time. By his general level of disinterest, Raph took him for Sir Eddard Ty, Fourth Lord of the Towers. Raph was starting to get the feeling that these people didn't like him very much.

"My apologies. I did not mean to give offense." He had but no point in saying that. "If you'll allow me a question. What is the Namahsii's interest in all this? It is my understanding that once the Sha'Dral is invoked it must be carried through."

"That is true if it is a valid challenge. It is the responsibility of the Namahsii to determine if this is indeed a valid challenge." Sir Geir's voice seemed to indicate that there was, in fact, some doubt.

"And if it isn't?" Raph doubted he was going to like the answer.

"Then we will take the appropriate measures." Raph was correct. He did not like the answer.

"You claim to be the Heir to the Fox. I was not aware that the Fox had any children." Sir Ferris Trelgrove, representative of the residents of High Town spoke pointing out the hardest part of Raph's story to prove. Which was ironic since at the moment Alistair stood only a few miles away.

"He doesn't."

"Oh, then why name you heir? How do we know that

171

you speak the truth? That you are Tah'Mer?" Sir Trelgrove's questions came in rapid-fire succession allowing Raph no time to respond.

"Don't be ridiculous that he is bound by the Sha'Dral is proof enough of that his lineage was part of the covenant. But the first question has merit. How do we know that you are the Heir of the Fox? Surely there is something that you can tell us that will prove your claim." It was nice to know that Sir Garret's disdain was not just directed at Raph.

"He said that if I told you anything you would know that I wasn't."

"Well, that certainly sounds like Alistair. True, cryptic, and completely unhelpful." The Lady Tam said with a casual familiarity. Did she and Alistair have a history together?

"I'm inclined to believe the boy." The grinning man on the far left came to his defense. Considering the cheapness of his clothes and his comparably upbeat mood. Raph took him to be Cass Kline, representative of Low-Town.

"Of course you believe the boy. You'll believe anyone with manners as horrible as yours." The other woman on the council joined in for the first time. Guildess Corwynn, Guildmaster of the five crafts and the representative of mid-town on the Namahsii. Raph had to stop himself from doing a double take. Alistair had described her as being a ferocious negotiator and a woman who was good to the letter of her agreements, nothing more nothing less. What he hadn't described was the woman herself. The Guildess was in her early thirties by the looks of it. He did not mention that she was an Amazonian brunette who spoke with a smoldering alto. If Cass was impressed by his fellow council member he didn't show it.

"Why council woman you wound my pride. I've always believed that my sense of decorum was beyond reproach." The representative for low-town pantomimed a wounded heart that earned him a look of stern disapproval from his fellow council members.

"Enough" Sir Geir did not raise his voice but the rest of the council was still as soon as he spoke. "The boy is here in front of us. That is enough for us who know to verify that his blood is part of the covenant. Whether or not he is the Heir to the Fox is irrelevant to the matter at hand even if it is relevant to the incessant scheming of this council. Xan'tah'Mer has told us his version of events. And Raphael here has told us his. If either version is true one would have the right of challenge and since both call the other a liar they both have the right of challenge there as well. The Sha'Dral is valid and this council has no standing to interfere in it." The rest of the council stayed silent, but, from the looks on their faces, Raph guessed that while this was the outcome they expected it was not the outcome he wanted. The Lady Tam was the first to disturb the stillness that sat over the room.

"Very well. The Knight Protector speaks the truth if not wisdom. We cannot break the ancient laws. Not even to save our own necks. Know this Raphael Carpenter if you kill Xan'tah'Mer there will be no preventing a war with the North. If you live this city will burn."

Raph stood there, not knowing what to say. One more impossible weight to bear. His life for a city. A city for the universe. Raph held himself steady as the collective gaze of the council bore into him but he could not bring his eyes to meet theirs.

"There will be a Masquerade tomorrow night at my home Raphael Carpenter. You and your retinue shall attend it. Xan'tah'Mer will also be in attendance. Considering the potential consequences for the city, the people of Ardoth deserve to see the participants of this Sha'Dral first hand. I will offer you some free advice. Attend and keep your mouth shut. It seems to get you into more trouble than you are capable of handling. Remember that it is my job to protect this city. From all potential catastrophes. Give me an excuse and I will see you dead for the good of us all, but so long as you stay within the law my honor will protect you. This is all I will speak on this matter." Sir Geir's back straightened and he assumed a more ceremonial tone.

"You have heard our words. The words of the Namahsii. Go out into the world armed with the wisdom that you did not possess before and prepare for what is to come."

Chapter 11

Masquerades

They gathered together in the common room of the Mended Eagle at quarter to seven. Lux had been so nervous that he'd been dressed an hour before that. Billy was so nervous that he'd been dressed a half an hour before Lux. Raph, on the other hand, felt completely calm. It was a fact that rather surprised him. But having faced down the Namahsii the previous day and with the Sha'Dral still to come, not to mention all of Alistair's training; it was nice to have a night off. He was from New Orleans after all, it was unnatural to go two weeks without some kind of a party.

Sir Geir had sent over a wide variety of suitable attire earlier in the day accompanied by his personal tailor. This was fortunate, as the clothes they'd been traipsing about in wouldn't have made for very good evening wear. Plus they were starting to get smelly.

All in all, it had been a rather good idea on Sir Geir's part.

Alistair picked out a high collared coat of deep red with gold trim for Lux. Apparently, red and gold were the colors of Alistair's house and the coat was the appropriate uniform of noble's body man. Then the tailor and Alistair put their heads together and decided upon a loose fitting dark purple jacket with long tails and maroon shirt for Billy. For Raph, they picked out a bright yellow jacket and leather plants of dark blue. Raph thought he looked ridiculous. At least the pants made his ass pop.

Alistair looked quite dapper in his own way, looking like a cross between Bruce Lee and Bruce Wayne in a form-fitting black button down shirt with a Chinese collar. A bright red fox was emblazoned over each breast. When Raph commented on his sharp looking apparel Alistair smiled at him and simply said "Well I have been away for quite some time. It wouldn't do for me to look shabby now would it?"

A large carriage pulled up to the inn as the last bell chimed seven. Which was weird. Under no circumstances is a carriage picking you up not weird.

After an exchange of a few uncertain looks, the four of them climbed inside. An inside that was surprisingly roomy. The four of them were not small men and Raph had expected them to be packed in like sardines or at least like Southwest passengers. The extra leg room didn't guarantee comfort, unfortunately. Between his ridiculous leather pants and an interior covered in enough velvet to be farcical Raph was rather uncomfortable actually. The

Comment [G]: Inserted: ,

Comment [G]: Inserted: ,

Comment [G]: Inserted: ,

Comment [G]: Inserted: -

Comment [G]: Inserted: ,

Comment [G]: Inserted: ,

leather he could have dealt with but the feel of velvet really weirded him out and it always had. Raph had never figured out how why nobody else felt that way. Thankfully the ride went by quickly, with only a minor bit of jostling from the uneven road underneath.

When they arrived there were servants everywhere, including one to open the carriage door. What they stepped out to was an impressive display.

The Knight Protector's house was closer to a castle than a mansion. Standing four stories tall and at least two football fields wide. The entirety of which seemed to be made out of one solid piece of obsidian. As Raph stood under the stars in the evening sky it was easy to see that Sir Geir's residence was, in fact, darker than night itself. Intimidating was the word that stuck out in Raph's mind.

They moved toward the entrance in a predetermined order. With Lux leading the group, invitation in hand as was customary for a servant. With Raph coming behind him with Billy and Alistair on each shoulder. The invitee and his worthy companions was how Alistair had put it.

Despite spending all of his life in New Orleans Raph had never been to any of the city's famous balls. He was still only nineteen after all and at least on their Earth Alistair had never really traveled in those particular circles. So this whole event was rather new to him. It felt like prom except here he would be the only awkward one. Well, him and Billy. At least they'd be awkward and out of place together.

Lux presented their invitation to a brightly dressed man standing in the doorway. Alistair took the opportunity to lean down and whisper some last words of

177

Comment [G]: Inserted: ,

advice to Raph and Billy.

"Remember we are about to enter a viper's den of iniquity and intrigue. The slightest slip may cost us all our lives." Raph had to bite back a chuckle. How could any place with this much silk be dangerous?

"Alistair, relax. It's just a ball."

Alistair gave Raph a look that could have withered stone.

"And the Titanic was just a boating accident."

Raph was just as glad that he didn't need to explain the reference to Lux.

They walked in through the doorway and waited at the top of a massive set of stairs while the man in the brightly colored clothes, Raph didn't know what to call him, went to announce them to the gathering.

The ballroom was enormous. The stairs flowed down and rippled out in size until they came to the marble floor below. A high arching ceiling painted sky blue gave one the impression of being outside while tall stained glass windows gave Raph the distinct feeling that he was in a church. Two long buffets were set up on either side of the room leaving the entire floor wide open for dancing and mingling. One long raised table was set up opposite the stairs from the far side of the room. Raph presumed for the Namahsii and their guests. In front of that was a bandstand where you could say the band was already in full swing. If by swing, you meant they were playing an extremely dour waltz. From their positioning on the landing, they could see all of it and Raph guessed that had been the architect's intention.

The music faded and a trumpet blast punctuated the

Comment [G]: Deleted:,
Comment [G]: Inserted: .
Comment [G]: Inserted: ,
Comment [G]: Deleted:,
Comment [G]: Deleted: i
Comment [G]: Inserted: d w
Comment [G]: Inserted: ba
Comment [G]: Inserted: h
Comment [G]: Inserted: .
Comment [G]: Inserted: ,
Comment [G]: Inserted: I
Comment [G]: Deleted:a group of ins
Comment [G]: Deleted:rum
Comment [G]: Deleted:t
Comment [G]: Deleted:list
Comment [G]: Deleted:were
Comment [G]: Deleted:,
Comment [G]: Deleted:i

air.

In a loud, crisp voice Raph heard his name and began to walk down the stairs.

"Raphael Ignatius Carpenter, Heir to the Fox with his companions William Bordeaux and...." The man, a troubadour maybe, stopped short as he looked up and back at the paper to make sure what he had read was real. He looked back over his shoulder and Raph could see the awe in his eyes "..........And Alistair Ret'Mier; Servant of the Seven Worlds, Wizard of the Barren Council, Defender of the Gate, Last Light of the Fallen," by now the entire gathering had grown silent and were staring at the newcomers as they descended the staircase, "The Fox of Avalon".

A murmur ran through the crowd. Excitement and curiosity mixed with anxiety and fear. Tension suddenly sat heavy in the air. It took everything Raph had not to look back over his shoulder and throw a snarky quip in Alistair's direction. But with every eye in the room staring at them it was probably better if he stuck to the script. And the script said that Raph was to remain dignified and aloof as he was greeted by his hosts, the First Lord of the Tower and his wife.

"Greetings and be welcome in my home young Master Carpenter. I bestow upon you and your retinue the protection of my house during your stay with us." While it would not be fair to say that the rigidity left Sir Geir's voice then it did seem to abate enough to infer a more relaxed tone. "I see you have brought the Fox to see our hen house for himself. I am not sure what I am to make of it other than to thank you for your efforts to protect our

evening from boredom." The woman on Sir Geir's right
made a strange harrumphing noise and gave the man a
slight pinch on the arm.

"Husband, you're trying for funny again. I told you
not to do that. Especially not with one so young." The
stern man's lip twitched into a brief smile that was gone
as quickly as it came. Raph found the exchange rather
sweet.

"Raphael Carpenter. Lady Robyn Geir. My wife."
Lady Geir was a tall woman, almost as tall as Sir Geir
who was only a few inches shorter than Raph himself.
Her features seemed at odds with her husbands. Where he
seemed to have a face of stone, hers was rounded with big
rosy cheeks. In the same way that Sir Geir could be
described as gaunt and sinewy but not skinny, Lady Geir
could be described as full and robust but not fat. And,
though they seemed like opposites, that was the real
connection between the couple. Both of their bodies
looked as if they were accustomed to hard work. A
feature that set them apart from a great deal of the other
nobles in the room.

"A pleasure to meet you, M'lady. You are most
gracious to welcome us into your home."

"The pleasure is mine Master Carpenter. These
parties do get ever so stale and I believe you and your
entourage will ensure that tonight stands out in my
guest's minds. Be welcome and enjoy every courtesy of
our house."

Raph nodded and moved to the side. Billy quickly
followed him having muddled through polite greetings to
Lord and Lady Geir. Raph barely paid Billy any mind as

180

Comment [G]: Inserted: ,

Comment [G]: Inserted: ,

he was anxious to hear all he could of Alistair's interactions with their hosts.

"Ah and here he is The Fox himself. If I remember correctly I believe I am supposed to have you arrested and hanged. If this was any other city on Avalon you most certainly would be." Raph nearly choked the Lord Protector's words. Alistair took them in stride.

"Then let us both be grateful that we are in Ardoth and wisdom rather than fear rules here."

"Yes, it does. Nonetheless, I will allow foolishness to stay my hand. Be welcome in my home Alistair Ret'Mier. Remember I too was at Balktier. My family owes you a debt for what transpired that day. But be wary the law is the law and I can bend it only so far."

"Thank you, Sir Geir. I will not abuse your hospitality."

Alistair shook his hand and moved to Lady Geir who was staring dumbfounded at her husband. Alistair took her hand and gave it a quick kiss before moving past. Raph raised an eyebrow as his godfather joined them.

"Well, that was interesting. Anything you'd like to share?"

"No. Not particularly."

"What's Balktier?" Apparently, Billy had been eavesdropping as well.

"A memory." Raph couldn't help but snicker at the non-answer.

"Wow cryptic much?" Alistair did not rise to the bait. So Raph moved on. "Right so what do we do now?"

"Now? Now we mingle." His Godfather had a glint of mischief in his eye.

181

Comment [G]: Inserted: ,
Comment [G]: Inserted: ,
Comment [G]: Inserted: ,
Comment [G]: Deleted:s

****

It reminded Billy of the first dance he'd ever been invited to way back in junior high. The men and women were far better dressed sure, and they certainly were much better dancers, but for Billy, those differences were superficial ones. At the heart of it, the two remained the same. He was in a room full of attractive people wondering what the hell he thought he was doing by showing up here and ruining their beautiful aesthetic. He hadn't blamed his eighth-grade classmates for their sideways looks and snickers and he didn't blame these people for their sneers. After all, it was hard to get angry at someone for thinking something when you yourself are thinking the exact same thing.

As soon as they entered Raph and Alistair had been caught up in a whirlwind of people. Billy had used the distraction to sneak over to the buffet. It wasn't that they hadn't been eating well at the inn it was just that Billy was used to certain standards in his culinary adventures and weird vegetable gruel wasn't quite up to those standards. Billy expected that the Lord Protector would put out an impressive spread and he wasn't disappointed.

The smell of roast meat filled the air. Billy wasted no time fixing himself a plate. Buttered garlic chicken, brazed turkey leg, and something that looked like ribs but was possessed of a distinctly yellow tinge. Billy bit into this first and was rewarded with a flavor reminiscent of sweet and sour pork. It was good to get some real food into his stomach. He had just filled his mouth with a delicious doughy thing that was like a dinner roll but sweeter when he saw her.

182

Comment [G]: Inserted: ,
Comment [G]: Inserted: ,
Comment [G]: Inserted: ,
Comment [G]: Inserted: -

May. In a gorgeous gown of green and blue. Billy had never seen anything like it. The colors seemed to swirl and melt together as she moved. It was absolutely breathtaking. She was breathtaking.

Several simultaneous thoughts ran through Billy's mind at that moment. *Why is she here? Did she see me? Did she see me stuffing my face with dinner rolls? Wow, she's beautiful. How the hell did they get the colors to move like that? How fat do I look right now? She saw me and she's disgusted and I'm going to spend the rest of my life alone.*

Panic seized him. It was not the completely rational panic of being attacked by fireball wielding maniacs from another dimension. Nor was it the fearful panic of finding out your best friend was being forced to fight a duel to the death. It was not even the cold, slow panic you get at the realization that nothing in your world made sense anymore. No the panic that seized Billy then was something far worse and far more normal than all of these. It was the panic of a boy who likes a girl and has convinced himself that he's going to say or do something to ensure that she never feels the same way about him.

Quickly Billy set his plate down and headed in the direction opposite May as fast as he could, trying awkwardly to keep his face obscured from her as he went.

Unfortunately, this meant that he was not paying much attention to where he was walking. He realized this about two seconds after he clumsily bumped into a behemoth of a man. Billy began a plethora of apologies that managed to get jumbled up in one another so as to emerge from his mouth in the form of what could

Comment [G]: Inserted: ,

Comment [G]: Inserted: ,

generously be called word sludge.

The man simply glared silently down his scary, clearly broken in a few brawls in his day nose at Billy.

"….So to summarize I'm very, very sorry." Billy gave a weak smile hoping for acceptance and dismissal.

Instead, the stoic silence continued. The man's perfectly constructed beard filling Billy with dread. He wondered if they chopped off people's heads on Avalon. It seemed like that would be a thing around here.

"You came here with the Fox and his heir. You are their companion?" The intimidating, matter of fact growl caught Billy off-guard.

"I'm their friend. Well, I'm Raph's friend. Alistair is more like an uncle that I'm kind of scared of." Billy knew that wasn't what he should have said, but thinking before he spoke was not a luxury Billy often afforded himself.

"I am Sir Garret. Third Lord of the Towers. I met your friend when he came before the Namahsii. He lacked manners as well." Great. One of the Namahsii. Billy had the best luck ever.

"Oh. Ya." Realizing that was not a complete sentence on any planet he tried to complete the thought using his word maker thing. "He can be like that sometimes."

Sir Garret gestured to someone behind Billy to come towards them. Billy could only assume that it was a pair of guards coming to take him away. He wondered what the dungeons were like. Cold probably. Billy heard the footsteps behind him and braced himself for all manner of unpleasantness.

"William Bordeaux, may I introduce to you my

184

Comment [G]: Inserted: ,

Comment [G]: Inserted: ,

daughter Lady May Garret." He hadn't prepared himself for that particular manner of unpleasantness.
Summoning every fantasy novel he'd ever read he tried his best to be courtly.

"A pleasure M'lady." Billy attempted a stiff bow and just barely managed to keep himself from falling over.

"Lady May will escort you around the party tonight and teach you proper Ardothi manners. You travel in infamous company Mister Bordeaux. Perhaps we should all strive to keep your clumsiness from adding to the intrigue this evening. May." Sir Garret gave a quick nod to his daughter then left them without a further word.

"Hi."

"Hi."

"So your father is one of the Namahsii."

"Your friend is the heir to the Fox."

"Well to be fair I was friends with Raph long before either one of us knew Alistair was the Fox."

"And I was my father's daughter long before I knew what the Namahsii was."

"Touché."

"What?"

"Good Point."

"Yes, I thought it was."

"So what do I call you? Lady Garret? Lady May? Something else?"

"May is fine. Lady Garret is my mother and I've never been fond of Lady May."

"I think Lady May is quite nice." Billy blushed when he heard the words aloud.

"Just May. Please."

"Oh. Okay." Billy hesitated at the chastisement and desperately groped around in his head for what to say next. Coming up blank he lamely put the onus on May. "So what do you want to talk about?"

"Well, I found some new books about Merlin. I think there are some cool things in them that aren't part of the normal accounts."

"Oh good." Billy's excitement was almost enough to make him forget his embarrassment.

"Let me tell you about what I found...." And just like that, she was off on a verbal tear. Leaving Billy no option but to try and keep up.

***

"Shall we dance?" The voice was strong and hot like smoldering steel. Inviting you in while warning you of the perils ahead. It was an impossible voice. A voice Raph knew should not be here. And the fact that it was could mean nothing good. He should scream for Alistair and get as far as he could from that voice. Because more than any other trait, that voice was sultry.

"Faye...." It was her. He knew it before he even turned around. The only thing that shocked him was that he wasn't really shocked at all. At this point, Raph wasn't sure if shock was something that he was capable of feeling anymore. He turned around to face her.

He was incorrect. He absolutely was capable of feeling shock. The incredibly flattering, low cut emerald gown Faye was wearing had corrected him of his misconception in a hurry. It also left him stammering like an idiot. Again.

"Wha...what are....."

"Oh now I know you're surprised to see me but really you're going to need to gather your wits a bit. A lady enjoys a man who is confident and articulate not one who falls to pieces every time she puts on something nice." Three times now she had surprised him. In New Orleans, in his own dreams, and now here, on a parallel world. But this was once too many. The first time had looked like a coincidence, their own little meet-cute. The second time he could have written off, it was a dream after all, why wouldn't he dream of the gorgeous mystery woman who flirted with him. But now she had overplayed her hand. Being here meant she had known all along and had manipulated him from the start. Raph hated being manipulated. No more stammering idiot. She wasn't a potential love interest. She was part of the game. The game that he was playing for his life. Fine then. Time to step it up a notch.

"You're right my apologies. My brain was having a hard time deciding which was more unexpected. Your beauty or your presence here. Now that it's made up its mind I should be much more capable on all fronts." Faye or whoever she actually was took the compliment in stride because of course she already knew everything Raph had just figured out and revealed herself anyway.

"May I ask what the final decision was?" Gracious and reserved. Just like every other noblewoman in the place. Except she most definitely wasn't. Well, Raph hoped not. If the other noblewomen here were like her then Alistair's 'den of vipers' comment had been a serious understatement.

"You may, but I am afraid that I must be less giving

of my answers until I've received a few of my own."
Raph may be a sucker for a pretty face, but he knew Faye
for what she was now. And just because he didn't believe
in manipulating people didn't mean he wasn't good at it
when he needed to be.

"Very good. You're beginning to learn. A game
then. An answer for an answer. Very well let us begin."

"Okay, who are you really?"

"Ah not so fast, you haven't answered my first
question yet."

"Very well, your beauty."

"How very sweet but not the first question I asked."

"Which was?"

"Shall we dance?"

"It would be my pleasure."

He took her hand and led her to the dance floor. He'd
been watching for a good deal of the night and the steps
weren't all that different from a waltz. And thanks to five
years of ballroom dance lessons Raph could waltz. Raph
could waltz incredibly well.

He took her right hand in his left and placed his right
high on her back. He waited for the downbeat and stepped
into the fray. Raph moved confidently, smoothly and it
surprised her. She didn't let it show on her face but Raph
could feel it in her body. She'd expected him to stumble,
to trip, to struggle; she'd been prepared to lead. Raph
smiled. Alistair had always told him to be a man of many
talents, you never knew what might come in handy.

"You pick up the steps quickly. Faster than I would
have expected." She relaxed now, a silent
acknowledgment to go along the verbal one that he knew

what he was doing. Dancing stopped being something they were doing and became simply their state of being.

"Oh just trying to play catch up. It seems everybody else has been dancing this dance for a lot longer than I have." Her eyes glistened under the light of the candelabra. Raph sent her into a graceful spin before bringing her back in close to him.   As they continued to move around the room Raph picked up the pace of their rotation. Occupying more space and making Lilith's gown twirl majestically.

"I can't wait to see what happens once you get a bit of experience under your belt."

"I think it will take me less time to remember that you haven't answered my first question yet."

"Ah yes, what was that again?"

"Who are you really?"

"My name is Lilith."

"That doesn't tell me what I want to know."

"You'll need to be craftier then. My turn. Who are *you*?"

"You know who I am"

"Perhaps. But I want to see if you know who you are. Answer the question."

"I'm Raphael Carpenter."

"That doesn't tell you what you need to know."

"Then I'll need to be craftier won't I?"

"Yes, you will. My turn."

"I just answered your question."

"And I yours. Yes, you will need to be craftier." She smiled a rather lascivious smile as he twirled her again. "Come now Raphael you were doing so well."

189

Comment [G]: Inserted: a

Raph may have gotten wise to her game but it didn't mean that she had suddenly stopped being a beautiful woman. It just meant she was a beautiful woman who couldn't be trusted and was blatantly trying to use her innate sexuality to manipulate him. Sometimes cold logic was as effective as a bucket of ice water at least as far as hormones were concerned.

"Ask your question."

"Who do you trust?"

"The universe." Lilith missed a beat then. Just enough to throw her out of the dance's rhythm, but Raph managed to keep them in-step.

"What are we playing: Mah, Na, or Ret?"

"What makes you think we're playing the same game?"

The music stopped and as did the dance.

"Well thank you, Raphael that was most exhilarating, it's always nice to have a partner who knows how to lead." Without waiting for a response she turned and walked away from him. He called after her hoping to get the last word.

"My pleasure. It is, after all, what I'm here for. Isn't it?"

Lilith looked back over her shoulder and threw him a wicked smile.

"I think that's entirely up to you." And then she was gone. Lost in the crowd.

*****

Jack had to hand it to the boy. He knew how to handle himself. Both in the council chamber and on the dance floor. And how brazen of Lilith to appear here

190

without any sort of disguise. Maybe she was hoping that everyone would be too busy looking at her dress to see her face but it was still a bold move. And while it was commonly believed that Jack favored boldness the truth was that he enjoyed subtlety just as much if not more. These were dangerous days for bold moves.

It was why he had taken great pains to avoid Lilith's eyes since she had arrived. While his disguise might be enough to fool the majority of the Knight Protector's distinguished guests there were two here who would only need a glance to unmask him. Lilith and the Fox. Hmm, that was a rather amusing notion. Lilith and the Fox. Like a children's book.   Lilith and the Fox. On second examination the thought was rather haunting really. The two of them in the same room at the same time. Dangerous days indeed.

Which was exactly why it was so important for Jack to make friends.

"Xan'tah'Mer, Emissary of the North and dueler of some renown. I found your performance in the council chambers the other day to be quite illuminating." Illuminating was the polite word for it. The man was as arrogant as any three kings alive without the wit to match. Still, he had a certain charm about him when he chose to use it. Which seemed to be only for a fairly narrow group of nobles he deemed worthy of his attention. Luckily at the present juncture, Jack was one of those nobles.

"You honor me sir but I'm afraid that at present your council more closely resembles a Pagentman's farce than a ruling body."

"Yes well, we all must make do with what we have.

191

Not all of us can be ruled by kings after all, no matter how preferable it may be at times."

A flash shone in Xan's eyes and Jack knew he had been right. Xan was not here to negotiate a peace, he was here to ferret out potential allies for the occupation. The man had the subtlety of a sixteen-year-old boy under the moonlight. Just as well Jack had led with that ham-fisted king talk, any coyer and he might have lost the boy.

"It is our belief in Candar that all nations should bend knee to a king. Preferably one of the Tah'Mer."

"That belief shows wisdom. Sometimes I wonder if we here in Ardoth would benefit from such a system. Unfortunately, our current affiliations with the Southern Alliance precludes us from making any such adjustments to our existing political structures. As I said we must all make do with what we have."

"And sometimes we make what we have into what we want." Oh, this was just too easy. Jack had already lost all respect for this buffoon but now he was starting to lose respect for all of Candor. How much self-loathing would a nation have to have to allow any member of this man-child's gene pool to rule them?

"Another philosophy that I share. Under the right circumstances, that is. Am I to infer that such circumstances might not be that far off?"

"Who's to say what the future holds?" He winked! Oh, Holy Eight He winked! Jack actually had to bite the inside of his cheek from laughing at this fool.

"Indeed. Please excuse me. A man in my position must make the rounds but I have found this conversation most enlightening. Thank you Xan'tah'Mer."

Comment [G]: Inserted: -

Comment [G]: Inserted: -

Comment [G]: Inserted: ,

Comment [G]: Inserted: ,

With that, he took leave of the North's Emissary to
Ardoth. And took away another insight. Whoever had
sent this man was not a fool at all. What better way to get
such an oaf out of your hair than to send him somewhere
where is oafishness was exactly what was called for. No
matter Candor's ruling family was a problem for another
day. Though a day not that far off.

Raph had spent most of the night trying to wrap his
head around his conversation with Faye, or Lilith more
accurately, certain that there were layers upon layers
hidden in her responses. Some of his dancing partners had
been more conducive to his pensiveness than others.
Unfortunately yet another beautiful woman of some
renown was demanding his full attention at the moment.
Amelia Corwynn, Guildess of the Five Trades, danced in
his arms wearing a skintight purple dress with a plunging
neckline and enough jewelry to fund a small island nation
for a few decades.

Luckily for him, her verbal sparring was a little less
impactful than Lilith's.

"So young master fox how go your preparations for
the Sha'Dral? Well, I hope?"

"They go well yes."

"Then you believe that you will win the day?"

"I don't know. But it's not like I have any other
options. So I'll win because otherwise, I'll be dead."

"A very pragmatic view."

"Thank You."

The music began to slow and Raph guided them to
the edge of the dance floor.

193

"Thank you for the dance. If you emerge from your ordeal triumphant perhaps we can have another." She smiled at him as she let go of his hand. Like a wolf smiling at a sheep. Under normal circumstances, such a smile would have unnerved him. Hell if a woman had smiled at him like that back on Earth he would have shit himself with fright. Unfortunately for him, it didn't even crack his top ten of unsettling things about tonight. Raph had a feeling the Guildess was a tad overconfident about her abilities to swim in the waters she found herself. Or maybe Raph was just projecting. He had, after all, had a drowning sensation since he'd gotten to this town. All of these thoughts he kept to himself and instead found himself summoning all his southern charm to merely say:

"It would be my pleasure Guildess Corwynn."

He stepped away from the Guildess and took a glass of wine from the serving man passing by. Dancing always left him parched and the double duty of the verbal two-step he'd been playing with these ladies all night only enhanced his thirst. He would have preferred something chilled, but anything in a pinch at this point. And he doubted that he would have been able to get a seven in seven on this world anyway.

He took a sip of his wine and appreciated his first free moments of the ball. Guildess Corwynn and Lilith had not been his only dancing partners that night. Lady Tam had stolen him away for two dances but her attentions had seemed aimed at drawing out as much about Alistair as she could. It was a grilling that would have done an episode of Law and Order proud. There had been others too. Pretty girls and beautiful women of all

Comment [G]: Inserted: ,
Comment [G]: Inserted: ,
Comment [G]: Inserted: ,
Comment [G]: Inserted: ,
Comment [G]: Inserted: woul
Comment [G]: Inserted: A
Comment [G]: Inserted: .
Comment [G]: Inserted: ,
Comment [G]: Inserted: -
Comment [G]: Deleted:a
Comment [G]: Deleted:'
Comment [G]: Deleted: be

types. All trying to catch Raph's eye and get his tongue moving. At nineteen Raph wasn't a virgin but he wasn't exactly experienced. The truth was in the last two hours he'd gotten more attention from women than he had in his entire life.

Under normal circumstances, he'd be drunkenly making out with anyone of these girls and feel the luckier for it. But he'd already learned from "Faye" tonight just exactly a pretty face could hide. There's a certain kind of maturity that comes from staring into the eyes of someone who wants to kill you. There is a whole other level of cynicism you get when you look into someone's eyes and they're still deciding whether you'd be of more use to them alive or dead.

Of course, after a while, they stopped sending women and started sending men. That had actually been much easier to handle as the boys seemed more inclined to believe that he wasn't interested. Or perhaps they didn't want to push the issue because on Avalon that lifestyle simply required more discretion. That would be too bad, but Raph was too concerned with other things at the moment to get riled up about gay rights on a parallel world. In any case, having rejected every potential suitor in the place, Raph finally had time to catch his breath while the powerful men and women of Ardoth regrouped and planned their next approaches.

He looked around the room in an effort to see if his friends were drawing as much attention as he was. Alistair seemed to have gathered two large crowds. One completely surrounding him and hanging on his every word, and another standing a little ways off, staring at

Comment [G]: Inserted: ,
Comment [G]: Inserted: d
Comment [G]: Deleted: s
Comment [G]: Inserted: ,
Comment [G]: Inserted: ,
Comment [G]: Inserted: ,
Comment [G]: Inserted: ,

him in mortification and gossiping amongst themselves. Billy, on the other hand, had managed to hide himself away in a corner and was conversing with a very pretty girl. *Good for him* he thought and then immediately worried that Billy might be falling for the same honey trap that the nobles had been trying to set for Raph. That thought made him afraid and angry at the same time. Afraid that Billy might have let something slip and anger at the idea that someone would take advantage of his friend that way.

Raph took a step towards the pair before he stopped himself and took a breath. Odds were if Billy was going to say something that was going to compromise them he would have already said it by now and Raph going over there wasn't going to fix anything if that was the case. And if it wasn't the case then Raph was going to end up acting like an ass to the first girl who'd ever shone a genuine interest in his best friend. So really going over there was lose-lose with the added disadvantage of letting everyone in the room know Raph though Billy was their weak link. *Better to just let it go.*

So Raph turned his attention to see if he could spot the fourth and final member of their party. Lux's job had been to see if he could find out anything from the various servants and attendants that were working behind the scenes of the masquerade. Which meant he'd need to blend in with the servants by pretending to be a servant himself. There had been some discussion as to whether he should pretend to be Alistair's man or Raph's. The argument was made that having a man would help Raph's reputation and working for Raph would allow Lux to

Comment [G]: Inserted: ,

Comment [G]: Inserted: ,

Comment [G]: Inserted: ,

Comment [G]: Inserted: ,

believably say he knew nothing of what Alistair was up to. So they decided for tonight Lux was Raph's valet. Raph didn't really know what a valet did and if he would be expected to help out with the party. So far Raph had yet to see Lux in the main ballroom but given how full his dance card had been up till now that didn't mean a whole lot.

After taking a good long look around the expansive room Raph let his eyes settle on the servant's entrance hoping to catch Lux going in or out in some capacity.   A couple of minutes went by without any luck before someone coming through the doors caught Raph's attention. He did a double take before realizing that it was not in fact Lux. The man was too skinny and just a bit too short to be his friend. But Raph's eyes lingered on him nonetheless.

Something about the man stuck out in Raph's mind. No one else around seemed to be paying him much mind. He was a servant after all, why should anybody in this ballroom give him a second thought. Except he wasn't a servant, at least he didn't carry himself like one. It was what Alistair had warned Lux about. That stride was too purposeful, too commanding and it was headed right for Sir Geir.

Like everyone else, the Knight Protector was oblivious to the man. Deciding something was most definitely wrong Raph began to move at an angle to intercept the imposter. But the dance floor was crowded and he was too far away to close the distance in time.

Raph saw the man reach into his sleeve and reacted on instinct.

Comment [G]: Inserted: ,

"MOVE!" His voice thundered through the room, freezing the band and turning all eyes towards him. Raph felt the molecules around him come alive as he pushed the air with everything he had at Sir Geir.

The blow knocked Geir back about ten feet back and onto a table but succeeded in getting him out of the way of the throwing dagger that had just taken the man he was talking to in the shoulder.

"Assassin!" That got people moving. Unfortunately for Raph some of those people were moving towards him and they did not look happy. *Crap. They think I'm the assassin.* Raph had barely finished that thought when something very big and heavy tackled him from behind. It hurt. A lot.

The tackle itself wasn't that bad. Raph the former football player was used to taking hits like that. It was slamming into the marble floor that knocked the wind out of him. The two hundred twenty plus pound man on his back was not particularly helping him get it back either. On the plus side, Raph was gaining his first insights into the various fashions of Ardothi footwear.

"What are you doing you fools? Get off of him."

"But M'Lord he tried to kill the Knight Protector."

"No, he didn't you idiots. He most certainly saved Sir Geir's life from a blade to the heart. Look."

A few seconds passed.

Then a few more seconds passed.

Finally, Raph heard a grunting noise and a release of pressure as his tackler released him and stood up.

Raph immediately jumped to his feet and scanned around for the would-be assassin but it was no use. The

Comment [G]: Inserted: ,

Comment [G]: Inserted: ,

man was long gone by now.

"I'm afraid he would have gotten away in all the confusion."

Raph's gaze settled back on the man who had vouched for him and saved him from a potentially dangerous situation.

"I think unfortunately he has Sir Ty. Thank you for the timely intervention. It was appreciated."

"Those same words I think I should be saying to you Raphael Carpenter. You appeared to have saved my life." Sir Geir's voice was crisp and clear above the chaos of the room, completely unshaken by the events of the previous minutes.

"I was just trying to help Sir Geir. I'm sorry I couldn't think of a subtler way to do it."

"Nonsense, I'm alive aren't I." Sir Geir walked over to where the knife intended for him had struck the man he had been conversing with instead. "Which is more than I can say for Sir Ricton here. A wound to the shoulder and dead already. Poisoned Blade. Poor bastard. At least it was quick, thank Merlin."

"Yes, thank Merlin indeed." All eyes went to Alistair as he joined their discussion. "Thank him for Raph's keen eye and quick thinking. Without them, this city might have followed you down to hell Sir Geir."

"Flair for the dramatic aside I would say that was exactly the villain's intent." Soldiers who had been stationed around the estate began flooding into the ballroom and Sir Geir left their makeshift council behind to issue commands to the incoming troops. "I want the entire city shut down, including the First and Second

Comment [G]: Inserted: ,

Comment [G]: Inserted: ,

Gates. Post guards at every intersection and roving bands of three to drive this fiend into the light. This man tried to kill me in my home and murdered a noble of this city. I want him found and I want him taken alive."

"I'm afraid that will not be possible Sir Geir."

Xan approached them with two of his guards in tow. One of whom was carrying a body over his shoulder like a sack of potatoes. He flopped the dead man unceremoniously at the Knight Protector's feet.

"We saw him kill a soldier as he fled. Knowing him then for the assassin we gave chase and cornered him. He pretended to surrender then went for a knife. I'm sorry I reacted on instinct to protect myself and my men. The fireball that I unleashed will make it harder for your men to identify him. Again you have my sincerest apologies for my failings."

Xan did not appear to Raph as being sincere in the slightest but Raph had to admit that may just be due to his profound hatred for the man.

"You kept this treacherous bastard from escaping and acted to defend the lives yourself and your men. No need to apologize for that. We have other ways to find out who the wretch was working for. It appears I have incurred two debts tonight. To two men who are destined to fight to the death. A shame. Can you not be persuaded to put aside this challenge?" Sir Geir looked sincere in his regret. At least sincere enough to give Raph pause. Of course, Raph wasn't the one who needed to be convinced to call off the duel.

"Nothing has changed. This man has impugned my honor and he will die for the insult. If anything I believe tonight has proved the worthiness of my cause." Xan's words were almost comical in their arrogance.

"Ya. You took a life and I saved one. I think that proves something all right. C'mon Alistair let's grab Billy and Lux and go. There's nothing else for us here tonight." Raph extended his hand to their host who gave it a hearty embrace. "Thank you Sir Geir for your hospitality and please that Lady Geir for us as well.

"I will as I am sure she will surely want to thank you for your attendance and particular for saving the life of your husband. I will gather some guards to escort you home as well as a pass to get you past the gates. Find your friends and they will be waiting for you at the doors."

Raph nodded and walked towards where he saw Billy and Lux milling about by the servant's door. Alistair matched his stride.

"You were awfully quiet once Xan showed up with that body," Raph spoke quietly making sure that only his Godfather could hear him.

"I thought it best at that point to simply observe."

"And what do you think?"

"You first."

"I think it was pretty curious that Xan was the one to find and kill the assassin with no one but his own men around. And I find it doubly curious that he did it in such a way as to make sure the man couldn't be identified. Is that what you think?"

"I think I raised a very bright young man."

They gathered up Lux and Billy and headed back to the Mended Eagle for a not very good night's sleep.

Comment [G]: Inserted: ,
Comment [G]: Inserted: t
Comment [G]: Deleted:t
Comment [G]: Deleted:.

Chapter 12

Sex, Lies, and Library Scrolls

The fallout from the ball could be felt throughout Ardoth. A crackdown would be the polite way to describe it. Turns out Ardothi lords get a little persnickety when you try to murder them in their homes. Anger was to be expected along with some extra security but Raph thought the only thing that kept this from becoming an Orwellian nightmare was the lack of cameras.

The City Watch was out in force and daytime identity checks had been put into place at both the Mid- and High-Town gates. The refugee problem, which had already been spiraling out of control before they had arrived in Ardoth, had now escalated from irritation to security threat. Sir Geir had ordered the gates shut to new visitors. Not even the other Lords of the Tower could order them opened. Of course, that didn't stop people from trying to get in. If you walked the city walls in the morning you were bound to find the bodies of desperate people who had fallen while trying to climb the walls. More than a couple of those bodies had been found with arrows in them.

Of course, Raph was getting all of this information second hand from Lux and Alistair since he was stuck inside for the foreseeable future. In what Raph could only consider a show gratitude for Raph saving his life, Sir Geir had posted extra guards at the Mended Eagle. "In order to ensure the safety of Raph and his party." At least that's what the message that had come with the guardsmen's lieutenant said. The guardsmen were also under specific orders not to allow Raph to leave the Mended Eagle without an armed escort. An armed escort that in the current climate seemed to do a better job of attracting and inciting trouble than protecting him from it.

All of this had the effect of making Raph a prisoner, unable to go outside without causing some kind of commotion.

So while Raph and his exploits were arguably the biggest topic of conversation in Ardoth, he wasn't able to go to the bathroom without an armed escort.

The only respite he got from his guards were his training sessions with Alistair. In what had been a very enjoyable conversation to watch his godfather had pointed out to the guards that if something came along that he couldn't protect his godson from then there was a very good chance that the same thing would leave the guards as bloodied corpses. The lieutenant hadn't been

203

Comment [G]: Inserted: ,

Comment [G]: Inserted: ,

Comment [G]: Inserted: e

Comment [G]: Deleted: a

happy about it but he had not pressed the issue. As apparently arguing with the Fox was seen as the height of futility on Avalon. It was a change of pace to have Alistair's reputation do them a favor for once.

But outside of his training sessions, he was stuck in the inn, watching the city go to hell through the comfort of the common room windows.

"Raph are you listening?"

"Hmm?" Raph turned back from the window and found three pairs of eyes looking at him.

"Are we interrupting your daydreaming?" How Alistair managed to make himself sound disappointed and passively aggressively angry simultaneously was a stroke of mastery that Raph was sure he would never be able to replicate. Maybe it was something you only learned when you become a parent. Whatever his secret Alistair always knew how to make Raph feel guilty for even his most innocuous trespasses.

"Sorry, I was just thinking about the ball. It doesn't make any sense. Why would the Shak'Tah'Noh go after the Knight Protector? Sir Geir and I have barely spoken. Why would they think going after him would help them get to me? What do they gain?" The question had been gnawing at him for days.

"While I would not dismiss the involvement of the Shak'Tah'Noh in all this out of hand, have you considered my dear boy that perhaps the whole incident had nothing to do with you at all? There are matters completely independent of you occurring in the city at the moment. Perhaps you're not the only person that a select group of people would like to see dead. I would imagine

204

assassination never really goes out of style in a city like this and what better way to demoralize a people before an invasion than to kill their leader? Ardoth was already a powder keg and it feels like the murder of Sir Geir was supposed to be the match."

Raph let the thought roll around in his head. It was rather arrogant of him to think that the assassination attempt was related to him. It was hardly a reassuring thought that other people were just as likely to be killed by shadowy figures as he was. Maybe he and Sir Geir could start a club. The please don't try to kill us anymore club or PDTTKUAC for short. Obviously, they were going to need a better acronym.

Still, there were things that bothered him about the whole thing.

"You think Xan had something to do with this?" Raph really didn't like that guy.

"I don't know. If the North truly sought to end the current conflict peacefully why send Xan. They'd have to know someone of his temperament could only inflame the situation. Unless that's just what they want. A reason to go to war."

"But the Namahsii aren't stupid they'd have to see that too."

"Exactly, and while Sir Geir is intent on standing up to the Northerners this city has changed hands so many times over the last hundred years there are deeply rooted families loyal to both the North and the South here. And some deeply rooted families who are loyal to whatever side is most convenient. Perhaps one of them acted to make the Northern takeover of Ardoth go a bit more smoothly. Hoping that their initiative would be rewarded by their new masters."

"There something else strange that I only just realized. Right after the attack, the guards tackled me to the ground thinking I was the assassin. They only released me when Sir Ty pointed out that I had in fact saved Sir Geir. He was right there talking to us but disappeared without a word right before you showed up."

"Hmm, that is interesting but not telling. There are a number of reasons he could have gone off. To check on someone's safety, to gather the other council members, to assist with the search. Still, it is worth keeping an eye on him. However, all of that is tangential to what we were originally talking about. Billy, go ahead with what you were saying." All eyes turned to Billy. Raph was keenly aware of how much each of those eyeballs made his friend uncomfortable. Acute stage fright was one of Billy's many quirks. The nervousness poured out of him in a verbal deluge.

"Um, ya. Right. Okay.....so you all know I've been spending an awful lot of time at the library researching everything I could think of about the Grail, Arthur, Merlin, really anything that even hinted at a connection to what we're dealing with. It's actually pretty amazing. They have books that go back thousands of years. I'm not even entirely sure they know everything that they have. I even found a book that detailed the eating habits of the first peoples of Avalon. They used to take bugs and boil them in this honey oil mixture…"

"Billy. The point." Alistair had always had far less patience for Billy's idiosyncrasies than Raph.

Comment [G]: Inserted: ,

Comment [G]: Inserted: e

Comment [G]: Deleted:i

Comment [G]: Inserted: ,

Comment [G]: Inserted: ,

Comment [G]: Inserted: ,

Comment [G]: Inserted: ,

The Seeker

"Oh right. Well, May told me at the ball the other night that she had found something interesting."

"May? As in Lady May. Sir Garret's daughter?" The mention of one of the Namahsii snapped everyone to attention.

"Yeah, she works at the library and she's been helping me out but I didn't know she was Sir Garret's daughter until the ball. So she told me she found something so I started looking into it and..."

"Billy, you've been investigating Grail lore with the daughter of one of the Namahsii?" To say the revelation caught Raph off guard would be understating things a bit.

"I told you I didn't know about her dad when we started but we can trust her. She doesn't even like her dad that much."

"That was not your decision to make Billy." Normally Billy would have shrunk at a rebuff from Alistair but not this time. No this time, for the first time that Raph could remember, Billy exploded in anger.

"Why not? Everybody else gets to make decisions. Raph didn't ask anyone else before he got himself into a duel. You do whatever the hell you want without telling any of the rest of us anything. Well, I made a choice to trust May and it worked out because if you'd all just listen to me for one minute I could tell you that I've found something and I think it's important." The outburst stunned the room to silence. Billy's face was a mask of sullen rage and while Alistair's demeanor could have given the sun chills. Lux was sitting in the corner trying not to be noticed or as it was colloquially becoming know, The Lux. It was up to Raph to calm things down.

207

Comment [G]: Inserted: ,
Comment [G]: Inserted: ,

"You're right Billy. We're sorry. If you trust this May then we'll trust your judgment. What did you find?"

The tension slowly went out of the room and Billy visibly took a few deep breaths before speaking.

"I'm not sure. It's important. I think. But well it may not be. There's a book of" Billy sentence stopped in its tracks as he searched to find the right word. Finally, he gave up. "There's a book. And supposedly it's written by Merlin himself. And it's full of all kinds of nonsense and poetry and visions that he supposedly had." Billy looked at them expectantly, clearly waiting for some reaction. Other than confused Raph didn't really have one. Alistair apparently felt the same way.

"I know of the book Billy. It is called the Dais'Deirdre but what does it have to do with our current situation?"

"Well, some Ardothi scholars believe it to be a book of prophecy pertaining to the Grail and the last scion of Arthur."

"And most believe that it is a book of nonsense not written by Merlin at all. But again why does this matter. There was only one copy of the book and it was said to be lost ages ago."

"True but that's what I'm getting at. In her, research May found a text that included one of the poems from Daysdeirder."

"Dais'Deirdre."

"Right. Anyway, I don't think it is a poem at all. I think it's a prophecy. And I think it's about us. Or well about Raph at least."

"A prophecy? Are we really to the point that we've

Comment [G]: Inserted: ,

Comment [G]: Inserted: ,

started listening to ancient prophecies?" Raph's incredulity couldn't help but interject itself into Alistair and Bill's exchange.

"Just listen. It goes like this…." Billy pulled out a book and flipped to a section of dog-eared pages. Clearing his throat he began to read.

> *"In Darkest Hour they shall Return.*
> *And Fight for Right as Worlds Burn.*
> *The Lion, the Fox, and the Faithful Friend*
> *Sooner or Later will all meet their End.*
> *Glory and Gain they seek these not.*
> *Still they search for what's been sought.*
> *Pie are squared on Adam's Chart*
> *After nineteen cakes he gets his start*
> *In the numbers lie the key*
> *Only in them can we be free*
> *Three of Four must be seen*
> *If the One is to find Thirteen*
> *Three of Eight will play their part*
> *When those rascally Seven have lost all heart*
> *Three of Twelve are much maligned*
> *Even possessed of towering mind*
> *Third of all will find your goal*
> *Just be careful and keep your soul*
> *The Dragon comes, so seek your way*
> *Three of one would like to play.*
> *Worlds and woe they may travel to see*
> *But here on Avalon they first bend knee."*

Alistair asked Billy to read the passage again just to make sure they hadn't missed anything. In Raph's mind, he was sure he hadn't. Which probably meant he had missed everything. Either way, it wasn't much help. Raph said as much.

"Billy this isn't even a prophecy. It's just a bunch of gobelty-gook. It sounds like a math professor's version of a practical joke." To Billy's credit, he took the skepticism in stride.

"Well yeah. I mean I guess. But I thought all prophecies sounded like gobelty-gook until they happen then everyone's all like 'oh ya that's what that means I totally called that dude.' So maybe we shouldn't totally rule it out just yet? I mean maybe it's not a prophecy at all. Maybe it's a puzzle."

Raph was not convinced and judging by the look on Alistair's face neither was he.

"Billy, what in any of this makes you think it has to do with us?"

"The first couple of lines. 'In darkest hour they shall return.' Well, you've been gone a while and Raph is supposed to be the return of King Arthur or at least his legacy. And 'The lion, the fox, and the faithful friend.' That's Raph, you, and me."

"Okay Alistair as the Fox is easy and I'll even give you the faithful friend. But how on earth am I the Lion? I don't even like lions. If I'm going big cat I'm going panther, maybe a tiger, but definitely not lion."

"Well, a lot of the Kings of England used lions on their shields maybe it's a reference to your heritage," Billy said.

"That seems like a bit of a stretch, Billy. You don't even know if this prophecy was even written by Merlin. It

210

could just be some wacky poetry written by a psych-ward patient who thought he really was Merlin. Or it could be a collection of random impressive sounding words that some con-artist put together to make a quick buck."

"But…" Billy tried to push his point further but Alistair cut him off.

"I'm afraid Raph's right Billy. Hundreds of scholars from a dozen worlds have tried to prove the existence of the Dais'Deirdre and most eventually come to the inevitable conclusion that it never really existed at all. I myself studied stories of it long ago and found nothing to substantiate its supporter's claims." Alistair's tone indicated that he believed that to be the end of the discussion. Either Billy didn't catch that tone or even more unusually he just didn't care.

"May thinks it's real and so do I."

Raph shook his head at his friend's petulance. A stubborn off between Billy and Alistair was just going to end in tears and Alistair was not prone to crying. There was enough outside pressure on them without adding internal problems to the fire. Raph needed to find a way to walk this back and keep it from becoming a thing fast. Luckily thinking fast was something he was good at. Well, most of the time.

"Okay fair enough. You've been the one putting in the long hours trying to find something to help us. If you think this is worth looking into then it's your call. Alistair's busy helping me train and if I don't win my duel all of this is moot anyway. But Billy this doesn't just affect you, it affects all of us. So I want Lux to go with you. If that's okay with him." The sandy-haired man

211

looked startled at the sound of his name but nodded his assent. "He's a neutral party in all this. If he thinks you're wasting your time or that this May girl is up to something he's going to tell us and we're going to have this conversation again. Cool?" Raph held out a fist to his best friend.

"Cool." Billy bumped it as a grin broke out on his face.

"Alright, that's settled for now then. Anybody have anything else? No? Good. Let's eat."

**

"You're not focusing."

Raph felt a sharp sting on the back of his hand to go along with Alistair's rebuke.

"I am focusing. But I'm also getting tired of getting switched by an invisible whip. The entire time you raised me you never hit me once. We come to Ardoth and all of a sudden it's whip'a'palooza. What gives?"

"You were a child then. Now you're an apprentice. There's a difference."

"Yeah, I have more welts now."

Raph got another sharp sting to the back of his hand. "Ow!"

"Apprentices don't get to crack wise."

"How do you even do that?" Raph had been trying for weeks to emulate Alistair's new favorite disciplinary too with no luck whatsoever. He just didn't want to say anything since he'd been practicing on Billy.

"Trade secret." His godfather didn't give him even a hint of a smile.

"Right. Because you keeping secrets has worked out

212

so well for us so far." Raph had intended the quip to be a bit of a barb but that would have required Alistair to understand sarcasm.

"You're right it has. Do you really expect to flick Xan to death? I believe we have more pressing things to focus our attentions on don't you?" The irritation was beginning to seep into Alistair's voice which in turn was irritating Raph.

"You never know. Maybe a well-timed flick could work as a distraction. The old fake out." Raph's verbal shrug managed to be the last straw for Alistair.

"Yes, exactly the old fake out. Because in the precious little time we have together we should concentrate on teaching you a harmless trick that will allow you to distract your opponent so that you can strike at him with the full force of all the skills you didn't have time to learn because you were mastering the art of the invisible pinch. After that, you can run a Statue of Liberty play while Xan roasts your innards in a swirling inferno of death. Personally, I think it's a brilliant strategy and I'm slightly embarrassed I didn't think of it myself." Raph was wrong. His godfather clearly understood sarcasm.

"Okay, Alistair. Point made."

"Yes, I believe it was."

"Statue of Liberty play?"

"I was bound to pick up something watching you play all those games over the years."

"Who Dat."

Together the two of them burst into laughter. It was a nice moment. Raph wished they had more moments like it. But too soon the laughter faded and Alistair was back to business.

"So far we've worked on the basics. Fire, ice, rock, and lightning these are easy. Let us move on to some more complicated things that you can try. It's possible a few of these might actually catch Xan off guard if you can pull them off. "

"I still don't understand why I can't just remove the air from around Xan. That seems like the easiest thing to do." It was more than a little horrible to stay awake nights thinking about how to kill someone. For so when you started comparing the difficulty of differing methods. This particular question had been bothering Raph for weeks. Cutting off someone's oxygen supply seemed so easy it was scary.

"I think you'd find if you attempted such a thing that it would not be easy at all. Quite the contrary, keeping someone from breathing the air around them would be incredibly difficult beyond even my skill." The answer was what Raph was expecting, after all, if it was an easy thing to do then everyone would be doing it. From what Alistair had told him they weren't so it must not be easy. What Raph didn't understand was why. He said as much to Alistair.

"I suppose it's time for a lesson in Bending theory." Alistair motioned for Raph to take a seat on the bench next to him. "We talked about the three stages of bending: believing, knowing, and being. What you also have to understand is that while the universe will manifest your will if you let it; that is also true for everyone else around you."

"I don't quite follow."

214

"Do you think about breathing or do you just do it?"

"I just do it"

"Do you think about existing in your present spot in space-time or do you just exist."

"I just exist."

"Precisely. When you attempt to alter your opponent directly that is what you have to contend with. Perfect being. Absolutely no doubt. Such understanding is almost impossible to match with your conscious mind, let alone surpass with enough power to alter the world around you."

Raph was beginning to get a handle on the concept. He couldn't command the cells of his own body to stop replicating. His neurons wouldn't stop firing just because he willed them to. Not with his own subconscious mind and autonomic functions working against him. How could he hope to accomplish that on someone else? Especially someone trained to think about the problem the same way he was. He nodded and Alistair continued.

"In order to understand what you are capable of doing at any given time you need to have a better understanding of your environment. Since at its core Bending is simply the manipulation of that environment to suit your needs." Alistair took a long swig of his water before continuing.

"Basically there are four types of worlds, bearing in mind the caveat that there are an infinite number of variations on these themes but I am trying to keep it simple for the purposes of this lesson.

The first kind of world is like Earth. Where the attractive forces between particles, what I refer to as molecular gravity, are particularly strong. Because of this strength bending or magic was not all that common and eventually became the stuff of legend and fairy tale. Nice stories to tell but generally believed to be impossible. So in addition to the stronger forces of molecular gravity exerted in that universe, it is amplified but the collective belief of everyone on earth that there is no such thing as magic."

"But if it's impossible on Earth how did you and those Shak'Tah'Noh do it?"

"A couple of factors played into that. The first factor, and the reason I chose to live in New Orleans in the first place, is that the city itself is a bit of a soft spot. It's a city with a rich occult history and a mysterious side. The people there tend to be more open to the unexplained, less tied up in what they know to be true. The second factor was that I had been living in that area for a long time slowly ingratiating myself into the area. Greasing the skids as it were. Getting the atoms around us more accustomed to changing form. And finally, there was no one else around. I doubt the Shak'Tah'Noh could have pulled off anything of that magnitude if there had been a crowd of skeptics around. Instead, on that street, there were two individuals who absolutely knew bending to be real and two young men who secretly hoped that such a thing existed."

"So Billy and I being nerds helped them try to kill us. Great."

"It wasn't that you were 'nerds' as you put it. It was that you both believed that there was something more out there. You were open to the possibility of wonders and so

216

Comment [G]: Inserted: ,

Comment [G]: Inserted: ,

Comment [G]: Inserted: ,

Comment [G]: Inserted: ,

wonders were easier to create around you."

"Still doesn't make me feel better."

"Take the compliment for what it is and let's move on." Alistair took another swig from his jug. Raph was starting to think that it wasn't actually water after all. "The second kind of world is like Avalon, where the molecular gravity is weak. Because of this weakness bending was a common thing or at least common enough for it to become accepted by the populations of these worlds as possible. And so the collective belief in some form of bending as magic amplified the inherent malleability of that reality.

The third and fourth types of worlds are conflicting viewpoints. Were molecular gravity is weak but the population believes bending to be impossible or molecular gravity is strong but there is a strong belief that the impossible can be made possible. In such a case, the collective belief works against the nature of the world making it harder or easier to bend to varying degrees.

Again these are merely a shorthand to help illustrate some basic principles of Bending. In an infinite reality, there are always exceptions.

It's also important to remember that those same forces also work on a more localized level. For instance, during the Sha'Dral itself, there will be a large crowd of people excited to see two Tah'Mer do battle. They expect to see fireballs and lightning and all that making it easier to do simple, flashy, elemental bending. But those expectations also work the other way making it even harder to affect your opponent directly."

"Well," Alistair exclaimed in a big huff of air as he

stood. "I think that's more than enough theory for now. Back to more practical things. On your feet. Let's go. Now how are you at dodging things?"

He spent the rest of his afternoon trying to bend while dodging fireballs from Alistair.

Raph came away from the experience convinced there were far better ways to spend an afternoon. Finally, as the sun dropped low in the sky and Raph was beginning to get singed more than not Alistair allowed them to call it quits for the night.

Exhausted from the days training Raph grabbed a plate of food from one of the serving girls and went straight up to his room. Closing the door he put the plate on the table and began to unbutton his now suitably crispy shirt. He looked up at the mirror and gave a shout.

Comment [G]: Deleted:ing

"Holy Shi-! Kara! What are you doing here?!"

He turned around to face her. She was in his bed, sheets up to her shoulders. Raph blushed. Unless he had gotten into the unconscious habit of leaving dresses on the floor he was fairly sure she was naked underneath.

"You saved me. I'm your servant now. I need to take care of your needs."

"Ahhhh..... you know when I had this fantasy I didn't realize it would be this fucked up." She looked at him blankly and he realized that 'fucked up' probably didn't translate. Which, considering the circumstances he felt was a little fucked up. Raph tried to keep his composure. It was difficult. There wasn't a ton of common sense knowledge out there on how to get a naked girl out of your bed. Volumes about getting them into your bed sure, but conventional male wisdom would

218

say once she's there just go with it. Sometimes Raph really hated trying to do the right thing.

"Kara you don't owe me anything."

"But m'lord without you that man would have taken me and killed me. I owe you everything." Raph had two simultaneous thoughts. That she was really, really sweet and that this was really, really wrong.

"No, you don't. I didn't help you because I expected something in return. Especially something like this." He wasn't sure why everybody couldn't get that.

"Does m'lord not find me beautiful?" *Great. Now I hurt her feelings.* At this point, Raph really wished that he was dreaming. He took a deep breath and tried to turn this whole thing into what Alistair would call a teaching moment.

"Kara you're a very attractive woman and under other circumstances, maybe. Who am I kidding? Probably. But not this way, not with you feeling that this is how you have to pay a debt to me. I stopped Xan because it was the right thing to do. I don't like bullies. People who prey on the weak and defenseless are the worst kind of scum. If you'd been old or a boy I would have done the same thing. If you had been anybody else I would have done the same thing. Nobody deserves to be treated that way and anyone who just stands by and does nothing is as bad as the people who do it. Worse even because they know it's wrong and still do nothing. So you know I really did it for me. Because if I hadn't I wouldn't have liked myself very much."

"But m'lord what can I do to please you. If you don't want my body I can cook and clean and do other chores.

Please m'lord I cannot stay here once you leave. I must go with you."

"Kara you're not property to be passed from one owner to the next. And you're not a trophy to be won and shown off. As for going with us, in case you forgot, I'm fighting a duel to the death in a couple of days. I may not be going anywhere."

"You'll win m'lord. I know it. The Eight will not let a man as noble as you fall."

"That's very nice of you to say but I don't think nobility is going to have much to do with it."

"Pease m'lord you must take me with you." She looked at him with eyes that broke his heart. There was fear there, mixed with sadness and pain. But there was also hope and utter devotion. She still saw him as a lord to obey, a master to serve. But she trusted him to take care of her. To make her life better than it had been. He wanted her to learn to stand on her own. She wasn't going to be able to do that if he left her behind. Whether he wanted it or not, whether it was right or not; he was responsible for her now. At least until she figured out that she was responsible for herself.

"Of course you can come with us. But not as a servant. As an equal. As a friend. Do you understand?"

"Yes, m'lord. Thank you."

"And quit calling me m'lord. My name's Raph."

"Yes, m'lord."

Raph let out a massive sigh. *Oh well, worth a try. Baby steps.*

"Okay, I'm going to take my dinner downstairs so you can get dressed. If you'd like to meet me down there

220

Comment [G]: Inserted: .

Comment [G]: Inserted: ,

Comment [G]: Inserted: ,

Comment [G]: Inserted: ,

when you're done you're welcome to. I don't know if you've eaten or not yet but the food's actually not half bad here." Raph grabbed his plate and headed for the door. "And Kara no more getting naked in my room okay?" With that, he walked out.

He shook his head at himself as he walked down the stairs.

Raphael Carpenter. Massive Tool.

Chapter 13

Sha'Dral

Raph rose early the morning of the Sha'Dral. Well, he didn't so much rise early as not sleep at all. Insomnia was a frequent companion of his when things weighed heavily on his mind. Oddly what was bothering him wasn't the thought that he might die today. Raph wasn't afraid of dying. Well, at least not any more than was reasonable. He had lived what he thought was a good life. He had stood up to a bully and helped out someone in trouble. If he was going to go out then in his mind there wasn't a more honorable way to do it.

No, what had kept him up all night was the thought of killing. That thought terrified him to his very bones. The funny thing was that while everyone had been so focused on getting him ready to not lose this duel that none of them had stopped to consider what it meant if he won it. He'd be a killer.

Raph knew that wasn't the same thing as being a

murderer. This was a 'me or the other guy' type of situation. But there was still a line that would be crossed. A line he would cross. A fundamental change in who he was. And this wasn't some movie where he could just stare dejectedly at his love interest in order for the audience to know that he had really struggled with the decision so it was okay. This was a burden he would carry with him the rest of his life.

The thing that really irked him was that he knew it was the best option. Even taking out all of the moral judgments over who was the better man between the two of them there was a simple fact to consider: If Xan died there might be a war and tens of thousands of people might die, maybe even a few million, there was no way to know; but if Raph died there was a chance that all of it could end. Everyone and everything. In the end, he had to kill Xan for everyone.

The logic of it should have made everything easier for Raph but it didn't. He felt selfish and cowardly. He felt as if he was using logic and nobility to rationalize a terrible decision. Raph wanted to tell himself that a brave man would admit that he simply wanted to live and if that meant savagery then so be it. Why wrap the impulse to survive in all these pleasantries? Be honest about it all. And so his thoughts went, spiraling downward and offering him no relief from the accusations of his soul.

The sun's first light trickled through the window. Raph stood and let its radiant beauty soak him to the bone. He felt warm and jubilant. Completely full of life. Doubts faded from him then. He had not chosen this. Any of it. The Shak'Tah'Noh had hunted him here. Ardoth had created a culture where the nobility could abuse those of lesser rank. And Xan was the one who had invoked a duel to the death. All Raph had wanted to do was stay alive and help someone who needed helping. For that, he didn't deserve to die. He deserved to see tomorrow's dawn. Certainly more than Xan did anyway.

"Screw it. The bastard did this to himself."

He finished dressing and made his way downstairs. A cold shower would have been nice but what are you going to do in a world without indoor plumbing. Raph allowed himself ten seconds to think about how much he missed home before putting it out of his mind. Feeling sorry for himself wasn't going to change anything. His body was here in Ardoth and if he wanted to stay alive it was where his head had better be too.

He turned the corner and walked into the common room where he found Alistair sitting alone sipping tea. On the table in front of him was a breakfast spread for two. It was too much for Raph. He burst out laughing. A serving girl gave him a look as she wiped down a table in the corner.

"Am I ever going to beat you to breakfast Alistair?"

"Perhaps. But not likely. I take breakfast very seriously. A man cannot face the day without proper nourishment. And a morning dose of bacon is a reminder that there are some truly good, noble things in this world worth fighting for."

"You've spent the last three weeks trying to cram the secrets of the universe into my head. Are you telling me now it all comes down to bacon?"

"Would it surprise you if I was?" A wry smile

touched his lips as he spoke. To be followed in quick succession by a piece of bacon and then another smile.

"Not even remotely." The sequence managed to get another laugh from Raph.

"Then you've come far. Whether or not it is far enough we will find out later. But for right now sit down and let a Godfather enjoy tea and bacon with his Godson."

Raph smiled as he sat down. It was a good feeling, being loved. He tried to enjoy it. Lux and Billy joined them as Raph put the finishing touches on his plate. Kara was waiting by the door for them once they'd cleaned up and headed out.

They were a strange group: a serving girl, a wizard, and three young men of varying shapes and sizes. As they walked, Billy tried to tell some jokes to lighten the mood which only led to him trying to explain Earth humor to Kara and Lux. It might have elicited Raph's third burst of morning laughter had he been paying attention but he wasn't. He was in the zone now. Focusing his mind on the task ahead.

The people in the streets parted for them and stared as they passed by. They made their way to mid-town without incident and indeed many who had seen them pass had chosen to fall in their wake. Raph grimaced at that. The Sha'Dral was a public spectacle and the people were not to be denied their rare opportunity to witness a blood sport. Especially one whose combatants were of an unknown quality to them. He was sure by know rumors about the night of the masquerade were all over Ardoth adding to the mystique of it all.

Upon their arrival, the crowd in tow merged with the one that had already gathered at the pavilion. In the few days since he'd been here last, they had erected a wooden grandstand for the more important of Ardoth's citizens. The closest comparison that Raph could draw was medieval fight night. It seemed like this was the place to see and be seen. Crowds didn't make him nervous and neither did this one. Not that it had to. The threat of his imminent demise was more than enough food for the butterflies in his stomach. Stage fright was an afterthought.

The people parted as he came near. Some sneering. Some cheering. But most just looked on in silence. After the first twenty yards, Raph started musing that he could have done with some walk-up music, maybe some Metallica. He smirked at the thought which the crowd seemed to take as some sort of a sign that he was ready for the duel.

Finally, they came to the dueling ring. A large circle, about twenty feet in diameter, lay at the center of the pavilion. Raph noted the irony that the only grass he had seen in the cobblestone covered city was on the ground specifically laid out for killing.

"Remember it is not enough to believe, not enough to know, you must be. When Sir Geir signals the start of the match the circle will be active. Try to leave it while Xan still live and it will kill you. It is being held by the whole of the Namahsii so it would not be wise to test its strength. Once you step into that ring I cannot help you. Xan may have more training than you do but Bending is more than that. It's about the sum of a person and their

226

relationship to the universe. Xan demands, he expects. There is great power in that, but also great weakness. You accept and understand. Use that." Alistair's words came quickly. Raph felt a bit bad for his godfather. This couldn't be easy for him.

Across the pavilion, Raph could see Xan entering with his retinue. The man was possessed of an arrogant calm. As he entered he received a similar mix of cheers and boos although there seemed to be more boos for Xan than for Raph. Apparently being a complete unknown was better than being a Northerner. Good to know. Raph felt a hand on his shoulder and knew who it was without turning around.

"Don't die, dude. That would be really uncool." Billy kept his tone light but he couldn't mask the fear in his voice.

"Thanks, I'll try not to."

Raph stepped into the circle and took his place opposite Xan. The man's eyes were full of disdain and hate. Hatred for anything not of his noble ancestry and disdain at having to interact with beings clearly beneath him. Raph closed his eyes and thought of his lessons. He was one with the universe. It was not enough to believe something was so, to know it, he had to be. The world around him was him and he it. It did not need to reshape itself because it had always been this way. Raph opened his eyes. He would win this fight.

The Namahsii entered the makeshift arena and took the highest seats in a special boxed off area of the grandstands. Sir Geir took the middle seat and motioned for the crowd to be quiet. When the murmur of conversation finally died down he rose to address the gathering.

"Citizens of Ardoth, we have gathered here to honor the ancient rite of Sha'Dral. It is the noblest of rites. The right of the Blood to settle their disputes before their fellow nobles and let the universe itself decide who has the best claim to continue living. On my signal I and my fellow councilmembers will raise the red ring, it will only lower again when two are reduced to one. As it was in the days of Merlin so shall it be today." Sir Geir looked at Xan who nodded an affirmative that he was ready. Then Sir Geir looked to Raph who also nodded his consent to begin. 'Here we go' was the only thought in Raph's head at the moment.

"Let the combat begin"

When Sir Geir finished speaking a red dome of energy came to life around them sealing Raph and Xan in with each other. Xan opened his mouth to mock Raph.

"You look nervous little foxling. Do you realize that your death is coming quickly? Well not too quickly. I must have my fun first after all." Xan punctuated the taunt with a fireball aimed at Raph's feet.

Raph dove out of the way barely, feeling the heat in his toes. Xan gave him time to stand up and face him before launching another fireball to Raph's right. Again he dove out of the way just in time. It was becoming clear to Raph and the crowd that Xan was toying with him.

"You know what I think? I think you're not really a fox at all. I think you're some jumped up bastard who let a little bit of Blood get him in way over his head." An invisible wall of air connected with Raph's stomach.

Then a breezy haymaker connected with his chin. Raph's vision blurred and he stumbled back a few steps before falling to one knee.

Not a minute into the fight and Raph was down. He was outmatched. A novice against a master. As his vision cleared he saw that Xan had turned his back and was facing his friends in the crowd.

"......it's just an embarrassment really. Some people really don't know their betters when they are staring them in the face. Ah well, we must all take our entertainment where we can get it."

Raph charged at Xan, hoping to take advantage of his inattentiveness. After only a step, he was seized upon by the air. Shackled again as he had been back on Earth against the Shak'Tah'Noh. For the second time in a month, Raph prepared to die. He struggled with everything he had to break free as tears welled up in his eyes. He didn't want to die like this.

"Don't cry little foxling. I've had my fun. It'll be over soon. How about I just start breaking things until we get to something important." Then Xan turned back to his friends. "Poor lad, never had a chance. Some drunk nobleman for a father and a whore of a mother. If she had really loved him she would have drowned him in a well at the first opportunity. Probably died herself that way after she got too old and too ugly for the brothels."

That was when Raph snapped.

He was tired of being hunted. Of being intimidated. Of being hurt. Of being lied to. He was tired of seeing power wielded by men of cruelty. He was tired of not knowing who he was supposed to be. But mostly he was tired of being powerless. And he would be damned if he would be killed by this fraction of a man, this woman-beating asshole. No, if Raph was going to die this little shit was not going to have anything to do with it.

Raph reached out with everything he had and welcomed the universe into himself. The atoms of the air and the earth reacted to him like a long lost friend finally returned home. He felt them all. As he had when he'd first arrived on Avalon. As he had when he'd first reached out to that tree in the forest. As he had when he first turned air into water. The universe was glad of him and Raph was glad of it. Raph did not command it. It was a part of him. An extension of his will. Of his being.

And so Raph was no longer constrained because he would not be constrained.

Xan turned back sensing something was wrong. Seeing Raph striding towards him he kept his calm.

"So you have some skill after all little foxling." Xan formed a wall of fire in front of him and sent it flying towards Raph.

Raph felt hot. And so the fire was mist and cooled him off.

Still, he strode towards Xan, whose eyes were now wide with disbelief. He began to create more fire but Raph did not wish it to be so and so it was not.

"First of all not a foxling, or a fox for that matter. I'm a man and a far better one than you." Raph bound his foe with air. "Second of all, you do not speak of my mother. Ever." He slapped Xan with the wind. First on the left cheek. Then on the right. "Finally you treat people with respect. All people. Whoever they are." A backhand this time, made of the blood and flesh of Raph's own right hand.

He turned and walked towards the spot where his companions were watching. Alistair looked pleased, Kara looked aghast, Lux looked impressed, and Raph wasn't sure how Billy looked but he thought giddy disbelief was as accurate as anything else. Raph sensed the javelins of ice rocketing towards him before they had even completely formed. They disappeared before they got within five feet of him. Raph even had time to smirk at the trope.

"This is over." He announced in a clear, authoritative voice. And with a wave of his hand the glowing dome that surrounded them disappeared.

Chapter 14

Ambush

That's when all hell broke loose. In the heartbeats between Raph bringing down the dome and Raph stepping into the triumphant embrace of his friends the grandstand holding the Namahsii and assorted members of the Ardothi nobility exploded in a fireless sonic boom that sent bodies and splintered wood everywhere.

Screams of terror erupted from the crowd. Bolts of lightning reigned down randomly upon the gathered onlookers, killing somewhere they stood. Gigantic balls of fire and ice came at them from all sides. Bedlam had broken out on the dueling grounds and it seemed as if nature herself wished them all dead.

Raph's first instinct was to turn to Xan, expecting the blowhard prince to be behind the cowardly attack, but one look told Raph that Xan was just as surprised by the ambush as he was. Panic seized him. The calm Raph had gained in the dueling circle disappeared and with it went his new found powers. If this wasn't Xan's doing then there was really only one other possibility. The Shak'Tah'Noh had found them.

Raph looked around. Trying to keep his fear from overwhelming him. He turned just soon enough to see a giant ball of ice hurtling towards him. He tried to will it out of existence like he had Xan's fireballs but it was no use. He was afraid and that meant he accepted his danger as real. He was seeing the world as the Shak'Tah'Noh wanted it to be. And even though he knew that he had no clue as to how not to do it.

Realizing he was helpless he tried to dodge, but his hesitation cost him as the ice ball connected with his right shoulder. Pain ran through him and he knew in an instant that his shoulder was dislocated. Raph forced himself to keep moving, certain that the Shak'Tah'Noh had seen him. He found cover behind a large chunk one of the upturned grandstands and braced himself for the follow-up attack that was sure to come at any moment.

After a few seconds, he realized that there wouldn't be one. The Shak'Tah'Noh hadn't seen him, the ice ball had simply been part of the initial onslaught. It didn't mean he wasn't still in grave danger, but it did mean that he could take a second to assess the exact nature of that danger.

Chaos reigned on the dueling grounds. From what Raph could spot there were at least a half dozen Shak'Tah'Noh not including however many of them had stayed in the shadows to continue their indiscriminate

Comment [G]: Deleted:g

Comment [G]: Deleted:ic

Comment [G]: Inserted: ,

shelling of the pavilion.

Raph tried to spot Alistair and the rest, but found it impossible to make sense of the cacophony of images that bombarded him at the moment. Logic and reason had no place in this madness. Raph watched as the woman was consumed by a fireball. Her screams lost in the roar of murderous rage emanating from her attacker.

Then Raph saw something that his eyes could make sense of. The woman from the inn who had berated Alistair was standing not thirty yards away with her bow raised at him. Before he could shout she had loosed an arrow. Raph froze. He wasn't sure if he would have been able to react fast enough to dodge an arrow or if it wouldn't have made any difference but the truth was he just froze up. He felt the whoosh of air as the arrow flew over his left shoulder. She missed. Raph heard a gurgling sound behind him. He turned to find Xan there with an arrow through his throat.

She hadn't missed. Judging from the dagger in Xan's hand she had just saved his life. Bea, her name was Bea, he finally remembered. Bea had just saved his life.

Raph forced himself back to alert. Just because she had saved him from one threat didn't mean there weren't others. He grabbed the blade from Xan's still twitching hands which if he'd spared even a second to think about was a little bit creepy. Luckily he didn't have a second to think about it.

A bolt of lightning struck a few feet to his left, sending Raph diving in the opposite direction.

"So you're the Arthur-Son. My name is Darina and I'm going to be the one killing you today." Raph looked up to see a tall dark-skinned woman dressed in all black staring at him as he pushed himself to his feet. "Funny I thought you'd be better looking."

Raph could hear explosions all around him. He had no idea where his friends were and had lost track of Bea when he had hit the ground. He was on his own against one of the Shak'Tah'Noh. Last time that had happened it had not gone well for Raph. He needed to play for time and pray that Alistair could appear out of nowhere and save his life again.

"That's okay. So did I." Raph took a step back as the woman approached him with a slow, deliberate sway.

"A sense of humor. Good, you'll need that where you're going."

"And where exactly am I going?"

"Oblivion." The woman who called herself Darina was close now. Only a half dozen yards away.

"Nice sentiment but if you were going to kill me you would have done it by now."

"Oh, would I?" Faster than Raph could register a small blade came flying at him. Slicing his right arm halfway between his elbow and his shoulder. "You see I'm a bit unlike the rest of my ilk. They glory in using the powers of creation to wreak havoc and carnage. Personally, I think the irony appeals to them. But Me?" A second blade flew from Darina's hand and winged Raph's right thigh, dropping him down to one knee. "I like to watch the blood flow. I want to feel it's warmth in my hands."

"Yay me." Raph could feel the blood leaking out of him, rolling down his arm and leg. He tried again to

235

recreate what he had done in the circle against Xan but couldn't. If something didn't change in the next few seconds this woman was going to kill him. In desperation, he tried to stall her. "So if you're so different from them then why join up at all? Why not go independent? Surely a woman with your skill set could kill anyone she wanted."

"Sometimes it's just a matter of scalability. Enough talk. Time to---------"The Shak'Tah'Noh's head pitched forward mid-sentence as her eyes rolled back into her head and her body fell to the ground in a lump. And where Darina had been now stood Bea holding a rather large piece of timber.

"Come."

"That's not the line."

"What?"

"You're supposed to say 'Come with me if you want to live'"

"I took your wanting to live as a given." An arrow flew from her bow as she spoke. "I can leave without you if that is not the case."

A fireball exploded to Raph's right and he decided he'd picked a bad time to be witty.

"No, I'm good. We can go now."

*****

Laughter erupted from Jack's throat. This was glorious. The smell of blood filled the air. Lightning and fire flashed across the sky. People running about scurrying this way and that. Absolute madness. Oh, this was just positively delightful.

One of the attackers caught sight of Jack's manic

Comment [G]: Inserted: ,

Comment [G]: Inserted: ,

glee and decided it was inappropriate for the occasion. A dozen arrows of ice came flying at Jack. Fire raged forth from Jack's hand and met the arrows head-on, vaporizing them and creating a veil of mist to hide himself in.

Quietly he moved through the mist while his frantic opponent shot fireballs in all directions. Jack hated fireballs. They were far too impersonal. He was close now. With a quick yank on the man's hair, Jack exposed the man's throat and his blade struck home.

A knife to the throat was vastly superior to a fireball any day of the week. For one thing, the smell of blood was much more sensual than the smell of burnt flesh.

Jack took a closer look at his felled foe. Dark robes, tattoos on the left hand. Shak'Tah'Noh. Disappointing. Where Jack composed beautiful medleys of chaos and corruption the Shak'Tah'Noh were rather one-note in their motivations. They were just so predictable. And dull. Ah well not everyone can be a winner.

Jack looked around for any other potential dangers in his immediate vicinity. It was always incredibly irritating when you wanted to surprise an enemy and that enemy surprised you instead. It just seemed like such a rude thing to do on a battlefield.

The chaos of the initial ambush had died down now and settled into two distinct fronts. Some of the attackers were concentrating their attention on the Fox, while across the field Sir Geir seemed to have rallied the benders amongst the nobility to protect the others while they ran.

Nobody seemed to be paying any attention to Jack. Which was really quite insulting when you stopped to think about it.

So now the question was what did Jack want to do about that?

Jack wanted to play. That's what Jack wanted to do about that.

The screams of a young woman caught Jack's attention. Now Jack was not usually one for chivalry but there was a good chance those screams indicated there was someone Jack could kill so he decided to investigate. Besides, it sounded like the woman was cute. Jack didn't like other people killing cute women.

Carefully he moved amongst the grandstand's debris following the sound of the screams, taking extra care to be silent and unseen like any good hunter.

It did not take long to locate the source of the screams.

Thirty yards in front of Jack he saw her floating in the air, spread eagle, the tatters of her clothes barely hanging on. Blood ran down her, emerging from several shallow cuts around her body.

A few feet away, admiring his craftsmanship, stood one of the Shak'Tah'Noh. A Shak'Tah'Noh of middling height and age. Jack hated non-descript people, he found them so dull.

Jack took a moment to contemplate the situation.

On the one hand, he hated to interrupt someone who was obviously enjoying themselves. It just seems incredibly impolite. He knew that if the situation was reversed and he was torturing some young woman he wouldn't want anyone interrupting his fun.

On the other hand, Jack had walked all this with

238

Comment [G]: Inserted: ,

Comment [G]: Inserted: s

Comment [G]: Inserted: ,

anticipation of killing something and Jack wasn't exactly known for putting others needs above his own. Plus it really annoyed Jack that the Shak'Tah'Noh were always toying with their kills. Like a cat with a mouse. They can never just get the job done. They had to torture and gloat every damn time. It's why they were always losing.

That line of thought got Jack's blood up enough to make a decision. A man was allowed his fun in the privacy of his own home, but if you insisted on making a public spectacle of it then you should expect the public to participate. Besides Jack firmly believed no young woman should die before enjoying a night of passion with him.

With absolute calm, Jack pulled one of his spare daggers from its hiding spot. He wasn't going to risk losing his favorite dagger after all.

He flipped it over in his hand, feeling the blade in his fingertips, readying it to throw.

Now, most people wouldn't be able to throw a dagger precisely at thirty yards.

Jack was not most people.

Also, Jack cheated.

It was actually pretty easy to do when you were bending the blade and the air around it to keep it flying straight and true.

Still, he felt a good deal of satisfaction when the dagger struck home, taking the Shak'Tah'Noh right in the ear. The man screamed as he fell.

Jack reached the downed man not long after his blade, having broken into a sprint as soon as he'd let it fly. Pulling the weapon free of its cranial lodging Jack

239

Comment [G]: Inserted: n

Comment [G]: Inserted: ,

used it to slice open the man's throat, letting the blood flow out of him. Jack really enjoyed cutting open people's throats. It also had the added benefit of silencing any annoying screaming by severing their vocal cords. Two birds. One stone. It was really just one of the most efficient and enjoyable ways to kill someone.

Jack wiped the blade on the grass and slipped it back into its hidden sheath before turning to the girl.

She was a bit of a wreck. Shivering and sniveling. Jack removed his own shirt and gallantly wrapped it around her. It wasn't much but it was a far sight better than the tattered rags her own clothes had become. If she happened to become aroused by his glistening sculpted torso then so much the better.

"Thank you, M'lord." It dawned on Jack that he had seen the mousy brunette before. Around the council chambers.

"I know you."

"Yes, M'lord. I am Sir Garrett's daughter, May."

Sir Garrett's daughter. See Jack good things come to those who kill. In his head, Jack beamed at the thought of a Lord of the Tower owing him his daughter's life. But on his face, Jack remained dour weighing down his otherwise buoyant features with worry and concern for her safety. Not too much worry though. He didn't want to make himself unattractive. Just grave and full of hidden depth.

"Yes of course Lady May. We must get you to safety. I will escort you clear of this madness."

Jack helped her to her feet and together they set off away from the sounds of battle.

240

****

Billy was losing his shit. He'd thought that two fireball wielding assholes attacking him out of nowhere was frightening. Well, a dozen fireball wielding assholes attacking him out of nowhere was exponentially more terrifying. If ever there was a time that one was entitled to lose one's shit Billy felt as if this was such a time.

And it all had been going so well too, he lamented. That lamentation was cut short however when he saw a lightning bolt headed straight for him. Billy put his arms up to cover his face and waited for the pain to come but it never did.

"Billy get down!" Alistair's scream was barely audible above the myriad of malicious noises that surrounded them but Billy heard him and obeyed getting as flat to the ground as one of his rotund nature could.

Shouts and explosions were happening all around him. Billy wanted to close his eyes and wish it all away but he knew that might get him killed. So instead he forced himself to keep his eyes open watching Alistair fight to keep them alive.

And boy Alistair could fight. Three Shak'Tah'Noh stood before him. No longer concerned with creating pure pandemonium it now seemed as if their attackers were concentrating their efforts on bringing down Alistair. They clearly knew as much about Alistair's history as Billy did because they looked completely unprepared for the hurt he was raining down on them.

They threw everything thing they could think of at him. Fireballs, lightning, ice, rocks, and other things that Billy couldn't even recognize. Alistair took it all dodging it or throwing it right back at his foes.

And as they dodged their own attacks boomeranging on them Alistair pulled his staff out of his robes and pressed his advantage. With a flick of his wrist, the small cylinder extended out in both directions until it reached its full six feet of length.

Charging he swung the full length of it at the head of the nearest Shak'Tah'Noh who was too busy dodging a boulder to see the real attack coming. Alistair's staff connected with the man's skull right above his temple. The vicious blow sent the man spinning through the air before landing unmoving on the earth a few feet away from where he had started.

Unlike Billy, Alistair's had not waited to see what had happened to his first foe as he had allowed his momentum to carry him forward towards his next target.

The second Shak'Tah'Noh had made it past his own fireballs and had anticipated Alistair's strike at his knees, deflecting it with a long curved blade. Metal screeching cut through the air as the weapons put pressure on each other.   Forcing the hands holding them into an upward arc.

Alistair whirled as they broke narrowly spinning away from the blade's follow-up strike.

Armed with a pair of metal batons, the third Shak'Tah'Noh was in the mix now making it a two on one fight. If that fazed Alistair he didn't show it.

"Come on then."

Alistair's opponents accepted his invitation, rushing him in tandem. Standing his ground Alistair thrust forward at the Shak'Tah'Noh on his right who knocked

Alistair's strike off target with his batons. Alistair leaned into the momentum of the block, turning it into a full spin.

As he spun he swung his staff high deflecting the curved blade coming at him in a downward attack. Showing off an amazing amount of control Alistair brought the staff back and aimed a quick forward strike, catching the blades owner square in the nose. Bloodied and dazed the first Shak'Tah'Noh staggered to the side, unable to continue his attack.

Taking a short, sliding-step backwards Alistair swung his staff down and back bringing it all the way around for a downward block of the baton headed for his midsection. Pivoting on his front foot and letting his hands slide down the length of his staff Alistair took a swing at the unprotected head of his second foe.

But the Shak'Tah'Noh had anticipated the move. Instead of standing his ground he did as Alistair had done; rolling with the deflection to create space. The man with the batons came out of his roll swinging, apparently hoping to surprise an off-balance Alistair. But if Alistair had ever been surprised in his life Billy had not been there to see it. Instead, he met aggression with aggression.

Now Billy had seen a lot of martial arts movies in his day. But what he saw now was a master's class. The two men ceased to be men and simply became two spinning blurs, improvising a choreography of parries and thrusts where one misstep meant defeat or death. It was too much for Billy to process. Then everything went from super speed to slow motion as Alistair narrowly avoided a baton to the face. He swung his quarterstaff with his full weight, connecting just underneath his opponent's chin like an uppercut from a heavyweight champion. The Shak'Tah'Noh's feet left the ground as his eyes rolled into the back of his head.

Coolly, Alistair spun again. Letting the full length of his staff fly out ahead of him. The curved blade of the first Shak'Tah'Noh cut through the empty space that Alistair had occupied only moments before. The surprised look on the man's broken face lasted less than a second as Alistair's staff struck home, cracking open his remaining foe's skull.

The three Shak'Tah'Noh were all down now.

Letting out a long breath of relief Billy stood and began to walk towards Alistair.

Billy felt a sharp pain on the back of his head.

Everything went black.

Chapter 15

Divide and Escape

The last deep orange light of dusk was fading from the barred windows when Raph heard the agreed upon knock against the cellar doors. Tensely he walked up the creaky wooden stairs and undid the heavy iron chains and lock securing the doors. Bea was inside in a heartbeat, pushing the doors shut behind her and grabbing the chains out of his hands to secure them again before Raph even had time to register his relief at her return.

After their initial flight from the dueling grounds Bea had stashed him here; in this poorly lit, cold, horror movie-esque basement. And while she'd been out doing god knows what Raph had spent the day pacing around his cramped confines scared out of his mind that every sound he heard was a Shak'Tah'Noh preparing to break down the doors and murder him where he stood.

No jokes. No flippant remarks. No hyperbole. Raph had spent the day alone. Alone and in mortal terror. It was not a feeling that could be described. It had to be felt and Raph prayed that he never had to experience again. Because he was quite certain if he ever did it would break him.

With the chains pulled tight and the lock firmly back in place Bea moved past Raph and down the stairs. Raph followed unsure of what else to do. Bea had saved his life. Twice. On top of that Alistair had seemed to trust her. Raph could be arrogant and stubborn but he knew when he was in over his head. And he was definitely in over his head. Whatever this woman told him to do he resolved to do it without hesitation or complaint.

"Well, it seems like it's not just the Shak'Tah'Noh who are after you now. Sir Geir has the entire city watch out looking for you and your companions as well under the pretense that you were somehow involved in the ambush. Sir Geir can be a fool but he's usually got his head on straight. More likely the rest of the Namahsii forced his hand this time. In any event, they want you brought in for questioning and that is going to make it harder to get you out of the city."

"Harder, but not impossible." Raph couldn't keep the hope out of his voice.

"No, not impossible. Put these on."

Raph did as he was instructed and threw on the outfit that Bea had brought him. They stank like his freshman locker-room but considering the state of his own clothes he really couldn't argue.

246

Comment [G]: Inserted: ,

Bea stood there in silence as he undressed. Raph tried not to blush as he changed. It wasn't like a woman had never seen him in his underwear before, but Bea was too old to be in his age range romantically and too young to be maternally platonic. Maybe. It could have been something else. He wasn't really sure. He was a nineteen-year-old male, after all, he didn't really need a reason to feel awkward.

Finally, he was dressed and they headed out. They crept through the darkness in complete silence, keeping themselves to the deeper darkness of the city's shadows. Those corners and alleys bereft of even the faint illumination of the stars. Bea moved with precision, following a mental map that Raph did not possess. All Raph could do was follow her lead and try not to give them away. But Raph was a city boy and unlike his fiasco in the forest with Alistair this time he managed to do his part and keep his footing.

To Raph's surprise, they were heading away from the gate separating Mid-town and Low-town and back towards the central market district. Raph wasn't sure why but he wasn't about to make noise about it. Literally or figuratively.

Eventually, they made their way to the back door of one of the larger shops just off the market square. Bea stopped and put her hand up.

"Wait here. Don't Move." Bea's voice was barely a whisper.

Raph stayed where he was as Bea moved around the corner and across the alley. He was tempted to peak his head around to see what Bea was doing but thought better

of it. If there was one thing Raph hated in stories it was
when the 'in over their head' protectee ignored the
instructions of the 'clearly able to handle themselves'
protector. That always ended in trouble. And Raph had
more than enough trouble without tempting fate. So Raph
stayed exactly where he was and waited for Bea to return.

He didn't have to wait long. No more than two
minutes later Bea had returned. Saying nothing she
motioned for Raph to follow her. She led him to an
unadorned backdoor. Two knocks, a pause, then three
knocks. The door opened immediately and an elderly
woman motioned for them to enter. The inside was
almost as dark as the outside but Raph thought he could
make out boxes and crates stacked throughout the place.
So they were in some kind of storeroom or warehouse
then.

Bea lowered the hood to her cloak. Gently she took
the old woman's hands in her own and gave her a small
smile. "Thank You for this Alena."

"No need to thank me, girl. You've more than earned
a few favors from me over the years. And I'm never one
to default on a debt. Especially not a debt of honor.
Although I'm not so honorable at to want to spend the
night with the city watch down my neck. So let's stop all
this yammering and get you on your way. Come on come
on. You too boy, if I had to guess I'd say you were what
all the fuss was about. No point standing around looking
dumb when there are things to do." Alena hustled them
further into the warehouse not even pausing for breath as
she did.

Alena directed them to a stack of large crates on the

248

Comment [G]: Inserted: ,

far side of the warehouse and the two women started moving them aside.

"Well boy what are you waiting for? Me to throw my back out saving your life?"

"No Ma'am." Raph put himself to work. The boxes weren't heavy and, in no time at all, they were stacked in a neat pile a few feet away. As he went back for the last one Bea stopped him with a hand. Alena smiled a toothy grin that was short a few teeth.

"That's right not this one. This here's a special box made it myself. A good box for making things disappear one place and reappear someplace else. Some call it magic, I call it good business."

She lifted the lid to the crate and stuck her hand inside. A few seconds later her hand emerged from the box, looking as if it was holding something. What it was Raph couldn't tell. She began to pull on her invisible string and the bottom of the crate lifted out, revealing a rope ladder on the other side and a hole in the floor underneath.

Alena held up her hand and motioned Raph over to look. Laying in her palm was what looked like a single gray hair except now that Raph was closer he could see that it was connected to the crate's false bottom.

"Thinner than anything you'd pluck off your chin and stronger than iron. Bought it off a Traveler a lifetime ago. He called it 'Balentari' but I just call it my little super-string. Best deal I ever made." The evidence of Alena's statements was found in the way she gently held the thin string.

"What did you pay for it?"

249

"One glorious night of debauchery." The aged woman gave him a wink and a smile. "I wasn't always this old you know. In fact, he was a rather handsome one that Traveler probably would have bedded him anyway. Yes, sir best deal I ever made."

Raph wasn't exactly sure how to respond to that. Luckily he didn't have to as Bea finished securing the rope ladder and told them she was ready to descend in her own curt fashion.

"If you two maidens are done recounting the steamy exploits of your youth we should get moving. Time is not our friend tonight."

And so they left Alena and began their descent.

When they reached the bottom of the rope ladder they stood in complete darkness. A spark appeared in Bea's hand followed by the full light of a torch.

"Follow."

They moved through the damp tunnel at a quick march. Drops of something thick and heavy occasionally fell on Raph. He tried to wipe them off quickly and assure himself that they were nothing more than water. The stench and general ickiness lent doubt to that assumption.

Twenty minutes later they came to another rope ladder. Bea set the torch on a protruding wall mount and began to climb the ladder.

When they reached the top Bea gently pushed open the trap door a crack and looked around before closing it.

"Quietly."

Bea opened the trap door all the way this time and pulled herself up and out. Raph gave her a second to get clear then followed her.

He emerged in a small storeroom that was cluttered with all manner of pantry items. High spirited music accompanied by the noises of a drunken crowd could be heard a few rooms off.

"Slouch, avoid eye contact, do what I do."

"Okay"

"Also, don't speak."

Raph started to say okay again but stopped himself and simply nodded instead.

Bea looked at him uncertainly for a long moment before giving her own nod of approval.

They exited the storeroom and entered a long hallway. The music got steadily louder until it, and indiscriminate shouting was all he could hear.

Raph followed Bea into a large common area, at least three times the size of the same room at the Mended Eagle. Size was not the only difference between the two common areas. The Mended Eagle didn't have half naked women entertaining its patrons. The girls occupied three stages that were scattered throughout the room. Two were positioned in the middle of the room, a little ways apart from one another. For these two, the word stage was being generous. They looked more like converted picnic tables. A bronze-skinned buxom brunette danced on each, wearing outfits that a belly dancer would have found revealing.

The third stage was an actual stage (well that might be a stretch but Raph had seen bands gig on worse.) Built on to the same back wall that Raph and Bea had just emerged from. And here, just in case you preferred variety, was a pale blonde of much slighter stature than her compatriots.

And now Raph faced his own personal moral conundrum. As a heterosexual nineteen-year-old male, hormones compelled him to take a long look anytime a woman starting taking off her clothes. As a properly raised southern man possessed of manners and a healthy respect for women, he wanted to look away out of respect. But he also was a feminist, or at least thought he was, and as such believed that a woman had a right to do whatever she wanted with her body and if she wanted to show it off that was her prerogative and he was really disrespecting her choice by placing his hang-ups on her and not looking. Then again as someone not overly experienced in the whole not fully clothed women department gawking at boobs with a bunch of drunken middle-aged men was definitely awkward and weird. Oh, and his life was in danger and he probably should be concentrating on following Bea anyway.

All of that ran through Raph's head simultaneously. It wasn't easy being nineteen.

He was doing well until a roar of delight came from the crowd and Raph turned on instinct to look. The blonde had finally dropped the veil she'd been playfully hiding behind and was now completely bare to the crowd. Tattoos covered her body in a way that invoked the artwork Raph had seen on the Knights who had passed him on the road into Ardoth. But where those mosaics had been a collection of empty landscapes the dancer's tableau served only as a backdrop for more erotic fare.

The thing about not watching where you're going is that you run into things. And sometimes those things

Comment [G]: Deleted:o

Comment [G]: Inserted: ,

Comment [G]: Inserted: e

Comment [G]: Inserted: f

Comment [G]: Inserted: ,

Comment [G]: Inserted: -

Comment [G]: Inserted: -

Comment [G]: Inserted: -

don't particularly like being run into.

"You spilled my drink."

Uh-oh. While Raph might be new to Avalon he was not all that new to drinking establishments and no matter what world you're on when a gruff voice says 'you spilled my drink' you're in for a long night.

"Oh, I'm really sorry about that. How about I head to the bar and buy you another one. Let me just grab my friend she has my wallet." Raph tried to move away from the disgruntled barfly but his friends blocked his way. Ya, this was not going to end well.

"Listen, guys, it was an accident. I don't want any trouble okay."

"Then I guess you shouldn't have spilled my drink."

And then what Raph was really afraid of happened.

"Hey, I recognize this guy. He's one of the ones the watch is looking for, from the whole Sha'Dral mess this morning." Drunken Goon Two was even more belligerent than Drunken Goon One which was saying something.

"There's a reward for you. Posters said alive. Didn't say nothing 'bout bruised." But Drunken Goon One has all the wit in the relationship.

Out of the quarter of his eye, Raph could see Bea inching closer.

Drunken Goon One gripped Raph's shirt tight. It was a good hold, right inside his chest, giving the man leverage. Any offensive lineman would have been proud. But Raph was a linebacker and a damn good one at that. He knew how to get off a block.

"You know on second thought I don't think I'm going to be buying you that drink."

With all the speed and strength he possessed Raph
brought his arms up, striking his assailant in the soft spot
of his wrists and breaking his hold on Raph.

Without slowing their momentum Raph brought his
arms around in a tight windmill motion and exploded his
hands into the man's chest as if he were hitting a practice
sled.

From start to finish the move took a fraction of a
second and left Raph unmolested and the drunk asshole
falling backwards over his chair. Coach would have been
proud.

"Duck."

Without a conscious thought, Raph dropped to one
knee. Bea's quarterstaff came swinging over his head just
as he did landing powerful successive blows on the
drunk's two friends.

Raph felt another hand grab his shirt pulling him up.
From its smallness, he could tell it belonged to Bea.

"Come on"

Chaos had erupted in the tavern. Raph's little
skirmish had turned one spilled drink into twenty and
things had escalated quickly from there. Twenty feet from
the exit Bea and Raph were now caught in the middle of a
full-on bar brawl.

Raph followed Bea as she swung her staff wildly
keeping the unruly patron's around the pair at bay as they
moved towards the door. Raph still had to duck and
dodge the various glasses and cutlery that were being
hurled their way but luckily most everyone who was
aiming at them was well past plastered.

One unlucky drunk managed to end up between Bea

and Raph but by now Raph had up a head of steam and needed only to lower his shoulder and keep his feet moving to bowl the man over.

Thirty seconds later they were outside. Unfortunately so were a lot of people. It had been less than five minutes since Raph had bumped the first idiot's drink and the brawl had already spilled out into the streets. It seemed all that built up pressure the Namahsii had been keeping a lid on was finally spilling out.

To the band's credit, the music never stopped.

"Going so soon Arthur-Son?"

The voice sent chills through Raph's spine.

Time seemed to come to a standstill as he turned to face the Shak'Tah'Noh.

The Emaciated Man stared at Raph with the empty eyes of death.

Individual fights moved around him in slow-motion. Brawlers and thugs who had no idea how much danger they were actually in.

"You didn't really think you could escape us did you?"

A ball of glowing orange-red energy began to form in front of the Shak'Tah'Noh.

Parts of it dripped to the ground melting the cobblestone street beneath it as it did.

Then the Shak'Tah'Noh made a sudden gesture and the molten ball was headed straight for Raph.

Before Raph could be immolated by said ball of lava Bea tackled him to the ground.

"Run." She screamed at the top of her voice.

And so Raph did. He ran faster than he ever had

before in his life.

"Not in a straight line you fool!"

The warning came too late as something hard as a rock struck Raph between the shoulder blades and sent him tumbling to the ground. Falling next to him was a chunk of earth the size of a bowling ball. Raph really hated being right. That was definitely going to leave a mark.

Comment [G]: Inserted: a

Comment [G]: Deleted:c

But Raph couldn't afford to stay still. Rolling to his left he concentrated on throwing up a wall of solid air behind him. It wasn't great but good enough to stop the next boulder from taking off his head while he scrambled to his feet.

Bea had turned and was firing arrows back towards the Emaciated Man.

They turned to ash before they got within a yard of him.

Once Raph got to his feet Bea turned and ran not waiting to see if Raph followed.

But follow he did.

Again Raph ran for his life. But this time he zigged and zagged, making himself a hard target.

In his mind, he held firm to the image of a steel curtain of air behind him.

It must have worked since nothing managed to hit Raph or Bea from behind.

But behind wasn't the only direction from which they could be attacked.

Thunder rumbled in the sky as unnatural clouds began to form in the clear night sky.

"Shit. Shit, shit, shit." Raph did not like where this

was going.

BOOM.

Lightning exploded from the heavens blasting Raph-sized craters in the ground in front of him.

BOOM.

BOOM.

BOOM.

Each successive blast came closer and closer to frying Raph like a chicken wing but somehow he managed to just evade each strike. He'd never been luckier in his life.

"Left" came the shout from Bea.

Raph took a sharp left try to make his turn as sudden and abrupt as possible. He lost speed this way but he feared a rounded turn would have made him too predictable a target. As he pumped his legs to get back up to full steam he looked up and saw the gate. The same one that he had come through almost a month ago. Except that time it had been open and he had only been figuratively running for his life instead of you know actually running for his life.

The guards manning the gate seemed to have noticed the two lunatics running at them like bats out of hell and were sounding the appropriate alarms.

Raph was twenty feet from the gate and five feet behind Bea when his luck ran out.

BOOM.

The ground beneath his feet exploded upwards into the air.

End over end Raph went tumbling to the ground. Collecting cuts and bruises along the way.

Raph got to his knees just in time to see a cannonball of molten heat head straight for him....

..... and turn to mist.

Turns out the city watch had a couple of Benders on the payroll after all.

They met the Emaciated Man's assault head-on with some gigantic fireballs of their own.

Raph scrambled clear of the skirmish; ducking and sprinting to where Bea was braced against the heavy stone of the city walls.

"You're still alive. Good." She hid it under a mask of cold apathy but Raph could sense the immense relief in her words. It was enough to make him blush.

A scream ripped through the air as one of the Watch's non-Bender's burst into flame. The smell of burnt flesh filled the air. Raph wanted to be sick.

The Emaciated Man cackled and redoubled his attack.

He sent a ball of electricity at one of the Benders, who dove to his right and countered with a missile of ice and stone.

The wayward ball of electricity struck the main gate and blew it to hell.

"Now. Move." Bea ran through the newly formed gap and Raph followed with all the speed he could muster. He was half expecting to get shot full of arrows on the other side but when his feet touched dirt he felt himself to be remarkably free of holes.

Bea didn't let up now that they were on the outside of the city walls. She ducked and dodged as she led them through the refuge tent-circle that formed Ardoth's outer

Comment [G]: Inserted: -

Comment [G]: Deleted:.

city.

The refugees gathered around small campfires gave them little notice. Most were looking at where they had come from where the sounds of battle could still be heard.

But as they reached the tree line the sounds began to fade. Raph started to believe that they'd made it clear without anyone chasing them. Bea must have felt the same way because once she made it to the trees she finally stopped.

"Good. The city watch isn't completely worthless after all." The woman was ridiculous. While Raph was panting and pacing with his hands over his head completely out of breath Bea seemed to have barely broken a sweat.

"So…what…now?" The words came between long wheezes.

"Now we have a long night of marching in front of us."

She turned and moved into the forest.

"Great."

Raph took three deep breaths and followed his protector into the darkness.

****

Billy awoke with a massive headache. While not usually one to complain he was really getting sick of getting hurled about by crazy wizards. Not to mention the fireballs. He looked down to see that his clothes were more than a little singed and quite covered in ash. He crossed his fingers that chimney sheik was in style this year. He got a bit squeamish as he lightly touched the

259

blisters that had developed all over his body including, as he began to uncomfortably realize, on some rather delicate bits of his person. Yes, it was safe to say that he really was getting rather sick of these people and their damn fireballs. For being able to shape the world around them into anything they wanted these wizards certainly had limited imaginations. Then again Billy guessed he should be grateful, out of everything they could choose to use to attack him with gigantic fireballs were probably amongst the easiest to dodge. He tried to remember what happened and how he got to wherever he was but the whole thing was a bit of a jumbled mess in his head.

Blinking away his blurriness, Billy sat up and looked around. He was outside and he was moving. *I'm on a cart!* As many of Billy's thoughts did that realization came with much more excitement than perhaps was warranted. On the other hand given his recent circumstances any thought that wasn't a variation of 'I'm about to die' seemed worthy of his exuberance.

There was a sudden jolt and pain ran through all his aforementioned delicate bits.

"Ow!"

"He's awake." It was a woman's voice. It took Billy a second to place it as Kara's.

The cart rolled gently to a stop and a few moments later Alistair appeared in Billy's vision.

"How are you feeling?" The older man didn't wait for Billy's response. His hands were all over checking Billy over with the thoroughness of a seasoned physician.

Add that to the seemingly endless list of skills Alistair possessed. Sometimes it frightened him to think of just how many things he didn't know about his friend's godfather. On the other hand, if Billy stopped to think it kind of frightened him how much he didn't know about everything.

"I'm fine. Just a bit of a headache."

"That tends to happen."

"How long have I been out?"

"More than a day."

Then something occurred to Billy.

"Where's Raph?"

"We don't know."

"Is he ok? Is he alive? Do the Shak'Tah'Noh have him?" His voice grew steadily more panicked as he played out scenarios in his head.

"We don't know." Alistair's voice wasn't any more reassuring the second time. "After the ambush, there was no sign of Raph so I gathered you up along with Lux and Kara and made for one of my safe houses. Sir Geir declared us all suspects and ordered that we are to be arrested on sight. Well, except for darling Kara here who was kind enough to help us escape the city. You may have noticed the smell?"

Now that Alistair mentioned it, he noticed that they indeed smelt fairly awful. They smelt a lot like shit in fact.

"It's a long story. Probably better if you don't ask."

Billy smelled his clothes again and decided Alistair was probably right.

"But where are we going? Raph's trapped in the city somewhere all alone. We have to help him."

"Actually I don't believe that to be the case. The

main gate out of Ardoth was attacked last night from inside the city. The wall sustained major damage and there are rumors that Bender's were involved."

"Shak'Tah'Noh."

"That is the most likely explanation yes. During the attack, two figures were reported as escaping through the gate and heading through the outer camps at a dead sprint. One of whom matched Raph's description rather closely."

"Oh."

The anger and worry went out of Billy's sails. Truth be told he was rather exhausted. This whole conversation seemed to be taking way more out of him than it should be.

"So, we're headed in the right direction now?"

"I believe so yes."

"Well. Good. I'm going to go back to sleep them."

"Okay."

And Alistair's grim grin was the last thing Billy saw before he let himself fade back to black.

When Billy came to again the migraine-inducing glare of day had faded and starlight filled the sky. He was still sore and covered in blisters but his second sleep had restored much of his strength. Which was good because now that he thought about it a bit he was pretty sure he had just slept off a concussion which seemed like the opposite of what should happen. Before Billy could freak out about that bit of hindsight his stomach growled and told him his appetite had been restored as well.

He climbed out of the cart and found the group had started a fire and had begun to make camp. Kara was feeding the horses and Lux was setting out his bedroll.

Comment [G]: Inserted: ,

Comment [G]: Inserted: -

Still, a bit wobbly Billy took his time walking over to Lux, making sure to put one foot in front of the other. Eventually, he took a seat on an old tree trunk next to Lux.

Comment [G]: Inserted: ,

The sandy blonde gave him a once over.

"Good to see you up and about. How do you feel?"

Billy feigned a smile.

"I'm fine," Lux responded with a sarcastic grunt. Apparently 'fine' was recognized as a multiversal non-answer. "Where's Alistair?"

"He went out scouting. I told him I could do it but he insisted and one does not win an argument with the Fox.

Billy was still a bit put off by the whole Fox thing. The Cult of Alistair around here was just weird.

"Any sign of Raph?"

"No."

"What about the Shak'Tah'Noh?"

"No, nothing."

"Does Alistair still think we're going in the right direction?"

"I don't know. Why don't you ask him yourself when he gets back?"

Billy wasn't completely thick. He knew when he was annoying the hell out of someone.

"Sorry I will. I'm just worried about Raph."

"You saw him in that duel. You know that he can handle himself. Trust that all is well and it will be." Lux was right. As much as Billy didn't want to admit it. There was no use assuming the worst. He might as well wait till he knew enough to worry properly. Worrying properly was Billy's wheelhouse after all. For now, he just had to

263

get himself up to speed with current events.

"So what happened? I don't remember much besides the fireballs and the people trying to kill me." And even that was a bit hazy Billy decided not to add.

"It was crazy. I've never seen anything like it. There were Shak'Tah'Noh everywhere. The Namahsii were caught completely off guard. If it hadn't been for the Fox we all might have died. Alistair fought six Benders all by himself. From everything my father told me of the Traveler's Wars that should be impossible. But the Fox he did it like it was nothing. Like he wasn't even trying. Eventually, Sir Geir rallied the city guard and the nobility to fight back but they took heavy losses. I think most of the city's Benders went north with that army we saw back in the woods."

Billy remembered Alistair facing down three attackers fairly easily but six still seemed like a ridiculous feat.

"Why would they attack all of a sudden? So publicly. It doesn't make sense."

"My father has a saying he's fond of repeating: 'Never try to understand the minds of devils, for that way leads to damnation.' I think perhaps its best not to dwell on such things."

Billy only nodded at that. Lux was right but that didn't mean that Billy wasn't going to dwell, it was in his nature. He had thought things couldn't get any worse and yet here they were, worse.

Billy didn't have long to dwell however as Alistair picked that moment to emerge from the trees in a manner that was suitably startling for everyone else.

264

> **Comment [G]:** Inserted: ,

"AAHH!!" was the cry from Lux as Billy fell off his stump. Only Kara out of the three of them kept her cool. Which was probably good since she was the one holding the horses.

"Shhh. Quiet. Gather your things. Quickly." Alistair's voice had an urgency to it that discouraged questions.

"Good. Now follow me." And Alistair made for the trees. Away from the horses and the camp.

"What about the cart?" Apparently, Lux's curiosity was less discouraged than the rest of them.

"Leave it."

"What is it? A dragon?" Lux tried to keep the fear from his voice. He failed.

"Oh, my dear boy there are worse than dragons in these woods."

****

"This is an outrage!" the Guildess was attractive when she was flushed. At least that was Jack's opinion. "How can there be trade if no one's allowed in or out of the city? Do you know how much money the guilds are losing every hour those gates are shut."

"Given the price gouging that I've heard of on the black market, I would imagine not nearly as much as they'd have us believe." Sir Geir raised a hand to stop the response coming from Guildess Corwynn. "However your point is a valid one. Unfortunately for the guilds, the safety of this city and its citizens are higher on my priority list than their pocketbooks. When I feel that the city is secure I will open the gates. Not before."

Jack tried his best to look like he found all of this

politicking extremely tedious, which wasn't hard because he did. He just also needed to remain attentive and alert for opportunities to exploit. It was a hard line to walk. He wished he could have brought his own stimulation into the council chamber but after his last exuberances Sir Geir had banned alcohol and women from the council chambers and Sir Garret looked to have far too delicate sensibilities for Jack to bring a man in. Though if Jack guessed correctly Sir Trelgrove might just enjoy that kind of show.

"And what precisely is being done to secure the city Sir Geir? A week ago an assassin comes to your home and makes a brazen attempt on your life in front of the most consequential members of our city. Then three days ago this very council was attacked by agents of chaos at the conclusion of a sacred rite, an attack that ended the lives of several of our citizens and that of the Northern Ambassador to these lands. That same night suspects wanted by this council for that ghastly affront blasted their way out of the city leaving a gap in our main gate the size of my favorite carriage. The hole has not yet been repaired. I do not feel secure oh Knight Protector and I am not alone in my unease." Jack really admired the way the Lady Tam could combine polite passive aggressiveness with brutal honesty.

"Arrests have been made." Sir Geir, on the other hand, was less than impressive in his obtuseness.

"Arrests? Of course, you've made arrests but rounding up the usual rabble hardly constitutes doing something."

"That usual rabble as you refer to them Lady Tam

are the backbone of this city, its craftsmen, and laborers. As the representative of Low-Town, I strongly object to these arbitrary arrests. This is nothing but an effort by the city watch to find a scapegoat for its recent failures." Cass Kline rarely spoke in this sessions. It might have to do with the way he was treated like insignificant peasant scum by everyone else in the room. Still, one vote in seven had its uses.

Lady Tam concurred, sort of. "As reticent as I am to agree with Representative Kline I'm afraid that I must. A long overdue sweep of the streets will not provide us with the answers that we need. The Fox and his Heir must be found and brought before this council for questioning."

"We have no indication that the Fox or the young Master Carpenter had anything to do with these attacks other than to be present when they took place. Which as I may remind you could be said of every member of this chamber." Sir Garret defending his mentor. Or perhaps something else?

"Bah, the Fox is involved all right. The Fox is always involved." All of this was rather interesting. The fear and awe with which these people spoke of Alistair Ret'Mier was astounding. Jack had reached a certain level of infamy across the multi-verse but he doubted anyone spoke of him in such a way. His own encounters with the man suggested that he was formidable but still a man who won or lost with the role of the dice just like the rest of them.

"It's of little consequence now. Xan'tah'Mer is dead and with him dies any chance of peace. We must prepare for war." The Knight Protector made a not so subtle

Comment [G]: Inserted: ,
Comment [G]: Inserted: ,
Comment [G]: Inserted: ,
Comment [G]: Inserted: e
Comment [G]: Deleted:l

attempt to move the conversation along. Luckily for him, Jack was more than willing to comply.

"Yes, my report we haven't gotten to talk about that yet. Our troops look so impressive out there. I really don't believe that we have anything to worry about."

Sir Geir was not as convinced.

"Your report is full of praise in its assessment of Wizard Carl's preparations. Though there seems to be a particular emphasis on his statements of confidence and on his dinner spread. I must confess that the council and I were looking for something a bit more substantial to place our trust in."

Good, that's what I was hoping for. "I don't understand Sir Geir. It's all there in my report. Wizard Carl is completely convinced of victory. And the bit about the food was meant as a reassurance. After all, if Wizard Carl is capable of such a lavish welcome under such trying circumstances then he must have everything well in hand. Mustn't he?"

"No he mustn't" It was the first time Sir Garret had spoken all afternoon. "What he must be is a fool. As you've all seen in Sir Glaive's report we are at a severe disadvantage. It will take all the luck and skill our forces have and even that might not be enough. To think otherwise would be dangerous and foolhardy."

"Agreed." Sir Geir and Sir Garret on the same side of a military matter was a hard thing to argue against.

Jack feigned frustration bordering on a tantrum. It was fun to pout.

"Well if you all so against poor Carl why not remove him from command and replace him with the *far more*

268

Comment [G]: Inserted: ,

capable Sir Garret." Jack made sure to let the sarcasm drip from that last bit.

"Seconded" Jack put on his best shocked face at Sir Geir's play.

This was the tricky bit. You see it was one thing to get a vote of no confidence passed. It was quite another thing to get one passed while appearing to oppose it.

Sir Geir was an old campaigner from way back. He felt nothing but disdain for untested braggarts like Wizard Carl and society dilettantes like Jack. He had also opposed the Wizard Carl's appointment from the start. He was a Yea. The Lady Tam and the not-a-lord Kass were on different ends of the spectrum politically and economically but both respected competence above all. They were two Yea votes.

Sir Garret, ever the man of honor, would abstain since the vote involved him personally. Sir Trelgrove was a stupid man who cared more about perception and the trappings of power than actual leadership he would vote Nay. As would that incorrigible dilettante Lord Ty.

So it all came down to the Guildess Corwynn. She would make an enemy of Sir Trelgrove and his powerful friends with a Yea vote but she would not retain her station if the city fell.

It was a hard choice.

An uncertain one.

A gamble. For her and for Jack.

Jack loved to gamble.

"Yea"

"Then it is decided. Sir Garret will relieve Wizard Carl of his duties and personally take command of our

269

forces at Rel'Tah'Ver." The burly man gave a solemn nod at the sound of his name. Trelgrove looked aghast as if someone had mortally wounded him. Jack merely shrugged and went back to eating his grapes.

"If there is no other business?"

Sir Geir took a long look around the room.

"Then this council is adjourned" He struck his gavel to make it official. Jack was envious. He quite liked gavels and the striking of gavels. They made a very satisfying knock. Very official and commanding. Jack decided he would have to get himself a gavel. He detested being envious of people. Such an emotion should be beneath him.

Speaking of things that should be beneath him....

"Guildess Corwynn I found your arguments in council today quite compelling." Jack flashed her one of his finest roguish grins while moving in such a way as to isolate them from eavesdroppers. "Perhaps we can arrange a meeting later to discuss them at greater length."

The Guildess gave him a smile of her own. Something proud and playful but with a fair bit of disdain. It looked good on her. "My lord flatters me."

"Is it flattery to speak the truth? If so let me be an honest man so that I may always be called flatterer."

"I think my lord that you would do well to stick to flattery and leave honesty for those whose options are more limited than yours."

"Our options are only as limited as our imagination my dear Guildess. It is important to keep an open mind in all things less we let life grow dull."

"And would you presume to open my mind good

Sir?"

"I simply wish to explore the many ways in which our interests might align. Why right this moment I can think of a myriad of positions I could take that would be mutually beneficial to all parties involved."

"Well, that does sound promising. Very well then my lord. You will come tonight. I will tell my guards to expect you at eight."

"It will be my pleasure."

"Yes I'm sure, but I hope it will be mine as well."

With one last skeptical look, the Guildess exited the council chamber.

Jack did not miss the fact that Lady Tam was keeping an eye on him. He would deal with her in time. For now, Jack decided he'd best get something to eat. He had a full night ahead of him.

Comment [G]: Inserted: ,

Comment [G]: Inserted: ,

Chapter 16

Fine Young Androphagi

By Raph's count, it had been almost three days since his duel against Xan and the subsequent ambush by the Shak'Tah'Noh. And it had been almost a whole day since Bea had stuck him in this cave and told him not to leave it under any circumstances. She was beginning to make a habit of sticking him places and telling him to wait. It was rather infuriating.   And it was making him a little stir crazy. Not that it wasn't a nice cave as caves go. Actually, it was quite spacious. Still, it was a cave and Raph was rather accustomed to the many entertainments of twenty-first-century earth. A Nintendo DS wouldn't have hurt to pass the time. Instead, he was stuck deciding whether Plato or Luke had the more fitting allegory for his present situation.

That wasn't all that he had time to think about. During their frantic escape from Ardoth Raph hadn't had much time to consider what had happened to the others. He'd been worried about them for sure, but the terror of his own situation had let him be easily persuaded by Bea's hollow reassurances that they were sure to be just fine. Now that he was alone with the stillness of the cave he could feel a slow steady panic building inside of him. Even if he trusted that Alistair could take care of himself, and he did, that didn't mean that Billy was okay.

They could have become separated somehow. In fact, Raph couldn't even be sure that Billy had survived the initial chaos of the ambush. He could have been burnt to the crisp by a fireball and there was no way for Raph to know. It was deeply upsetting and sitting around this cave wasn't exactly helping him find his Zen.

Raph walked to the rear of the cavern and sat down cross-legged with his back to the wall. It still irked him. After tapping his inner badass to make Xan look like a fool he had almost completely lost his ability to Bend. If it hadn't been for Bea he would be dead four or five times over. Raph had to face the fact that this was his life now. There was no going back to New Orleans and the Portent's End any time soon. And if he ever wanted to get back there again, hell if he wanted to spend his life anywhere other than a cave or a basement, he needed to learn how to defend himself. And that meant mastering the ability to Bend.

He closed his eyes and ran through the exercises that Alistair had taught him. Visualizing the cave around him. Reaching out the atoms and particles that made up the fabric of reality and acknowledging them as an extension of his own being. With the connection established he began manipulating the molecules. Rearranging them to become what he wanted, to become what was to be. Raph sat there practicing for hours, turning air into water into fire and back into air again.

"Impressive. You've got quite a bit of potential. Now if you could only pull something like that off in a fight, you might actually have something." Everything disappeared in a flash as Bea's voice caught Raph completely off-guard. "That's your problem, the slightest distraction and you lose focus. Too bad all you have in a fight are distractions."

"Bea you're back." Raph didn't even try to keep the excitement from his voice.

"An astute observation. No wonder all of creation bends to your will." Bea walked over to one of the other cave walls and slid down it with the grace of a large hunting cat.

"What did you find out?"

"Later. First, we're going to talk about what just happened."

"I had it, then I lost it. What's there to talk about?" Raph wasn't in the mood to discuss his numerous failings as a Bender. And when Raph wasn't in the mood to discuss something he tended to become a bit churlish.

"I would think how not to lose it would be a start."

"You know you don't talk much but when you do almost none of it is helpful." Well, maybe not churlish so much as sulky and mean.

"It's more helpful than feeling sorry for yourself and

getting both of us killed." Bea's voice was even. What she said wasn't an attack, it was a fact.

"You're right I'm sorry. But how exactly are you going to help me? You can't Bend can you?"

"No. But I can fight. Done right they're the same thing."

Raph found that hard to believe. And said as much.

"Believe what you will. Bending is supposed to be about maintaining your calm and opening yourself up to the world around you. Putting yourself in complete harmony with your environment. Any properly trained warrior seeks that same harmony in battle."

"Well, great then. There are two things I can't be, a bender and a properly trained warrior." Bea stood slowly and let a pause hang in the air before speaking her next words very deliberately.

"You petulance is tiring."

"No my petulance is petulance. Try to keep up."

A sharp crack thundered through the air as a surge of pain rushed through Raph's face.

"You slapped me."

"No, I backhanded you. Try to keep up."

Raph started to open his mouth but thought better of it. After all, only an ungrateful idiot gives undeserved lip to someone who has repeatedly risked their life for him and is the only reason that he is alive. And only a complete and utter moron does it again immediately after being popped in the mouth for the first infraction.

Raph may have been an idiot but he wasn't a moron.

"Good you have a modicum of sense. Stay here." Bea left him and walked out of the cave. She returned a

275

Comment [G]: Inserted: ?

Comment [G]: Deleted:

Comment [G]: Inserted: the

Comment [G]: Inserted: ,

Comment [G]: Inserted: are

Comment [G]: Inserted: T

Comment [G]: Inserted: .

Comment [G]: Inserted: ,

Comment [G]: Deleted: t

Comment [G]: Deleted: 's

Comment [G]: Inserted: ,

few minutes later carrying two long pieces of wood. Each one coming in somewhere between Bea and Raph's height in length and about two inches thick in diameter. She held them together side by side and compared their heights before tossing the taller of the pair at Raph. He caught it out of reflex.

"That seems about your size."

"About my size for what?" Raph wasn't sure what was going on. He thought that she'd gotten up to gather firewood. She walked towards him, stopping when there was about three feet between them.

"You've got a future as a Bender. That's fairly obvious. But it takes more than being a Bender to become a Traveler. In fact, most Travelers can't Bend except on the loosest of worlds like this one. One day you're going to find yourself against a will or world stronger than you and on that day you're going to need to know how to fight. You'll need to learn how to use as many weapons as possible but we start with the bow staff. Every world has different dangers, different weapons. Swords, arrows, guns, grenades. These tend to be the most prevalent but even those have variations on each world that can get you killed for your ignorance. But a bow-staff? A bow staff can be found or made on practically every world with ease. Master it and even the most desperate of situations can be turned to your advantage. That's why a Traveler's best friend is his bow-staff. It is said that the Eight could Bend a staff into creation. Simply summoning it from thin air when they were in need of a weapon."

"That's amazing."

"Since I highly doubt you'll be doing that anytime soon we will just have to make good with these." She moved her body into a fighting stance as she gave him

276

Comment [G]: Inserted: ,

instructions.

"Put your right foot forward with your knee slightly bent." Raph did as she instructed. "Now with the staff on the open side of your body position your backhand about a hands width up the bass of the staff and your front hand should be the length of your forearm from that hand like that." Raph watched then emulated the way she held her staff. When he was ready she continued her instruction.

"In this position, we both have our guard up. The first basic move I will teach you is a simple deflect and strike. By pushing the back end of your staff up and in you get underneath his guard. Then push it down and away." She demonstrated the move. Her staff looping around Raph's before pushing it away. "Now I have a clear line. I push forward with my back hand while letting the staff slide through my lead hand." The end of Bea's staff now sat an inch away from Raph's chin.

Bea demonstrated a few times before having Raph try. On his third attempt, she stopped him.

"You're too big. The key is subtlety. Small, controlled movements or you leave yourself open for a counter move. Again."

They practiced like that for a couple of hours. Bea teaching him a move. Raph doing it incorrectly. Bea correcting him. Eventually, Raph got to the point where he could string a couple of attacks and defenses together and they could spare a bit. Raph was sweaty and exhausted by the time Bea allowed them to stop for the night.

Raph had no thoughts at all as he drifted to sleep

He awoke to the not so gentle shaking of his person by Bea. Groggy and sore he wiped the sleep from his eyes and tried to make the world coherent. The cave was still

Comment [G]: Inserted: ,

Comment [G]: Inserted: ,

Comment [G]: Inserted: ,

dark but the first light was beginning to peak over the horizon.

"Get ready we leave in ten minutes."

Raph made a big production of standing, looking around himself for anything he might want to pack up and take with him, then running his hand through his hair to flatten it out.

"Okay, I'm ready."

Bea pulled a stale loaf of bread out of her rucksack, broke it in two and tossed Raph half before tying up the sack and throwing it over her shoulder.

"Good we'll eat as we walk."

"Sounds like a plan." Raph tried to keep the sarcasm out of his voice. He didn't succeed. To be fair he hadn't tried very hard.

The half loaf of bread didn't make it very far. Which was too bad since it had been the only thing distracting Raph from the torturous walk. At least Bea called it a walk. Raph was fairly certain that when the grade became this steep it became a climb. He considered raising this point but decided it was probably better if he didn't. Bea was irritated enough with him already without bringing semantics into it.

Their major conflict was rooted in the fact that Raph just generally sucked at nature stuff. The particular nature stuff he sucked at included but was not limited to: moving quietly through forests; moving quietly through fields; moving quietly over hills, and moving quietly while crossing moving water. Really the only thing he was good at was not tripping over tree roots, which makes sense to anyone who has ever walked on a New Orleans sidewalk.

Unfortunately when you're pointing out that you're really good at not tripping you've already lost the argument.

The argument being that Raph's inability not to be heard by every living thing in a three-mile radius was very likely to get the both of them killed.

For Raph's part, he was really trying to be all stealthy woodsman. It's just that, to assert the earlier point, he generally sucked at nature stuff.

They'd been walking for a couple of hours when Raph thought he heard a sound in the bushes behind them. Before he could react Bea's hand was over his mouth with a finger raised to her own lips in what Raph thought must be the universal wilderness sign language for 'Quiet something's about to jump out of nowhere and try to kill us.' But people trying to kill him was becoming old hat to Raph at this point. So rather than panic and look wildly around for danger he attempted to remain perfectly still and kept his eyes locked on Bea for an indication of what he should do next.

Stillness hung between them. Glacially she moved her finger away from her mouth and up over her shoulder towards the bow staff strapped to her back. At the same time, Raph could feel the muscles in Bea's hand relax against his lips, no longer the tight clamp against speech they had been only a few seconds prior. Still, Raph kept silent as her hand came completely free of his mouth. Uncertain of what to do Raph remained where he was as Bea moved past him, never leaving her crouch.

A minute passed like this, with Bea behind him and Raph frozen in place. A light tap on the shoulder sent

Comment [G]: Inserted: ,

Comment [G]: Inserted: ,

Comment [G]: Inserted: ,

shivers running up and down his spine, but he held himself together enough to not jump out of his skin at the shock. Carefully he turned to Bea, a little too pleased with himself that he had managed to avoid screaming his lungs out like a frightened child.

Bea motioned him forward and pointed down the slope of the mountain to spot on the path about fifty yards behind them.

There were four men there. Three dressed in the uniforms of regular soldiers and one fitted with what appeared to be Traveler's gear complete with two long wooden sheaths on either side of his hips.

"A scouting squad. Probably up here to make sure that their rear lines don't get harassed by a bender they can't see."

"We should just keep moving forward," Raph argued in a voice as soft as the rustling leaves.

"No, at some point we're going to run into danger ahead and we can't deal with whatever that might be with these bastards on our flank."

"But they're not even looking for us. They're here for the battle." Raph did not like the idea of making any more enemies than he already had.

"Doesn't matter. They're soldiers and we're not wearing their uniform. Best case they take us prisoner and try to sort it out when the dust's settled. Worst case......" Bea merely shrugged as she let her sentence trail off. Raph got the point.

"Fine, but no killing. They're just doing their jobs."

"Do you think that the two of us are such talented fighters that we can take on four men of war and just

Comment [G]: Inserted: ,

Comment [G]: Deleted:.

decide in what condition we will take them? After the blood you've seen are you really that naïve? I will do what I must. I aim to keep the pair of us alive. Beyond that, I make no promises."

Raph started to say something else but thought better of it. When you're in over your head you listened to the experts and when it came to survival Bea was an expert. Instead, he let her lay out their plan.

"They'll come up in a one then three formation. With one of the soldiers scouting ahead and the remaining two protecting the traveler. It's a tactic specifically designed to protect their best fighter in case of an ambush like we're planning."

"So then how do we take them?" There was no incredulity in Raph's voice just cold analysis. Now that they had agreed on a course of action there was no point in doubting in it.

"That depends. Do you think you can Bend right now?"

"I'll be fine when we first attack but after that, I don't know."

Bea digested that for a second. Raph wished he could offer more but he thought it best not to overpromise in situations like these.

"Stay here." She pointed to a large rock a few dozen meters ahead of the scouting party. "When the lead scout reaches that rock, do whatever you must to take him out."

Raph nodded his acknowledgment of her orders. "And what are you going to do?"

"Stop the rest. Hopefully, the Traveler isn't a Bender."

281

"And if he is?"

"Then we will most likely be dead five minutes."
And with that bit a reassurance Bea disappeared into the brush.

Raph cleared his mind and focused on the world around him. He felt the molecules in the ground beneath him, the atoms in the air, the protons and electrons in the rocks and trees. He let awareness fill him replacing the blank space in his mind with a high definition depiction of the universe that surrounded him.

Rather than open his eyes, he watched the scout's approach with this new sight. As the soldier got closer Raph concentrated on the currents in the air, focusing them, strengthening them. When the man hit Bea's mark Raph unleashed the wind, viciously driving the scout into the rock and knocking him unconscious.

Bea did not miss her cue.

The woman moved with a grace that was heedless of the armor she wore. The second scout fell before Raph even registered that Bea was in motion. With a quick twirl, she flung her bow staff out wide in a sweeping motion towards the third scout.

He ducked it. But Bea brought the staff fully around and took the man's legs out from under him. Another change of direction by Bea smacked the man square in the chin on the way down.

And like that Bea was one on one with the Traveler. Raph assumed that if he was a Bender he would have revealed himself by now. But if Bea was any indication not being a Bender didn't make a Traveler any less deadly.

Bea and the Traveler circled each other slowly.
Taking the measure of one another. The Traveler feinted
left with is staff before pivoting to a powerful sweep on
his right.

Bea was prepared and caught the swing with a
vertical block. A loud crack splintered the air as the two
staves clashed.

Bea dropped her bottom hand and kicked her staff
upwards forcing her opponent's staff over her head,
moving into a crouch as she did so.

Pivoting to her left she swung her staff in a tight arc
towards the traveler.

The traveler had recovered and pulled off an
impressive block and counter that left Bea staggering
backwards. Raph watched as this continued for a long
while.

Back and forth the two worthy opponents fought
each pressing their momentary advantages only to be
rebuffed by the skill of their opponent.

Eventually, they fell into a rhythm. The crack of
wood on wood becoming as steady as a drummers beat.

Raph stared at them unsure of what he could do to
help. Certain that anything he did would backfire and put
Bea in danger.

But this was Bea and Raph's help wasn't necessary.
Her opponent stepped on a small rock, half the size of
Raph's fist, and lost his footing for a moment.

A moment was all Bea needed. She pivoted her
weight and spun a quick strike at the opposite leg. The leg
that now was holding the majority of her foe's weight.
The blow caused him to lurch to his right even as Bea

spun again and struck him on the back of the head.

The man stumbled to the ground and tried feebly to grasp at Bea before one more blow to the head knocked him out for good.

Raph was so intent on Bea's battle that he didn't notice the blade at his throat until it was too late.

"Impressive as always Beatrice, but be a good girl and put down the staff or I'm afraid I'll have to kill your new boy toy." The voice was brash, arrogant, and unnervingly flippant.

Intense hatred filled Bea's eyes. Her mouth curled into a snarl. In the time they'd been together Raph had yet to see her be anything but calm and cool. She looked as if she was ready to go into a full animal frenzy now.

"Balyn." She choked on the name. Like it was a poison she was trying to spit up. She took a fighting stance and Raph feared for his life. If she made a move he had no doubt his life would be over a second later. With disgust, she dropped her quarterstaff to the ground.

"Take them."

Men in armor came running at Bea from behind Raph. She didn't put up a fight as they seized her arms. She fought her head free long enough to meet Raph's eyes and give him a slight nod of her head.

Then a bag came down over his head and all he could see was black.

Well shit.

Sometimes two words were all you needed to know that you were completely fucked.

****

"There are worse than Dragons in these woods."

284

The Seeker

Alistair's words filled Lux with dread even now hours after they'd been spoken. The deep dark of night hung over them like a cage. Every sound, every movement a harbinger of terror and death.

Fear radiated from Billy and Kara. Their heads constantly moving. Their eyes wide with fright. Lux could hear their teeth chattering. There was no thought to their actions. Their movements were mechanical. They were running on pure adrenaline putting all of their hope in the man they were following. Trusting in Alistair to keep them alive.

And the Fox led them further into the woods.

Uncertainty filled him. He knew that it shouldn't but it did anyway. The Fox was a legend. The greatest Bender of his generation. The most feared Wizard of the Traveler's Wars. Without Alistair Lux's father would have been dead a dozen times over. Which meant that Lux directly owed his own existence to the man. He had sworn his service to the Fox. Sworn to obey and follow his commands. But the truth was even after spending the last month with the man Lux barely knew him. And it's hard to give anyone your complete trust when bad things are coming for you in the night.

A twig snapped and Lux's heart nearly jumped out of his chest.

He snapped his head around to see that it was only Billy who somehow managed to look sheepish, mortified, and terrified all at the same time. Apparently, Raph and Billy came from a world filled with cities and mechanical transports that moved you from place to place so they had never needed to learn basic woodcraft. Lux just couldn't

Comment [G]: Inserted: ,

285

wrap his head around that. For him, the thought of them being adults without such basic skills was just impossible. What kind of world was it where they didn't need to bother with the things that Lux knew were essential to his survival? Even Kara, a big city serving girl moved better than Billy.

The thought of Kara brought Lux's eyes instinctively to her. Her honeyed skin seemed to glow in the moonlight even as she struggled to keep her dress from getting snagged on the various roots and branches of the forest. Her features were soft and rounded but her face bore an unmistakable look of determination. The way she endured her troubles and indignities without complaint impressed him. There was a certain nobility about her. She was strong. Maybe not in her arms or her legs. But in her heart. Where it counted.

Lux turned his gaze away from her and directed it back out into the woods, keeping his eyes scanning for threats. There was an unnatural tingling in the hairs on the back of Lux's neck. He had the feeling that they were being watched and had been for some time.

His body tensed. He wanted to believe it was just his imagination. His fear and anxiety playing trick on him in the dark. But he knew it wasn't. They were no longer simply running to avoid trouble.

Whatever Alistair had been afraid of had their scent now. Someone or something out there was hunting them. They weren't going to make it out of these woods without a fight for their lives.

Lux didn't need to see the Fox's upraised hand to sense that the others had stopped.

The Seeker

He saw their eyes first. Red surrounded by bloodshot white, burning embers of hate and malice. They came closer indistinct forms coalescing into tangible singular figures, almost as if they were wild spirits reverting to their human form for the kill.

Their skin was as black as the night that had given birth to them. They were children of the dark just as surely as Lux was his father's son.

Hunger and lust filled their faces. Wild smiles and silent laughter revealing teeth that had been sharpened into points. They wore next to nothing, only some sparse bits of leather covering sensitive areas.

Kara and Billy each carried a small hunting knife to defend themselves with. Even if they knew how to use them Lux doubted that they would be much good against these creatures.

His eyes met Alistair's and he immediately understood. This fight was up to the Fox. Lux's job was to keep Billy and Kara alive while Alistair worked to end it as quickly as he could manage. The Fox was not afraid for himself. He was afraid for those put in his charge.

Lux wished he could be so confident in his own survival.

Unholy screams ripped through the dark.

Lux readied his bow and desperately tried to keep his fingers from trembling.

Figures moved just beyond his vision.

Alistair reached into his cloak and pulled out a small cylinder.

There was a metallic sound, like a sword being pulled from a sheath and the cylinder expanded out to its

Comment [G]: Inserted: d

Comment [G]: Deleted: s

full length.

"Everyone. Behind me." Came the Fox's command. "Hear me craven beasts of the Sunken Moon. I am no easy prey for you to feast upon. Leave. Now. Or the only blood you taste this night will be your own."

Alistair's words were met with silence.

A stillness possessed the night until even the memory of Alistair's words had faded.

Lux held steady. Listening carefully for anything that would give the creatures away but the only sound he could hear was the thundering of his own heart.

Then the screams came again.

And with them came the creatures.

They exploded out of the trees with inhuman speed. Far too fast to be anything other than blurry visions of death.

Lux let loose his notched arrow but it struck nothing but air and bark.

He reached back for another arrow already knowing he wouldn't be in time.

The creature leaped at him and was inches from Lux's face when a blast of fire hit it in the stomach and sent its burning body into a faraway tree.

Somewhere behind him Kara screamed.

He turned to help but Alistair got there first, spinning his staff with deadly accuracy. A resounding crack thundered through the air as he caught one of the creatures beneath the chin, breaking its jaw.

Lux could only watch as Alistair whirled his staff with breathtaking finesse, keeping himself between the three remaining creatures and the party. He spun it around his back then swung it in a wide arc forcing his foes to keep their distance, never allowing his staff to stop spinning or lose momentum.

Having taken note of their fallen comrades the creatures eyed the Fox warily. Lux tried to line up a clear shot but they were too fast and Alistair kept getting in the way.

With a blood-curdling screech, they came again, rushing Alistair all at once. The Fox again swung his staff wide only this time he kept only his right hand on the weapon giving him two advantages. The first being that the extra length gained from the one-handed strike surprised his attackers. The staff clipped the second creature on the shoulder and sent it careening into the third leaving only the leftmost foe to deal with. The second advantage of the one-handed strike was the ball of flame that erupted from Alistair's free left hand which struck that left most foe square in the chest and kept going leaving a rather large hole where the creature's torso and previously been located.

Alistair didn't look back as he squared himself against his remaining two opponents, resuming a two-handed grip on his weapon.

"LUX!"

Billy pointed over Lux's shoulder as he shouted. Lux turned and let loose with an arrow not bothering to aim. He struck the blackened, burnt in the shoulder but the blow didn't slow it down. Lux threw up his bow as the beast landed on top of him. He froze at the terrifying sound of wood snapping in its jaws. In two chomps the thing was through and only Lux's hand at its throat kept it

289

Comment [G]: Inserted: a

Comment [G]: Inserted: ,

Comment [G]: Inserted: -

Comment [G]: Inserted: -

Comment [G]: Inserted: '

Comment [G]: Inserted: -

from biting off his face.

Frantically Lux reached around him for something, anything he could use to defend himself.

He felt the shaft of an arrow and clawed at it till he could get a good grip on it. Then with all his strength, he plunged it into the beast's eye.

It let out chocked off scream twitching and jerking on top of him as the last light went out of its remaining eye.

With a shove, Lux pushed the lifeless body off of him and scrambled to his feet.

He got to them just in time to see the Fox launch fire at the last remaining creature. Its burning, still-living corpse ran howling into the night.

Silent space had replaced the cacophony of mayhem that had existed only a few moments before. Alistair stood leaning on his staff, Kara was sobbing silently to herself, and Billy was silently rocking back and forth with his hand over his mouth.

And nothing else moved.

It was over.

Lux let out a long exhale and looked at the monster he had slain.

Except now that he looked it wasn't a monster at all. It was a man.

A twisted perversion maybe. But there was no mistaking it. Grotesque as he was he had been a human being and Lux had killed him.

Shame bubbled up inside him. He felt as he wanted to vomit. His hands shook.

They were trying to kill us. All I did was protect

290

Comment [G]: Inserted: ,

myself and my friends. Lux repeated that though over and over in his head. It didn't stop his hands from shaking.

Alistair walked over and put his hands on Lux's shoulder. This time the tremors did stop.

"They are called Androphagi. Or more commonly the Phage. Cannibals. They massacre their way from world to world, devouring the flesh of their victims believing it to give them supernatural abilities. They are less than human but because of their belief, they are also something more. They are the foulest of creatures. From the start, this could only have ended in death. Theirs or ours."

Alistair's words were meant to give Lux comfort and reassurance. They did not. He had acted in self-defense. He knew that. But the thing that Lux also knew now with absolute certainty was that if he stayed with the Fox eventually he would have to kill again. And that thought more than any other frightened him.

Comment [G]: Inserted: ,

Comment [G]: Inserted: ,

Comment [G]: Inserted: ,

Chapter 17

Casualties

Raph was starting to think that adventure mostly consisted of sitting around waiting for other people to do things. On the other hand, considering how often he was trying to escape from people who wanted to capture or kill him there was a good chance he wasn't doing it right. At least this time the bad guys seem more interested in Bea than in him. They were probably still going to die but he felt a little better knowing this time it was because of somebody else. Raph had also decided that adventure meant taking your wins where you could get them.

He was about to start singing "Always Look on the Bright Side of Life" when the guards finally came for him. He wasn't sure how long he'd been a prisoner at that point. Couldn't have been more than a day. Time tended to run together when you're left alone in a tent tied to a pole. And considering that all of his pre-tied to pole time had been spent marching around with a hood over his head Guantanamo style he was really rather unsure of what exactly the hell was going on.

"On your feet."

Raph did as he was instructed. The guard cut the rope around Raph's wrists before coming around to face Raph. He placed the knife under Raph's chin and looked him square in the eyes.

"Any trouble and I gut you. Understand?" It was the cold detachment in the man's voice that sold the threat.

"Yes."

"Yes, What?"

"Yes, I understand."

"Good. Follow me." He nodded at the other two guards who took up a flanking position on either side of Raph. Then he gave Raph one long up and down look before turning and walking out of the tent. Raph, being new to the whole prisoner thing and not wanting to make waves, followed.

The camp was odd to Raph. Not that the camp itself was odd it just felt odd to Raph. Yet again he found himself completely out of his depth. He'd never seen this many people camped in one place. In fact, the only time he'd ever been out camping at all was when he'd gone with a group of friends the summer before his senior year. His greatest accomplishments there had been catching a fish and making out with Stephanie Parker in that order.

None of which was particularly helpful in his present circumstance. He tried to do what every good hero would do in his situation, look around and memorize everything he saw in order to come up with some ingenious escape plan, but it was kind of impossible when you didn't even know the names of half the things you saw.

Hell Raph wasn't even sure whose camp he was in. It wasn't as if he'd gotten an information pamphlet to go with his bonds. Though there was a great idea. Little brochures entitled "You and Your Dungeon" or "Who's holding you Prisoner and Why" Raph thought his personal favorite would be "3 Easy Steps to Preventing Rope Burn."

Comedy he could do. Breaking out of a heavily fortified encampment not so much.

He thought about trying to Bend his way out but the risks were too great. For one he didn't know if he could in the first place. If he tried and failed they'd kill him on the spot. He also had no idea if there were Benders in the camp (given his luck there had to be) or where the hell they were keeping Bea. All in all his best option was to wait and hope something broke in his favor.

They brought him into a wide extravagant tent that was five times the size of Raph's bedroom back in New Orleans.

Sitting in an ornate chair with a goblet in his hand was a thin sinewy man who landed somewhere in the grey area between middle-aged and elderly. He was dressed in fine silk robes that reminded Raph of pictures he had seen of the ancient Greeks and Romans. Gold and silver rings laid on almost every finger. If captivity and the repeated pointing of sharp objects at his throat hadn't already put Raph off these guys that would have. Raph never trusted a man who wore jewelry. They almost always turned out to be assholes.

To the asshole's right stood a man who looked to be in his late thirties to early forties. He was built like a distance runner, plenty of muscle but no real bulk and certainly not an ounce of fat. He was blonde and blue-eyed and just a few inches shorter than Raph. So a Nazi and an asshole then. There was no way this interrogation was going to go well for Raph.

"Bring the prisoner forward." The one on the right spoke and Raph recognized the voice as belonging to the man Bea had called Balyn.

"Tall. Well Built. Soft Hands. You do not have the bearing of a soldier. And certainly, you cannot be Tah'Mer. So who are you boy to be journeying out with such infamous company?" The man in the chair spoke haltingly; stopping after every sentence to cough into his handkerchief.

Raph considered carefully his response. The truth would either get him killed or make him a valuable prisoner and he honestly had no idea which it would be. Claiming to be Alistair's heir again might help but the last time he'd done that he'd ended up in a duel to the death. He didn't know enough about this world to lie about anything for more than three seconds so he doubted he could talk his way out of this. He had no play. If he spoke up he was screwed. So he kept his mouth shut.

Balyn must have seen the decision to be stubborn in Raph's eyes because as soon as it was made the bulky man walked over and delivered a backhand that had Raph seeing stars.

He staggered backwards for a couple of steps but

managed to stay upright. The taste of blood filled his mouth.

"Answer the question."

"And miss out on getting smacked again? No way Jose." The second blow was worse than the first but Raph was prepared for it this time and kept himself rooted to where he stood. Raph was proud of himself. He'd managed to stick to his plan of keeping his mouth shut for almost a whole minute. Well, almost a minute. Thirty seconds really but who's counting.

"Insolence is not a virtue."

"Neither is balding but you don't see me judging you for your failings now do you." Normally Raph wouldn't go for such an obvious target but his head was spinning a bit too much to be clever and obstinate at the same time.

"You speak bravely for a one who lives or dies at my command Traveler."

"I took a class. 'How to piss off anyone at any time.' That reminds me do you guys have any pamphlets? I'm new to this whole prisoner thing. Will there be an orientation?"

The third blow dropped Raph to his knees. He let his tongue do a quick check of his mouth. All of his teeth were still intact. So far. He started to laugh.

Now Raph did not consider himself a tough guy. He'd played football and been in a few fights at school sure. But all of those fights had been about protecting Billy and none of them had lasted more than a few punches. He'd never really experienced a beat down before. By all rights, he should be crying his eyes out at this point.

296

Comment [G]: Inserted: ,

Comment [G]: Inserted: ,

The thing is though, while Raph may not have considered himself a tough guy he did consider himself a stubborn one. A stubborn guy who really hated bullies. A stubborn guy who really hated bullies and read an inordinate amount of Harry Dresden and Peter Parker stories.

If one knew this about Raph (and knew who Harry Dresden and Peter Parker were) then one might find Raph's next words fairly predictable. If one did not know this about Raph then it would be quite easy to believe that he was, in fact, a rather tough guy.

"So Baldy, can I call you Baldy? So Baldy are you just gonna sit in that chair all day or are ya gonna come down here and get in on the fun?"

Balyn reared his hand back to strike Raph again but Baldy the Asshole stopped him with a subtle wave of his hand.

"My name is Eadric Tah'Mer. You may call me My Lord."

"Ohh fancy. But I've got to wonder, doesn't it get a tad incestuous if y'all go around calling each other Tah'Mer?"

"Our legacy must be preserved. Is it not so where you come from?"

"Who said I come from anywhere?"

"Do not play word games with me, Traveler. So far I have no interest in you beyond your association with your companion. You would be wise not to do anything to change that."

"So you guys don't like Bea huh? I could see why. She does tend to lack my interpersonal skills. But what has she done to piss you off so much? Wouldn't be your prom date?"

"I tire of this. Take him back to his tent. Perhaps a night of being cold and hungry will temper his wit."

"Oh, I don't know. I get pretty cranky when I haven't eaten. Anybody got a Snickers bar?"

Balyn finally got to land that fourth blow and it left Raph seeing stars as he was dragged back to his tent. Roughly, his guards re-tied him to his pole before resuming their posts outside. Alone with no one else around he finally did decide to start singing "Always Look on the Brightside of Life" He made it to the refrain before passing out.

****

Billy was tired. In point of fact, Billy was quite a few magnitudes beyond tired. In his vast thesaurus of a brain, he could not come up with a word that could appropriately encapsulate the level of tired he had reached. His entire body ached and burned. All he wanted to do was close his eyes and die. It was a reasonable request. After the Phage attack, they had marched the rest of the night and well into the next day. That Billy had survived it was a miracle deserving of its own holiday.

Oh sure there had been breaks but none long enough to get any real rest, let alone sleep. Twenty-four hours of marching would be near impossible for anyone. And he hadn't even had the worst of it. While Billy had been sleeping in the back of the cart recovering from his injuries the others had put in a full day's travel before they'd had to run from the Phage. That they were still moving forward was an inhumane feat that was

Comment [G]: Inserted: -

Comment [G]: Inserted: ,

Comment [G]: Inserted: ,

Comment [G]: Inserted: ,

Comment [G]: Inserted: ,

completely incomprehensible to Billy.

> **Comment [G]:** Inserted: p
>
> **Comment [G]:** Deleted:b

Eventually, they came to a hole in the rock face. Leaving the trail behind Alistair veered right into the cave. Luminescent rocks produced a faint blue light that guided their way and Billy soon came to the realization that they were not in a cave but a tunnel. As the others looked around in wonder at the beauty of the cave Billy fixated on what they might find on the other side.

What Billy saw when they emerged from the tunnel was not any of the things he had been imagining. Melded together with the forest was a gigantic estate. The main house was twice the size of any of the plantation houses Billy had seen around New Orleans. It was made completely of wood and seemed to blend seamlessly into the surrounding scenery. There were a few smaller structures scattered around it ranging from the size of a shed to a small house. High up in the trees were a string of walkways that circled the perimeter, beginning and ending at the third story of the main structure. Faint blues lights came to life as they approached like a thousand fireflies had suddenly woken up.

It was really freaking cool.

"What is this place?" The question came from Lux but Billy had been about to ask the exact same thing.

"It is my home. At least it was. One of my father's houses I inherited it when he passed. Though as you know I have not been here in some time." Alistair's tone was heavy and laden with sorrow. They knew better than to push for more of an explanation.

"It's so beautiful." The soft, high voice caught Billy off guard. He was fairly sure it was the first time Kara had spoken without being spoken to.

The group silent as they made their way over the short distance to the house.

Alistair opened the front door and they all stepped inside. The interior of the house was every bit as majestic as the exterior.

"So what do we do now?" Billy asked.

"Now we wait for Beatrice and Raphael to join us." Alistair put his pack down just inside the door.

"Beatrice? The woman who threatened to kill us at the inn?" It was only Billy's surprise at the response that kept the incredulity out of his voice.

"Yes. I believe she is the one who helped Raph escape through the gates."

"You think the woman who threatened to kill us helped Raph escape and is with him now?" Lux had found Billy's missing incredulity.

"Yes, and she wasn't really threatening to kill you she was merely being melodramatic." Alistair moved around the place slowly. Like an actor getting a feel for a stage.

"Okay well if that's the case shouldn't they have been here ahead of us?" That ever-present nervousness began to build up in Billy again.

"I wouldn't think so. Remember because of the Phage we haven't stopped for nearly two days. If they were on a regular pace or more probably if they were being unusually careful they might not be here for another few days."

Alistair made a valid point but Billy's worry train had already left the station. Luckily he was far too

300

exhausted for it to get up a proper head of steam.

"There are beds upstairs for everyone but I'm afraid the kitchen is likely to be bare. I haven't been here in quite a while. We'll have to subsist on stale bread for one more night and send Lux out hunting in the morning."

Billy wasn't sure if Alistair was reading his thoughts or if it was just that everyone felt exactly the same way but the thought of a bed put everything else out of his head.

Billy followed the others upstairs. He was far too tired to join in Lux and Kara's looks of awe and wonder. He made for the first open door, saw that there was a bed inside, and immediately laid down. He was asleep before his head hit the very expensive looking pillow.

****

Her hips moved with delectable grace, swaying hypnotically to the exotic sounds of the orchestra. Not too fast, not too slow, just the steady rhythm of sex and comfort. She was talented. Dancing in that special way that made each man believe that she moved only for him. Absolutely enchanting.

The scent of stale beer mixed with the pervasive aroma of pipe tobacco to form a rather repugnant fragrance common to taverns across the multiverse. What made the smell of this particular tavern unique was the added stench of desperation and treachery that assaulted the nostrils for no extra charge.

He smiled. This place reminded him of home.

"I gotta say, Jack. I've heard some stories about a certain handsome young Lord with certain appetites. And those appetites put me in the right frame of mind to start

301

G.R. Linden

reminiscing over my good friend Jack. And now here you
are looking to enlist my services in a job that involves
some of those lord muckity mucks of overcompensating.
A smart man might start putting some pieces together.
Might start thinking you've got some mischief afoot." The
big, burly man stroked his long grey beard as he spoke, a
blank white eye twitching in its socket while its
mismatched partner of dark hazel constantly scanned the
room.

Jack had always been fond of Dras Ursidae. He had a
habit of seeing things that other people didn't. The
delicious poetry of that appealed to Jack. The man also
had a habit of always keeping things interesting and that
was the highest praise the Purveyor of Pandemonium had
to offer a man. He smiled. He hadn't come here with the
expectation of a game. It was exciting.

"A smarter man might know nothing at all."

"Aye. True, true. But I ain't never done wrong by the
Bard of Bedlam and he ain't never done wrong by me. So
it might be that the smartest of men might just make an
offer."

"Might be. Might also be that the dumbest of men
makes an offer. It really all depends on the offer doesn't
it?" A bellow of laughter erupted from deep in Dras'
belly.

"That it does. That it does." Dras let his laughter
subside before leaning in for a conspiratorial whisper.
"See, way I figure it whatever you're up to is going to end
up one of two ways. Either you are going to do what you
came here to do and leave when it's done in which case
knowing you there is going to be a good bit of chaos and

302

opportunity for a man with his wits about him; or you are going to make a play for a piece of the pie which again knowing you would have to be a pretty big piece to make it worth your while."

Jack nodded along with the man's reasoning.

"On the whole, your logic seems sound."

"Thank you, now you came down to offer me money to do a job. So based upon the previous assumptions I'm telling you that me and mine will take care of this thing of your sans wage."

"That's a very generous offer. But you understand, given the lifestyle choices that the two of us have made, that I might be a bit apprehensive at the prospect accepting such a favor."

"Oh, I can assure you that my understanding of such matters is absolute. Rest assured I will make my intentions clear. In return for my services and those of my men, I ask merely for the opportunity to be included in your current endeavors. A tip-off to opportunities created in the aftermath of said endeavor or in the event of a pie seizure I humbly request a position in the hierarchy of pie management such as it were."

"Your proposal is intriguing and not only for its colorful phrasing, though that is most appreciated as well. It is not often that I am afforded the opportunity to converse with a man of such linguistic prowess. Tell me since I have money aplenty what do I have to gain by agreeing to your more creative pricing model?"

"Ah, a fair and insightful question such as befits a man of your station. May the Eight in their wisdom grant me the eloquence to promulgate my response in a manner worthy of your inquiry's grace. On the one hand, if you are planning on leaving this lovely metropolis in a bit of a stir there is nothing to be lost in giving a tip-off in payment as you will be well on your way out by the time I make use of any such information. On the other hand, if you decide to stay, having established yourself as a prominent figure in this fine city, you will have responsibilities. Some of those responsibilities will require delegating. Some of those responsibilities will also come with perks that a man of your stature might take for granted but that a man like myself might find fresh and invigorating. After all, you can't sail a whole ship by yourself. You need a crew. Preferably one whose hands are as bloody as your own."

"Your arguments are persuasive." Jack paused for effect. Slowly tracing a finger around the rim of his glass before lazily lifting it to his mouth. Its amber liquid tasted sharp then warm. Gently he placed his glass back on the table. After all their banter the silence sat in the air like an infection. Eating away at Dras' reserve. Sweat began to run down his forehead. The silence was of Jack's making and thus he was far more resistant to its corrosiveness. He let it sit there, devouring them both until finally he too succumbed.

"Agreed."

The air came rushing back into the room.

"Excellent! I'm glad that our negotiations have come to a satisfactory result. Tell you the truth I've never been a First Mate before. I'm looking forward to it. Now about this job what is it I can do for you."

"It's actually a rather simple task. I simply need you

Comment [G]: Inserted: ,

Comment [G]: Inserted: -

Comment [G]: Inserted: ,

Comment [G]: Inserted: ,

Comment [G]: Deleted:,

Comment [G]: Deleted:o

to intercept a delivery for me." Jack's manic grin turned wolfish as he shared the details with Dras.

****

Raph awoke tied to a pole. Again. He promised himself if he ever got home he was buying one of those sleep number beds and never leaving it. It was the dead of night and he had a roaring headache. Which was either a side effect of poor neck support or getting punched in the face multiple times? At least he didn't have a black eye or if he did at least it didn't seem to be impairing his vision. When you're being held captive on a parallel earth by super hardcore military dudes you have to focus on appreciating the little things.

He tried working on the ropes around his wrist again, more out desperation than anything else. They weren't going to give and even if they somehow miraculously did he hadn't exactly figured out what his next move should be. Even so, he kept fiddling with his bonds, after all, you never know when you might get lucky.

"My, my, you do have a habit of getting yourself into trouble. But I suppose the handsome ones always do."

Raph jumped at the words. Well, he jumped as much as one can while sitting tied to a pole with your hands behind your back.

"Lilith!"

Raph practically shouted her name such was his surprise. Then, hearing himself out loud and realizing what he'd just done, his eyes went wide and he instantly looked at the open tent flaps expecting the entire camp to come flooding in at any moment.

"Oh relax. I've taken care of that. No one can hear

Comment [G]: Inserted: ?

Comment [G]: Deleted:

Comment [G]: Inserted: ,

us." Still, she moved swiftly as she spoke. Not hurrying but certainly not wasting any time.

Raph could smell orange blossoms as she bent down next to him and undid his bonds.

"How did you know I was here?" Raph said in a hushed whisper. Lilith may have taken care of the noise but there was no point in testing her assertion. Well, at least not any more than he already had.

"That would be telling. And I believe we've already covered that." Raph had a feeling that he was hoping out of the metaphorical frying pan and into the proverbial fire. Lilith was not to be trusted but as a general rule when a beautiful woman shows up to break you out of jail you try not to ask too many questions.

"Follow, stay close to me, and try not to succumb to any more cries of exuberance at my presence; it is far more difficult for me to cloak the both of us than just myself so we will need to be quick and subtle." She paused and gave him an appraising look. "But perhaps later I can make you say my name like that again." Raph was really hoping that it was too dark for the incredibly hot sociopath to see that he was blushing.

Lilith made to exit the tent and Raph was ready to follow her until he remembered something rather important that he had forgotten about. Bea was still somewhere in the camp.

"Wait we have to help the woman I was with."

Lilith gave him a quick shake of her head.

"There's no time. We must go. I can't keep both of us hidden for long."

Raph wasn't sure what Lilith's game was but he

knew she was playing one. Bea had risked her life for him and these people obviously didn't like her all that much. Leaving her would be both wrong and stupid. Either one would have been enough to sway him. Both made him as stubborn as a mountain.

"I'm not leaving without her. Help me or leave me; up to you."

For a second, really just for a fraction of a moment, Lilith's omniscient seductress mask slipped and Raph saw the hate and rage that lived beneath it.

Then it was back with a pleasant smile that frightened Raph even more.

"Of course. I would never expect you to leave your friend. Do you know where she is?"

That was a very good question.

"Um no. But she can't be far. I mean wouldn't they keep all of the prisoners together?"

Lilith gave a shake of her head. A teacher disapproving of a student before answering her own question.

"She is three tents down on the left."

"Oh, well if you knew why ask me?"

"Because there will not always be somewhere around with all the answers and if you do not begin to ask yourself the right questions you will die for lack of foresight."

"Point taken. Can we rescue Bea and get the hell out of here now?"

"As you wish."

Finally, they did exit the tent. Raph bent low and stepped carefully through the camp in his best impersonation of stealthy. That is until he looked over to see that Lilith was walking upright and practically strolling along. Acting as if she didn't have a care in the world.

It was counter-intuitive but Raph forced himself to move as she did, trusting that she knew what she was doing.

They found Bea exactly where Lilith had said they would. Three tents down on the left.

Two soldiers stood guard next to the tiny flap that served as the tent's entrance. Lilith whispered something in their ears and the men slouched down into a deep sleep.

Lilith pulled the flap back and motioned to Raph to go in.

Bea did not look good. Raph was no medical expert but he was fairly sure the term "pretty fucked up" applied. Bruises and cuts covered her face and arms. She was gagged and dried blood matted her short red hair to her head. Her clothes were intact and Raph prayed that meant what he hoped it meant.

Whatever they had done to her had not dulled the sharpness in her eyes. As soon as they entered her gaze locked on them, following their every move.

Raph motioned for Lilith to untie her while he removed the gag. It took her only a second longer than it took him.

Bea said nothing once she was free. She simply stood and rubbed her wrists.

In the softest whisper, he could muster Raph asked her if she was okay. She simply put a finger up to her lips and nodded. She eyed Lilith wearily but seemed to accept her presence for the time being.

Together they moved out of the tent and into the open air. The camp was still. Apparently, they had caught a break and everyone there had the exact same bedtime.

It was two more rights and a left before Raph realized that not quite all the soldiers in the camp had said goodnight.

Four guards stood watch over the exit from the tent maze they had lost themselves in. Raph was certain there would be even more soldiers patrolling the perimeter.

"Can you get by them?"

"On my own yes. With you two along no."

"Well, then we are going to need a distraction."

Lilith frowned for a moment before her face returned to its customarily wicked smile.

"Wait here. Run when you see my signal."

"What signal?"

"Oh my dear boy, can't you tell by now when a woman is sending you signals."

She turned and walked away while Raph was still fumbling for a response.

Instead, Raph said nothing and shifted his gaze to Bea. She was holding up okay and was standing up straighter by the minute. She looked at him, then at the direction Lilith had gone, and then finally back him, this time raising a quizzical eyebrow.

Not knowing what else to do he simply shrugged. Luckily for Raph, Bea weighed her need to know against their need to not be heard by anyone and prioritized the latter. It was painfully obvious to him however that they

Comment [G]: Inserted: ,

Comment [G]: Inserted: ,

Comment [G]: Inserted: ,

Comment [G]: Inserted: ed

would be having a lengthy conversation sometime soon.
If they got out of there alive that is.

The too tense silence didn't last long as they
received Lilith's signal loud and clear.

Now when Raph had said that they were going to
need a distraction he was thinking about letting some of
the horses loose or knocking over one of the tents with its
soldiers still inside. Something easy that would cause a
bit of a fuss while they got away. Apparently, Lilith had
envisioned something a bit grander in scale.

The explosion blinded and deafened him at the same
time. He felt Bea pull at him and he started running in
that direction. After a few seconds, his sight and hearing
returned accompanied by a feeling of pity for whatever
poor bastards had been closer to that blast than he had
been.

As far as distractions went it was a doozy. Raph
doubted there was anybody in the camp who wasn't
dealing with white spots in their vision at the moment and
if there were they certainly weren't going to be looking in
Raph's direction anytime soon.

He was about a hundred yards from the promised
land when that assumption proved to be incorrect.

The earth rumbled under his feet. Trees exploded
upward from Aging from saplings to centuries-old
sentinels of oak in mere moments.

Raph skidded to a stop as he was suddenly blocked
by a wall of bark and bramble.

Bea did the same although far less awkwardly.

"Is there any way through?"

"No. Can you Bend?"

Raph could here shouting closing in on them. He closed his eyes and reached out to the world around him. The air, the earth, the wall of wood and thorns; they were all connected. He tried to envision their path without obstruction. Seeing only air in front of them. But try as he might he couldn't make what he saw in his head reality. He hung his head in shame.

Comment [G]: Deleted:h

"No."

"Then it's a good thing I'm here." Lilith's lithe figure appeared out of thin air. The only apt comparison Raph had that came to mind was a Romulan ship de-cloaking.

It was more than a little unsettling.

Lilith whispered something he couldn't hear and the branches began to part. Forming a narrow tunnel for them to escape through.

"Well, what are you waiting for? Run."

Bea went first, showing neither fear nor surprise. After a moment's hesitation, Raph followed.

Once he was inside, he didn't stop moving letting the adrenaline coursing through him do its thing. His legs were pumping like pistons and Raph reached that point of optimum physical exertion where you also achieve complete mental clarity. And that's when he realized something.

"Aren't they going to follow us?" He yelled between breaths. Hoping Bea or Lilith could hear him.

"Did that though just occur to you? Do not worry, I have taken care of it."

He didn't stop to think just how ominous that sounded. Just like he didn't stop to think about how he could hear Lilith as clearly as if she was standing next to him and how she did not sound even the tiniest bit out of breath. Those were things that could be put on the mounting list of concepts, confusions, and terrors that would keep him up at night later when he had time for insomnia.

Bea got clear of the wood wall first and didn't stop until she reached the actual, not crazily sprouted out of nowhere, tree line.

Raph caught up with her only a few seconds later.

They stood at the edge of the clearing; a ten foot high, twenty-yard thick wall of burning timber between them and their pursuers.

With Bender's around they'd get it under control soon but Lilith had bought them what they needed; time and distance.

Raph looked over his shoulder to thank her but she was nowhere to be found.

"She's long gone. That kind never sticks around. Come on let's get going. We're not far from where we need to be and being long gone from here when they put out that fire isn't such a bad idea."

Comment [G]: Inserted: s

****

Grey clouds filled the sky while thunder rolled in the distance. There was a storm coming. Billy looked around. He was standing on Neutral Ground somewhere on St. Charles. There were crowds everywhere. He could see Voodoo BBQ off a ways down the street. He could hear a marching band start up as someone shouted "TUBAAAAA!!!!!"

He ducked reflexively as beads went flying past his head. Mardi Gras. Billy recovered from his near miss and took a look at the floats going by. It only took him a second to realize it was the Muses parade. That meant it was either the Thursday or Friday before Fat Tuesday. He never could remember exactly when Muses rolled. Raph had always been better at keeping track of the Krewes.

"Well this looks like rather a lot of fun, no wonder you and Raph wish to return here so badly." The voice startled Billy. He turned to face its owner.

A big behemoth of a man stood in front of him. Tai was different than Billy remembered him. He was still huge of course. But he also seemed somehow more solemn and yet also more alive, if that was something that was even possible.

"Tai what are you doing here?"

"I think the more appropriate question would be what are you doing here."

"It's Mardi Gras. Where else would I be?"

"Think back. Where were you before?"

"I was in bed at Alistair's house." The other shoe dropped. "On Avalon."

"Yes."

"So I'm not really here. This isn't happening. I'm dreaming."

"Well yes and no. You are dreaming. But this is also what is happening right now back on Earth."

"That doesn't make sense it was October when we left Earth. We've only been gone a month. I knew Mardi Gras was going to be early this year but not that early."

"Time tends to move differently on different worlds. But that is a rather complicated discussion for another day. We do not have much time and there are more important things to discuss."

Thunder and lightning ripped through the sky. The storm was getting closer.

"Okay, like what?"

"Like the Grail."

"Um. You're right that's more important."

"I thought so."

"So where is it?"

"Unfortunately it's not that simple."

"Why not?" Billy's tone was not full of sarcasm or accusation but rather it possessed a rather rare breed of sincere befuddlement.

"Because there are rules." Billy began to speak. "And before you ask part of the rules are that I'm not allowed to talk about the rules."

"So why are you here?"

"I'm here so that you can answer your own questions."

Billy thought about that for a second.

"That means you think I already know the answers I just don't know that I know them."

"That is a shrewd progression in logic."

"So what do I know? What do I know that I don't know I know?" Billy stood there grasping at straws while the crowd around him screamed for the people on the floats to throw them beads. Then it hit him. "The prophecy!"

Tai said nothing as Billy began to work through the

prophecy in his head. He hadn't realized he'd been reciting it out loud until he got to the last line.

"Worlds and woe they may travel to see, but here on Avalon they first bend knee."

"The first step to finding the Grail is here on Avalon. But I don't know anything about Avalon. Pretty much all I've seen is Ardoth."

"I tore apart the library there was absolutely no mention of Ardoth in the anything having to do with the Grail."

Billy really felt like an idiot. "Because if you were going to hide a weapon with the power to shake the multiverse why would you advertise where everyone should start looking."

"Okay stop that's getting really annoying, even by my standards."

Tai stood there and said nothing. The thunder roared again, even closer this time. Tai looked at it apprehensively.

"You must hurry we don't have much time."

"Okay so the key to the Grail is in Ardoth, but where? It's not exactly a small town and there are no obvious landmarks other than the Towers."

"The huge mysterious towers? The ones that date back to Merlin? The ones no one has ever been able to get into? The ones that seem to have no discernible purpose? Those towers?"

Someone threw a shoe from one of the floats. Just as he had when he had ducked the beads earlier Billy moved with the instincts of a native New Orleanian. With nearly two decades of parade going experience behind him he reached up and snagged the toss by the heel. And as he did suddenly everything made sense to him.

"Holy Shit."

"Precisely."

The thunder roared and lightning flashed across Billy's vision. The storm was so close now. Too close.

A desperate look came across Tai's face. He grabbed Billy by the shoulders.

"Billy listen to me. You must fight through what is coming. You must tell Raphael what you know or all is lost. You must tell Raph!"

Then Tai was gone. And all that was left was the Storm.

316

Chapter 18

Choices

Bea was right about not being too far from where they were going. After only a few hours they came to a large rock face. Instead of going around it Bea ran her hands along it searching for something. Her hand paused. Evidently, she had found what she was looking for. She motioned for Raph to follow then seemed to disappear into the mountain.

Raph was too tired to be startled and decided that with everything else he'd seen in the past month disappearing into solid rock wasn't really all that weird. He ran his hands along the rough slab as Bea had. He took a few steps forward and making sure his hand kept touching the rock.

And then it wasn't. Raph ran his hand over the craggy façade and again it was touching rock until it wasn't. He took a breath and walked into the blank spot in the wall, stepping into a tunnel of blue light as he did.

Well, tunnel of blue light wasn't an entirely accurate description but the tiny crystals embedded in the walls gave one that impression. If he hadn't been tired, beaten, and generally fed up with feeling tired, beaten, and fed up he would have been rather impressed with the beauty of it all.

Bea led the way and Raph was even more grateful for the illumination when it became clear that portions of their journey would require him to bend down to avoid hitting his head. Walking face first into the ceiling at this point of his journey was probably the very definition of an unforced error.

The tunnel was not a large one and they soon emerged from it to the sight of a small woodland area that was dominated by a spattering of small buildings and one large mansion-house. More blue lights lit up the night.

This time Raph actually did take a moment to appreciate the beauty of it all.

"Someone is already here. Stay back until I tell you it's safe." Bea said softly in a way that made sure her voice did not carry to whoever this 'someone' might be.

By now Raph knew better than to argue with the expert tracker and all-around bad-ass so he stayed put as instructed. But truthfully he wasn't scared. He was just tired. Even if they were in trouble he wasn't sure he'd be able to muster the energy for a fight. Instead of worrying

318

Comment [G]: Inserted: ,

then Raph decided to focus his energies on trusting that his friends were here.

He watched Bea as she moved casually through the trees using them to shield her advance from whoever might be looking on. He was certain that he would have to explain Lilith and their escape to her at some point. But he was just as certain she was going to need to explain to him Balyn and their capture. That woman was more than just a closed book. She was a closed book locked in a vault that had been dropped in the Marianas Trench. He wondered what Alistair knew about her that the rest of them didn't.

Raph lost sight of Bea then. Somewhere amongst the trees. She reappeared a minute later holding Lux by the scruff of his neck. Relief flooded through Raph then. The others were here and they were all right. Everything was going to be okay.

"Hey! Let go." The blonde man fidgeted but put up no real resistance to Bea's grip. Raph started walking towards them.

"Lux!"

"Raph! You're alive. Thank Galed!" Lux started to run towards him and Bea had to let him go before she got pulled along with him.

The two young men embraced and Raph thought he was going to suffocate in the bear hug Lux trapped him in. It was rather touching. Raph definitely considered the guy a friend but they hadn't known each other all that long. Raph chalked it up to quick bonding during close calls.

Finally, Lux let him go. Raph noticed something off

in his face. Something wasn't right he could see it in Lux's eyes.

"What's happened? What's wrong? Where are the others?" Raph shook Lux's shoulders as the questions fired out of his mouth at light speed.

"It's Billy. He's- Raph he's sick. We can't wake him."

"Where?"

Lux pointed to the big house at the center of the estate.

Raph didn't remember starting to run towards the house. All of a sudden he just was. He was running faster than he ever had in his life. Faster than he had on any football field. Faster than he had from the Shak'Tah'Noh or from the Northern Camp. He ran without thinking. Moving on pure instinct.

His friend was in trouble.

Raph burst through the doors to the main house.

There was a shriek and a crash and his head snapped towards the noise.

Kara was standing there with a tray at her feet and tea spilling everywhere.

"Raph!"

"Where's Billy?"

"Upstairs. Raph he's-"

Raph didn't hear anything else Kara said. He made for the stairs and bounded up them two at a time.

When he reached the top he made for the first open door he saw, stopping short of the threshold.

After running all the way here he found that he was terrified of walking into that room.

He took a deep breath and did it anyway.

Raph's heart dropped out of his chest.

There on the bed lay Billy. He looked pale. No not pale, white. He looked a ghastly shade of white. Sweat covered his face to the point that it was almost dripping off of him. He was tucked beneath several layers of blankets. Alistair sat next to the bed holding Billy's hand.

"Raph-" There was pain in Alistair's voice. Pain and grief and sorrow. That more than anything broke Raph.

He had faced down a lot in the last month. But the sight of his best friend in that bed, the hopelessness in his Godfather's voice, it hurt like nothing he had ever felt before.

"Alistair. Wha-What happened?" Raph's throat felt rough as he spoke the words. His eyes began to water.

"He's been poisoned. I don't know when or how, but he's been poisoned. That I'm sure of." His godfather's soft voice was heavy with sadness and regret.

"Can't you do something? Heal him somehow. Use the force or whatever the fuck it is you do to make him better." Anger began to boil up within Raph. Anger and fear.

"Raphael I can't. Healing by way of Bending is difficult in the best of situations. Without knowing the real cause of his sickness and more importantly without him being conscious to help with the process there's just no way to help him that way." Alistair would not meet Raph's eyes as he spoke

"That's bullshit and you know it, Alistair. You're always holding out on me, not telling me the whole truth because you think you know best. Not this time. This is Billy. You're going to help him or so help me god

321

Alistair...." Raph didn't realize he was screaming until he heard his rage echo in the silence.

"Raph please..." Finally, the Alistair looked him in the eyes. The great Fox of Avalon was weeping. "I don't know how to help him. I swear I don't."

Raphael embraced his godfather and tears flowed from him too. Eventually, the tears stopped coming and Raph was forced to ask the question that he had never wanted to ask of anyone.

"How long does he have?"

Alistair regained his own composure and gave a small solemn shake of his head. "If his condition doesn't worsen? A week at best. Maybe less."

"So what do we do?" The despair was audible in Raph's voice. As audible as the resignation in Alistair's response.

"We pray for a miracle."

Alistair left Raph alone with his best friend.

****

The fickle light of day faded from the room, replaced by the immutable cloak of night. Grief muffled the sounds of life emanating from some distant world. A distant world it must be, because his world did not stretch beyond this room. It was here, trapped by four walls and drowning in melancholy.

For two days Raph had sat in this room, waiting for some sign that his friend might recover from the sickness that consumed him. There seemed to be no such sign coming. If anything Billy's condition had worsened. His fever had spiked and he'd taken to moaning in his sleep.

The others came by occasionally. Sometimes to check on Billy and sometimes to check on Raph. Kara brought him food and did her best to get him to eat. Alistair came with fresh cold towels every couple of hours in an effort to keep Billy's fever down. Bea wandered by every hour or so and watched him from the hall, never coming inside. It was Lux that Raph most appreciated though. When he wasn't out patrolling the perimeter he came by and sat with Raph telling the occasional joke. They were mostly awful and not very funny at all but Raph appreciated the effort all the same. Mostly because he thought Billy would have.

"It's funny. People always thought I was the one who looked out for you. Made it seem like you were my sidekick or my pet or something. Just a stray I picked up and decided to take care of. But they never got it. They never saw you for who you really were. For what you brought to the table. The consummate optimist. The true believer. You're my rock, Billy. You always stand up for me, always have my back. You believe in me and make me believe in myself in the process. You came here, risked your life, and wore yourself down without complaining because of me. Because of our friendship. People don't do that Billy. They just don't.

I remember first semester freshmen year, not even a month into school, we were in Mr. Gisen's honors algebra class. It was a game day so I was in a shirt and tie and I got up to the board to solve a practice problem and I get the whole thing right except I forget to carry a four. So my factoring is off and my answer comes out wrong. An honest mistake. I was just moving too fast, not double checking my work. Mr. Gisen smugly corrects me and the whole class starts giggling. Whispering things like 'jock' and 'meathead', acting like I'm just some stupid football player. They were mean and my feelings were really hurt.

> Comment [G]: Inserted: ,
>
> Comment [G]: Inserted: ,

But after class, you stopped me at my locker and you told me they were just jealous because I had a lot of things going for me and they only had the one. You promised me that we'd work hard and set the curve on the next test just to piss them off. And we did. We did so well Mr. Gisen had to give us a hundred and ten percent just to fix it so his favorites didn't end up with C's."

Raph leaned in and put his hand on Billy's. It was hot and clammy. He gripped it. Not too hard but tightly enough that he hopped Billy knew that he was there.

"A man cannot be said to succeed in this life who does not satisfy one friend."

Tears filled Raph's eyes as he squeezed his friend's hand.

"Isn't that how the quote goes? I can't remember. You were always more of a Thoreau fan than I was."

Suddenly Billy's head began to shake and he started mumbling as if he were having a nightmare.

"The Lion-" The words came out as a rasp, all scratchy and dry. Raph leaned in close to try and make out what Billy was saying.

"Billy?" Raph stood and tried to steady his friend.

"The Lion, the Fox and the Faithful Friend." Billy began thrashing around, flailing his arms and jerking his head from side to side.

"Billy?" Raph was scared. He didn't know what to do. "ALISTAIR! SOMEONE HELP!!"

"On Avalon, they first bend knee." At first, Raph didn't know what Billy was talking about. He was too worried to let the words register properly. But after a few seconds, he realized why they sounded familiar.

"The prophecy. Billy, can you hear me? What about the prophecy?"

"The towers…. So stupid….. It's in the towers." The sound of his friend's voice managed to cut him like a knife and fill him with hope all in the same moment.

"Billy, can you hear me? It's Raph. It's gonna be okay buddy. Can you hear me?"

"Gotta tell Raph….It's in the towers…..There all along."

Then as abruptly as he began Billy stopped and became completely still, fading back into a deep sleep. Raph put his hand to Billy's forehead. He was burning up.

For the first time in two days, Raph left Billy's side. Screaming for Alistair as he did.

****

Quietly and carefully Lux moved through the dense foliage. He'd been out here for hours, scouring the woods for any sign of potential trouble. From the way things had been going since he'd joined up with the group trouble really meant anyone who wasn't them. If there was a faction on Avalon the Fox hadn't made an enemy of yet, Raph probably had. He didn't blame them. It just made life a lot more interesting.

Lux wasn't thrilled being stuck on these patrol duties but with everyone's attention focused on Billy someone needed to take care of it. At least he wasn't alone. Bea was out here somewhere and even though she always insisted on scouting on her own it was still nice to share the workload with someone. Especially someone as good as Bea. She'd gotten the drop on him multiple times since they'd started. It was as annoying as it was impressive.

It made him anxious staying in the same place this long. The Shak'Tah'Noh were out there somewhere.

G.R. Linden

Along with two armies that wouldn't much care what they had to say if they were captured. Lux would have preferred to put some distance between them and all of that.

Comment [G]: Inserted: ,

Comment [G]: Inserted: ,

But Billy's life was in danger and they didn't seem to have much of a choice. Even if that were not the case he had promised his father that he would follow and obey the Fox and this was the path the Fox had chosen.

He wondered what his father was doing right now. At this time of night, he was probably already in bed. Or maybe he was sitting up, wondering what adventures Lux was having. A little more than a month adventuring and Lux was already homesick. He knew he could leave anytime he wanted. Just up and walk away. Nobody wanted him dead. In fact, he doubted that any of their enemies actually knew his name.

But no matter how much he might want to go home he knew that he couldn't. If he abandoned his friends he would never be able to look at himself in the mirror again. Let alone stand to see the look of disappointment in his father's eyes.

No these people were his friends and what they were doing was important. He had sworn to follow the Fox. It was his own fault if he had been too naïve to understand the enormity of what that really meant.

He was about to head back when he spotted a piece of torn clothing on a nearby branch. Lux paused and took a deep breath. This had just stopped being a normal patrol. Taking extra care with every step me moved to the ragged strip of cloth.

The piece was too ragged to have been deliberate.

Meaning he could probably rule out it being placed here as a marker or signal. He checked the ground around it. There were multiple tracks some of which appeared to indicate that someone was running away from someone else.

That was not a good sign. Cautiously he followed the trail taking great pains to ensure no one could get around him while also vigilantly checking to make sure he did not accidentally stumble into whoever it was he was following.

The process was slow and arduous. It took him nearly an hour to travel what he normally would have covered in ten minutes.

His patience and persistence were rewarded with the most horrible sight he had ever seen. A sight that he would have given his eyes never to have seen in the first place.

The camp held five tents. Two on each side and one at the head. Smoke still rose from the smoldering fire. Body parts were strewn about everywhere. Carelessly, as if they were toys left behind by a petulant child. They were mutilated and deformed. It was impossible for Lux to determine how many people they had been.

His stomach turned and he had to swallow down his own vomit. The whole scene reeked of death. Rancid flesh and stale blood.

His eyes watered at the stench. At least he tried to tell himself that was all they watered from. If he could have he would have curled up into a ball and wept.

Despite that, he moved in closer to get a better look. He didn't think he could feel any worse but as he was able to examine the mutilated body parts more closely he realized he could. Because they weren't just mutilated. They were partially eaten.

And now Lux knew what had happened. One of this group had gone off. For firewood, for a piss, didn't matter. Because they'd encountered one the Phage. They'd run and led it straight back to their friends.

Lux's heart was ready to beat out of his chest. He wanted to turn and run. He wanted to scream. Either of those would get him killed. Worse. They'd get him eaten alive.

He took as deep a breath as he dared and focused his thoughts on everything his father had ever taught him. Despite himself, he took one last look at the image that would haunt his nightmares for a lifetime and faded back into the woods.

He'd been moving for about a quarter of an hour when the sound of rustling leaves made him freeze. Lux focused all of his attention on listening to the area around him.

He could definitely hear leaves moving and branches being broken.

Slowly he pulled out his hunting knife. Careful not to let the metal scrape against the edges as he did.

Lux waited like that blade drawn, crouched in the bush, heart beating out of his chest. He waited like that for a lifetime praying to every deity he'd ever heard of that when they found him he would die quick. He waited like that until the forest neighed.

The noise startled Lux which was impressive considering he'd been waiting for supernatural cannibals

Comment [G]: Inserted: ,

to jump out of the bushes and eat him.

And then it neighed again.

More confused now than terrified Lux stood and made his way to the sound.

And standing there, drinking from a tiny creek, was a great big white mare.

She had scratches all over her body and blood covered a good deal of her coat. If Lux had to guess a good amount of that blood belonged to her previous owners back at the camp.

All reason said to leave the poor thing out here to fend for herself. Lux wouldn't be able to move quickly or quietly with her in tow. But if he left her out here the Phage might find her and eat her and no amount of logic could make Lux leave any creature to that fate.

"Come on girl, I guess you're coming with me."

It was well past midnight when he finally made it back to Alistair's.

The others were waiting for him. All had worried looks on their faces and it made him feel a little better that they cared. That feeling was especially strong when he looked at Kara and the tears she was trying to hide. But only a little better. After what he'd seen he knew he'd never be the same man again. They went inside and so he could tell them his story. He just hoped when he was done they weren't as terrified as he was.

****

"I confirmed what the boy said. It's the Phage. A horde of them. And they are headed in this direction. I counted at least two dozen there could be more. " Bea set her cloak and staff down on the heavy wooden table.

G.R. Linden

"Thirty I would guess. Seven families of five make up a host. And we killed one family on our way here." Alistair was drinking tea at the far side of the table. At some point, Kara had dug out an antique serving set.

"Are they responsible for what happened to Billy?" Raph held out hope that there might still be another path than the one he had chosen.

"Perhaps." Alistair cleared his throat. "Almost certainly. And I don't believe their presence here to be an accident."

"You think they tracked the poison here and waited till they had the numbers for an overwhelming assault." Bea did not phrase her words as a question.

"It seems the most likely scenario." Alistair's cup made a jarring ring as he set it down on the small plate in front of him.

"Is there anything they can do or anything they have that can cure Billy?" Raph felt he knew the answer before he even asked the question.

"I doubt it. No. These are creatures of destruction and death. It would not occur to them to make someone better." Alistair stood and began pacing back and forth in front of his chair.

"Then nothing's changed. I leave tonight." Raph's statement made his Godfather stop and glare bullets at him.

"What is he talking about?" Bea hadn't moved from where she had set her things down. The only concession she had made in her rigid posture was to fold her arms over her chest.

"Billy said something in his sleep. He said the Grail's in one of the great Towers of Ardoth."

"That is not what he said. You told me he repeated

330

Comment [G]: Deleted:e

some phrases from the prophecy and then just repeated towers over and over again. That is not nearly the same thing as clearly stating the Grail is in the Towers." Alistair was trying to be logical but he couldn't keep the edge from his voice.

"You weren't there. You didn't hear him. I know Billy. I know what he was trying to tell me. I'd bet my life on it. And I'm pretty sure he just bet his."

"Even if he was trying to tell you the Grail was there. You have no idea if that's true or not. At best it's a guess at worst it's a fever dream that ends with you both dead." This time Alistair's exasperation was plain for everyone to see.

"I'm going Alistair and that's that."

"When do we leave?" The question came from Bea and might have been the closest thing to affection he'd ever seen the woman show.

"We don't. I do." Raph leaned back in his chair and tried to look confident. He very much doubted that it worked. Especially considering Alistair's reaction was to walk over and get right in his face.

"Don't be a complete fool. You're a terrible woodsman. And since every guard in the city has a description of you there's no way for you to get in without being arrested. On top of all that you have no idea what to look for once you get there. One of us must go with you." Raph stood and walked away from his Godfather.   When Alistair was done he turned back around and addressed the whole room.

"No. If that many of these Phage are coming here you'll need all of you to protect Billy and each other. I don't need a woodsman I can take the horse Lux brought back. Nobody here rides better than I do I would bet.

331

Besides I have a feeling I'm going to pick up some help along the way."

"Raph-" Alistair was almost pleading with him now.

"Trust the Universe Alistair. I can do this." Raph tried to keep his words gentle and free of the fear that lay just under his calm features.

"He's right. We can't move Billy and it will take all of us to face the Phage. Even if we manage it the boy will die without the Grail. You brought him here and drove him to this quest. We can spare only one and he's the one it has to be." Raph was thankful for Bea's support.

Alistair looked around the room and saw that he had been overruled. He shook his head sadly and conceded defeat.

"Fine. It is decided then. Raph will go after the Grail while the rest of us defend the estate. Let's not waste any more time talking about it then. There are preparations to be made."

Raph had gotten his way but as he prepared to go he noticed that his godfather could not look him in the eye.

****

The wine danced on his tongue, decadent and delectable. Which was more than could be said for some other things he had partaken of this night. Jack enjoyed the feel of the goblet in his hand, watching the ruby red liquid swirl as he did. It was a subtle pleasure, one capable of adapting to any situation. Sadness, remorse, contentment, whimsy. Whatever your mood your psyche could take this sensory information and use it to accentuate those feelings. It was rare that Jack found a behavior that versatile. It reminded him of himself.

Which might explain why he enjoyed it so much.

There was a light rapping at his bedroom door.

Jack threw a robe over himself and answered.

"Sir Trelgrove to see you m'lord."

"Hmm a day earlier than I expected. Eager beaver that one. Yes, thank you please show him to the sitting room and inform him that I will be with him presently."

"Very good M'Lord."

Jack had been expecting the man since his performance at the last council meeting but he thought it would take another bit of news before he was ready to make his move. Jack yawned. Sir Trelgrove was going to be boring and predictable. Jack hated boring and predictable but he forced himself to remember that it was early days yet. All of this maneuvering was really just a way to put himself in position for the game to come. Against players much more worthy of his skill. He channeled his boredom into his character and headed downstairs.

Jack entered the sitting room with a flourish, studiously combining the fawning society fob with the disinterested entitlement of nobility. It was an air that was almost impossible for anyone to imitate and yet came so naturally to those born to wealth and power. But Jack was not anyone. Jack did it with aplomb.

"My dear Sir Trelgrove what an honor it is to welcome you into my home. You must forgive my delay I needed to make myself presentable for such an esteemed guest."

The thin man rose to greet him with a rather weak handshake. Jack matched it and lessened his grip by a hair. Allowing the other man to be the stronger of the pair. Sir Trelgrove wouldn't notice anything peculiar, in his mind he was the superior creature here. Jack wondered how many firm handshakes had resulted in this man's instant ire.

Out of everyone on the council, Jack liked Sir Trelgrove the least. It was unfortunate that he was the most likely of them to make it out of this alive. Jack made a note to himself to remember to kill this man once he was done with him out of principle if nothing else.

"It is you who do me the honor, Sir. You are after all one of the Lords of the Tower and I a mere councilmember."

"Mere? Nonsense. You represent the High-town. You are the voice of the real power of this city. Why we even give the rest of the rabble a voice I will never understand but tradition is tradition I suppose."

"Nonetheless I thank you for receiving me at such a late hour."

"Of course what can I do for you tonight?"

"Well, I was hoping to get your read on the current state of the council. It seems like events have been spinning out of control of late and given your recent support of the Wizard Carl in our most recent vote I thought that you and I may be cut from a similar cloth."

"Yes, I thought that whole vote was rather insulting. After all hadn't I just been to the camp? It was all there in my report. The Wizard Carl was completely confident in his abilities to win the day and send those northerner's scurrying. And then Sir Geir has the audacity to doubt my assurances and sends his pet Sir Garret to go steal the

334

Comment [G]: Inserted: a

Comment [G]: Inserted: ,

glory after the Wizard Carl has done all the work. It's completely unacceptable. It's worse than that its bad manners."

"My sentiments exactly. That is why I came to you. Sir Geir is out of his depth. It's obvious to anyone with sense enough to see it. And perfectly understandable. The attempted assassination at his home, the attack on the Sha'Dral, the threat of invasion it's enough to overwhelm anyone but the greatest of men. He could have handled all once I'm sure but he's not a young man anymore. We need someone with fewer years weighing him down. Someone who can see the big picture. Someone with fire."

"With fire yes. Yes, I like the sound of that but who? Lady Tam is ill-suited to leadership and Sir Garret is Sir Geir's creature through and through." Jack took a pause, and spoke quietly and with great reverence. As if he had just this moment been given a divine epiphany. "You Sir Trelgrove. You are the man to lead us through such trying times."

"You are too kind and I admit I have considered the possibility but I am meant to be more of an adviser to greatness. A humble servant to this great city. You on the other hand. With your style and your charm and your clarity of vision. This is what you were born for."

"Me? Why Sir Trelgrove I would hardly know where to begin."

"And that is why you will have advisers."

"And what about Sir Geir?"

"These are perilous times. We must be prepared to turn tragedy into opportunity."

Comment [G]: Inserted: .

Comment [G]: Inserted: ,

Comment [G]: Inserted: -

Comment [G]: Inserted: ,

Comment [G]: Deleted:,

Comment [G]: Deleted:a

Jack did not respond. Careful to appear as if he were pondering the man's words with the profound wisdom of a shallow mind. Trelgrove had pushed as far as he would tonight which as it turned out had been pretty far. Let the man see his contemplation and take it as a win. There was no point in pushing it any further. After all, he had just shown up unbidden at Jack's door and expressed a desire to do exactly as Jack wished him to do. It wasn't his fault he didn't understand that.

Apparently, Jack's acting job was a good one because his visitor began to make his exit.

"I will take my leave. All I ask is that you think on my words and prepare yourself for the possibility that Ardoth may need you and need you soon."

With that Sir Trelgrove allowed himself to be shown out.

Jack took another moment to enjoy the feeling of his wine goblet between his fingers. He smiled, finished the glass, and went back upstairs.

"Who was that?" His companion had awoken and was waiting for him by the bedroom door. Her naked body seductively outlined by the flickering candle she held.

"Just one of the servants looking to get an advance on his pay."

Jack let his robe drop to the floor letting his new conquest enjoy her own eyeful.

"Really? Because it sounded like Ferris was trying to get you to make a move on Sir Geir."

"Now Amelia you weren't eavesdropping were you?" He turned her around and gave her rough slap on the ass. "Because that would require me to punish you."

She pressed her body back into his as his hands reached to caress her breasts, kneading them as she arched her back for him.

Jack made sure she could feel his hot breath working its way up her neck.

When he began to tease her earlobes that's when she moaned.

Breathlessly she begged "Yes punish me Lord Protector. Punish me"

He shoved the Guildess Corwynn down on the bed and began to do just that.

These people were so easy.

****

Raph rode hard and fast. Covering in a night's ride what had taken him days of walking through the dense underbrush. If Bea was right then the Northerners and the Southerners would be far too busy with each other to pay him any mind. As for bandits if they could catch him they could have him. Raph was a man possessed.

Horseback riding, ballroom dance lessons, philosophy, and fantasy literature. All things that had come in handy lately. All things Alistair had encouraged him to pursue growing up. Insisted upon in the case of horseback riding. Alistair had been training Raph all this time. Every time he thought he had made peace with his Godfather's lies a new one came to light and pissed Raph off all over again. There would be no forgiveness this time. Not if Billy died.

Raph pulled up at the sight of a lone rider blocking his path ahead. It was dark, but even so, there was no

337

mistaking that silhouette.

Which was good since Raph had been expecting her.

She seemed to have a habit of showing up when he was in trouble or about to be. It seemed only logical that she would appear now as he was stupidly rushing headfirst into an entire city full of danger. The truth was he needed her help desperately and had been counting on it. He just needed her not to realize that just yet.

Cautiously he eased his horse to where she was waiting for him.

"I don't have time for your games right now Lilith. I have to get to Ardoth and I've no time to waste." To prove his point he tried to edge his horse by her but Lilith re-positioned her own gelding to block him.

"I know that's why I'm here. The Southern army is defeated. The Northern army prepares to march on the city. In a few hours, Ardoth will begin prepping for a siege. Do you really believe that you can make it through that on your own? Let me help you. I know ways into that city that even the Knight Protector cannot fathom."

"And why should I trust you? What do you get out of this?" Raph felt like every cliché hero asking their one-time nemesis to be their ally. Except this wasn't a comic book or television show character doing a heel-turn. This was Billy's life on the line and these questions needed to be asked.

"The only thing I've ever wanted. To help you achieve your destiny." She looked sincere. On the other hand, she had looked sincere every time Raph had ever seen her so maybe Raph just wasn't fully cognizant of what looking sincere actually was.

338

Comment [G]: Inserted: ,

Comment [G]: Inserted: ,

"Why? What do you gain?"

"My continued existence. The Shak'Tah'Noh would end it all. Myself included. You will need many allies in the days ahead. You may not have the luxury of liking them all."

"Perhaps, but I'll need to be able to trust them."

"And what about the Fox? Do you trust him?" The question brought Raph up short. "He has told you far more lies than I have. I revealed myself willingly, without duress. He only shared with you who he really was, who you really were, when forced to by circumstances."

Raph really hated that she had a point. Sensing Raph's hesitation she pounced with the only argument that she had needed to make.

"I have laid out my good intentions but the truth is that they don't matter. If you want to save your friend, you need to get into the city. You do not know how to do that. I have told you that I do. Trust me or not. Believe me or not. On your own, you have a zero percent chance of success. With me, it's higher. So you will accept my offer."

Comment [G]: Inserted: ,

Everything she said was true. And he had already done that math before leaving Alistair's. But he needed her to see him struggle with the decision. It was the only way to keep her from realizing just how far she had gotten her hooks into him. After a long pause, he gave her his answer. Hoping he hadn't overacted the moment.

"Fine. Let's Ride. You Lead."

So they rode. A few times Lilith slowed her horse in an attempt to converse but every time she did Raph sped on by her. Forcing her to retake the lead. He wasn't in the

339

mood for talking. And he most especially wasn't in the mood for a verbal sparring match. He had no idea what laid ahead but he doubted being edgy and pissed off would do him any good.

Dawn was beginning to break over the horizon and The Four Great Spires of Ardoth had just come into view when Lilith led them off the road and to a little farm. She hopped off her horse and led him to the stables. Raph did the same.

"These people are friends of mine. They'll take care of the horses until we come back for them. From here we go on foot."

"I was afraid you were going to say that."

Raph stroked his mare gently and made sure she was all set up for a proper rest before stepping outside the stable. Lilith appeared a few minutes later and without conversation began to walk back towards the road.

"You know what I don't get?" Raph was as surprised as Lilith that he had started speaking.

"No. What don't you get?" Surprised or not at least she was willing to play the straight woman for him. It was possible she was bored.

"I don't get how you guys always have a network of spies everywhere. All of you. Alistair, Bea, you, every sage or savvy fantasy character I've ever read about. Everybody has this vast network of people who owe you favors. How do you maintain something like that? It just seems ridiculous to me."

"Well I don't know about everyone else but I manage it by providing people with my services when they are at their most desperate and making my price so

340

Comment [G]: Inserted: f

high that they are forever indebted to me."

Raph gulped at that explanation. It hit far too close to home.

"So basically what we're doing now is a regular occurrence for you?"

"This? No this is special. Great men have great needs. And I would only go to such lengths for a great man."

That seemed like as good a time as any to let the conversation die.

It took them almost a full day of walking to reach Ardoth. Raph did not say another word the rest of that walk.

When they arrived at the gigantic tent city at the edges of the city Lilith led them off the road and toward the fringes of the makeshift encampments.

Somewhere along the way she picked up a shovel and handed it to him. Raph was too bewildered to react.

Finally, they stopped. She stomped on the ground twice before moving back and pointing to where she had pounded her foot.

"Dig."

Raph looked around but it was already beginning to get dark again and no one was paying any particular attention to them so he did as he was told.

A few minutes later and he heard the tell-tale clang of metal. He shoveled off a bit more dirt before Lilith came over and gently pushed him out of the way. She reached down and pulled the trap door up.

The last daylight was fading fast and Raph could barely see the faintest outlines of a rope ladder like the one he used to get out of Mid-Town after the ambush.

Raph wondered just how many secret ways there were in and out of this city.

"Well, are you just going to stand there looking handsome or are you going to get that cute little butt moving."

Raph begrudgingly responded to the sexual harassment and carefully began his descent of the rope ladder. Being able to see would have been a plus but he was able to handle it all right even in the dark.

When they reached the bottom Lilith lit two torches and handed one to Raph, effectively killing his night vision just as his pupils had adapted.

Still light was better than no light.

Raph was fairly sure that they were in a secret tunnel and not a sewer. Which was too bad because at least the sewer would have had an excuse to smell this bad.

Lilith began to walk and Raph followed in silence.

Raph had never been great at distances but he guessed they been at it for about a mile when the tunnel began to slope upwards.

It was another half mile before they came to the end of the tunnel and a giant metal door.

Lilith whispered a few words and the door creaked open. She motioned Raph on ahead of her.

He left the tunnel behind and entered an empty basement that would have been large enough to rent out as an extra room.

He turned back to Lilith as she was starting to shut the door behind them

"No, you're going back." Raph made his voice cold

as iron. He called it his 'Don't Fuck with Me' voice when he practiced it in the mirror back home.

"Don't be silly I'm coming with you. You need my help." Apparently, he should have practiced it a bit more.

"Wrong I needed your help. Past Tense. I needed you to get me into the city and now I'm in the city. Congratulations you kept your word but from here I go it alone."

"Don't be an arrogant fool. You don't know what awaits you. What you might face. A Bender for a month and you think you can take on alone something that has killed off everyone else who has sought it."

"Yes. Because I'm supposed to. And I'm guessing Merlin's invitation wasn't meant for Arthur's heir plus one. So I'm going it alone because I think if we both go we both die." Lilith seemed almost convinced by this argument. Too bad Raph didn't care about convincing her. "Also I still don't trust you and I don't need to be worrying about a knife in my back while I confront unknown dangers. Besides I have a job for you."

"A job. What do you take me for? Your errand girl?"

"You are going to back through that tunnel, back the way we came, and all the way back to Alistair's house. I'm going to assume you know the way. Billy needs protecting. The Phage may already have attacked by now but you are going to make sure they survive."

"The Phage? You want me to fight those *things*?" Raph had been prepared for Lilith to present him with any number of reactions. He had not anticipated terror. Too bad. Ally or not his sympathy had worn thin.

"You want my trust you do this and you do it right.

Or we're through forever. Do you understand?"

"Yes."

"Good."

The two of them stood there staring at each other until Lilith made an exasperated noise and opened the door, going back the way they had come.

Raph waited a good, long while before deciding that she had really gone to do as he had asked before exiting himself. The stairs in the corner took him up and out a cellar door and into the cool evening air.

It took him a minute to get his bearings before he realized he was in Mid-town somewhere. Looking up at the towers he picked the one closest to himself and headed towards it.

It was fully night now and the stars shined brightly in the sky. The streets were mostly empty and there wasn't a hint of the city watch anywhere. Consequently, it took Raph no time at all to reach the nearest tower.

He hadn't gotten close to any of the spires before but now that he was here he was overcome by the scale of the thing. The base took up more than a city block and when he looked straight up he couldn't see the top.

"Okay so let's see if I can get inside you."

Raph snickered at himself.

"Phrasing."

He walked around every side of it. Feeling his hands against its unnaturally smooth surface trying to find anything that would let him get inside. When he'd gotten back to where he'd started he hadn't really gotten anywhere at all.

Then he tried every password, phrase, saying he

could think of from open sesame to merlin rocks and came up empty. Finally, it occurred to him that he was an idiot.

"Only the blood of Arthur can find the cup."

Raph went over to one of the nearby storefronts, found a brick with a sharp edge, and gave himself a slight cut across his left hand. Once the blood started trickling out of the cut he placed his hand on the Tower's smooth stone and waited.

The stone shifted back and soon other stones began to follow suit, creating a tall narrow doorway in the wall face. Raph looked around to make sure he wasn't seen before stepping through the doorway. The stones slammed shut behind him and for a brief moment, he was surrounded by darkness before the walls themselves began to light up with a translucent blue.

On the far wall was a small elevator with a stone lever next to it. Well, 'elevator' was a generous way to describe it. It was really a rectangular wooden box with a guard rail instead of a lid. Four ropes were attached to it. Made out of a thick silvery material that Raph didn't recognize. Overall it looked like the type of thing a seven-year-old would make to get his dog up to his treehouse.

But being that he was now locked in a stone tower with no other discernable options, Raph didn't see how he had any choice.

Out of everything really what are the odds that this is what kills me?

Raph had hoped that would be a comforting thought. It wasn't. Still, he gingerly climbed into the elevator and mentally prepared himself to pull the lever.

Comment [G]: Inserted: ,

Comment [G]: Inserted: '

Comment [G]: Inserted: '

Comment [G]: Inserted: ,

If you don't do this you're trapped and Billy dies. So really what have you got to lose?

Raph took a deep breath. Got a good grip on the guardrail. And pulled the lever.

His stomach dropped as the rest of his body flew upwards.

Complete panic came over him while his senses were completely overwhelmed by the velocity at which he was traveling towards the rapidly closing ceiling.

He wanted to shout some clever last words but the acceleration kept him from being able to scream.

In what can only be described as the start of a miracle or the end of a very mean practical joke the elevator's brakes kicked on and rapidly slowed his ascent while still matching his momentum enough that he didn't go flying through the air as it came to a stop at the top of the tower.

Fighting back a sudden case of acute motion sickness Raph opened his eyes. And was surprised by what he found.

Chapter 19

Trials and Tribulations

Raph stood in a small empty room at the very top of the tower. And he knew it was at the very top of the tower because a strip of glass as tall as his hand ran around the room and when he looked out it all he could see was night.

And the tops of the other towers.

"So.......What do I do now?"

The tower rocked and there was a flash of blinding light.

When his vision came back into focus Raph was surprised for the second time in minutes.

In the middle of the room, really cutting the room in two, was a giant wall of crackling blue energy.

A giant wall of crackling blue energy that looked just like the portal Alistair had opened to bring them to

347

G.R. Linden

Avalon in the first place. He looked around the room for
some other egress but found none.

"Well, I guess that answers that question."

Raph considered his options.

Then Raph came to the conclusion that he was not in
possession of an overabundance of them.

He tilted his head slightly and shrugged his
shoulders.

"Fuck it."

Raph walked into the wall of liquid blue.....

........And found himself in some sort of ancient
tomb.

At least that's what it looked like to him. Although
it's not as if he had a lot of experience with ancient tombs
outside of having seen all three of the Indiana Jones
movies multiple times.

But in this case, the stale air, cobwebs, and masonry
were about what you'd expect in the "sacred burial place
of kings" department.

Oh, and the four Raph sized stone sarcophagi that
stood against the walls of the room.

They were a bit of a giveaway.

Each one was chiseled to emulate a creature with the
body of a man and the head of a lion.

As Raph looked around the room a realization hit
him.

Four Walls.

Four Solid Walls.

The portal was gone.

Raph was trapped in this room.

"Okay. Maybe I shouldn't have said fuck it."

Raph didn't panic. There was no reason to go to all

Comment [G]: Inserted: ,

Comment [G]: Inserted: ,

348

this trouble just to bury him alive. There were easier ways to kill him (like that crazy ass elevator).

Which meant this wasn't a trap. It was a test. And if it was a test then Raph could pass it and get himself out of here.

He walked up to the nearest sarcophagus with the intent of examining it for clues but when he got close its eyes began to glow a deep shade of red and a deep, gravelly voice spoke out of nowhere.

> *"My features never change*
> *And I never wear a mask*
> *But each would describe me differently*
> *If you were to ask."*

For once Raph felt like he had caught a break. He could do riddles. One of the first things that he and Billy had bonded over was The Hobbit. They used to have riddle duels like Frodo and Gollum. And while Billy had more book smarts than him, Raph had always been the better lateral thinker. A skill that was absolutely essential to solving riddles. Raph had rarely lost those duels. And he wouldn't be stumped here either.

"Truth. The answer is truth."

The eyes dimmed. Raph hoped that was a good thing. He looked around the room but absolutely nothing had changed. He hadn't expected it to. After all four sarcophagi meant four riddles. Given that he didn't really want to bother with the math on how long his air would last down here he hurried to the next sarcophagus. Getting close to this one had the same effect as the first one only here the eyes glowed green and the voice was more of a baritone than a bass.

> *"It can come in an instant*
> *Or take a lifetime to gain*
> *It does not sit beneath the murk*
> *Rather it rises as the bigot's bane."*

Raph considered the second riddle carefully. The last line set him on the right path but it was the third line that gave away the one true answer out of a couple of dozens. He double checked his answer against the whole stanza before speaking it aloud.

"The answer is understanding."

Again the eyes dimmed and the creepy lion-man sarcophagus thingy was silent. Raph really hoped he was getting these right.

"Right. On to lucky mummy number three then shall we."

The third sarcophagus' eyes glowed yellow and it spoke in the voice of an elderly woman. Or rather it didn't speak so much as the disembodied voice that was emanating from its general direction did.

> *"It can take many forms across the years*
> *Touching all no matter how clever*
> *When found you cannot imagine life without it*
> *And when it is lost it will remain with you*
> *forever."*

Again Raph knew the answer almost instantly. The truth was there was nothing specific in this riddle that guided him to his response. But taking every line of the stanza together and considering the nature of the previous riddles the answer seemed obvious to him. If this had been a math exam he would have gotten in trouble for not showing his work. Luckily it wasn't a math exam.

"Love. The answer is Love."

Nothing exploded and he wasn't dead so he took it as a win and moved on.

The fourth and final sarcophagus followed the pattern of the previous three. Its eyes glowed blue and its untethered voice called out in crystal clear soprano.

> *"I am both the path and the destination.*
> *A faithful companion through which all is translated.*
> *Within me you will find the answer to all questions;*
> *Without me, you will never be sated."*

The Reverse Sphinx's riddle was less of a riddle and more of a philosophical musing. Which was a problem. Because unlike riddles philosophical musings tended to have more than one right answer. The stanza could be referring to any number of things.

Hell, just to start with the answers to the three previous questions would all work.

Raph really enjoyed it when a mental tangent provided him with a useful solution.

"Love, Understanding, and Truth. You are all of those things because they are all the same thing. There's no need to choose. What you possess of one you possess of all three."

A blue portal appeared before him. Raph had no idea where it led, but again it didn't seem like he had much of a choice. Stay here and die or step through and take his chances on the other side. He took a deep breath and stepped into the blue.

****

Preparations went quickly. The Fox wasted no time formulating a plan and giving instructions to the rest of them. In fact, the Fox had spent so little time formulating a plan that Lux was forced to assume that Alistair had spent a great deal of time anticipating an attack similar to the one they were about to defend themselves against.

Lux tried not to dwell on that thought. Especially when there were far more disturbing things to dwell on at the moment.

The plan was for Alistair to hold the front door while Bea and Lux held the canopy walkways and provided cover with their bows from above. Kara would stay in the basement with Billy. If the Phage overran the others Alistair had given her a magic button that he said would lock Kara and Billy in while destroying the house on top of them.

Apparently, this button was linked to a mystical putty Alistair called See Four that he had been setting up all over the house. Lux was not so sure about this but he recalled his father's tales of the Travelers' War and remembered that the workings of Benders was far beyond him.

While Alistair and Bea had been busy with that, Lux had been strategically placing quivers of arrows all around the canopy walking path he would be firing from when the attack began. In yet another example of The Fox's foresight, Lux had found ten quivers with thirteen arrows apiece in the basement. Basement was a loose term, there were enough weapons and supplies lying around that it was far more accurate to call it an armory than a cellar.

Comment [G]: Inserted: ,

Comment [G]: Inserted: ,

Comment [G]: Inserted: ,

Comment [G]: Inserted: a

Another indication that he had been preparing for a siege like this for a long time. Lux supposed it wasn't paranoid if you eventually had to use your preparations.

Nervous energy coursed through him. His last encounter with the phage sat heavy in his thoughts. In that fight, Lux had barely survived one of the Phage while Alistair had held off the other four. He would need a far better showing if he hoped to live through their next attack.

Lux returned to the basement to grab the final group of quivers.

Billy was laid out on a cot in the corner. Kara sat next to him holding a cold compress to his head. Lux caught her eyes following him around the room until her eyes caught his eyes catching her eyes and both of them looked away embarrassed.

He grabbed what he had come down for and began to head for the stairs.

Lux hesitated.

The Phage could attack at any time and there wasn't really time to waste.

But if something did happen Lux didn't want to risk missing his last chance to talk with her. Even if it was only for a few minutes.

She watched him as he walked towards her but Kara said nothing as he approached.

"How is he?"

"Worse. He burns to the touch. If Sir Raph doesn't hurry I fear he will not be in time."

"Raph will return. It's up to us to make sure we're all still alive when he does."

Comment [G]: Inserted: ,

Comment [G]: Deleted: ,

Kara opened her mouth to speak but closed it again without uttering the words she had intended to share. Her eyes drifted past him. Focused on some distant object only she could see.

She took a deep breath and spoke a far simpler question than what she had been unprepared to ask before.

"Is there anything I can do to help?"

There was an earnestness in her eyes that Lux had never seen in anyone else before. She was scared of course but she trusted in the rest of them to protect her.

Shame welled up inside him. When Raph had first stepped in and saved Kara from Xan that fateful afternoon Lux had tried to stop him. Tried to tell him not to get involved.

How could he ever have not wanted to help someone as sweet and caring as her?

"Knowing you're down here, looking after Billy, is help enough."

She nodded. It was a slow, subtle movement of resignation. Her head turned back to her charge and Lux began to leave. Without looking at him she made a request.

"Tell me that it's all going to be okay."

Lux tried to infuse his voice with all the warmth and hope he could muster but he feared that he fell well short of comforting with his response.

"It's all going to be okay."

The words felt hollow as he spoke them.

He hurried out of the basement, not wanting to sit in his embarrassment. He had work to do and Kara was

354

Comment [G]: Inserted: ,

better off without his sloppy attempts at reassurance

It took him what little daylight there was remaining to hide and secure the remaining quivers around the walk. Satisfied that his various caches of arrows were as ready as they would ever be he headed back to the big house and down the stairs to the dining room.

As he turned the corner to get his next assignment he found Bea and Alistair in the middle of an intense conversation.

".....And you think this mystery woman is who Raph is hoping will show up to assist him?"

"She could Bend. And she had little interest in saving me. She was there to assist the boy. We would not have escaped without her."

"I find that hard to believe. I've not known a Northern camp capable of holding you any longer than you wished to be held. Who were they?"

"Balyn" her voice got soft "and Eadric."

"I'm sorry Beatrice."

"I don't want your pity."

"That wasn't what I was offering."

"Whatever you're pushing keep it to yourself. I've set explosives at the tunnel entrance. Multiple trip wires for redundancy. It should give us a few minutes warning and take out a couple of them in the process. I'm going to go double check my weapons."

She stormed out of the room without waiting for a response from Alistair.

"You can come in now."

Lux practically jumped out of his skin. He was about to ask how the Fox had known he was there before he remembered his father's warnings about the futility of questioning a Bender. He remembered another old adage about a Bender's temper and decided to begin with an apology instead of a question.

"I'm sorry I didn't mean to eavesdrop. It sounded private and I didn't want to interrupt."

"Most of what you heard was benign. As for the rest, I will trust to your discretion as I did your father's. Have you completed your tasks?"

"Yes, sir."

"It's okay to be nervous Lux. I think you'd have to be crazy not to be."

"It's just that there are so many of them. The odds just seem to be against us."

"Take a seat." Alistair pointed to one of the chairs at the dining room table and pulled around another chair for himself.

"I'd like to tell you a story. A very long time ago, on a day much like this one, your father and I were trapped on a world with no way out. The enemy was at the gate and they outnumbered us four to one. The attack came that night. Like you, your father had the high ground. He saw that the enemy had burst through our lines and was about to slaughter the civilians we had sworn to protect. He tried to signal but we were pinned. We wouldn't have made it in time. Brun tied a rope to his arrow and rode it down into the fray, cutting off our foes from their targets. He held that door against twelve of their number. When we finally reached him a dozen corpses lay at his feet. Your father saved lives that day. No Bender could have done better."

"He never told me that story."

"I see your father in you. You have his resolve. And his courage."

Alistair put a hand on Lux's shoulder and looked him square in the eye.

"I believe in you. Your father believes in you. Do you believe in you?"

"Yes, sir."

"Good. Now get some rest. Bea will take the first watch and I will wake you when-"

There was a loud explosion in the distance. The ground rumbled and the house shook as the Fox bolted towards the front door as he screamed.

"Positions!"

Lux took off up the stairs and out onto the canopy walk.

He could see them in the distance.

Indistinct figures of death and rot swarming over the forest green.

He raised his bow and pulled an arrow from his quiver.

Then he took three deep breaths and remembered his father.

The Phage had come.

****

Raph emerged back in the tower, or rather a tower. A quick look out the window let him know that he was now in a different tower than the one he had started in.

As the portal he had just exited snapped shut with a thunderclap another portal open in front of him with a blinding flash.

It was enough to leave him blind and deaf for a minute.

When his senses eventually did normalize he again was staring at a single blue wall of shimmering energy.

"Oh good, there's more of those."

In a situation like this if you can't be sarcastic what can you be?

Knowing before he looked that there were no other ways in or out of the spire Raph looked anyway and confirmed that this was indeed the case.

"Right. Let's hope this one's not as eager to kill me as the last one." Raph had a feeling that this would not be the case. But he stepped through the light blue portal anyway.

And emerged in a grand hallway lined with mirrors.

Without turning around Raph knew from the explosive noise that the portal that had brought him here was already gone, but turn around he did and to no surprise he found a simple stone wall cutting him off. Being right was getting to be annoying.

Forward through the hall of mirrors was the only path available to him.

"I guess it's time for a little personal reflection."

Raph felt a moment of relief that no one had been around to hear that particularly cheesy one-liner.

With a fair amount of trepidation, Raph began to walk doing his best to keep his head on a swivel as he did so.

He wasn't quite sure yet how these mirrors were going to cause him bodily harm but he was pretty certain that they were. Of course, if he was lucky the whole thing

Comment [G]: Inserted: ,

could just be one elaborate prank set up by Merlin or whoever to psych him out.

Raph considered that for a second then decided that would piss him off more than one of these mirrors trying to kill him.

Raph considered *that* for a second and decided that he was in a really weird headspace and recent lifestyle changes were probably driving him a bit crazy.

As he started to move past the mirrors he saw his reflection in them. Or at least that's what he thought he saw.

When he passed an image of himself with a bowler hat on, he did a double take.

With fresh eyes, he looked at each of the mirrors. In them, he saw himself but not *him*, him. Rather variations on him. Skinnier, fatter, short hair, long hair, clothes of all kinds, one of them even had on an eye patch.

An eye patch.

Like a pirate.

He'd always wanted to be a pirate.

"Interesting aren't they? All the lives we could have led. All the choices we could have made." Raph's head snapped from the mirror to the startling new voice.

Another of his reflections was standing there. Only this doppelganger was made of flesh and blood. And Raph didn't particularly like the vibe he was picking up off himself.

"I don't know. I'm pretty happy with my life choices so far."

"Are you? You don't think that maybe if you had made a different set of choices, walked a different path

Comment [G]: Inserted: ,

Comment [G]: Inserted: ,

maybe Billy wouldn't be dying right now. Maybe if your mother had made better choices she wouldn't be dead."

The words were clearly meant to press Raph's buttons. And maybe the bit about Billy would have. But way too many people were bringing up his mom these days. It was just way too heavy handed, he expected better of himself. So instead of getting all emo angry rage face, Raph did what you should do to anyone who's actively trying to get a rise out of you. He laughed in his own face.

"Wow, I'm kind of a dick. You must be from a reality where I have no friends"

His double swung hard with his right and Raph barely had time to step back. As it was he caught a glancing blow to the jaw.

That hurt less than the follow up left hook that left him reeling.

Raph knew that if he didn't get his act together this fight would be over soon and with a result not to his liking.

He let the momentum of the second punch carry him around to a full three-sixty, dropping to one knee as he did.

Raph gathered himself before exploding upward and outward at his opponent. Head up, legs driving through his target just like he'd been taught. A pure tackle.

Raph followed up with something that he'd never actually been taught but had seen enough MMA to know it was what he needed. The Ground and Pound.

Raph rained blows down on his own evil face. Wailing on a creepy maniacal grin that he hoped he himself had never worn.

If the pummeling was having an effect on his twin it wasn't showing whereas Raph's hands were quickly becoming bloody and raw as he punched what felt like stone.

If you've ever been in a fight you understand they are not the long protracted battles you see on television. They're fast. Because brawling takes a lot out of you and eventually one tired guy finishes off one totally exhausted guy.

Twenty seconds of throwing down big time punches and Raph was exhausted.

That's when DoppelRaph made his move.

The double barely missed Raph's kidney with his first punch and landed a jab to the face with his second.

Raph rolled off and away and the two men got to their feet at about the same time.

Raph's arms felt like lead but he got them up in a defensive position anyway.

He could have really used some evil villain monologing right now to give him an opportunity to rest but his foe stayed silent and pressed his advantage.

Raph backpedaled staying out of range of a jab-jab-uppercut combination. He countered with his own right-left-right set of jabs. They landed but did no damage to his evil self.

DoppleRaph took the blows and let Raph get in close.

His powerful push kick caught Raph right in the chest.

Raph went flying backwards, smashing a mirror as it

broke his fall.

His double let out a grunt and nearly tripped over his own feet.

A flash of insight and Raph realized he might be going about this fight completely the wrong way. *He's a reflected image. His power comes from my unrealized reflections.*

Raph tested his theory by shattering the mirror closest to him.

Again his doppelganger staggered.

"Gotcha."

Evil Raph roared as he lunged for Raph's neck.

Raph fell back and kicked up his leg up, using his double's momentum to flip him through the air.

Scrambling to his feet Raph began to run throwing mirrors to the ground as he did. All toll he counted twenty-two. Eleven on each side of the room. He'd broken five more for a total of seven when Evil Raph tackled him from behind.

Raph hit the ground hard and his breath flew out of him. He didn't wait to get it back.

Instead, he quickly threw two successive elbow shots behind him and rolled out from underneath himself.

He tried to stand but his double grabbed at his ankle and kept him on the ground.

Raph started kicking at his evil face until the familiar fingers digging into his leg let go.

He got to his feet and picked up the closest unbroken mirror, the last in the row nearest him and swung it at his doppelganger. The mirror shattered along with the three it and evil him went crashing into.

362

The Seeker

Eleven down, eleven to go.

Raph used the time he'd bought himself to sprint down the second line of mostly unbroken mirrors.

Twenty seconds. Another seven mirrors.

Raph was now back where he had first arrived with his bad self just getting to his feet on the other end of the hall.

Hurriedly Raph broke the three remaining mirrors on his side of the hall. He was pretty sure that in the last mirror he broke he was a cyborg.

He wondered if somewhere in another universe Pirate Raph and Cyborg Raph were having this same fight.

Twenty-one mirrors down. One to go.

The one Evil Doppelganger Raph was standing in front of.

Raph smiled. Fourth Quarter time and all he needed was a sack to win the game.

The two Raphs ran at each other, but where DoppelRaph jumped in the air for a flying superman punch Raph did what he did best. He used a spin move and made a beeline for the quarterback.

"See ya. Wouldn't want to be ya." And with that schoolyard taunt, he smashed the last of the mirrors.

His doppelganger shattered into a million tiny little shards of glass, screaming as they fell to the floor.

Raph stood there panting as silence fell over the hall of broken glass.

"Well, I really hope that was the boss of this level. Oh magical wall of shiny blue, where are you?"

His ride appeared right on cue. Which was a little

Comment [G]: Inserted: ,

Comment [G]: Inserted: ,

disappointing.

"What no bathroom break?"

Raph had kind of been hoping for a bathroom break.

In protest, he took a few minutes to catch his breath. When his lungs stopped feeling like fire every time he inhaled he decided it was the best he was going to get and stepped into the blue.

****

Like a pack of starved half-mad wolves they came.

A Horde of the Phage.

Running on all fours they swept through the woods with inhuman swiftness, heightened speed and agility on frightful display.

Lux took his position on the left side of the second story canopy walk. He saw Bea draw her bow on the opposite side. Alistair stood between them, on the ground guarding the main entrance to the house.

Alistair did not look at them but shouted orders knowing they were there.

"Hold!"

Explosions ripped through the trees as the Phage triggered more of Bea's trip wires.

"Hold!"

The explosions did nothing to slow the cannibals advance. The swarm was almost upon them.

Lux tried to remember everything his father had taught him about archery and combat. The importance was to stay calm and breathe regularly. Pick out your targets. Shoot where they will be not where they are.

"Hold!"

They were close enough now that Lux could make

out individual members of the Horde. Their faces were twisted with hate and rage. And hunger.

"Fire!"

Lux loosed and took the Phage closest to him in the eye. He felt a sudden flush of heat that told him the Fox had taken his own command literally. Unholy screams filled the night.

Lux pulled and loosed as rapidly as he could without sacrificing accuracy for speed.

Of his next five arrows, one was a headshot, one struck torso, two struck limbs, and one missed altogether.

None dropped their target.

The Phage had noticed him now. Or at least the ones with arrows sticking out of them had.

Five of their number broke off from the pack and headed towards him.

They were a lot harder to hit now that they were actively trying to dodge him.

When he had emptied his quiver he dropped it and picked up the spare by his feet.

He slowly and deliberately gave ground towards his next arrow stash, firing every time his plant foot stepped behind him.

The Phage began to climb the trees around them, skittering upwards towards the canopy and his hanging walk.

Still, he fired arrow after arrow after them as they ascended finally felling one of the bastards. It had only taken two arrows to the same eye socket to do it.

Lux tried to sneak a peek at Bea and the Fox to see how they were doing but every time he managed to knock

Comment [G]: Deleted:1

Comment [G]: Inserted: ,

one of the climbing Phage down to the ground another had recovered and was closing fast. Lux was forced to assume that his companions were still alive. If for no other fact than if they fell he would follow them in a matter of minutes.

Again he switched out his empty quiver for a stashed full one.

The first arrow from his new quiver took one of the Phage in the neck. It choked on its own blood as it fell back to earth.

Lux drew and loosed again catching a Phage leaping from the tree to the walkway in midair. It spun as the arrow took the creature in the shoulder canceling out its momentum and causing it to crash to the ground as well.

The third and fourth arrows joined a pair from the previous quiver in the side of the third Phage to reach the top of its climb. Enough for the thing's entire side to rip open and its innards to fall out.

Still, the horrible creature would not die, slowly crawling towards him, teeth gnashing at the air.

Lux put arrows five and six of his new quiver threw its eyes.

The Phage was still.

Lux was starting to think this was his lucky quiver.

Suddenly the tree the Phage had been climbing exploded in a burst of lightning and fire.

The same tree that was holding up the other end of the walkway Lux was currently standing on.

He turned, put his bow over his shoulder, and ran as the remains of the tree tumbled to the ground. The walkway began to dip and he could feel the wood

Comment [G]: Inserted: .

Comment [G]: Deleted:i

Comment [G]: Inserted: ,

planking giving way beneath him.

While he was still a few feet away from the roof's edge he leaped into the air.

Everything slowed down as the walkway gave way beneath him and he flew through the air. He could hear the sounds of battle all around him but his mind was focused on one thing.

Making it to that roof.

Lux realized he was going to be short.

Then everything sped up.

****

Again Raph found himself back in a different spire than he had been in previously. He closed his eyes and covered his ears in anticipation of the sensory overload to follow. Even with those precautions, his ears were still ringing when the requisite fireworks show was over.

Raph opened his eyes to the familiar sight of another crackling portal and smiled.

"Well, at least we're establishing a pattern."

He stepped into the pool of blue energy and onto yet another strange world.

And standing there, in all its fire-breathing glory, was a dragon. A very large, very scary looking dragon.

"Well, Fuck."

Suffice to say that Raph was not overly pleased with this turn of events.

With his head on a swivel like any good linebacker, Raph scanned the area around him for cover. To his right, about thirty yards away, was a group of large rocks that looked big enough to protect him. Raph broke into a full-on sprint, leaving nothing in the tank, hoping to outrun

Comment [G]: Deleted:t
Comment [G]: Inserted: ,
Comment [G]: Deleted:hr
Comment [G]: Deleted:ugh
Comment [G]: Inserted: -
Comment [G]: Inserted: ,
Comment [G]: Inserted: -

the dragons notice.

He barely made it without becoming barbeque. In fact, the back heel of his left boot was more than a little singed. Raph ducked as close as he could to the largest rock of the formation sheltering him but made sure not to touch it for fear of burning himself. Even taking that precaution the heat was close to unbearable. It had only been a few seconds but much more of this and he might just get baked alive.

Raph tried to block out all of the distractions and open his mind up to the world around him. Hoping that if he could Bend he might just be able to get himself out of the mess he found himself in. Unfortunately being slowly cooked alive by a fire-breathing dragon was not overly conducive to keeping one's focus. So first he concentrated on the heat, or rather he focused on there being no heat.

Breathing in and out slowly he concentrated on one thought over and over.

It's a cool summer's day.
Breathe in.
It's a cool summer's day.
Breathe out.
It's a cool summer's day.

The heat was gone. Raph had faced far worse days during a New Orleans August than what he felt at the moment. Now that he had handled that problem he moved on to the next. Making sure the dragon didn't eat him while he figured out why the portal brought him here.

It seemed a little too on the nose that he was supposed to slay the dragon. If he was that was pretty

368

Comment [G]: Inserted: ,

messed up. Poor guy probably didn't even want to be here. Then again a tiger probably didn't like being in a cage, didn't mean you'd be any less eaten if you fell in with it.

Raph wished he could just talk to it. Infinite worlds and getting a talking dragon was just a step too far. Reality sucked sometimes. Even when you can bend it to your will.

Sensing a break in the dragon fire being breathed in his direction Raph risked poking his head out for a second to attempt a proper appraisal of his situation.

The dragon had indeed stopped its attempts at barbeque Raph and had begun pacing back and forth. Now that Raph had a moment to look where he wasn't running for his life he could see that the dragon had a gigantic manacle attached to one of its hind legs.

The chain was attached to the large tower behind the poor guy. A tower that was scaled down replica of the obsidian tower Raph had come from back in Ardoth. Looking up Raph could see a blue light shining out of its top. Raph began to realize the challenge before him. It was simple, get to the top of the tower and get through the portal.

All he had to do was get past the dragon and climb sixty stories of smooth obsidian. No problem whatsoever.

Raph went back to his hiding spot behind the rock and tried to think this through. The first test had been a group of riddles to work out. It was about using his head. The second test had been about facing his reflection, about the nature of his soul. Mah'Na'Ret. Heart, Mind, Soul. This test was about his heart. But what did that mean?

Raph tried to run through all the things that heart was synonymous with. Bravery, courage, boldness, love, compassion.

That's it. The thought came to Raph all at once.

There was only one option here that would require all of those things: He had to free the Dragon and ask it for a ride.

Since that seemed insane, Raph ran through his thought process again. Unfortunately, he came to the same conclusion the second time through as well.

"Well, if you're going to make a mistake, make sure you make it at full speed." Somehow his football coach's old axiom seemed appropriate given the circumstances.

Except, in this case, he'd be doing the exact opposite. Making a mistake at the slowest speed he could manage. Raph thought it was the commitment to bone-headedness that really mattered.

With every bit of body control, he could muster Raph slowly and carefully moved out from his hiding place behind the rocks and into the open.

"Heeyyy Buddy" Raph tried to put on his best friendly baby/animal talk voice without making himself sound too patronizing. After all just because the dragon couldn't talk didn't mean it wasn't smart. Raph would hate to be eaten simply because he had come off as condescending.

"How we doing fella? That chain looks a little painful. How about we get you out of that thing?"

The Dragon looked at him. Smoke fumed from its

370

Comment [G]: Inserted: t

Comment [G]: Inserted: ,

Comment [G]: Inserted: ,

nostrils. Raph hadn't been incinerated yet. So that was a good sign.

To Raph, it felt as if hours passed as he moved closer to the enormous winged creature. Raph's body was so tight it ached. Sweat practically dripped from every pore. Raph was deathly afraid that any sudden movement no matter how small would startle the dragon. Turning his would be devourer into just his devourer.

Eventually, he made it to the manacle. The dragon's head turned to watch him. A single eye as tall as Raph taking his measure.

Raph tried to put the threat of imminent digestion out of his mind and focus on the problem at hand. The manacle was made of the same smooth obsidian as the tower. There was no lock or mechanism that he could find.

He wondered for a second if it was another puzzle but decided it probably wasn't. After all, that wasn't the point of this particular exercise.

The last time he'd had to get through this obsidian he'd had to bleed on it.

"Well, at least this time I don't have to cut myself." He rubbed his hand over one of the various cuts on his body from his fight with DoppelRaph and placed it on the manacle.

Immediately it fell away and the dragon was free.

The magnificent creature roared and began flapping its wings. Taking to the air and knocking Raph to the ground in the process.

Raph crawled clear, the gale force of the dragon's wings keeping him from standing upright.

Comment [G]: Inserted: ,

Buddy took to the skies, enjoying his freedom. (Raph had decided that the dragon needed a name and he thought Buddy the Dragon had a nice ring to it.)

A few minutes later he returned nuzzling Raph in thanks. Well as a snout could nuzzle an entire person half its size. It was awkward. Raph got a little covered in dragon snot.

Still, it was pretty cute.

When Buddy was done he sat back on his haunches and waited for Raph to speak.

"So Buddy I guess you know a bit about how all this works." Raph pointed to the top of the tower. "Can I get a ride, big guy?"

Buddy snorted what Raph assumed was assent.

When he was positioned on Buddy's back and not charcoal Raph took that as confirmation.

"Okay. Let's go!"

He patted the Dragon twice on the back and Buddy took off.

Slowly they gained altitude and speed as they circled the tower. They were moving pretty fast by the time they got to the top.

So fast in fact that Buddy went right by it. Way, way by it.

"Uh, Buddy? I think we missed my stop." Raph shouted to be heard but wasn't sure if his words reached his new friend.

Their ascent stopped well above the tower's top. They floated there for a minute wings flapping before Buddy gradually began to point his nose downward.

"Oh shit."

Raph grabbed on for dear life.

"BUUUUDDDDYYYY!!!!!"

They went into a dive.

Raph had never been skydiving but he imagined the rush must be similar, except that here instead of a parachute he had packed himself he had a dragon he'd just met.

Buddy smoothed out the dive easily. Decelerating so as not to buck Raph off. Snorting to himself as he did.

Apparently, Buddy the Dragon was a practical joker.

Raph leaped from the back of the dragon to the top of the tower. It was an action that every fantasy novel he had ever read made seem like an afterthought. Just a ho-hum thing the heroes did to advance the scenery. Like opening a door or walking outside. But jumping from the back of a dragon to a rooftop three hundred feet in the air is not ho-hum. It's fucking terrifying.

Though still slightly less terrifying than the nosedive he'd lived through only moments before.

Raph hit the stone hard and went into a half intentional half 'shit I might have just sprained my ankle' roll.

That roll stopped about a foot away from the far edge of the tower.

Raph freaked out a bit when he saw this and rapidly crab crawled back towards the tower's center.

He stood up when he stopped shaking.

"Real nice Raph. Escape a tomb, beat up your freaky evil clone of glass, make friends with a dragon, then accidentally roll to your death. You're the coolest."

The surprise flash of light made him fall on his ass.

"THAT IS GETTING SUPER ANNOYING!" he shouted to absolutely no one.

He waved at Buddy as he flew away before stepping through the standard issue blue portal and back to the fourth and final tower.

After the usual shenanigans, the old portal vanished and a new portal was waiting in front of him.

"Ooo. Shiny."

He gathered himself. Whatever all of this was about was probably on the other end of this trip.

After all, he'd run out of towers.

"Once more unto the breach."

> Comment [G]: Inserted: ,

Chapter 20

The Cup and the Sword

Raph exited through the pool of blue energy and stepped onto another world. It was night here. Soft, red clay lay beneath his feet and a cloudless, moonless sky reigned above his head. Impatiently he waited for his eyes to adjust to the thin din of starlight that blanketed the barren land surrounding him. In the distance lay a mountainous silhouette defiantly unaware that it stood as a sharp contrast to the theme of emptiness that seemed to preoccupy the rest of this particular world.

The portal collapsed shut behind him and again Raph found himself with only one reasonable path. Forward.

"Right first thing when I get back I'm looking up 'Big Blue Portal Thingy's' at the library."

With that glib remark, he began moving towards the

darkened shape in the distance.

As he walked Raph tried to keep track of how far he had gone in case he needed to go back but he couldn't seem to manage it. Even counting his steps seemed beyond him. In some moments he felt like he was moving swiftly, covering great distances in no time at all; other times he felt anguish overtake him as eons seemed to pass between each step forward.

Raph's senses were lost. Overwhelmed by waxing and waning of time itself. He yearned for relief but found none. His mouth was dry, his stomach empty. Other urges rose up in him as well. Primal lust, a need for flesh to fulfill flesh flowed through his veins causing his muscles to ache and nerves explode with fire. But, even as his body burned for pleasure, his eyes grew heavy, insisting on his exhaustion, begging him to just rest for a moment. Every instinct, every human need that Raph had ever felt within him had been activated in the same instant. It was torture as he was denied relief from them again and again.

And then he stood before his destination and everything was still. His body and time restored in the same instant. Both operating under normal parameters again. Shaken, Raph took ten deep breaths before moving.

Directly in front of him was an opening in the rock face. He entered it. Stepping carefully, he navigated a narrow walkway between the sharp granite jutting out around him. As he passed through it, he emerged by a lake. Beautiful white sand gave way to calm blue water. Majestic in its serenity.

"Welcome, Raphael." The voice hummed with

Comment [G]: Inserted: ,

Comment [G]: Inserted: h

Comment [G]: Inserted: ,

Comment [G]: Inserted: ,

Comment [G]: Inserted: ,

power, like a Mezzo-Soprano before a performance, warmed up and ready to take the stage. His name hung there, in the space between the light touch of angelic femininity and the deep, hidden power of an earthly goddess.

Easily she emerged from the still waters of the lake. With a grace that would outshine any queen she took her first steps onto land; her blue, flowing gown perfectly dry.

Her eyes took her fill of him. Appraising every small detail. Joy and delight cascaded from her, the exuberance of a mother whose wayward son had finally come home. It would have been easy to be overawed by such a presence. Expected even to be overwhelmed by her. But these were not the words that described Raph at that moment. All he felt was warmth.

"Thank You. Welcome to where?"

"The universe has many hidden places. This is one of them. You've visited another one in a dream I believe?" Her blue eyes sparkled in the sun like the light bouncing off a gentle wave.

"How do you know about that?" It was not surprise, but curiosity that prompted the question.

"Like many of my ilk, I deal in secrets and unknown things. Lilith Fey is not nearly as shrewd as she believes herself to be. I have been watching you for a very long time, Raphael. I am pleased that we have this opportunity to meet." She smiled and extended a small hand to him. Raph took it and felt the tender softness of her grip, firm and delicate at the same time.

"It's a pleasure. Although I have to admit you

377

Comment [G]: Inserted: ,

Comment [G]: Inserted: ,

Comment [G]: Inserted: ,

Comment [G]: Inserted: ,

G.R. Linden

weren't what I was hoping for." The honest words slide out of him and he did not fear that they might insult her.

She tilted her head at him and her smile took on a note of sadness.

"You sought to find the Grail here in the hopes of healing your friend. A noble quest." She let go of his hand and turned back to the lake. "A noble quest indeed. Tell me what do you know of the Grail?"

"Not a lot. Most of what I did know was based on Earth legends. And it seems like those tend to be…" Raph hesitated for a moment looking for the right turn of phrase "…limited in scope."

Lyrianna chuckled at that. Raph wasn't sure how he knew the Lady's name but somehow he just did.

"Yes, your understanding of this universe of ours has expanded exponentially over the last few weeks hasn't it? Suddenly knowing things you shouldn't can take some getting used to." Her smile grew as she continued. "You may let your mind at ease, The Cup is here and it has the power to heal your friend. But The Cup is not The Grail. Or at least not all of it."

"What does that mean?" The relief at her words mingled with his confusion. The Cup was the Grail. At least that's what every legend he'd ever heard had said. Of course, he had just admitted that those stories were limited.

"It means what it means. The Grail is a collection of thirteen pieces of power and wisdom. If you hope to defeat the Shak'Tah'Noh and their master then you will need to assemble all thirteen. If you fail to do so, leave but even one out, and we will all fall to ash. All the

378

Comment [G]: Inserted: ,

Comment [G]: Inserted: a

possibilities of tomorrow burnt out of us in one brilliant flash." Lyrianna's face darkened at the last. Raph felt as if someone had dropped a shroud over his soul. Then the feeling was gone and Lyrianna was smiling again.

"The Cup is a map of sorts. A guide that will help you to locate the other pieces. I believe your friend warned you that this was a possibility."

"Leave it to Billy to figure something out that I don't get until it's literally staring me right in the face."

"Yes, he's bright that one. I've taken a shine to him as well. He will play his part in what is to come. But he cannot do what must be done."

"And I can? No. I'm taking the Cup. I'm going to make sure Billy's alright and then I'm out."

"Do you believe it to be that simple?"

"Why can't it be?"

"Because you know better. Because without the bitter cold we can never find comforting warmth and without the searing flame we cannot know cool relief. Because you are who you are."

"What? What am I? The great-great whatever-son of King Arthur. Why should that matter to me? Why should that change the choices that I make?"

"I have noticed in my observations that you often fail to hear what has been said. Refrain from using your brain so much and try using your ears for a change. It might just save your life someday."

She turned again to face him. Her eyes disassembling him. Striping away the extraneous until nothing was left but his naked soul.

"I know you, Raphael Ignatius Carpenter. I know

379

Comment [G]: Inserted: ,

you of old. The blood of kings may run in your veins, but that will not define your legacy. Not any more than it did theirs. You are who *you* are. The tipping point between all the decisions that have come before and all of the possibilities yet to pass. Between the empirical and the mystic. The masculine and the feminine. Order and chaos. Life and Death. Because you are the essence of choice itself."

"I don't feel like the essence of anything."

"We rarely do."

"So if I am all of those things how am I supposed to save everyone?"

"Be careful in your choices. Remember that while everyone can be saved, you can't save everyone."

"I still don't understand."

"Understanding is a journey without destination." Finally, her eyes pulled away from his.

"Three gifts will I give you to assist you in that journey. The first is what you seek. The Cup." A satchel appeared over Raph's shoulder. He felt a weight against his hip. Reaching into the bag he pulled out a large goblet covered in pictures and writing. Lyrianna handed him three vials full of a clear liquid.

"Pour one of these vials into the Cup and make the afflicted drink. They will be healed of any injury or malady. Three vials are all I have to give and so three lives are all that you may save. *Callen*a *Fayier.*"

"Callena Fayier?"

"Choose wisely." Raph nodded at the instructions.

Satisfied Lyrianna walked to the edge of the water and reached her hand beneath the gentle lapping waves. It emerged again gripping a golden hilt. From the water, Lyrianna pulled forth a great sword, radiant in the light of the midday sun.

"The second gift I give you is that of the Sword. Known to you as Excalibur. Its edge will never dull, its blade will never break, and its bearer will never falter so long as the one who wields it does so with a noble heart. May it serve you as it did your forefather. In peace and in justice."

Raph took the sword with great reverence, overawed by its majesty. Carefully he took the sheath and tied it over his shoulder so the sword was secured on his back. Hilt up towards the sky.

"My final gift is the gift of prophecy. One of your allies is an enemy and one of your enemies an ally."

****

"You have your orders. Please relay them to your commanders. Dismissed." Jack took a long swig of his wine as he watched the officers leave before turning back to the giant map of the city and outlying territory that had been rolled out on the buffet bar.

Jack had created his own private war room in the dining hall that his poor dearly departed wife had left him. He'd made sure to make it look haphazard and hastily assembled. Wouldn't want anyone to think he'd been prepared for anything.

"The Lady Tam to see you, my lord." His servant intoned droll as always. Jack had been expecting this visit. Looking forward to it really.

"Yes, show her in."

The Second Lord of the Tower entered with a slow deliberate pace of command that had been perfected over

381

Comment [G]: Inserted: ,

Comment [G]: Deleted:e

Comment [G]: Deleted:h

Comment [G]: Inserted: ,

the decades. That precise mixture of grace and power that was usually reserved for large hunting cats.

She looked at him, then over the room, then back at Jack before speaking.

"I see you have heard then."

"Yes, a complete disaster. Our forces have been completely routed. The Northern army makes for Ardoth. We must prepare for a siege." He let a small note of panicked bravado enter his voice. It was a hard sound to get right. Jack had been forced to work at it over the years. Jack moved to offer the Lady a chair.

"Though that is a rather pressing concern it is not the thing to which I was referring." Lady Tam moved absently but with the deliberate intent of keeping the dining room table between them.

"Oh?"

"Yes, and you know it. Sir Geir and Sir Garret are both missing. In fact, Sir Garret never made it to his rendezvous point with our forces. As a result that idiot the Wizard Carl remained in command ensuring our defeat. And now Geir is missing and I find you here taking it upon yourself to rally the city's forces despite the duty being mine to assume." Jack feigned shock at the insinuation.

"I was merely setting some simple and necessary matters in motion Lady. I assumed no authority and did not mean to offend. I was merely attempting to be helpful in a time of need." Now he assumed a deferential posture and made his face show that he felt appropriately chastised.

"I know who you are Jack Smith"

In an instant, Jack transformed. His stance straightened but became easier. His amber eyes

Comment [G]: Inserted: ,

Comment [G]: Inserted: ,

Comment [G]: Inserted: ,

brightened and went wild. His face relaxed and his natural, impish grin took over. The Lady Tam was no longer the only large hunting cat in the room.

"Oh, my dear Lady Tam that is unfortunate. I was really getting to enjoy your wacky antics. I'm afraid I'll have to kill you now."

"I've beaten you to it oh Bard of Bedlam. I've taken the liberty of poisoning your wine." The Lady Tam had the face of one who was extraordinarily pleased with herself as she nodded towards the cup in his hand. Jack let her savor the moment before burning all of her dreams to ash.

"Yes you did, unfortunate that. You killed my favorite redhead. What was her name? Beth? Bailey?.... Kirily! Yes, that was it Kirily. Poor girl. Red had a penchant for the red you see. Broke into my private stock. Got herself killed. Well, you know how it goes. The wine in my hand, however, is a gorgeously light white from Boonwahee. It has just the tiniest bit of a fruit flavor. Like kiwi. Would you like to try?"

The Lady Tam simply stood there looking aghast. It was Jacks turn to savor the moment this time.

"But....But...But...."

"And you were absolutely right. At my request, an associate of mine intercepted Sir Garret before he could save your forces from the bumbling of that fool Carl. Sir Geir's disappearance, however, was the sole providence of Sir Trelgrove I'm afraid. You know that peacock seems to think he can turn me into his own personal puppet ruler. Probably meant to kill you next, the bastard. It will be my honor to rob him of the pleasure."

Jack set his wine down carefully on the dining room table and strode towards her. The Lady Tam took two

G.R. Linden

steps back. It was not enough. In one swift move, Jack
pulled out his belt knife and buried it deep in her innards.
She gasped and sputtered as Jack twisted the knife. Small
drops of blood appeared on the corner of her lips. Slowly
the life began to go out of her eyes. Jack pulled her in and
gave her a deep passionate kiss before yanking his blade
free and letting her body drop to the floor. Jack wiped a
bit of the Lady Tam's blood from his mouth as the rest of
it began to pool on the floor.

"Well, that just won't do."

Jack stepped gingerly around the body and grabbed a
white cloth from the table in order to wipe off his hands
and boots.

*Now, what is that servant's name Alexander?
Kentral? ....?*

"Fredrick!"

It took only a moment for the man to arrive in the
dining room. And only another moment for the man to
turn an unappealing shade of pale.

"Yes, M'lord."

"Ah, Fredrick. Excellent. I remembered your name.
That's a big step up for you." Fredrick was staring at the
corpse of the recently departed Lady Tam. "Yes, you
noticed that. I'm afraid the Lady Tam attempted to kill me
and so I was forced to respond in kind. Fortunately for all
parties involved, I have better aim. Unfortunately for us, I
do tend to be a bit messy. So if you wouldn't mind
cleaning all of this up and dumping the body somewhere
outside the city walls I would be most grateful. Also, do
try not to be seen. I'd rather not have to try to explain all
this in the middle of a siege." The man's face grew paler
by the second but he nodded agreement.

"Oh and Fredrick, the Lady Tam here sought to

384

Comment [G]: Deleted:to
Comment [G]: Inserted: ,
Comment [G]: Inserted: ,
Comment [G]: Inserted: ,
Comment [G]: Inserted: ,

betray me and she was quite a bit cleverer and quite a bit more important than you are. Do you understand me?" Jack hoped he wasn't being too subtle. It was always a shame when someone didn't understand that you were threatening them.

"Yes, M'lord."

"Good. Now if anyone needs me I'm going to go look over siege preparations. It's important to be seen saving the city. Otherwise, how will people know to give me the credit?"

****

Lux flew through the air absolutely sure he was about to die.

His chest hit the timber ledge that was the main house's roof and his hands scrambled to find anything to hold. His fingers found the remnants of the canopy walkway supports and held on for dear life.

Slowly and with great effort Lux pulled himself up to the roof, denying gravity its glory.

He checked his back and made sure he was still in possession of his bow and quiver.

Next, he took stock of the battle.

Broken and torn bodies were strewn about everywhere. Alistair was engaged with a half dozen phage but twice that number lay at his feet.

Bea had forgone her bow for her quarterstaff and still held firm on her side of the canopy walk but was being pressed hard by a pair of Phage.

Lux pulled an arrow from his quiver and was about to assist her when she looked his direction.

"To Your Left!!"

Bea's warning came just in time. A group of three

Phage had started climbing the walls in an attempt to get at him. Lux loosed taking one right between the eyes. It fell, screaming as it did.

Comment [G]: Inserted: -

Lux reached back into his quiver for another arrow. The two remaining Phage had reached the rooftop and were bounding towards him.

He loosed and took the left one in the shoulder. He drew two more arrows in quick succession and put them through the thing's head. It dropped twitching.

The last Phage was almost upon him. He reached back for another arrow but his quiver was empty.

The Phage leaped at Lux, coming for his throat. Lux threw his bow at the thing and tried to draw the short blade at his belt.

The bow forced the Phage to shift direction mid-leap but it managed to swat at Lux's hand with enough force that he lost his grip on his blade.

Lux dropped into a roll to keep some space between him and his attacker but forgot his bearings for a moment.

The roll sent him further away from the house and back towards the fallen canopy walk.

Lux was now trapped against the roof's edge without a weapon of any kind.

The Phage lunged at him. Lux tried desperately to move out of the way, diving to his right hoping the man would move past him and over the side of the building to the battle below. But Lux had never been that lucky. Sharp pain flooded Lux's mind as the Phage's claw-like hands opened up a three-inch gash along his right side, his blood began to puddle on the bricked roof.

The Phage stood above him. Lux tried to think of a

way out of the situation, but he was too tired. Too hurt. His last hope as the fatal blow began to fall was that the Fox might still save him. But as the things teeth came speeding towards his neck he realized that was a false hope.

"NOOOOOO!!!!!!!!!"

The high pitched squeal froze the Phage mid-attack.

A tiny ball of fury flew across the rooftop slamming into Lux's executioner.

The blow was not much.

But it was enough.

The Phage was not mindful of its surroundings and took a step back where there was none to take.

He hung there for a second, wildly waving its arms in a futile attempt to stop its inevitable descent.

Its screaming started before its fall but they ended together.

Kara stood there like a statue. Staring over the edge at what she had done.

Later Lux would look back and think it a rather morbid and inappropriate thought but at that moment he was absolutely sure that a more beautiful creature had never existed on this or any other world.

"Kara." Stunned she didn't register Lux calling to her.

"Kara." He tried one more time.

"KARA!"

Finally, she seemed to come back to reality.

"Lux?" slowly her head turned away from the empty space beyond the roof's edge.

"Oh, Lux! You're hurt."

"I'm okay."

"No you're not, stay still let me look at it." She ripped off his already torn shirt and pressed it against the bleeding hole in his torso.

"You saved me." His words were soft and full of tenderness.

"No more than you saved me." She leaned into his body, her soft lips touching his. Electricity filled him. He forgot about all his wounds and pains as he lost himself in her embrace. It was wonderful.

There was a cough.

Startled the pair pulled away from each other.

Bea was standing over them. Lux had almost thought that the stoic woman had been smiling.

"It's over."

****

"Remember three time you may use the Cup. Once for what was, once for what is, and once for what will be. *Callena Fayier.*"

Lyrianna lightly touched his face with her hand. It was a sad touch. A touch full of understanding and regret and longing and warmth. It was an apology and a promise. It was love. Raph closed his eyes and let himself feel the universe unfold before him. Worry and doubt faded away, replaced by wisdom and understanding. And suddenly he had something he hadn't had in a long time. Something he'd managed to touch upon when he was facing down Xan. Raph had clarity.

And then she was gone. But his understanding remained.

Raph stood there enjoying the residual glow of the

388

> **Comment [G]:** Inserted: r

Lady's presence. Finally, he let out a large exhale and turned away from the lake's edge. Carefully he strapped the sword to his back, picked up the satchel Lyrianna had left him and walked out the way he had come. He knew before he exited the alcove what he would find there and he was prepared for it. For them.

Outside, four of the Shak'Tah'Noh were waiting for him.

He recognized two of them as the emaciated man and the brute from when they had attacked him outside the Portent's End. The other two had been part of the ambush at the Sha'Dral. A woman with ratty black hair and her face filthy with dirt and grime. And a man of middling size who seemed decidedly non-descript.

The four Shak'Tah'Noh were spread out in a staggered semi-circle designed to give Raph nowhere to run. Grinning ear to ear the four clearly believed him trapped and easy prey. Slowly a smile began to creep onto Raph's face as the emaciated opened his mouth to speak.

"You have something of ours Arthur-Son. Give it to us and we will make your death quick and painless."

Raph felt serene. At peace in a way that he never had before. Everything around him was alive and pulsing with energy. The molecules that made up the air and the earth stood ready to make happen his any request. At that moment he was in possession of a deep, mystical understanding of the universe that few would ever touch upon: What is. Is. What is is also a choice.

But just because he'd touched upon a sliver of enlightenment didn't mean he couldn't enjoy a little banter.

389

"Cliché School called. You forgot to pick up your diploma." Rat-hair and Non-descript seemed startled. They clearly expected him to be more cowed by the odds. Their mistake.

"Seriously guys. You've been trying to kill me for over a month now and I've yet to hear a witty retort out of any of you. And frankly, I'm disappointed. I like my villains with a little chutzpah, a little panache. You know maybe if you enjoyed your work a little more you could dedicate your life to something other than bringing about complete nothingness."

"Kill him." The emaciated man was clearly not impressed by Raph's wit.

"Pithy and to the point. I can respect that."

Fire and lightning came at him from four directions. Raph didn't run. He didn't duck and he didn't hide. Raph stepped into the attack. Feeling the energy, he reached out to it and formed a vision of the world in his mind. Heat and electricity coalesced into a single stream. Raph turned and let the stream rush past him before calling it back. Whirling around and swinging the deadly energy like a biker chain against his attackers.

Raph caught Nondescript on the rib cage, ripping cloth and leaving a nasty burn. The man fell back with a scream but Raph had already moved on to his next target. A flick of his wrist sent the rolling wave of fire and lightning towards his remaining three attackers. Before it could strike home it became water and splashed to the dirt harmlessly.

At the same time, the ground beneath Raph's feet exploded upwards, rocketing him towards the sky. He

jumped backwards turning the water soaked dirt into ice
as he did. Causing Rat-hair and the Emaciated Man to slip
and fall.

But the Brute kept coming.

"You're dead." Not much for words apparently.

Raph dodged to the side and barely avoided the
Brute's fist which was now covered in two-inch steel
spikes.

"You know what I'm going to do. When this is all
over I'm going to buy you a joke book." The Brute swung
around and crushed a fist into the dirt where Raph's torso
had been a moment earlier.

Raph used a gust of wind to push himself backwards
and put some room between him and his attackers.
Emaciated was back on his feet and rushing towards Raph
but luckily Rat-hair was still on the ground.

Raph tried to take advantage of the more favorable
odds by launching a wall of fire at the pair but it
dissipated before it made it halfway to his target.

"I don't know if you guys celebrate Christmas here
or not but I really hope you're disappointed when you
don't get a card from me this year." Thousands of steel
thorns were rocketing towards Raph now. Raph focused
his mind on the steel thorns. And then they were flower
petals.

Raph realized it had been a stalling tactic. All four
Shak'Tah'Noh were on their feet now, though it gave
Raph a little comfort that Non-Descript seemed to be in
pretty bad shape. Again they spread out in a half-moon,
forcing Raph back towards where he had emerged from
the enclave.

And it was exactly where Raph wanted to be.

The realization had come to him back by the lake. These Shak'Tah'Noh were thugs. They used lightning, ice, fire, and metal in their attacks because it's all they understood. They saw a destructive force and they emulated it. They lacked imagination.

But Raph was a nerd.

A nerd who'd grown up in a bookstore.

Imagination was his wheelhouse.

Hot magma began to ooze up out of the ground behind the four Shak'Tah'Noh trapping them in a half moon of Raph's own.

Rat hair came at him in a rage but pulled up screaming only five feet later having run face first into a pocket of super-heated air Raph had placed in front of her. Her screaming stopped when her breathing did.

The others only watched as their companion succumbed. Then they turned their attention back to Raph. All three of them were smiling.

Raph was not.

They moved together now. Slowly, methodically checking for invisible traps and tricks.

Raph was not about to give them that luxury. Magma and super-heated air were not his only weapons.

Sure that it wouldn't take much more to knock Non-Descript out of the fight Raph focused his attention on him.

Putting up an ice wall to slow down the Brute and the Emaciated Man, Raph ran full speed at Non-Descript who responded by hurling a pair of fireballs towards Raph's head and torso.

Raph dropped into a baseball slide, turning the ground beneath him to ice in order to keep his momentum.

Seeing his fireballs miss, Non-Descript tried to move and counter; but Raph was moving too fast. He barreled into Non-Descript's legs like a two hundred twenty pound bowling ball. The two men went flying through the air. Limbs tangled.

They hit hard but Raph ignored the pain and rolled clear on instinct. Which was good because he narrowly avoided the flying boulder that now occupied the space he had been in. Non-Descript was not so lucky.

Two down. Two to go.

The Brute and Emaciated Man had cleared the ice wall and were facing him together.

Neither one looked particularly disturbed that they had just ground one of their own to a pulp.

"What's the matter Arthur-Son? No witty repartee? No snarky remarks? A little blood and gore and you lose all your... what did you call it? Chutzpah?"

A thousand specks of light came at him. It was the same tactic that they had tried on Alistair back outside the Portent's End. Raph concentrated and turned the volley of flares into mist.

Raph's chest exploded in pain as it was struck by a ball of ice the size of a barstool.

Staggered he fell back. Reflexively he put up a wall of flame, trying to protect himself from the certain follow-up strike.

The next attack came in the form of steel spikes flying through the air like daggers. All Raph's wall of flame did was super-heat them.

One spike struck home, burying itself in Raph's right thigh. The others left him with cuts and burns on his arms and sides.

The strap on his shoulder had been cut and Excalibur, still in its sheath, fell to the earth next to him. Even if he knew how to use a sword Raph doubted he had the strength left to wield it anyway.

Bindings of air picked Raph up off the ground.

"Tsk. Tsk. Right back where we started aren't we Arthur-Son. But this time there is no Fox coming to save you."

The Brute sent an electric current through Raph's body making him cry out in pain.

"No last moment heroics. Just the bleak inevitability of the abyss."

Again the Brute shot lightning into Raph's veins. Again Raph screamed

"Do you understand now? Free will is an illusion. No matter what path we take it all ends like this. In darkness and despair. The game is rigged. So why play? Why fight what will always be?"

The Emaciated man was right. No matter what Raph did, no matter how far he came, he always ended up like this. Trapped in invisible chains. Mocked by evil men. Made to feel weak and powerless.

But he wasn't weak or powerless. Lyrianna was right. It didn't matter if he was descended from Arthur or not. He was Raphael Ignatius Carpenter. And he wasn't going to let his friend die. And that was all there was to it.

The Brute charged up for another electrocution.

Raph closed his eyes and thought of his first lesson with Alistair.

Reaching out with all that he was, he let his pain leave him and felt the molecules around him, the fabric of reality that tied everything together. He saw the world as it was and how he wanted to be and then he saw that they were the same thing.

"Because I choose to."

Raph opened his eyes and the water above The Brute's head came crashing down on him right as he released his pent up electric shock. The combination fried him where he stood.

Air no longer held him. Raph dropped into a roll. He grabbed the hilt of the sword and pulled Excalibur free of its sheath.

He didn't know a lot about swords but he did know the most important part......

"But he said…" The Emaciated Man gasped.

……. the pointy end goes in the bad guy.

The life faded out of the Emaciated Man's eyes and silence enveloped the world.

Raph pulled Excalibur free and used his shirt to wipe it clean before returning it to its sheath. This was when Raph realized he was bleeding. A lot.

Carefully he pulled the steel-spike free of his leg and made a makeshift tourniquet out of the remains of his shirt. At least he tied the cloth tight right above the wound. He was pretty sure that was how it was done.

Once he'd taken care of his wound he put the sword back over his shoulder, tying a simple knot where the band had been cut but the rouge spike. It wasn't great but

395

it didn't need to be.

Raph took one last look around. Letting the remnants and the horror of it set in his memory. He'd killed people today. For the rest of his life, he'd never not be a killer again. That thought felt heavy on his soul.

With a glance, the magma ring Raph had created turned to rock.

He crossed it in a daze. His thoughts were elsewhere.

Raph did not know how long he had walked before he came to the blue portal. Nor did he bother to look behind him to check.

Without hesitation, he stepped through it and back to where he was needed most.

Comment [G]: Inserted: ,

Chapter 21

The End of the Beginning

Raph emerged from the portal battered and bruised but alive. Kara and Lux rushed to his side, gently placing his arms over their shoulders, each taking some of his weight. How they had found him he had no idea, but considering how the day had gone so far he was way too tired to ask. Solving the mysteries of the shiny blue portal thingies could wait for another time. A time when his best friends life didn't hang in the balance.

A cacophony of questions fired forth from his friend's mouths; their worry and excitement making them oblivious to the fact that they were talking over one another. Wearily, Raph raised a hand to quiet them.

"Billy, just take me to Billy." Lux nodded hesitantly and Kara's mouth became quite tight. But they kept quiet and the three of them got moving. Raph could feel the Cup banging against his leg as the satchel bumped up and down with every stride he took. Carrying Excalibur and the Cup together made for a heavy load, but even in his weakened state, Raph bore the weight well.

He could see them exchanging worried glances as they walked, stealing looks at the sword over his shoulder, wondering just what had happened to him. Their curiosity was understandable. And eventually, he would answer their questions. Well, most of their questions. But there would be time to sort through all that later. Right now he needed to save Billy. Nothing else mattered.

Fires raged in the woods around them. Raph assumed they were the remnants of the battle with the Phage. Apparently, he wasn't the only one who'd had an interesting couple of days. Kara and Lux seemed to glow when they looked at each other. Raph pegged it as that euphoria that comes from the realization that you may yet live to see another day. That feeling was the only thing that was keeping Raph's legs going at the moment.

The walk took them ten minutes longer than it should have, but Raph couldn't move any faster than he was already and he didn't trust the Cup to be out of his sight for even a moment. Not even with Lux or Kara. He only hoped that the delay wouldn't cost Billy his life. Raph tried to think happy thoughts. Given how long it had taken for them to get this far there was no statistical reason why they should fail now when they were so close.

398

Comment [G]: Inserted: ,

Comment [G]: Inserted: ,

Comment [G]: Inserted: ,

Lux took them to the main house and opened the door as Kara helped Raph inside. He walked over to where the others were huddled around Billy, who was just lying there unconscious in the sitting room. Carefully Raph knelt and pulled the Cup out of the satchel the Lady had given him.

Alistair was standing over his shoulder now, his towering shadow giving Raph a terrible sense of foreboding.

"You found it?" It was the obvious question. The only question really. Unfortunately, he knew now that it wasn't that simple.

"Yes and no. I found the Cup and I have a way to heal Billy. But the Grail is much more than any of us ever imagined." Raph pulled one of the three vials he had been given out of his pocket, taking pains to ensure that the others in the room would not see that there was more than one. It shamed him not to trust them but he believed Lyrianna when she said there was a traitor in their midst. He would have to keep the extra vials a secret for now until he knew more about what he was really up against.

Raph uncorked the vial in his hand and poured its cold, clear contents into the Cup. He let it settle for a minute, hoping for some outward sign that it was working. When none came Raph decided he would just have to trust. He motioned for Kara to hold Billy's head up and gently Raph pushed Billy's mouth open before pouring the contents of the Cup down his throat.

It was not easy for Raph to hold the Cup there. It should have been. Holding up a cup to pour water is no great trial. But Raph's hands were trembling and it took all his willpower to keep the Cup from spilling out its life-saving contents.

Raph made sure Billy swallowed every drop before pulling the Cup away from his lips. And then they waited. Raph could feel his heart beating in his chest at an impossible rate. Could hear the sniffles that Kara was unsuccessfully trying to hold back. Could see the grim faces of Bea and Alistair.

"C'mon, C'mon. Work. C'mon Billy. It's time to wake up now." Tears began streaming down Raph's face as he began to face the very real possibility that he had gotten here too late. He could feel Alistair's hand grip his shoulder, trying to comfort him.

"Raphael, I'm sorry."

"NO!" Raph snarled at Alistair as the tears flew from his face. "He has to live. Lyrianna said he would." Raph gripped the unmoving body of his best friend.

"Did you hear that Billy? The Lady of the Lake herself said that you were going to live. So you are." Raph was beyond hysterics now. "You hear me?! You're my best friend and you're going to live."

Billy's body began to shake. Not in the manner of an epileptic episode but in the way your body does in the long stretch after an even longer sleep.

There was a sharp intake of breath and then his eyes shot wide open. Gasping, Billy grabbed Raph's hand and squeezed it tight.

"It's alright. You're back."

Billy laid his head back on the pillow and gradually his breathing slowed down to a more natural level. Raph tried to subtly wipe the tears from his face but Billy noticed. He turned his head so that he was looking directly into Raph's eyes.

"What's the matter? Did I miss Taco Tuesday?"

Raph's laughter filled the room.

****

Lilith watched as the boy left the portal with his companions. The Cup was out in the open, meaning that the Grail was up for grabs. The power to shape the destiny of every world that would or could come to be. The boy had served his purpose. For the third time, she was tempted to take the initiative and simply kill him where he was. He was dangerous. That he was still alive was proof of that. If she killed him now it would remove an obstacle from her path and give her a head start on the others.

Of course, there might be complications. Things about the Cup she might not yet know. Things that might require the Arthur-Son. Also, it was a good policy not to anger the Fox. And killing his godson would do exactly that. No, she would not kill him. Not yet. His death would rob her of too many options. And when you play the long game it's best to have options. She smirked as a pool of blue appeared in front of her. *Plans within Plans.* Lilith took one last look around and then stepped through the portal leaving Avalon far behind her.

****

Jack was rather pleased with himself. He was alive and he'd gotten to personally end the life of at least one person who had tried to kill him. He wasn't entirely sure what other people would call it but for him, that was a good day. Worthy of a drink and screw. *Remarkable* he

Comment [G]: Inserted: ,

Comment [G]: Inserted: ,

Comment [G]: Inserted: f

Comment [G]: Inserted: ,

Comment [G]: Deleted:t

Comment [G]: Inserted: ,

thought to himself, *I am always so fucking horny after a kill.*

"M'Lord" It was Jack's bald, fat, short serving man. Jack didn't even bother trying to remember his name this time. One must always have a servant who is far less attractive than oneself. That way they accentuate rather than distract from your own magnificence. Also in case of a honey trap, it's far easier to tell when an unattractive person suddenly starts getting laid. Jack wondered why such common sense wasn't a universal practice in the courts of Avalon. And Jack had fucked enough servants, male and female, to know that it wasn't. The need for eye candy should never outweigh the need for security. Oh well, foolishness to ponder on another occasion.

"Yes?" Jack's tone was curt and authoritative. He was quite proud of himself.

"Well, the rest of the Lords of the Tower are dead my lord." *I know I killed half of them* was what Jack wanted to say. He decided that would not be the most prudent of responses.

"And?"

"That makes you First Lord of the Tower and the Knight Protector M'lord. The rest of the Namahsii send word that they have no objections to your ascension. The city of Ardoth is yours to command." *Interesting* was the thought that came to Jack's mind. That he did not have a problem saying.

"Interesting."

"Orders M'Lord?" *Oh, so many possibilities.*

"Send messengers to all of our allies. Tell them Ardoth stands and war beckons. A siege is upon us and

Comment [G]: Inserted: ,

Comment [G]: Inserted: ,

their assistance is required."

"Yes sir" Jack's bowling ball of a servant turned on his heel and headed quickly towards the door. Just as he reached it Jack had another thought.

"Oh and once that's done I would like you to send up a feast fit for the Knight Protector of Ardoth to be served by the ten most attractive members of the household staff. It seems I've worked up quite an appetite." A devilish grin swept across Jack's face.

"Yes, M'lord."

****

The message had arrived early this morning along with word of their victory over the Ardothi army. He'd read it over at least two dozen times since. His brother was dead. Killed in a cowardly betrayal. Xan'tah'Mer would be avenged. This Raphael Carpenter would die a slow and horrible death.

****

"Alistair, can I talk to you for a minute?" The sun was slowly creeping up over the horizon. Raph had brought his godfather up to the roof where he thought that they would be out of earshot of the others. Alistair stood next to him. The two of them on the roof looking out at the world.

"Billy's going to be fine Raph. He's already almost made a full recovery. He just needs rest and a couple of good meals and he'll be back to clumsily knocking things over in no time." Raph looked at his godfather and wondered if he was going crazy. But the signs were all there if you stepped back enough to see them.

"Alistair, I think we've been played." His godfather

tilted his head, a quizzical look coming over his face. But he said nothing so Raph continued running through everything that had happened since that first night at the bookstore. "Think about it. If the Shak'Tah'Noh had wanted me dead they could have done it easily back in New Orleans. Walked up and fried me with a fireball on my walk home one day. Better yet they could have used a gun and it would have been chalked up as just another mugging gone bad, nothing mystical about it. Even when they did attack they had their chances to kill me and didn't take them. Didn't even maim me. They just beat up on me till you showed up and saved me."

Alistair was nodding along but Raph was uncertain if he was really following.

"All of that leads us here to Avalon. Where we were safe until we got to Ardoth and weren't sure where to go next. Then they attack, yelling about the Grail and me, but not attacking with any order or coordination just causing maximum carnage. Except for Billy who was knocked unconscious for a second time. But we got separated so I didn't know Billy was in trouble until later once he'd recovered. Instead, we come here to your estate. The Shak'Tah'Noh don't attack us on the road here. I arrive and find Billy poisoned. Again this time nobody is hurt except for Billy who is attacked with an incredibly gradual yet completely fatal narcotic. And now I have no choice but to find the Cup if I want to save his life. The Shak'Tah'Noh get in and out of your camp without anyone noticing anything and all they do is poison Billy with something so slow acting that I literally have weeks to find the Cup and cure him?"

Comment [G]: Inserted: ,

The Seeker

"But the Shak'Tah'Noh didn't poison Billy. The Phage did." Alistair's response was more academic than incredulous.

"Really. Because I've talked to all of you who were there. No one remembers him being hit and there wasn't any sign of a wound on him. No, I think the Phage were working with the Shak'Tah'Noh."

"The Androphagi work for no one but their own hunger."

"Fine, then they were tricked or influenced or something but it's all too perfect to be coincidence."

"Raph you've had a traumatic few weeks. Perhaps you are making connections where there are none?" Raph shook his head at his godfather's words.

"No, because then conveniently we find out that the Grail not only is on Avalon of all the places in an infinite universe but it's just a couple of hundred miles away from where we are. In Ardoth back where we came from. Back where I'm not sure we were ever supposed to leave. Long enough that we'd have to hustle to make it in time but close enough that Billy should survive long enough for us to make it. Always keeping us moving without allowing us time to stop and think what was really going on. "

"That's a lot of speculation Raphael."

"There were four Shak'Tah'Noh waiting for me after I recovered the Cup Alistair."

"Four? And you killed them all?"

"I did what I had to do. That's not the point."

"Then what is?"

"This whole thing was staged, Alistair. They didn't want to kill me they wanted me to find the Cup. And it seems pretty clear they knew where it was the whole time. Hell, they might have been the ones who dropped the hints for Billy and me to find. I'm sure of it Alistair. As sure as I've ever been about anything in my life. The question is why? What do they gain by activating the one person they think is capable of stopping them?"

"I don't know Raphael. But I do know that whatever their motivations they want to destroy everything. Leave nothing but the void. And I believe that whatever the circumstances that led us here you are the only one who can stop them. And if they were the ones who put you on this path then so much the worse for them."

"Alistair you said we were fighting for choice. But what choice do I have? Prophecies and legends and now I'm supposed to be some savior out of a fairy tale. You said the universe is infinite. So I'm not the only one. I'm not the only descendant of Arthur. Hell, I'm not even the only Raph Carpenter. There are other versions of me out there. Why can't they do this? Why should I believe that I'm the only chosen one?"

His godfather took a long, audible breath and turned to look Raphael in the eye. "You're absolutely right. You are not the only one who can do this. There are other descendants of Arthur Pendragon. And if not them, then there are other versions of you who might take up the fight. I could take you back home right now and we could go about our lives; shelving books and helping customers all the while wondering whether or not today was the day the world was going to end.   You are not trapped Raph. There is always a choice. Always agency. What is the greatest evil that has ever been?"

Comment [G]: Inserted: ,

Comment [G]: Inserted: me

Comment [G]: Deleted:I

Comment [G]: Inserted: ?

Comment [G]: Inserted: ,

Comment [G]: Inserted: a

Comment [G]: Deleted:.

Comment [G]: Deleted:e

"The apathy of a good man." He turned his eyes back to the rising sun. "All right Alistair. I'll do it. I'll fight."

End Book One

Made in the USA
Columbia, SC
29 October 2018